bloodbrothers

Morgen Leigh

Electric Zoo Media • Colorado Springs, CO

bloodbrothers

Copyright © 2020 by Morgen Leigh Thomas
Original cover image by Daley Thomas, © Morgen Leigh Thomas
Author photo and illustrations © Billy Sobolik
Cover design © 2019 by Rashed Al Akroka
Interior design © 2019 by DeAnna Knippling

ISBN: 978-1-7343006-8-0

Library of Congress Catalog Number: 2019919313

All rights reserved. This book or any portion thereof may not be reproduced or used in any manner whatsoever without the express written permission of the publisher/author except for the use of brief quotations in a book review. While all attempts have been made to verify the information provided in this publication, neither the author nor the publisher assumes any responsibility for errors, omissions, or contrary interpretations of the subject matter herein. Any perceived slight of any individual, group, or organization is purely unintentional.

Printed in the United States of America

First Edition
First Printing, 2020

Electric Zoo Media
PO Box 25044
Colorado Springs, CO 80936

for Pop, who taught me to believe in myself
and
for Chelsea, who always seems to know the right thing to do
and
for Will, who beats back the shadows every day to shine
his light on the world

This story was inspired by Johann Samuel Lucero.

part one

Friendship is the most worthy
of human ties.
A man loves his friend's soul,
and to do that
he must have a soul himself.

-DeBuffon

prelude

June 21, 1983

Joe Schell stood in his bedroom, the cream-colored carpet recently vacuumed and smelling of some putrid floral deodorizer that made his throat burn. He looked at his naked body in the enormous mirror on the west wall. Sporadic lightning strobed through the darkness, making his eyes hurt. Outside, the sky unzipped, as it so often did in the Pacific Northwest. Wind whipped through the maple leaves, sounding like crashing waves.

Joe raked his long hair down over his face and listened to the inevitable wails and whispers in his head. Flashes of light showcased the scarred intricacies of his flesh. Strategic gashes and cuts—experiments, mostly. A rosebud on his left pec. A detailed carving of the girl on the other, still fresh and oozing. Perfectly round burns on his belly, like crop circles showing the way.

He heard the question and pointed at the boy in the mirror, simultaneously reflected and embodied. Joe's teeth clenched so hard it stung his jaws.

"Yeah, it'll hurt," he seethed. "It should hurt. That's the fucking point." He lit a Camel and inhaled, holding the smoke deep. A TV preacher's southern quacking drifted up through the heating ducts—some inane sermon about fornication, masturbation, sins of the flesh.

Spiral ruts engraved into his right thigh. Three missing fingernails, two others bruised from the clenching. Wings etched into his bony shoulders, the cuts deeper on his collarbones.

Joe got his Bible from the desk drawer, opened it, tore out a page, and taped it to the bathroom mirror. He'd highlighted the passage weeks ago. *The wicked must suffer.* Bright yellow to match the tile. He flicked the smoldering butt into the sink just as his mother let out a resounding "hallelujah, brother!" downstairs.

He had one picture of Norma Schell. In it she held a small child, smiling, content. The kid in the picture wasn't him. It was the first one. The dead one.

The double-edged razor glinted with manic flickering as lightning flashed. Joe held the bit of stainless steel close to his face, put out his tongue and licked it, tasting metal. Tasting blood. The wails and whispers intensified. A child's cry.

"I hear you," Joe breathed. "I always fucking hear you."

He set the blade on the edge of the bathtub and went to dig under his bed for his mother's gardening trowel, the one with the sharp point. Her favorite.

"For-ni-ca-tion," preacher man warned.

Joe eased down into the empty bathtub and sat cross-legged, elbows propped on the edge, chin resting on his balled fists, and listened to the storm and the preacher's hypocrisy rage in synchronized symphony. From this vantage point, he could see his reflection in the huge looking glass across the bedroom, pale image framed by the bathroom door like a macabre still life. Beyond his reflection, the boy cried big, fat, pathetic tears.

Joe lifted the garden spade from the tile floor and brushed fresh dirt from the edges. She'd been out there again. Digging. Burying. Secrets and lies.

The sharp point bit into his right side just under the ribs, tearing a wide, jagged gash and releasing a fall of blood. Joe drove it in harder, deeper. A third thrust and the point buried itself into several layers of flesh. Gasping, exhilarated, Joe let the trowel clang into the tub, never taking his eyes off the weeping boy beyond the glass. *The wicked must suffer. It's the only way.*

Joe picked up the razorblade, felt the meager weight of it against his fingers, and marveled at the truth that such a small thing could have so much power. The blade sank easily into the soft skin at the base of his palm, but Joe hesitated, realizing he had to break eye contact with the kid in order to follow the vein. The boy beyond the glass blinked tears onto his round rosy cheeks, ruby lips stretched wide in an anguished scream that only Joe could hear. He'd shut Alex out a long time ago.

"Mas-tur-ba-tion!" preacher man hollered.

Joe watched his hand drag the blade through the tender, translucent skin of his arm. A serpentine trail of blood bubbled out fast, turning the freshly scrubbed porcelain bright red. The smell, like wet leaves and intimate places, made his skin prickle and tighten with excitement. Thunder reached down, rocking the house. Joe stopped the blade at the nook of his elbow and looked up to make sure the boy hadn't run off like the coward he was. There he stood, as pale and bewildered and annoying as ever, frozen in time and memory, small hands clenched under his chin, mouth twisted in a confused grimace, eyes leaking.

Joe seethed the hot, humid air through clenched teeth. "Alex can't hear you anymore, so shut the fuck up. You have to watch it and feel it. All of it." Sweat stung his eyes. He started to tremble and didn't know why.

Crimson bathed his thigh as he cut deep into his other arm. Joe's head felt light and heavy at the same time and he rested his cheek on the edge of the tub. The yellow tile didn't seem so yellow anymore. It looked darker, more orange, more russet, more bloody.

Joe peered out across the bedroom at the mirror, which seemed closer now. "Don't look at me like that," he said, the boy's image wavering, fading. "Can't hide anymore. You're tormenting me, and it has to stop. Just go easy, okay?"

Joe tilted his head and watched his essence puddle on the tile. The glimmering pool caught his reflection, trapped it there like a photograph. In that frozen picture he saw his dad, weeping into thick hands. Saw his dead brother, and Alex's too, playing catch in bright rainbow beams of light. He saw Alex, shoulders slumped and shaking with grief as white feathers rained from a black sky.

"Forgive me," Joe slurred, drawing circles in the puddle with his finger. The images went dark.

Clenching blood-dipped hands under his trembling chin, the boy in the mirror sent a scream into the vastness. The glass of the mirror shook violently in its frame.

Preacher man's voice rode on a red wave. "Sins of the flesh."

The smell hit Alex first. Sweet-sour. Salty. Bitter. Thick. The taste of fresh blood and sweat hung heavy on the hot, humid air. He took deep, steady breaths and tried to talk himself out of knowing what he already knew, what he saw before seeing it.

Just inside Joe's bedroom door, Alex looked through a violet haze toward the adjoining bathroom. Wet air swirled in a rainbow of moving color. A halo of light framed the open door and Alex saw blood, saw Joe, saw life dripping away. He looked down at his shoes, anchored to the cream-colored carpet, polished and new, the Band-Aids on his heels making them feel tight. Perspiration poured from his armpits, soaking through his tuxedo, making the itchy fabric cling to his skin. His fingers vibrated. He stared at his feet and wondered why they weren't moving, wondered what the Florsheim people would say if he got blood all over his new shoes. *Reason for return? Failure.* They'd probably make his mom pay an extra cleaning fee.

A pulsing roar filled his head and he realized it was his own heartbeat. His nerve endings fired with the persistent message to *move*, to *do something.* A distant sound came from deep within his weary mind—a whisper, a groan, a sigh—

the undeniable truth that Joe was just beyond his reach. Always just beyond reach. Downstairs, the preacher raged about God and redemption, Jesus and salvation, from Mrs. Schell's brand new nineteen-inch Curtis Mathes TV set, the one she'd won at the church raffle a few weeks back.

I shouldn't be here. I should be in the middle of number seventeen. Second movement. The Hunt. Always gets me a standing O.

A heavy weight pressed stale breath from his lungs. One shoe lifted, hovered over the clean carpet. *Move,* he told his legs. Thick air rushed like a wave, slowing him, trying to force him to his knees. Alex swam through the room, pulled at the ribbons of color, blinded by fear and Joe's life raining down in fat scarlet drops. Far below, preacher man's rapturous voice rose and fell with the adrenalized exertion of his message. He warned of fornication, masturbation, and sacrificing salvation for simple sins of the flesh.

"Sins of the flesh." Alex hadn't meant to say it out loud, but the words trailed from his thoughts and hung in front of his eyes in bright red flashing neon letters.

Blood streamed down the walls. Crimson patterns smeared across yellow tile. Flesh, torn and ruined and opened. A bit of glistening steel lit up with a blaze of lightning as a double-edged razor slipped free of Joe's slack grip. Alex wanted to turn away, to shut it all out, to forget, because he was good at forgetting. All this was inevitable anyway, wasn't it? Nothing he could do, really.

Reason for return? I stopped listening.

Bare, flayed flesh on hot palms. Joe's slick body pressed to his own. Blood dripping into rusted buckets. Lifeless, dangling limbs. Smiling gashes in flesh. Glassy, unseeing eyes. Fornication, masturbation, salvation …

A guttural scream tore out of his throat, rising from a forgotten place as a random realization settled heavy and thick.

This must be what a slaughterhouse smells like.

one

May 19, 1984

Kings

Norma Schell knelt on a cushion before the altar, holding an open Bible in her pudgy hands. She murmured to herself, lost in the onionskin pages of God's Word.

"I will haul you out and leave you stranded on the land to die. And all the birds of the heavens will light upon you and the wild animals of the whole earth will devour you until they are glutted and full." The woman pressed a soggy tissue to her brow. "Amen. Praise Jesus."

A rhythmic thumping drifted down the hallway, breaking the fervent calm of her devotional. She spoke louder.

"And I will cover the hills with your flesh and fill the valley with your bones. And I will drench the earth with your gushing blood, filling the ravines to the tops of the mountains!"

The drum-thrum grew louder. Norma clutched a framed photo to her breasts, black tears tracking through the layers of pancake and rouge on her cheeks.

"God would have forgiven you if you had asked," she said. "Then you wouldn't have had to leave, and the boy wouldn't be lost to the ways of Christ. But you are a stubborn one, aren't you?" She pressed her lips to the glass, leaving a fuchsia smudge, and gazed at the crucified figure hanging cross-corner on the wall above the altar. Her Savior, her Lamb. Flickering candle flame cast dancing shadows over the messiah's withered features, animating his sad, weary face.

"Yes, darkness will be everywhere across your land, even the bright stars will be dark above you." The walls vibrated with blasts from an electric guitar. Norma shook her head, nostrils flaring, and blotted her painted eyes.

"My hands do your bidding, my prince," she whispered. "There can be no forgiveness without the shedding of blood."

She lifted the knotted lash lying at her side, checked to make sure the razor bits sewn into the frayed ends were good and sharp, and got to her feet.

8:13am

Alex stared at the white structure topped with a chipping red slate roof and shivered in the morning sunshine. He rubbed his eyes. *Goddamn nightmares.*

Joe's was the only house on the block that stood high up on a hill and away from the street. Mrs. Schell's prize-winning madonna roses lined the entire two hundred-foot driveway. The flowery perfume always made Alex's head ache. Already feeling tired, he ambled a few more feet and was about to step onto the porch when he sensed movement behind the giant bigleaf maple in the front yard.

"Joe?" Alex squeezed between two thorn laden bushes and stepped onto the mowed grass. "That you?"

Nearing the maple, he heard a muffled voice. "Prepare to die, O slayer of monsters."

With a shrill holler, Joe leapt from behind the tree's thick trunk.

Alex stumbled back, startled.

Joe wore black from head to toe. His shirt was inside out, as usual. Streaks of red and black grease paint smudged his face and his long blond hair flew wildly around his head.

A child-sized bow and some small arrows stuck out of the *Batman* backpack slung over his left shoulder, too small now for Joe's broad, bony back. In each hand, he held the homemade wooden swords they'd fashioned when they were six. Worn out aluminum foil covered the sheaths and peeling black electrical tape wound around the handles. Alex hadn't seen those things in a decade, at least.

"A fight." Joe tossed Alex a sword.

"A duel." Alex caught the weapon, so small in his hand now, and assumed a combative stance.

"Prepare ye to die, O wandering thief," Joe intoned in an ominous voice, holding the sword in front of him, a playful smile on his obsidian-painted lips.

"Thou dost think much of thine self, O boastful knave," Alex told him with a smirk.

"Haha!" Joe lunged.

Alex jumped back with a grunt, then advanced, wooden swords crashing.

They swung at each other, the cracks of wood clashing with wood echoing. Alex was just beginning to enjoy himself, to let the veil of depression lift a little, when Joe, with a shattering war cry, raised his sword high above his head and charged. Alex sidestepped. Joe crashed to the ground amidst the sounds of splintering wood and crunching aluminum foil. Alex laughed as Joe rolled onto his back with an exaggerated groan. Alex put the sole of his faded black Converse on Joe's abdomen and looked down at him through the streaming sunlight. He lowered his weapon, worn point aimed at Joe's heaving chest.

"O mighty King Joseph," Alex said, a sly smile on his lips. "Ye are defeated."

"Indeed, Sir Alex. You must slay the beast," Joe whispered. He pulled the wooden point down to rest on his throat. "Do it swiftly, Alexander. End my misery. Do it now." He closed his eyes and stretched his arms out wide on the grass.

Alex stood there in stunned paralysis, restless shadows shifting at the corners of his memory. Flashes of torn flesh and rivers of blood zigged and zagged through his mind like lightning strikes looking for a target. The old piece of wood slipped from his grasp and fell to the ground. The growing weight in his chest made it hard to breathe.

"Goddamn it, Joe. What the hell was that?"

Grinning, Joe jumped to his feet and slapped Alex on the back. "It was a game, my friend. Like when we were kids. You loved sword fights, man. We always had a blast. Slaying dragons and each other? Yeah?"

Alex glared at him, face deepening from warm pink to angry red.

"We're not kids anymore," Alex said. "Why do you have to make everything so weird? Why can't you just chill the fuck out?"

"*Chill?* You want me to *chill*, Al?" Joe stared at him for a long moment and Alex thought he might try to push his thoughts into his mind, but they hadn't shared like that in a long time. Then Joe shrugged, smiled, and draped his long arm across Alex's shoulders. "Sorry, man. Didn't mean to freak you out. Sometimes I just wonder what it'd be like to be invisible, you know? Like Claude Rains in that movie we watched in Mister Burns' theater class junior year."

Alex's legs went numb. He had stopped listening the second the word *invisible* came out of Joe's blackened mouth. The word struck a chord of fear in his mind. He didn't want to think about it. He was tired of thinking about it.

Joe looked at him, sweat-streaked makeup running into his eyes—the same lost little kid look that had always gotten him out of running track in gym and made the girls want to take him home to mom.

Alex shrugged him off. "You're still coming tonight, right?"

"Naw," Joe said, backing toward the house, looking like some weirdo at a *Kiss* concert. "Got plans."

Alex's stomach flipped. "What kind of plans?"

"Oh, you know, a little praying for my soul, a little blood-letting, a little animal sacrifice." Joe shrugged, grinning like a maniac. "The usual."

Alex looked at the grass. "It's just easier when you're there."

Joe stepped onto the porch and wiped black makeup from his eyes. "I'm always with you, Rex. No doubt. You know that." He flashed a peace sign and a cocky grin and went inside.

8:43pm

Joe raked his blond hair out of his eyes and positioned the sharp corner of a razor blade just under his left nostril. Squeezing the pimple there, he leaned close to the medicine cabinet mirror and stopped.

Why do you do it? Why do you cut yourself, Joe? Dr. Rivers' soft voice had a benevolent tone.

"Shut up," Joe told the voice in his head. "I didn't invite you to this party."

He dragged the blade downward, cutting deep. Pus mixed with blood shot onto the glass. *Stitches,* he thought, but was too tired to thread a needle. The plotting and organizing—finding the most pristine patch of skin to allow the darkness to flow from—always got his blood moving. But once he cut, burned, *bled,* exhaustion set in like a hard-core sedative.

Fuck Dr. Rivers.

The howling inside Joe's head had started early, pulling his focus from repeated attempts to push good thoughts to Alex for his performance. Instead, as the day had gathered into deep shadows and storm clouds had mounted in the eastern sky, so had Joe's anxiety. Ubiquitous mutterings beckoned. He'd tried not to listen, tried not to hear their promises. *So much for that.* He smiled, the flesh of his lip pulling apart, revealing a viscous crevice. He worked the wound with his tongue, tasting metal and salt.

Alex would ask about the cut. Always did. "Cut myself shaving," Joe told his pale reflection, practicing the lost kid expression Alex and everyone else seemed to buy into most. Alex would believe him. Always did. He'd nod in fleeting concern and drop the subject, ignoring the fact that Joe had no facial hair except for the sparse patch just below his lower lip. Sometimes, in dreams, he still heard Alex's screams, still felt cold vaporous hands on his skin, pulling him away from the living and into the cadaverous shadows. The ache for that cool darkness had grown stronger in recent weeks.

"Pitiful," Joe said to his reflection.

Laughter sounded below. Mrs. Schell had offered to hold the monthly church social because Mrs. Dugan's boy, Charlie, had come down with the stomach flu. Chittery female voices drifted up through the heating ducts, commenting on the deviled eggs, the spinach dip and, of course, *the poor boy.*

"Is he still seeing that doctor? That, uh, proctologist?"

Joe scowled. *Yeah. Stick your finger up my ass, you stupid bitch. You'd like that.*

"Psychiatrist," Norma corrected. "No. He's not seeing him anymore. Waste of money. Satan's in him, nothing more."

"Oh, Norma, honey. You've been through so much. You are such an inspiration to us all. Remember, God doesn't give us anything we can't handle. Hold strong to your faith, sister."

"Praise Jesus," Joe whispered.

"Praise Jesus," said Mrs. Schell.

Mrs. Schell. That's what he called the woman who'd given him birth nearly nineteen years ago. Her voice grew distant for a moment then high-pitched cackling roiled up from the ducts again.

Joe bit down on his lower lip. Coppery blood ran into his mouth. He bit harder, feeling the tender tissue give way. *That's better,* his mind whispered, *slow and easy. Take your time. You are the Lamb.* Tears strained, but he refused to let them come.

A pattering rain mingled with the clucking below. The barrage filled his head, vibrating his insides like a thousand baby rattles shaken at once. Sucking at the swelling flesh of his mouth, Joe shuffled out of the bathroom, steadier now, mind quiet.

He thought about the drive home from the hospital that day. The scene replayed in his mind like a frantic cartoon, all color and motion. Mrs. Schell had dressed for the occasion, sporting a tight pink skirt and blouse and a wide-brimmed fuchsia hat pulled down over her bottle blonde head. Her lipstick had been an odd shade of orange—peach maybe— and she never failed to smear her teeth with whatever putrid color she selected for the day. Every time Joe had looked at her mouth he'd wanted to vomit, so he tried to focus on her stenciled eyebrows instead. Those crayoned tufts of hair never moved, even when she spoke. They arched above her blue eyes, creating a perpetual look of surprise, or judgment. Maybe pity, but he doubted that.

Fucking phony clowns.

He knew she'd bought the garish pink costume as a consolation gift to herself, the penitent and patient mother pretending to grieve over her sinful and wayward son. In truth, the purchase had been a celebration of his probable demise. Except he didn't die like he was supposed to. They had driven seventeen miles before she decided to part her brightly painted lips and say something.

"God will punish you," she told him, staring straight ahead, knuckles white on the steering wheel of her blue

Pontiac Bonneville, long peach fingernails digging into the flesh of her palms.

Joe glanced at the long, thin, white scars on the insides of his arms, feeling sick with failure. *He already has.*

Joe studied his naked body in the huge mirror, thinking he looked much like a corpse that had been rolled in jagged pieces of broken glass until every inch of its flesh was sliced open, drained of blood. Dark shadows smudged the hollows under his blue eyes. Ruby lips stood out against a vampiric complexion, in sharp contrast with dark eyebrows. He pulled his shoulder-length hair back and studied the nearly healed wire-thin scar on his neck. Cutting that close to his jugular had been a real kick in the head.

The looking glass left mere inches of wall space on all sides, with a frame of tarnished brass knobs and gnarled bars that hung off the sides in a riotous mess of metal. It seemed the mirror had always been a part of his room, although Mrs. Schell had bought it just three months before *the incident.* He'd heard the tale more times than he could count—God told her to purchase the monstrous accessory at a garage sale over in Grants Pass. She had thought it hideous but refused to disobey His command.

"His command," Joe mocked in the deepest voice he could muster.

He searched the piles of junk on the floor for a pair of long johns. More clucking erupted downstairs. Lightning sparked, strobing through the room in manic flashes, making his eyes hurt. He checked Wolfgang Rat's water bottle then leaned and kissed his poster of Marilyn Monroe goodnight.

"You and me, babe," he told her. "Someday."

He flashed Jimi and Janis, Marilyn's companions on the wall, a peace sign, opened the window wider, got into bed, and pulled the blankets over his head, hoping to be asleep before Mrs. Schell came upstairs. He didn't think he could handle listening to her pray at her bedside for things to be the way they were, praying for God to save her son from whatever evil had seized his young heart. Not that she truly cared. She performed the ritual more out of insane duty to her god and perfunctory maternal obligation than any true affection. He knew no amount of prayer could save him now.

Joe drifted toward twilight sleep. A freight train passed three blocks away, rattling the windowpane. A cool breeze swept raindrops through the window. Thunder boomed, but Joe didn't hear it. He was dreaming, and in his dream the mirror beside his bed became hazy, swirling with dancing pinpoints of movement as a small hand found its way through the glass and glided through the air. It reached down gently and placed a single fingertip on Joe's chest, then disappeared back through the glass, replaced by black birds flapping madly against a wall of liquid glass …

A shriek of violins jolted him awake. Joe swallowed, mouth dry, and reached for the open Coke bottle on the floor. He chugged it down and tossed the empty toward the overflowing bin in the corner but missed. *Gotta remember to drag those over to Alex's for return. Probably got about five bucks worth in there. Fucking hippie.*

The holy hypocrite party had ended, leaving the house quiet and creaking in the nocturnal wind. Joe got up and padded down the hallway to Norma's room. He pressed his ear to the door. Muffled A.M. talk radio played. She kept that shit on all night long. He opened the door a few inches and peered inside. She lay on her back, breathing heavy, an open Bible balanced on one mountainous breast.

Joe crept into the room and looked down at his mother. Without the mask of color on her face, she looked older than her forty-five years and absurdly harmless. A thin translucent scar trailed from just above her left eyebrow, across her browbone, and down to her outer cheekbone. The result of a car accident when she was ten, she said. Joe had heard the story ad nauseum when he was younger. Her father had lost control while driving over a narrow bridge on a Christmas trip to Minnesota, she said. They were the only two people in the car, she said. The vehicle had plunged into icy waters and he drowned. She had loved her father very much and he had loved her. She said when she met Marcus, he reminded her of her father. She said she loved Marcus and missed him deeply and wished he would come home.

She said a lot of things.

Joe let his hand hover over the scar on his mother's face. He traced it slowly with his index finger, seeing how close he could get without actually touching her. Then he traced the other lines, the result of life and godfear and penitence and rage. *They're like roads on a map to perdition,* Joe thought.

The radio host said something about humans using only ten percent of their brain capacity. Joe frowned. *No way, gotta be less than that.* He lifted the Bible carefully from his mother's chest and looked to see what she had been entertaining herself with before drifting off. *Song of Solomon.* One of his favorites. It created a sad melancholy in him, and he liked that.

Joe closed the leather-bound book, placed it on the nightstand and went to retrieve his poor widowed grandmother's hand crocheted quilt from the rocking chair by the chest of drawers. As he passed, he glanced at the crucified figure hanging above the altar in the corner and tried to ignore the wicked chill that wracked his spine. Joe covered his mother's rotund form with the blanket and brushed a few strands of straw-colored hair from her pasty brow. She'd been beautiful once, slender and fit. Happy. He'd seen photos. She didn't look like herself anymore. A result of life and godfear and penitence and rage.

Joe shuffled to the corner altar and looked up into the mounted martyr's withered face. He hung there like an embattled king watching over an artificial queen. Joe touched the figure's feet, the right nailed over the top of the left and warmed by flickering flames in glass cups. Shadows flitted around the room. Joe leaned to kiss the savior's stiff toes.

"Scars run in the family," Joe whispered. "Sorry, man."

He blew out the candles and left the room.

Norma had her nightly rituals.

Joe had his.

8:43pm

The violin bow hit the wall with an angry crack and came flying back like a boomerang. Alex stooped, picked it up and sent it spinning into the wall again, hoping it would break and he'd have a legitimate excuse not to play besides his lame hands cramping up every time he tried. The damn thing didn't break, no matter how hard he flung it at his Albert Einstein poster, which was heavily marred and pocked from previous episodes of frustration just like this one.

Alex gave up and sat on the wood floor by his bed. He looked at his fingers, curled stiff on his knees, and willed them to open. They didn't. They clenched up tight every time he picked up his violin or even thought about playing. It had been an issue for a few years but had gotten exponentially worse over the past year to the point that he'd had to cancel numerous performances, which pissed him off. He closed his eyes and breathed out. Light from the bedside lamp filtered through his eyelids and he noticed, without amusement, that the music notes prompting him to play in the first place were still there, dancing in the darkness of his mind like lunatic fairies. He tried, really tried, to hear the silence between them—the empty spaces where the magic lived—but it was no use. Alex grabbed the bow and held it in both hands with every intention of breaking it into as many pieces as he could before coming to his senses. He cast a sideways glance at Albert.

Great spirits have always encountered violent opposition from mediocre minds.

He looked at the *Star Wars* poster pinned up next to Albert. *May the Force be with you.*

Alex cracked a wry smile. Luke had loved that movie. The x-wing fighter jets flying through space had thrilled the hell out of his kid brother, and the fact that he shared a name with the young Jedi hero was bonus in Luke's book. When *The Empire Strikes Back* came out it was all Luke could talk about. When Vader sliced off Skywalker's hand, Luke jumped out of his seat and screamed *asshole!* at the top of his lungs, which made Alex uncomfortable in the crowded theater and Joe laugh until he fell out of his seat. *Don't go to the dark side, Ally,* Luke would say, gray eyes wide. *It sucks ass over there. Plus, you could lose a hand!*

Alex's shoulders dropped. He let out a tired breath. He stared at the bow in his useless hands. Buying the thing had been the only sign of encouragement his father had ever given him concerning his "sissy music" and, despite Joe's very vocal opinions on the matter, that meant something to him.

Alex placed the violin and bow back in their worn case and rubbed his face. Flipping the lid closed, he stared at the dull gold plate bearing his name—*Alexander Thomas Knapp*—and realized the letters, the name itself, held no more meaning than a puddle of mud. Not anymore. He pulled his nose, a habit he'd developed as a kid to help him think. Earlier he had listened to his mom on the phone, making excuses for him. He'd lost track of how many times in the last three years she'd had to repeat the same script … *No, he's not feeling well … yes, still very difficult … yes, I'll tell him.* Then the obligatory *thank you for being so understanding and flexible.*

Flexible. Alex hated that word. Flexibility involved pain.

"I'm a fucking idiot," he whispered.

A thunderous crack shook the house. Alex jumped. Raindrops battered the windowpane. The sky had turned as black and thick as old soot. Uneasy, he combed his fingers through his dark hair, rubbed his thumb along the callused fingertips of his left hand, and shuddered at the gloom.

Sudden flashes of bright light followed by a deafening boom of thunder. The room plunged into darkness. Alex's heart throttled. Panic took hold, pinning him in a vice grip. His pulse drummed. He tried to swallow, but found it impossible, mouth drained of moisture. He couldn't get enough air into his lungs. Darkness squeezed, gripped his insides with invisible hands. Shadows sprang to life, surrounded him, suffocating. His legs shook numbly. He crawled backward toward the wall, trying to remember Dr. Lyn's instructions. *Try to remain calm, take deep breaths through your nose and … and* what? Images of streaming blood and torn flesh strobed through his mind. Shadows leapt, reached into his lungs, wrung the air out. A sudden memory took hold, slamming into his head so hard he felt the room tilt, and he was instantly there …

Alex's arm stretched downward, reaching. Sand and dirt spilled onto a young boy's red face as he clung to the rocks and roots jutting from the side of the incline. The kid's legs dangled, useless, unable to find ground. Below him, dusty darkness.

"Hold on," Alex said. "Don't let go."

"Don't let me fall, Al," the boy pleaded. "Please don't let me fall."

"I won't, Luke. I promise."

Hanging in his harness, Alex kicked, tried to get closer, and sent a cascade of pebbles and sand into the boy's face, who began to choke, his throat filling with dust. The kid panicked, thrashing his legs, and then tumbled into darkness. Screams bounced back from cold canyon walls—

Save him, Alex. A woman's voice. Inside his head.

He was suddenly back in his room. A trembling breath caught in his dry throat. Alex slid along the wall toward the door and groped for the knob.

"Please," he gasped. "Not again."

Sweat stung his wide eyes, but he didn't dare close them. *Don't blink. Don't blink or they'll get you—suck out your soul and make you one of them. Don't. Blink.*

He turned the doorknob, a hoarse groan escaping his throat. "Mom?"

She was already in the hallway. Elizabeth tucked her arm around Alex's waist and guided him to the living room window where he could see the emergency lights at the railroad crossing in the distance.

"Remember," she coached. "The darkness doesn't last forever. There's nothing to be afraid of. The shadows aren't real. Deep breaths. Nose first then out through your mouth. Long exhales."

Tears of frustration and fear rolled down Alex's cheeks. *Please, not again.*

"You're doing better, hon," Elizabeth said, giving him an encouraging smile. "At least you didn't start screaming like last time."

May 20, 1984

In the dream, Joe dug, fingers unearthing bits and pieces at a time. Roses bloomed, their thorns like a crown around his head. Flesh tore loose in his hands, slippery so he couldn't hold on to the parts, the important parts, the parts that mattered most. Just as he settled one piece into place to make it make sense, the others would jump away, dragging bone and sinew out of reach and he'd have to chase them through the thorns. The thorns made him bleed and when he looked up all he saw were rings of thorns, like crowns hovering above his head. O mighty King Joseph, ye are defeated. Warm, saltsweet liquid filled his nostrils. He breathed in the flowery perfume until his veins ran thick with it, then got back to digging.

Joe woke with his hands clamped over his stomach. He ran to the bathroom and slumped against the tub, groping for the gold ring on the chain around his neck. Hot bile burned. He launched himself toward the toilet, but didn't make it, instead rocking onto his hands and knees, clear vomit spilling onto the floor. Below, he heard the front door open and close. Heavy feet pounded up the stairs. He tried to stand.

"Joe, get up. We have to—"

Alex stood at the bedroom door, sweatshirt and hair damp with perspiration from his morning run. For months he'd been claiming the physical exertion helped turn musicland upside down. Joe knew better.

"Jesus," Alex said. "You sick? What the hell happened to your mouth?"

Joe wiped his face with the sleeve of his gray long johns. He almost always wore them now, so Alex wouldn't see. "Cut myself shaving."

Alex left the room, muttering under his breath, and returned a moment later with a mop. *The mop.* Spatters of blood still stained the neck, standing out like accusations. Joe squeezed his eyes shut tight for a second then got up and fished in a pile of clothes for jeans and a T-shirt, found a Van Halen one that didn't smell too bad, and put everything on over his long johns, tying a plaid shirt around his narrow hips. Alex mopped with his back to him and Joe didn't blame him. He knew he was hard to look at these days, especially for Alex.

"Delivery day," Alex said. "Mary needs us to pull boxes from the basement. Up for a walk?"

"Yep. Gotta piss first." He traded places with Alex and closed the bathroom door, avoiding eye contact. Alex's worry hung on him like a heavy wet blanket and Joe didn't want to make it worse. He met Alex downstairs, poured coffee from the pot and lit a cigarette.

"You know I hate smoke. Makes me sick. And your shirt's on backwards. Can't even see Eddie's face. And there's a hole in the armpit."

"Want coffee?" Joe asked, ignoring Alex's complaints. Mrs. Schell had placed a twenty-dollar bill next to the coffee maker. Joe crammed it into his pocket.

"Missus Schell never forgets allowance day," he muttered. "She never forgets anything."

Joe drank cold coffee and snuffed his cigarette in a gleaming glass potpourri holder on the counter. He'd caught the stuff on fire once and had a good laugh at Mrs. Schell's flustered attempts to put out the flames with an oven mitt.

"I'll meet you outside," Joe said, heading for the stairs. "Forgot my board."

When Joe came downstairs, he found Alex standing in the foyer, gazing into the living room. Joe looked, too. He knew being in the house made Alex anxious and not only because of what happened. The place was like a shrine— dozens of paintings of Jesus and Mother Mary stared from the walls, plaintive and patient, among them a giant velvet portrait of the resigned messiah holding out bloody hands to anyone who might take them. A gold plaque affixed to the bottom frame promised *The Blood of the Lamb Saves.* Crucifixes were mounted on every inch of wall space.

"Remember when you went through the house and turned all the crucifixes upside down while Norma was at church?"

Joe grinned. "She ran out of the house so fucking fast, screaming that demons had taken over her holy home. She looked like a clown twirling down the driveway."

Alex grinned, too. "She wouldn't go back until Brother Adam came and blessed the living room. I thought she was gonna have a stroke."

"It's good to have goals," Joe said, trying to lighten Alex's mood, and was pleased to see Alex's smile deepen.

"Don't know how you live in this house, man. Even the smell is intense. What is that anyway?"

"Still lavender, dude. Like it has been our whole damn lives. Guess I'm used to it."

"I hate this house," Alex stated.

"I know," Joe said, reaching for the doorknob. They stepped into the crisp morning air.

"Sweet Jesus," Joe shouted. "We haven't done anything fun and rebellious and utterly fucked-up in a long time. Let's have a really good day, okay Rex?"

Alex nodded, eyes fixed on the house.

Joe followed Alex's gaze. "What? Paint peeling?"

"No," Alex said. "I just … the house seems different. It looks weird. Empty."

"Well, Alex," Joe said, drawing out his words as if talking to a two-year-old in the hopes it would ease Alex's mood even more. "The house *is* empty right now. Should we watch an episode of *Sesame Street* so Grover can explain the concept of *empty* to you?" He crossed his eyes and grinned his best jester's grin, feeling the cut in his lip pull a bit.

"You're a disaster," Alex said, smirking. "And you need to tie your shoes, so you don't crack open your fucking *empty* head."

Joe doubled over in laughter. He slapped Alex's back, gasping for air, then dropped his ragged skateboard, stepped on, sailed down the driveway, ollied off the sidewalk while leaping into the air to catch a handful of elm leaves, and wiped out in the middle of the street. He could hear Alex laughing hard.

"Told you to tie your shoes," Alex called.

Grinning, Joe flipped him off with both middle fingers and took a dramatic bow. He decided to annoy the hell out of Alex by whistling a hyped-up version of *Amazing Grace* all the way to Mary's front door. Judging by Alex's exasperated sighs, it worked.

The storyteller sat in her wooden rocking chair, chin on her chest, snoring softly and mumbling her dead husband's name. Her shoulders rose and fell with the steady rhythm of sleep-breath. A thick, gray braid draped over one shoulder to coil in her lap. Joe slipped Mary's reading glasses off her nose, rousing the woman from her slumber.

"Didn't mean to wake you," Alex said.

"Meh!" Mary waved a wood dust-covered hand as if shooing a bothersome fly, then wiped her hands on her smock. "I've been working since five. It's time for my walk."

"Watch it," Joe warned, a wicked glint in his eye. "People might start calling you One Who Walks Across Cutters Grove. They'll think you're out searching for some big secret."

Mary smiled her own mischievous grin. "And some might call you One Who is a Pain in the Ass."

Joe smiled. "Good one, Whitewing."

"Secrets abound. Don't they, Joseph?"

"You know it." Joe pulled a hacky sack from his pocket and he and Alex began kicking it back and forth between them.

"Story today, *gwiiwizensidog*? Or just passing through?"

"It's Tuesday," Alex said, concentrating on the footbag. "We came to bring up the boxes from the basement. They were delivered yesterday."

"Good," Mary said, glancing at the clock on the wall. "No hurry then. What would you two like to hear?"

"How about the sound of Alex crying like a little girl when I make him drop the sack?"

"Shut up," Alex said.

"You shut up," Joe said.

"Nothing changes," Mary said. She jumped in and intercepted Alex's pass, kicked the hacky sack to Joe, who back-kicked it to Alex, who missed. The footbag rolled under the couch and Alex dropped to all-fours to fish it out.

"Damn left-handers," he grumbled. "I can never win against you two. You do everything backward."

Joe and Mary high-fived each other and Mary yelled, "Southpaws for the win! As usual!" Smiling, she settled back into her chair, huffing a little. "Okay, which story today, my *gwiiwizensidog*?"

"How about One Who Walks, since we're on the subject," Alex said.

Joe groaned. "Jesus, Al, we've been listening to that one since we were born. Pick a different one."

"Excuse me if it's my favorite, dumbshit. You pick."

"*Songaona*," Joe said.

Alex shook his head. "And you call *me* predictable."

"*Songaona* it is." Mary filled her pipe with sweet cherry tobacco and held a flame to it, puffing until scented smoke swirled around their heads.

Alex kicked the hacky sack high. Joe caught it and crammed it into his jeans pocket. In unison, they slumped to the couch, propped their feet up on the coffee table, crossed their ankles, and closed their eyes. They'd been listening to Mary's stories about passionate love, fierce battles, selfless sacrifice, great journeys, and debilitating losses all their lives. This one was as familiar to them as their own skin.

Once, in the days of moonlight and dust, twin boys were born of separate wombs. One had skin the color of the white stones lying at the bottom of the riverbed, the other had skin the color of the black oil found deep within the earth's core. Each knew the other's thoughts and fears. Each held the other's lifepulse within his own chest. They shared a strength uncommon, knew the ways of one another's dreams, and spoke of traveling together into the deepest realms of the soul. This they called 'songaona,' the sharing, and Moon blessed them.

Makate, the son of Midnight, painted the hills every morning in a rainbow of streaming color, singing the songs of clouds and washing the sky with his tears. But Wabishk, the son of Dawn, floundered, struggling for breath and footing on this earth. Light always ran from him and the chase made him tired. Wabishk grew weak in his fight for light and eventually vanished, consumed by the darkness that is sometimes necessary. Day by day, Dawn dwindled into a matted hue and the hills lost color. Sky dimmed. Wildflowers paled. Makate was heartbroken at the loss of his brother, so lost that he refused to leave the hogan for fear that Darkness would consume him also. The people were very sad. They mourned for the rainbow hills and clean sky. They tried to entice Makate from his safe shelter, to no avail. Many moons came and went. One day Dawn did not come. With unbalance upon the land, the people suffered. Sickness took many, especially the babies. "If only Wabishk could be found," the people sang, mournfully. "If only Wabishk had fought a little harder."

But Makate knew it was not so simple. Makate knew the sweet seduction of Darkness.

In spring, the rains came and the wakwi sent Makate a dream. He dreamed of Wabishk trapped in a dark place and singing out for help. Sinister long-fingered hands held Wabishk down and fed him poisonous snakes, which coiled through his nostrils and back into his throat. But part of Wabishk kept singing, so Makate knew there was hope. Upon waking, Makate told the people that he would walk into night's core and retrieve his brother, who called to him in the drone of the loon's song and the difficult sighs of the wind. The only thing he would take for protection against the long-fingered demons, he told them, would be a white feather.

Stripped bare, Makate set forth with the white feather entwined in his hair. He walked and walked, thinking only of light. Then Darkness found him. The battle for Wabishk was fierce and bloody. Darkness held fast. Makate lost his way more than once. Soon, Darkness offered a proposition. The boy Makate listened carefully for any tricks.

"I have a compromise," Darkness said. "Trade your soul for your brother's and I will free him."

"The music of the land has grown silent," Makate explained. "Balance must be restored."

"His soul or yours," Darkness demanded. "Choose."

"Yes, I choose," Makate said, and began to sing the song of songaona to fortify Wabishk's spirit and make his heart strong. "Bezhigo nijichaagonnaan." Makate thought, my brother's soul and mine are one, and he took the battered Wabishk into his spirit, his essence blending with that of his brother.

Darkness roared, angered by the boy's courage and selfless love.

Thirteen moons after Makate struck out on his tireless journey, a stranger found his way to the people. His walk was familiar, yet his face unknown and deeply lined with the wisdom of the gods. The stranger's skin, painted with rainbows and the aura of the sun, illuminated the dim world with an amber glow. His long white hair brushed the earth at his heels, a single white feather entwined into the fine strands. He gathered the people into his arms, and they wept.

"I am Wabikate," the stranger said. "I am reborn, and I am strong. I bring balance to the land."

At that moment, Dawn returned in a blinding streak and harmony was reborn. The people sang in gratitude and bowed to Wabikate for his sacrifice. This they call songaona, the sharing. And Dawn blessed them.

"I still don't see why Makate had to die," Alex said. "Why didn't Wabishk just nut up and tell Darkness to screw off?"

"Jesus, Al. If you haven't gotten it by now, you never will."

Mary set her smoldering pipe in the bowl on the worktable. "Why do you think?"

"Makate came to an understanding," Joe said, "and it scared him."

Mary nodded. "I see."

"It scared him more than death," Joe whispered.

"Nothing's more terrifying than death," Alex countered.

"How would you know?" Joe snapped.

Alex tried hard to see into Joe's eyes, but Joe wouldn't

let him. He jerked his head just as Alex caught something there.

"So, where's our wish?" Joe stood and stretched his gangly arms overhead with a noisy yawn.

"*Aaniindi giwiishkobanjiganinaan*," Mary corrected. "You boys never forget your *wish*. I have you well-trained." She pulled a familiar alabaster jar from the cabinet and held it out. "Only one. You know the rules."

Joe reached in and extracted a black ball the size of a plump blueberry. He popped it into his mouth with a grand flourish and rolled it around his tongue, smiling.

Alex took one, closed his eyes, and put the black licorice ball on his tongue. Mary always granted one wish after every story. She said it was like prayer, only better.

"Well?" she asked.

"Whirled peas," Joe said, predictably.

Alex shook his head, a familiar sadness pulling behind his closed eyelids, and thought, *I don't want to be afraid anymore.*

"Ditto the whirled peas," he said.

"You two," Mary said, smirking. "One day you just might get what you ask for. Get to work. I'm going for a walk. I open at ten so no screwing around."

12:17pm

Joe climbed the branches of the bigleaf maple, his lanky form silhouetted against the stormy sky. Alex followed as rainclouds chased the sun into deeper shadow. Confrontations with Mrs. Schell were not high on their priority list, so they rarely used the front door of Joe's house anymore. Drops of rain dotted the red slate as Alex pushed the bedroom window closed, muffling a boom of thunder and sealing in the gloom.

"Gotta piss." Joe headed for the bathroom.

Alex sat in the desk chair. He stared at Wolfgang and wondered again how Joe could name the disgusting rodent after one of the greatest composers of all time, but also knew Joe had done it to irritate him. The fat rat ran on his metal wheel, tireless.

"What does this thing eat?" Alex called over the steady sound of urine hitting toilet water.

"Armadillos," Joe answered from the bathroom.

"I don't doubt it." Alex wrinkled his nose at the beast. "You're hideous."

Joe sat on the floor and lit a cigarette. "Hey, be nice to Wolfie. He's got a tumor."

Alex smirked. "Good."

"You know what else?"

"What?"

"That place is haunted, man."

Alex shot Joe a look, quelling the familiar impulse to shake him until he puked up all his secrets. He hated when Joe talked about Cutters Estate—*that night* at Cutters Estate. Joe had been bringing it up more than usual lately.

Alex heaved a heavy sigh. "Don't start with that bullshit. It never happened."

Joe rolled his eyes and shook his head. "You still don't believe what we saw? Jesus, most people pray for tangible evidence. Seeing is believing and all that crap. You see it and you *still* don't believe your own eyes. I thought you'd have accepted it by now. What the fuck?"

"There was rain and fog and it was dark. We couldn't even see the trains we went up there to watch. So, drop it."

Joe exhaled a steady stream of smoke. "The rain and fog weren't enough to hide that girl while she was being murdered right in front of us, Al."

Alex tried to quiet the hum in his head. Lightning flashed, followed by a raucous boom of thunder.

Joe opened his mouth then closed it again.

Alex squinted through the growing gloom. "What?"

"You're such a pussy, Al." Joe grabbed two Cokes from the crate on the floor, opened them with the bottle opener attached to the wall, and gave one to Alex.

Alex clenched his teeth. *I'm a pussy? You're the one sucking death like oxygen and I'm the pussy?* But he kept his mouth shut. He was a coward, the king of denial and avoidance—conflict, red meat, game shows, sorrowful memories, death. Whatever. He would never admit that he envied Joe's passionate understanding of death, *of dying,* and his reticent acceptance of the inevitable. Joe had embraced the Grim Reaper long ago, had kissed the Mighty Shrouded One full on the lips without flinching, had probably given Ol' Black a little tongue, too. Alex took a long swig of his soda. *It's not the death part that scares me, it's the dying part.* He turned and saw Joe looking at him.

There are worse things than death, Al. Way worse. Joe's voice was like a bell clanging inside Alex's head. Joe hadn't pushed his thoughts in so long Alex had forgotten how annoying it was. He tried to see beyond the long hair hanging in Joe's face and pushed back. *Like what?*

Like giving up your soul for the wrong reason. Joe took a deep drag and Alex could taste the smoke on his own tongue. Joe broke eye contact then, extracting himself from inside Alex's head. He snuffed his smoke on the sole of his shoe.

"You think I'm crazy, just like everyone else in this shit-small town."

Alex rubbed his eyes. Being in that space with Joe used to boost his energy. Now it drained him.

"You're not the crazy one in this house, man."

Joe smirked. "Yeah. Poor ol' Missus Schell with the possessed son. It's the devil in him! It's the devil, I say!"

Alex shook his head, trying not to laugh. The impending threat of the storm had set his nerves on edge.

"Hey, Al, ever consider matricide?"

Alex frowned. "Of course not. You *are* nuts."

"Me neither. I love my mama."

They burst into laughter.

Joe bounced on his butt like an excited preschooler. "She loves me, too. She doesn't even have to say it, I can see it in her eyes. Those sincere, compassionate, sympathetic—no, wait—*pathetic* eyes of hers." He brushed invisible tears from his cheeks in a dramatic flourish. "It's just so damn *touching*."

Alex laughed until his sides ached.

Joe pursed his lips, crossed his eyes, and patted Alex's knee. "God is the answer, son. Just look at what he's done for me." He grabbed non-existent breasts and plumped his lips in an obscene smile, dark eyebrows jumping up and down in maniacal dance.

Alex almost fell out of his chair. Still bouncing, Joe lit another Camel.

Alex wiped his eyes. *Why can't it be like this all the time?* He heard Joe's voice clear and liquid inside his head. *Because you're a chicken shit, Al, and you don't want to see.*

Alex slid to the floor and crossed his legs, facing Joe. *Okay. Let's play.*

Joe smirked, raking stringy hair out of his face. *What do you want to see?*

Whatever you want to show me, man. You know that.

Joe tilted his head, gaze steady. Alex sucked a sharp breath as an image of bloody brown hair and cut skin filled his vision. His senses flooded. He smelled mowed grass, wet and lush, scented blood on the wind, heard muffled cries of terror and bewilderment mixed with thunder—and tried to break Joe's hold. But Joe was stronger. Always had been. Alex didn't want to see this again, but Joe seemed intent on replaying the scene with fervor this time.

Stop, Alex thought and was surprised when Joe let go immediately. Alex slumped over, heart beating fast and hard. He could still taste the blood rain in his mouth.

"It happened, Al. Accept it."

"You put that in my head. It's not my memory. It's not real."

Joe scowled. "Okay, have it your way. Stay in your safe little world. But you know better. I can't make you see what's not true." He brought the cigarette to his ruby lips, cherry glowing hot in the dimming light.

"Jesus, that wipes me out. Didn't used to, but now …" Wiping his eyes, Alex glanced at his reflection in the looking glass—and blinked.

A drop of clear liquid slid along a lower brass curvature before dropping off and disappearing into the bedspread. Another droplet emerged from the glass, following the same path as the first. Alex leaned forward. He couldn't see a crack. The bead of water seemed to appear from nowhere. There was another and another.

"It's been doing that," Joe murmured.

Alex cleared his throat. "It's raining. You've got a leak in the roof and it's coming out of the wall behind the mirror."

Joe nodded, a faraway look in his eyes. "It's not rainwater."

Sudden fatigue settled deep in Alex's bones.

"They're tears." Joe's gaze met Alex's in the glass.

Alex raised his eyebrows. "Yeah, and I'm Eddie Murphy." He smiled then frowned when Joe didn't give up the joke.

"Taste it. It's salty." Joe nodded toward the monstrosity on the wall and gave Alex a shove.

"Okay, okay," Alex said, shaking his head. He stood up, hesitated, then leaned over Joe's bed and put his finger on the glass, damming the droplet's course.

Save him.

Alex jumped back. Her voice sounded as crisp and clear as it had in his room when the lights went out.

"Joe—" Something caught him, hitting his chest so hard he lost his breath. Tackled by an invisible force, Alex reeled backward and sprawled on his back next to Joe. Stunned, he lay there, gasping at the sharp pain shooting down his spine.

"What the fu—" Alex stared at the mirror.

"Look." Joe pointed.

Beyond the glass, a wave, thick and red, arced toward them. The ruddy crest seemed to move from very far away, from deep within the wall itself, growing bigger and closer, until it crashed silently against the glass of the mirror, filling it with a milky rust color. The thick substance clung to the glass and a figure emerged. Alex's breath hitched. He recognized the young woman's long dark hair—exactly as Joe had shown him again and again, saturated in blood, her light brown eyes filled with terror and shock. Beyond the surface of the mirror, she whirled and stumbled. She seemed to be looking for a way out of the glass encasement, a means of escape from the thick, menacing liquid. She fell to her knees, got up and fell again, hunting in desperation for an exit. She railed against forces unseen then raised her arms high above her head, mouth open in a silent scream. A dark rust wave rose up behind her. Alex watched, horror-struck, as the surge worked its way toward her, pulsating like an enlarged heart. The liquid engulfed her. Alex let out a yell and lunged at the glass.

In a flash of bright light, the woman's flesh connected with his and Alex's feet swung up from the carpet. In a violent pitch, he sailed across the room, through the open bathroom door and shower curtain, and crashed into the bathtub wall, legs dangling over the edge. Clear fluid saturated his left arm. Nauseating pinpricks erupted under his skin. Alex frantically wiped his arm and hand on his jeans and sat up, sure that the electric bolt had zapped his brain. A deafening heart-pulse filled his head. He scrambled out of the tub.

Joe sat stone still in the center of the bedroom floor, a deep scowl creasing his usually disaffected expression. "So, she's protecting—"

Alex heard something unfamiliar in Joe's voice. Sadness. Grief. Desperate, trembling regret.

"What is this shit?!" Alex's shout broke through the hum in his own ears, beamed down from a distant place. His words seemed broken, meaningless. His fingers tingled and he rubbed them as he stared at the mirror, anxiety mounting. *What the hell was that?!*

Joe's face looked odd in the dimness. Paler than usual, with strange dark shapes and lines contorting his features, as if something moved just below the surface of his flesh. His red lips quivered. He looked like a little kid who had just busted his grandma's favorite picture frame. Scared. Ashamed. Haunted.

"Look," Alex said, kneeling and grabbing Joe's arm too tight. "You have to tell me. I'm not letting you slide on this one, Joe." Darkness crept in. The rain fell harder. The air felt like wet wallpaper.

Joe wrapped his cold fingers around Alex's wrist and pulled his hand away. His eyes never left the mirror.

"The dream is back."

Alex leaned forward, keeping a watchful eye out for the soul-suckers that would soon be lunging from dark corners. Rain pounded the windowpanes.

"Like a movie," Joe continued. "Except, lately there have been variations. Instead of familiarity I feel emptiness, sadness. Loss. And need."

Alex pointed at the mirror. "What does *that thing* have to do with your dreams?"

"I don't know."

Alex shook his head. "Don't do that."

"What?"

"Don't lie. This isn't the first time this has happened, the first time you've seen her in that fucking thing." Alex got to his feet and flipped on the bathroom light. Pain jack-hammered in his skull, shockwaved through his shoulder joint.

"It's happened before," Joe admitted.

"When? A lot?"

"A few times now."

"Why?"

"Al, I don't know, but …" With a shaking hand, Joe pressed something into Alex's moist palm.

Alex squinted at the pendant, at the sterling silver bird's head with turquoise eyes, and shook his head. "What …?"

"I took it from Mary's when we were unpacking boxes today. You can see why, can't you, Al? You do remember we found a necklace exactly like this one embedded in the grass at Cutters Estate after that guy killed her, don't you?"

Alex clenched his jaw, pacing. He didn't remember. He was better at forgetting.

"It didn't used to be this way," Joe said, motioning toward the mirror. "Been real quiet since I tried— Just in the last couple of weeks it's been acting weird. Since the dream started."

Alex halted mid-step. "You've been having the dream for two weeks and you didn't tell me?"

Joe nodded, frowning. "Yeah. There's the small man with skin the color of coal—"

"—one of his eyes is white," Alex interrupted.

Joe squinted and Alex felt Joe's thoughts pour into him. *He dances in a snow-white desert—*

"—with an orange sun."

And there's a funky looking tree—

"—a Joshua tree."

He plays a drum and doesn't have a shadow.

Alex eased to the floor and leaned against the wall by the door. "Holy shit. I haven't had that dream since—"

"—our sixth birthday," Joe finished, swiping hair out of his eyes. "The day my mother came home."

two

May 21, 1984

Queens

Alex struggled to raise his head. Thick fog surrounded him. He waved his hand and watched mist trail from his fingers. He thought he should feel cold.

Two vague figures emerged from the dense air like skeletal trees revealed through a blanket of shifting gray. The smaller of the two moved toward Alex, body twisted and broken into odd angles. Bloodied bones poked through the torn flesh of its bent arms and legs. The concaved side of its head made its eye bulge in a grotesque bubble. The thing's head balanced precariously on its neck, which bowed out on one side in a purplish bulb. Blood gushed from a gaping head wound, soaking its sandy-brown hair and once white shirt. It shuffled forward, dust and dirt spilling from its nostrils, mouth, and ears. Slug-drunken, it turned to the taller figure and motioned for it to come closer.

The second figure moved like a stiff robot. Long, bubbling scars wound around its arms and legs in macabre spirals. Deep punctures on the creature's abdomen and wrists oozed blood and clear fluid, and dark shimmering scabs stood out on its chest and neck. Sinew, veins, and arteries popped through the skin of the thing's arms and face as Alex watched, horrified and unable to move. The surreal beings approached the bed he lay on and grinned, revealing broken, jagged teeth.

"Save us, Alex, save us," the creatures taunted, poking his chest with bloody nubs where fingers had once been. Their warbled words slurred together, sounding like a sinister hymn. Alex strained to shake off the grogginess and managed to lift one arm to push the closest creature. His hand sank into the thing's belly, soaking his arm with a viscous bloodshot liquid. The aberration laughed, black tongue winding from its mouth like an engorged worm, and pulled Alex's arm out of its body. Clenched in the fingers of his dripping hand, Alex held the monster's lifeless heart.

The creature grinned, singing in a static growl. "You have my heart and you still can't save me." As the phantoms faded, he heard their familiar voices speak again.

"We're waiting, Alex."

Then he fell through empty, dark caverns, twisting, searching, out of control. Blackness consumed him. He opened his mouth. Dust and dirt filled his throat. No sound came.

Alex jumped as if struck by a bolt of electricity and fell to the floor next to Joe's bed. Voices echoed in his ears. The dull hum in his head grew louder. Sweat drenched his hair. He pushed himself to his knees and looked around, disoriented, the surroundings familiar and not, and spotted the clock. Was it really nearly five at night? He needed to call his mom.

A voice trailed up through the air duct and after several long seconds of deciphering he recognized it as Mrs. Schell's. Her words, punctuated by the whistle in his head, rose and fell in angry jags. Alex got up and steadied himself. Pins and needles jabbed at his legs as he stood, holding the desk for support. He licked his dry lips and shuffled toward the door. Norma's voice grew louder as he made his way past the probing eyes of Jesus and Mary in the hallway and headed down the stairs, holding the railing tight.

"… and I don't want him in this house. It's bad enough I have one sinner living here. I won't have two!"

Norma stopped talking when she noticed Alex leaning against the kitchen doorjamb. He peered at Joe, who raised his stony gaze from the floor and looked at his mother's twisted painted face. His hands clenched, unclenched, clenched again. Mrs. Schell pointed a long pink fingernail at Alex. A forgotten curler clung to the back of her head, flapping with every move.

"*You* are not welcome in *my* home. I've told you before. I don't want you around my son. You're a bad influence."

The woman's nasal whine sang inside Alex's pounding skull and he winced. A familiar instinct kicked in, knotting his gut in a conflicted tangle of fear and disbelief. *Protect him. Keep him safe. If I don't do it, no one will.* Anger ignited.

"*Your son?*" Alex stepped forward, letting the fight overpower the flight reflex. Sensation returned to his legs, but they still shook, vibrating his entire body. "Got news for you, Sister Norma. Good mothers don't treat their sons this way."

Mrs. Schell snapped her heavily-mascaraed eyes back to Joe. "You see, Joseph? You see what you've allowed into my sanctified home? A spoiled, arrogant, insubordinate brat."

"*Disrespectful,* too," Alex said, with emphasis. He took another unstable step. Mrs. Schell stepped back, crossing her arms under her enormous boobs. The corners of Joe's mouth turned up slightly.

"And *insolent.*" Alex took another step. "And *discourteous* and *rude* and, oh yeah, *contemptuous.*"

Joe nodded. "That's a good one."

With each word, Alex took a step, until he was standing between Norma and Joe.

Norma had backed herself up against the kitchen stove. She glared at Alex, livid hate filling her painted eyes. A thick blue vein strained against the skin of her pancaked forehead.

"And *snotty*," Alex finished, cocking his head. "What did Joe ever do to you? Huh? He deserves better. Somebody who gives a shit. At least."

Mrs. Schell took a moment before she spoke.

"He knows exactly what he did. And *you* are nothing but a Godless heathen. A child killer."

Alex flinched. He felt the blood drain from his face.

Joe rushed at his mother. "Shut up," he seethed. "You have no right to say that."

Mrs. Schell's dark pink lips began to move silently, and Alex guessed she was praying. *Yeah, pray*, he thought. *Pray that I don't break your fat fucking neck.* Joe ran out of the kitchen, almost knocking him over. The front door slammed a moment later.

Alex stared at the woman while she whispered to herself, his presence apparently forgotten. A deep, nagging remorse spread through him and he couldn't stop his words.

"What happened, Norma? What broke you?" She ignored him, clasping her pudgy hands closer to her bosom.

"I know you can hear me," Alex said. He stepped toward her. "Tell me!"

Norma stumbled back and put her hands up as if warding off an attack, the curler flapping on her shaking head. "Thou shalt not kill, thou shalt not kill …"

Alex watched her for a moment, then leaned close enough to smell the mouthwash on her panting breath. "I'm not going to kill you, Norma. You deserve a much worse fate than that."

He wanted to slap her, to smear that clown makeup right off her stupid fat face. Fighting for control, he turned and headed for the front door, every step slow, agonizing. He had to use both sweaty, shaking hands to turn the doorknob.

At the bottom of the driveway, Alex surveyed the empty street. No sign of Joe, only the cool breeze and the sound of the Carpenters' barking golden retrievers four houses down. At the wail of a distant train whistle, an alarm went off inside his head. His pulse throttled.

The tracks.

He broke into a run, eyes watering as he raced down Knob Road.

"Nononono," he chanted, nearing the crossing. Warning bells clanged as the red and white guardrails began their descent to block the road.

Joe stood motionless on the opposite side of the tracks a couple hundred feet away. Alex looked over his shoulder and spotted the nose of a train rounding Hangman's Bend, a blind spot that prevented the engineer from stopping before hitting anything that happened to be on the tracks within fifty yards of the turn. The gridiron came into view, accompanied by another long moan. Joe stood very still, head down, clenching and unclenching his hands, and Alex had a fleeting vision of a gunfighter about to draw his weapon. He spun around, the locomotive, moving fast and picking up speed. Joe had chosen his position well. When they were kids, they always knew when to stop, when to quit the race and head home for some cherry ice cream. Now, Joe never knew when to give up, never knew when to let things go.

"Joe!"

Joe bolted forward, kicking up wet clay. Alex froze, imagining Joe's frail body going rigid as the train's iron impact sent him flying high above the trees. He willed his weakened legs to move, but they wouldn't cooperate. The train screamed, and a hot blast of air roused him like a harsh slap to the cheek. He ran, pumping as hard as he could, thinking, *I'm gonna die trying to outrun a fucking train.*

Joe ran on the other side of the tracks, far ahead. His long, skinny legs propelled him forward like a sprinter with a worthy competitor at his heels. Alex thought he heard Joe's voice on the wind, but the deafening roar of the train devoured all sound. The locomotive inched up, blasting acrid air, shrill whistle filling the world. And then, like an ominous charging black beast, the engine moved in to obscure the last fleeting glimpse Alex had of his friend, still running like hell to win the race. Of course, winning meant dodging in front of the train as it bore down and making it to the other side of the tracks unharmed. If one of them lost a shoe it didn't count.

"Joe!"

Joe's image was gone, replaced by rushing boxcars carrying waving bums and farm supplies. Alex slowed to an exhausted trot, the last surges of adrenaline fading as the train swept by, taking his energy with it. There was only a feeling of despair, coupled with a crippling desire to beat the shit out of Joe.

Alex stumbled across the tracks, nearly falling face-first into the gravel. Thick clay clung to his shoes as he walked, feet heavy and slick. The sun-washed smell of wild blackberries filled the air. He spotted Joe's size eleven prints in the reddish mud and followed them. Several yards up, he passed a dead fox lying by the tracks, a limp rabbit still clenched in its stiff jaws. Dead animals often littered the tracks, too slow or too afraid to dodge the charging locomotives. The fox's blood darkened the clay into a sickly maroon color. *The rain will wash it away later and predators will have your bones picked clean by midnight,* Alex thought. When they were little kids, he and Joe would haul carcasses home and Mary would show them how to make things with the parts. Joe got good at making arrows out of bones, sharp and painful, Alex knew. He'd taken one in the arm once, and one in the back of the knee that had landed him in the emergency room.

Alex stopped, almost tripping on his heavy feet. Joe's prints angled off and disappeared into thick stands of lodgepole pines and Douglas-firs lining both sides of the tracks.

"Asshole," Alex breathed, scanning the tops of the trees. The sky darkened as he watched. Rain clouds gathered. Cursing, he peered into the dense darkness of the Siskiyou Forest.

"Joe," he called into the woods. "Don't think I'll follow you in there, right? Stubborn fuck."

Eerie silence answered. Alex shivered, chilled, but realized it wasn't only from the cold. He suddenly felt eyes on him, watching, and turned to see a small owl perched at the center of a rail tie not more than six feet away. Alex let out a long breath, tension easing a little.

"A little early for you to be out."

The night bird stared at him with unwavering crystal eyes and cocked its head. Its white feathers ruffled in the soft breeze, giving Alex an odd sense of déjà vu. Steam billowed above the trees as another train sounded in the distance. Alex watched the owl, expecting it to take flight, but the bird didn't budge. It watched him, unblinking, with shining, translucent eyes.

"Get," Alex said, waving his arm. The bird cocked its head, looking at him sideways. The train rounded Hangman's and rolled into sight.

"Go," Alex said, raising his voice. He stepped forward and waved his arms.

The owl perched, statue-like with its head tilted, ignoring Alex's commands.

"C'mon, get off the tracks," he coaxed, stepping forward and kneeling down, the train fifty yards away now. The whistle sounded a second warning. Alex panicked. He dove at the bird, slipped on the wet clay, and crashed to the ground, landing on his right shoulder. A stabbing pain shot through his arm and up his neck. Letting out a yell, he rolled onto his side as the train swept by, blasting a steady stream of hot wind against his back. He lay there after the train passed, willing the wracking pain to leave his body, then gritted his teeth and sat up. The owl swooped low and yanked a few strands of hair from Alex's head before ascending into the steel gray clouds without a sound.

"Ow," Alex mumbled, getting to his feet. "What the hell."

Thunder ripped through the sky and Alex knew it would start pouring any second.

Eyeing the dark woods, he thought about what awaited him a half mile in. Cutters Grove Cemetery. He'd been to the graveyard just three times in his life—his father's funeral, Luke's funeral, and two days before Joe had decided to paint his bathroom a sticky shade of blood. The unbidden memory replayed in his mind like a videotape set on slow motion—Joe on his knees, stabbing at the grass and dirt with a gardening spade, his face twisted with the force he used to impale the earth.

"What the hell are you doing?" Alex had yelled, trying to wrench the shovel from Joe's grip.

Joe had been so resolved. "Digging my grave, Al. I've decided to assist Norma in my destruction, to go easy. No biggie. The world still spins. Want to help?"

Alex had felt like he'd been punched in the stomach. Something in Joe's tone, as if he'd just stepped off a thousand-foot cliff and suddenly realized the hopelessness of the situation in midair. But what had disturbed Alex most was the utter and complete quiet. Silence was something entirely different. Silence was the moment before something happened or someone spoke. Silence was the hush of an audience as the lights dimmed, the breathless silence following a particularly fine performance. Quiet made him think of death. Quiet was the last exhale of a dying person. Quiet was looking through Joe's open bathroom door eleven months ago. It had been so damn dark, and the quiet had shrieked like a dying harbinger. *Look. Look away. See. Don't see.* Joe was the most stubborn person he knew, but Alex took the prize when it came to looking away. He peered again into the dark woods and felt the darkness look back as anxiety began to boil in his veins. *You're such a pussy, Al.*

"Asshole!"

Thunder tumbled into the hills and it started to rain. Rubbing his sore shoulder, Alex turned and walked toward home, trying to lengthen his exhales all the way there.

6:38pm

Alex stepped into the foyer and eased the front door closed. Elizabeth sat at the kitchen table, staring at the wood grain, tracing the lip of her *World's Greatest Mom* mug with her finger. She sipped tea as he sat across from her.

"Hi."

"Hi," Elizabeth said, watching him through the steam. "I was worried. You didn't call."

Alex nodded. "Sorry. I lost track of time." He looked at the table. It wasn't a lie. He *had* lost track of time, or time had somehow lost track of him.

"Joe's having a rough time, isn't he?"

Alex nodded. She always knew what was going on. He never had to explain and was grateful because this time he didn't think he could.

"How did you know?" He wanted tea but couldn't find the energy to lift his arms.

Elizabeth sighed and pulled the rubber band out of her dark hair, letting it fall around her shoulders. Her hair was thick and healthy, eyes clear and inquisitive, and the freckles dotting her nose made her look much younger than thirty-eight.

"Well, you look like you haven't slept in weeks and you're covered in muck. You looked like this before Joe's suicide attempt. Except for the muck." She took a deep breath. "And I got a call from Norma warning me to keep my evil seed out of her holy home or she would charge you with trespassing."

Alex rubbed his eyes.

"Alex, look at me," Elizabeth said, setting down her mug and leaning forward. Alex looked at his mom's pretty face.

"I know you want to help Joe," she began. "I know you have this need to be there for him. You always have. You're a great friend, but I don't want you losing everything you've worked so hard for."

Alex frowned, puzzled.

Elizabeth leaned back in her chair. "I'm not panicked about what Norma is telling people—yet—because I don't think she holds that much influence. I'm more worried about the influence Joe has on you. You're off to Juilliard in the fall, Alex, and I don't want his problems to interfere with your future. It's already become an issue, more than once. And we live in a very small town. You know how obsessive fanatical people can be. They make everyone else's business their own."

"Jesus." Alex rubbed the bridge of his nose. "What's she saying?"

"She's telling everyone you're a satanist, a devil worshiper, that you assaulted her—" Elizabeth took a breath, "—and that you pushed your brother into the ravine as a sacrifice to the devil."

Alex's jaw dropped. He shook his head in disbelief. An electric jolt pierced his head.

"Perfect," he whispered. "Fucking perfect. I'm not afraid of her and she knows it. That's why she's saying that shit. Psycho-bitch." He stood up, took a few weak steps, and sat down again. He reached across the table and took his mom's hand, wishing he could crawl into her lap like when he was a little kid. He could barely sit up he was so tired. He rubbed the length of his nose, trying to get a grasp on his weary thoughts.

Elizabeth smiled. "I used to do that when you were little," she said. "Whenever you got upset, I would brush your tiny baby nose with my pinky very softly. It must have had some sort of soothing hypnotic effect because it always calmed you down. Your eyes would droop, and you'd fall asleep right there in my arms, no matter where we were."

She sipped her tea.

"You and Luke were polar opposites," she continued. "He was always so hyper, a lot like Joe. Nothing could calm him down, always buzzing around here yelling about one thing or another. He wanted wings, used to pray for them. To fly like—"

"Superman," Alex finished.

"You do what you can to support Joe," Elizabeth said. "But remember your priorities. Your music comes first, that's our agreement. You don't get a job, you write and practice and perform. Your dad's life insurance has allowed for that. Irony at its best. If you need me you know I'm here, but I swear to God one of these days I'm going to let that woman have it."

Alex's head felt heavy. "I need to figure out what's eating him. I can't let him down again."

"Joe needs professional help, Alex, not someone to assume responsibility for him. What Joe did wasn't your fault. You saved his life."

"Yeah, and he hates me for it," Alex said, shaking his head. "He's so different, Mom. He acts like he never feels anything."

Elizabeth nodded. "Abandonment is traumatic, especially for a little kid. They say it's worse than if the person had died because you know he's out there somewhere living his life as if nothing had ever happened. Marcus is a good guy. I guess living with Norma took a toll. I honestly don't have a clue how he did it for so long. But why he would leave Joe with her is beyond me. Apparently, child protective services didn't have a problem with her. She passed all those fol-low-up visits with flying colors."

"How'd they meet anyway? Norma and Marcus? I asked Joe, but he didn't know for sure."

"Saint Mary Hospital over in Astoria. She was some kind of nurse. Surgical, I think. Why?"

Alex shrugged. "Just wondering how their paths crossed. Talk about polar opposites, can't think of two more differ-ent people." He rested his cheek on the table. "A nurse, huh?"

"A regular Flo Nightingale. Hard to believe, I know."

"Wish I could remember why I went into Joe's house that night. It's still a blur. Mostly flashes of movement and col-or."

"You'll remember. Your mind is just protecting itself."

"Yeah, but why? From what?"

"You've had a lot to deal with the past few years, Alex. Like Doc Lyn says, give it time."

"That's something I wish I had more of." He closed his eyes.

Elizabeth's voice came from very far away and he could no longer grasp the meaning of her words. He felt a mat-tress beneath him and his shoes being pulled off.

"Love you, Mom." He turned onto his side and dropped quickly into restless sleep.

6:38pm

Joe stood under the tall maple and gazed up at its leafy moonlit branches, too exhausted to climb. He shuffled to the front porch and sat on the step. A distant train whistle screamed through the night and he cupped his ears and hummed, attempting to drown out the mournful noise. It faded, leaving only an evangelist's threats booming from the television on the other side of the front door. Mrs. Schell recorded all the Sunday morning sermons while she was at church and watched them all week every night before retiring to her room, where she read her Bible for exactly one hour. No more, no less. Then she prayed for an hour. Loudly.

The preacher's voice echoed from the other side of the door, "For only twenty-four ninety-nine salvation can be yours!"

Huh, Joe thought, *price went up.* He wrung rainwater from his hair and searched his pockets for a cigarette, found one, but it was soaking wet and crumbled in his fingers. Flicking it onto the grass, he stood up just as his mother yanked open the front door.

Joe leapt back. "Jesus."

"What did you say?" The yellow porch light lit up the spit on her caked lips.

Joe took a deep breath and crammed his hands into his jeans pockets, a devilish grin pulling at the corners of his ruined mouth.

"I said JEE-ZUS," he shouted, mimicking the tele-preacher's tone. He looked at her through clumps of wet hair and thrust his hands over his head, pumping his fists in the air. "JEE-ZUS! JEE-ZUS! Save me from my own wretched self! O' lordy, lordy, for I have sinned against YEE-OO!" He hopped from foot to foot and waved his hands in the air with the preacher singing back-up from the TV. Joe had heard this sermon so many times he was able to anticipate every word before it was spoken, so he sang along. He whooped and hollered and stomped his feet in a sarcastic interpretation of her favorite homily about redemption.

Joe was just beginning to get a good rhythm when Mrs. Schell's hand shot out and connected with the side of his head. He reeled, stumbling backwards onto the lawn, shocked that she had actually touched him. Along the way, he managed to get caught up in one of her madonna rose bushes. Thrashing and rolling with melodramatic fervor, Joe grinned, thorns piercing and scraping his skin. He chuckled, doing his best to get the most out of the situation, then stopped and looked at her livid expression.

"O why hast thou forsaken me?" he whined, holding his scraped and bloodied palms out as though pleading for mercy. "What did I ever do to you?"

Norma glared at him from the porch and buried her arms under her breasts. The blue vein made an appearance on her forehead, throbbing like an engorged worm. Her lipsticked teeth reflected the moonlight when she opened her mouth to speak.

"Why do you insist on embarrassing me?" Her voice sounded like frying bacon. "You'll pay for the way you treat me. Don't doubt that for a second. You'll pay in Hell."

Joe folded his hands, pressing sticky palms together. "An eternity in hell would be paradise compared to living here with you," he said, voice soft, steady.

"Leave. I won't stop you."

Joe concentrated on his hands and shrugged. "Yeah. Exactly. But somebody's got to give your sorry life meaning, Norma. Guess I got volunteered the day they let you out. And I don't break promises like some people do."

He stepped onto the narrow walkway and faced her. "In two years you can declare Dad dead. I'll get the money he left and be on my jolly way. In the meantime, why would I throw away twenty-three months, two weeks, and six days of free entertainment? I'm having a blast. Can't you tell? Besides, what would all your little church friends say, Norma? They wouldn't pay any attention to you if I left. There'd be no reason for them to come around. No one to tell you how rough you've had it. No one to kiss your ever-expanding ass. No one to feel sorry for you. You'd be lonely without me. And you know what else? I know you love me in your own sick, demented way. You think I don't hear you praying for my soul every single fucking night? You think I don't know that you're doing everything you can to save me? If that's not love, Mom, I don't know what is."

Norma's mouth twitched into a shocked grimace. "You don't know what you're saying. There's something wrong with you. You're crazy."

Joe hopped from foot to foot and flapped his arms, making his way toward her, hooting like an owl. She narrowed her eyes, nostrils flaring, and watched him approach. Joe stopped on the porch and squinted through the piss-yellow halo filtering from the outside light. Just looking at her made him want to laugh.

"Yeah, baby, losing my mind was the best thing that ever happened to me," he whispered, leaning close. "Wasn't going bonkers the most orgasmic experience you've ever had, Mother? Doesn't it just make you want to *fuck* everything in sight? I bet Jesus was a great lay in his time. A real free-love hippie. A regular Romeo. You'd love to fuck Jesus, wouldn't you, Mom? You can tell me. After all, you and I are very much alike." He snorted. "Aren't we?"

Her lips trembled. Her face burned as bright as her pink teeth. She backed toward the open door, watching him.

"I've got a secret," Joe continued in a hushed tone, moving toward her through the open door. "The night Alex found me upstairs was an unfortunate misunderstanding. Satan had been whispering in my ear all day long. He told me to slit your throat and drink your blood, to make you one of us, but I became impatient. I needed blood." He gnashed his teeth, licked his lips. "I couldn't wait so I turned the blade on myself and sucked my own blood from my veins. Demons crave blood, you know. You've been telling me that my whole life. Alex still doesn't know the truth. He thinks I actually wanted to die, when all I really wanted was to *kill*. Guess I got that impulse from you, huh, Mom? How did it feel holding him under the water, Norma, knowing his tiny lungs were filling with pond scum? Did he struggle? Or did he go easy?" Joe looked at her, eyes narrow. The televangelist's rhythmic threats pumped through his body. He began to shake.

Mrs. Schell crossed her arms again and cocked her head.

"My baby Isaac died because of *you*," she said, a chilling distance coming to her eyes. "You never lived up to the son your father lost. Never. You are small and weak. Your father did not love you. He felt obligated to you, nothing more. And because of you attacking my body from the inside like the malignant monster you are, my sweet angel baby Isaac just—just ..." Norma thrust her thick arms over her head and dropped to her knees, stenciled eyes filling with tears. "Oh, but glory, he is with you now, Lord! Praise God, he's sitting at the right hand of his father now! Oh, glory, glory!"

Joe's breath squeezed out. All the blood left his hands and feet and suddenly he felt very cold. The preacher's undulating voice banged against the walls of his skull.

"What did you say?" He stepped toward her, clenching his fists in time with the preacher's rising and falling chants. His teeth vibrated with the blasts of organ music blaring out of the television.

Norma lifted her chin, got to her feet, and tightened her arms around her midsection. A tight smile stretched across her fluorescent pink teeth, but it wasn't happiness that prompted the expression. Joe recognized it immediately when he met her stony eyes. The Cheshire Cat. An undeniable, indisputable look of euphoric gratification with a strong trace of insane glee. He'd seen it before, as a kid, always when she knew she had hit her mark. This time her aim was right on.

"What happened was your fault." She pronounced every syllable of every word. *"And you know it."* She turned and

stepped back into the house, leaving the front door wide open.

Every muscle in Joe's body tensed when she brushed by. It took all the control he could muster not to grab her by the throat when she moved within reach. His father's familiar words galloped through his head in a ghostly tone. *Be a good boy, Joey. Your mother's not well. Please don't do anything to upset her. She can't help it. We have to take care of her. Just help out and don't cause trouble. Do that for me, okay Joey?*

Okay?

Joe's hands clenched, unclenched, clenched again. He forced all the air out of his lungs then inhaled and held it, face turning bright red.

Okay?

Something exploded inside him, filling his head with a rushing roar. He ran into the living room and yanked the largest wooden crucifix from its holds. The pegs in Jesus's hands came loose. The messiah's metallic body swung upside down, held only by the screw driven through the tops of both feet. Joe found this almost as amusing as looking at his mother's pitiful, painted face, but his anger did not dull at the sight of the swinging savior. Joe looked up at the giant velvet painting on the wall and focused his gaze on Christ's vermilion-dipped palms, held out plaintive and searching.

Holding the cross in his trembling hands, Joe stepped to the blasting television and stared at the evangelist's face, as red as his own but streaked with tears and sweat.

"… as he promised on oath to you and your forefathers, you are to give over to the Lord the first offspring of every womb. All the first-born males of your livestock belong to the Lorrrrd. Redeem with the Lamb every first-born donkey, but if you do not redeem it, break its neck. Redeem every first-born among your sonssss …" The preacher wiped his forehead with a handkerchief. Joe's body shook.

"… and it will be like a siiiign on your hand and a symbol on your forehead that the Lor—"

Joe slammed the cross into the preacher's overly excited face. A loud pop broke the unexpected silence. Sparks sputtered. Broken glass sprayed the carpet. He lifted the crucifix again and swung it as hard as he could. He kept swinging until all the glass had fallen from the frame of Mrs. Schell's Curtis Mathes TV. Breathing hard, Joe dropped the hunk of wood to the floor and pulled a damp sleeve across his eyes. His chest tightened with every breath. His legs threatened to collapse as he headed toward the staircase. Mrs. Schell stood at the kitchen entrance with her arms still pushed under her boobs, putrid pink mouth pulled tight, nostrils flaring like a hard-run horse. Joe paused at the bottom step and looked at her, noticing a few stray strands of blonde hair sticking straight up on her head.

"I fixed the TV," he said. "It was making a terrible racket." Shaking, he pulled himself up the stairs, using the railing for support.

8:12pm

Joe sat on his bed, index fingers shoved deep into his ears, knees knocking together. The sound of the piano came through the vents and walls like an unstoppable bullet. His head vibrated with the pounding of the keys. The mirror shook and rattled, threatening to crack in a web of jagged lines. Norma screeched hymn after hymn at the top of her lungs, loud enough to drown out the sound of Wolfgang's grating metal wheel. She'd been carrying on for over an hour.

The familiar heavy ache had risen, prickling in his head and spiking down into his stomach where it bloomed hot and sharp like cactus needles full of fire. He gulped the stale air. He couldn't stop his legs and hands from shaking. He pressed his hands tighter over his ears, trying to subdue the unbearable racket and the faint wailing inside his head.

"Stop it. Shut up."

The noise rose to a deafening serenade—a million hornets buzzing, a thousand trumpets blaring, hollow and lonely. He slammed his skull against the wall and dug his bitten fingernails into the flesh of his forearms. He jumped to his feet and paced, pulling at his hair. Norma's off-tune honking carried through the house like the cacophony of a hundred tortured ducks.

"Shut up, bitch!"

Joe slammed his fist into the wall, beating at it until his wrist swelled. A bluish bulb rose on his arm and throbbed. He smirked, enjoying the dull ache.

"Shut the fuck up!" He banged his head into the door.

His leather jacket lay on the floor. Groping in the pocket, Joe pulled out a red lighter and held it in his trembling fingers. *Okay. Take control, goddamn it.*

The noise quieted a little. Joe breathed deep.

Why do you do it? Dr. Rivers pushed his glasses onto his veiny nose. *Why do you burn yourself, Joe?*

"Everyone is faced with choices."

So, you acknowledge that you're choosing to do this?

"Absolutely."

Joe pushed up his sleeve. The flame flared, beckoning, dancing, wavering with the cool breeze creeping in through the window. He held the fire close to his face and thought he saw himself there, features contorted in shimmering reds and blues, his head bobbing on a string, weightless, thoughtless, and he wanted to be the fire, wanted to be the heat and the annihilation it offered.

The blaze bit into his flesh, sending an exhilarating shock of precious pain through his body. He sucked in his breath and shivered, smelling the brackish-sweet aroma of himself burning. As he moved the flame back and forth under his forearm, an electric tingle filled him, and the summoning darkness called out. *Welcome back*, it groaned. *Stay this time.* The faint cries and hollow howls quieted, and he felt something inside break open, spreading warmth and calm throughout his body, numbing his mind. Bright blues and dazzling reds danced and shimmered in front of his eyes like colorful streamers in slow-blowing wind. The heat had entered him, flooding him to the core, igniting the anxiety and incinerating it to ash in his veins.

Calmer now, Joe groped on the floor until he found it. He pressed the triangular wedge of TV glass to his flushed cheek. *Control*, he thought, *nice and easy.* The glass reflected moonbeams pouring through the open window, calling to him seductively, saying his name in a child's whisper. He bolted up and yanked off his damp shirt, jeans, long johns, filthy socks. Turning the piece of glass over in his hand, he squinted at the sharp point, relishing the sense of power it offered. He'd decided the specific site a while ago but had to wait until his mind was quiet before beginning. He had drifted to another place, far away, where there were no hymns or preacher's threats or phony people with painted cartoon faces.

Fucking phony clowns.

Joe sat on the bed, placed the point on his sunken white chest and blinked sweat from his eyes. Pushing deep, he drew the sharp edge of the glass downward, past his navel to his pubic bone, relishing the stinging shock of pain. The faint ripping sound of his skin made him cry out in giddy abandon.

Why do you do it? Why do you make yourself bleed, Joe?

"It feels good."

It feels good to hurt yourself?

"It feels good to make the pain my own, to feel it outside instead of inside."

Describe the feeling you get when you make yourself bleed.
"These wounds heal."

Blood seeped from the cut, bathing his skin. A thin stream pooled in his navel before winding over his hipbone and spattering the bedsheet. Joe concentrated on the deep wound in his flesh, sure he could feel his breastbone when he probed the gash with his fingers. Lifting the sharp wedge, he placed the point on the left side of his abdomen and pulled it across his ribs to the pink scar Mrs. Schell's gardening spade had left eleven months ago. The edge cut deep on his protruding bones and the pain felt good, all his senses awakened at once. Hushed voices called, echoing from the darkness, beckoning, promising. He heard a child weeping.

Joe pressed the point into the center of his left palm and pushed, twisting and turning, gouging a dime-sized hole. Blood spilled onto his bare thigh. He repeated the digging motion on his right hand, relaxing into tranquil emptiness with each turn of the glass. As sanguineous liquid flowed from his wounds, the hate and anger he felt went with it, out of his body, taking him into shifting rays of warm amber light and lullaby music. Angels sang in his ear. Groggy, Joe slid off the bed, scooted to the middle of the floor, and lay flat on his back. He spread his thin arms out wide and crossed his ankles, hoping it would be Mrs. Schell to find him this time. Alex deserved better.

A stream of blood slid over his right side and under the curve of his back. He could feel blood pooling near his groin, trapped there by his jutting hipbones. Joe relaxed, concentrating on keeping his eyes open. He wanted her to find him staring unseeing at the heavens, an expression of relief etched on his face. Wanted her to be the one to close his dead, stiff eyelids, although he knew she wouldn't touch his body. Wanted her to see dried tear tracks on his cheeks but, as usual, he could not bring himself to cry.

I am the Lamb, Joe thought, listless.

Moonlight from the window illuminated his scarred body. The cross carved into his belly stood out like a foreboding neon omen against his pale skin. He could feel its heat blazing into his flesh, muscle and bones.

As Joe lay waiting for unconsciousness and eventual death, a droplet of clear liquid slid along a curving brass bar of the looking glass and tumbled to the carpet at his feet. Another droplet followed that one. Then another and another, until steady streams of saltwater wound along every curvature of every brass bar, cascading to the carpet uninterrupted. The noise below continued, but Joe's mind fell quiet, distant, vaguely aware of someone singing very far away, the sounds broken, unfamiliar. He repeated a familiar phrase in his mind—*there can be no forgiveness without the shedding of blood.*

Beyond the glass, the boy screamed in silent agony.

"Forgive me father," Joe whispered. Darkness came and he gratefully slipped into it.

three

May 22, 1984

Tears

Alex winced at the pain in his shoulder and neck. He pulled himself up, let his socked feet rest on the floor, and attempted to piece his thoughts into a picture that made sense. Elusive images flashed in his mind. Joe's mom. The train. The owl. Graveyard. Joe. Scared. He was scared, confused.

Shivering, Alex went to his bedroom window. Daylight filtered through the closed curtains, casting long, misshapen shadows across the floor and walls. He moved the drapery to one side and peered out at the sky. A frown creased his brow. He looked at the clock and realized it wasn't the next morning but late afternoon the next day.

"Shit," he muttered, sitting on the bed, rubbing his puffy eyes, shoulder twinging. Then he noticed his clothes. Streaks of red mud blotched his jeans and shirt; his socks had a rusty orange hue. Disgusted, he stood and stripped to his underwear, then pulled all the sheets and blankets off the bed and tossed them into the corner. Still trying to clear the fog from his mind, he headed down the hallway toward the bathroom. When he passed Luke's room he hesitated, then pushed the door open and poked his head in.

Cardboard boxes lined the walls. Mattresses stood on end against the closet door. The curtains were wide open. The remains of daylight streamed through the window. Luke's model airplanes and spacecrafts hovered above Alex's head, covered in dust and cobwebs. Flying was all his brother had ever talked about. He'd wanted to be a pilot, specifically a spaceship pilot, like Han Solo. An astronaut. Alex touched the model Millennium Falcon overhead, setting it in motion.

A wooden owl hung among the planes and crafts. Alex pulled the string swinging from its white belly and the bird's wings began an easy motion, flapping silently in the disrupted dust. Luke had been fascinated by anything that could fly—planes, helicopters, birds, bats. He'd spent months constructing the owl from scratch using his allowance money.

Alex's voice sounded hollow against the bare walls. "Wish I had your balls-out way of doing things, Lucas. Could use that right about now." He listened to the phantom echo of Luke's hearty belly laugh bounce from one bare wall to another. Alex gave the string another tug.

"Remember the rope swing with Dad? We spent more time hunting down the perfect tree to hang it from than we did swinging on the thing. Broke my ankle falling off that stupid swing and you got on my case, said I should've spread my arms out like a bird and just floated to the ground. You made it sound so easy, so possible."

Tears tried to come, but Alex wouldn't let them. He stood there awhile, staring at the motionless planes, then left the room, closing the door behind him.

Steaming shower water poured over him, easing the stiffness in his shoulder and neck. The bathroom door opened a crack and Elizabeth's voice interrupted his dark thoughts.

"I'm home," she called. "Feeling better?"

"Fine," Alex lied, rinsing shampoo from his hair.

"Hungry?"

"Starved." He turned off the water.

"Salad and tuna melts okay?"

"With fontina." He tied a towel around his waist and pulled the shower curtain open. Still dripping, he stepped out of the tub and put his arms around his mom.

"You're getting my clothes all wet," Elizabeth said, pretending to be irritated.

Alex kissed her cheek. "I love you, Mom. You're the coolest." He bent over and shook his head, spraying her with water. She fled down the hall, laughing.

"Avocado on mine," he called. "And tomatoes, please."

"Yeah, yeah," he heard her say. "And I want cukes and olives in my salad, so hurry up."

"You got it," Alex said. He stared at his haggard reflection in the fogged mirror and tried to comb out the cowlicks in his hair. It didn't work. He'd inherited his dad's hair, thick, dark, and unruly with a mind of its own. Giving up, he raked his hair back from his face and tossed the comb onto the bathroom counter before starting toward his room. He came to a halt in front of Luke's door.

"Hey, Mom," he called, reaching for the knob. "Okay if I shut Luke's door?"

"Of course," she said from the kitchen. "We always keep it closed."

"Yeah, but—" Alex's outstretched hand trembled. He drew back and frowned, staring at the shiny brass door handle, at his own weary image reflected there.

Elizabeth appeared at the end of the hall. "What?"

Alex startled. "Nothing." He shook his muddled head, grabbed the knob and pulled the door closed.

6:27pm

Alex trotted along the peaceful street, swinging his arms in big circles to work the stiffness out of his shoulder. Crickets twittered, singing a pre-dusk song. The cool damp air smelled good, washed clean of car exhaust and cigarette smoke. Leaves on the trees danced and ruffled in the slow-blowing wind. Alex thought about what he should say to Mary but couldn't decide on a good starting point. She'd always told him to come to her with his challenges, but he doubted a beautiful specter and a haunted looking glass were what she'd had in mind.

Mary believed in magic and when Alex was with her, he did, too. It was in the trees, the spirits of the smallest creatures, in the skies and in the oceans, she'd say. She'd been telling him stories all his life and after each one she'd give him a licorice, hold his small face in her cherry tobacco-scented hands, and plant a firm kiss on his forehead before sending him on his way. "Truth," she would say into his ear, warm breath smelling of anise and smoke. Alex wondered if Joe ever thought about those long summer afternoons spent listening to Mary's stories, eating oatmeal spice cookies and drinking cold cinnamon tea. He hoped so.

Mary's porchlight was always on, like a lighthouse beacon in a perpetual storm. Alex stepped over the threshold and closed the door. Bach's *Third Concerto* filled the air. The elder woman sat on a stool at her worktable in the far corner near the window. She wore dusty jeans and a purple sculptor's smock smeared with dried clay and paint and flaked with the shavings of her latest invention—a four-tiered wood flute that could be played by two people at once. Various tools littered the table and floor—hand saws, chisels, turners, mallets, clamps, sharpening stones, a lathe. Mary swayed with the music, eyes closed, a smile on her lips, long gray braid coiled in her dust-coated lap.

Alex slumped onto the world's most comfortable couch. He closed his tired eyes and watched vivid images play in the darkness of his wandering mind. He saw himself and Joe at the age of three. Alex had belly flopped off a swing and Joe had gone to help, unaware of another kid swinging right at him. The impact of the kid's shoe on Joe's face had knocked his front teeth loose, prompting loud wails. Alex lay where he was, a silent grimace frozen on his red face as he struggled for breath. Tears streamed down his dirty cheeks. A very pregnant Elizabeth had rushed to her son's aid, almost toppling over Joe's dad. Together, they laughed at the chaos.

That's how it had always been—Joe took the risks, ventured out, rescued people; Alex stayed at a safe distance, unwilling to step into the fray. Joe lived for the battle, thrived on it; Alex hid. When they were thirteen, Joe had slugged Matt McMurty in the mouth for calling Alex a sissy fag who played with violins instead of guns. Joe got sent to Principal Brainerd's office for that one, but it didn't faze him a bit and Dirty McMurty never said another word to Alex. That was the year Joe befriended Charlie Dugan who, as big as he was, would never defend himself against the bullies at school. Kids teased him about his size, his stuttering, his bright orange hair, everything. But Joe liked him, said Charlie would be a hero someday sure as monkey shit and just wait and see if he was wrong. Joe taught Luke how to defend himself with his wit and his smarts, and occasionally his fists, if it came to that. He enjoyed coming up with elaborate schemes to embarrass the losers who picked on his friends, but he was also never afraid to go bare knuckles with someone who deserved it. And he was good at it. He had always been the brave one, a defender of the weak and the meek, and he'd gotten his teeth knocked in more than once for it. Bravery always had its consequences.

Stupid kid, Alex thought, *always doing the right thing.*

"Story today, *niniijaanis*?"

Dazed, Alex opened his eyes to find the old woman staring at him.

"Where's Joe tonight?"

Alex shrugged. "Not my day to watch him."

Mary smiled, tilting her head back to look through the glasses perched on her nose. "You have an open soul,

Alexander. This is necessary if you want to help your friend."

"I can't help unless I know what's wrong with him."

"You already have the answers," she said, reaching for a turner. "You acquired them the moment you found Joseph dripping his life's essence from the cuts in his veins. Do you remember?"

"Remember?" Alex's voice cracked, and he cleared his throat. "I still have trouble with the details, but Jesus. I can't forget the blood. It was everywhere."

Mary reached for a small hand saw. "Did I ever tell you the story of the *nibowin jiibayag*?"

Alex tried to will the tension out of his shoulders. "Probably."

Mary peered at him over the top of her glasses. "The death guides. Spirits, both living and *beyond* living. They guide the dying to and in the *wakwi*. They help facilitate a good death."

Alex scowled. "There's no such thing as a good death."

Mary cocked her head, turning her attention back to the flutes. "Yes. For some people, you are right." She picked up a small wood file. "Is Joe still visiting hospice patients?"

"Yeah. He's obsessed. He talks to them. Don't know why he does that. I couldn't."

"It makes sense *why* he does it, when you think about it. Which you won't."

"What's that supposed to mean?" Alex stroked the bridge of his nose.

Mary peered closer at the flute. "It's *how* he does it that is more interesting. He shares something in common with them, don't you think? Knocking on death's door, watching the veils part between this world and the next. It makes sense when you think about it. Which you won't."

Alex got up, shoved his fists into his pockets, and paced. "How about if I tell you a story today? A story about two knights, one a trickster who loves to battle anything that comes his way, the other a coward too afraid and confused to know what the fight is even about."

Mary reached for another tool. "I'm listening."

Alex jumped to the middle of the room and gestured dramatically, swinging an invisible sword, shoulder pinging in sharp jolts. "There used to be a time when these two knights could battle any threat, especially the monsters in the dark. Seething, soul-sucking shadows that pounce when you least expect it. Those were their favorite. The fearless trickster knight understood the ways of the shadows, knew how to turn things around and banish them from the land of light, but the other knight, the cowardly confused knight, really didn't get it. His only objective was to keep the fearless knight safe, so the monster-slaying could go on."

Alex moved around the room, fencing invisible foes.

"Then one day the fearless knight let the confused knight see through his eyes, see what he saw. The confused knight looked into night's core and became afraid, while the fearless knight fed off the darkness there, mocked it even, taunted it, laughed at it. After that, the fearless knight had no trouble slaying the beasts, but the confused knight ran and hid. Sure, he could fight other battles—a war of words, a particularly evil queen—but darkness did scare him so."

Mary peered over the rim of her glasses. "So, what became of these battling knights?"

Alex halted mid-swing. "Well, the fearless knight joined the shadows, of course, because the confused knight was too gutless to stop him. The confused knight died inside. Fear turned him into a tired old man. He grew weak and the shadows, emboldened by the fearless knight's alliance, came for the confused knight also." Alex knelt in front of Mary, one hand on his chest, the other held out to her. "He just gave up, m'lady." He kissed her dirty fingers.

"He made his choice then."

"Guess so."

Alex dropped onto the couch and rubbed his face. "Sometimes I just want to beat the shit out of him."

"The fearless trickster knight?"

"Yeah."

Mary smiled. "That's a crappy story."

Alex offered a weary grin. "I'm not a world-renowned *aadizookewinini* like you. But I try."

Mary leaned toward him, piercing him with her knowing, dark eyes. "Hold fast to your fire, Alexander. Don't let go. It's the key to saving Joe, this heat you possess."

Alex frowned and rubbed his face. "You sound just like him. You both talk around the issue. All I want to know is what the hell is wrong with him and what I'm supposed to do about it."

"Good," the old woman said. "I'll tell you something, Alex. Joe is gone, halfway out of this world. Slowly, day by day, breath by breath, he retreats into himself. You still have some fight in you. He's the one running out of strength. His long battle with darkness has left him weak and blind. Joe is no longer capable of seeing anything except the emptiness, the colorless desert, the waiting place of the soul."

Alex's gaze snapped to Mary's face at the mention of the desert. "Is that what happened to Wabishk?"

Mary continued. "If abandoned, he will be devoured by it. You must fight for him, help him remember who he is."

Alex sighed. "You're not telling me anything I don't already know. He's messed up. I get that, but he won't talk to me. I don't even know where to start."

Mary's dark eyes fastened with his. "Begin with your own heart. What does it tell you? Truly. What whispers are you refusing to hear? What are you refusing to see? When you went catatonic after Lucas died, Joe dove deep. Remember? What did he share with you there?"

Alex shook his head and stood up, feeling irritated at the question that probed his mind and heart in ways he didn't like. "Th-that was all just a weird dream. My head was screwed up after Luke died."

"Yes. Your heart, too. It all works together, Alexander." Mary Whitewing resumed filing. Wind chimes sang in the soft breeze outside. The sound mingled with the music filling the room, making Alex think of faerie dust and faraway lands. He sighed in resignation.

"Okay, you know about the desert dreams and the—the woman."

Mary nodded. "Joseph came to me a few weeks ago with this challenge."

"Okay," Alex said, rubbing his nose. "I'm listening."

Mary leaned forward, expression serious. "You must free your heart of the burden it carries. Only then will you be able to help your friend fight. Only then will you be strong enough to bring him back into a world he has found too painful to face alone."

"He's not alone. I'm—"

"In many ways, you are just as crippled as he is," she said, scowling. "You must heal yourself before you can attempt to heal another." Mary paused. "How long has it been since you've traveled now? Three years?"

Alex swallowed. The question was both figurative and literal, he knew. When Mary had first explained to him about losing time, what was actually happening when he played his music, he didn't believe her. She'd told him it was then that his spirit took its leave to travel the Earth and heal those who suffer, that someone—or something— had chosen him to be the vessel through which music was channeled. She'd told him that only a few are chosen. Five hours in the mist often seemed only five minutes, true, but Alex still refused to believe her. He didn't feel chosen or gifted. He felt sad, alone, and utterly grounded. Like his feet would never again leave the dirt, not even to fly in his dreams.

"It's when we deny our Truth that we begin the struggle with darkness, as Joseph struggles, as you struggle now. It's easier not to fight, easier not to listen."

"Easier to hide?"

"Easier to lose yourself."

"Joe knows all this?"

"Oh, you know him. Joe is stubborn and will not believe." Alex nodded, solemn.

A deep frown pulled at the woman's aged face. "Think back, Alexander, to that night in the fog and mist. Think about Joe. Perhaps he is the fearless knight you believe him to be, but maybe not. Perhaps the fearless knight of your crappy story gave up his soul too easily to the darkness. Perhaps the confused knight followed too quickly."

"I can't remember everything that happened that night at the estate, Mary," Alex said, voice edged with fear. "You know that."

Mary wiped the wood dust from her hands. "Joining the enemy can be the most cowardly of acts. Sometimes it is smarter and more strategic to hide. But you can't stay in one place too long or they will find you. *You* know *that*." She waved her hand as if dismissing him.

Alex stood, perplexed and irritated, sensing a strange finality. The music filled his head with bizarre, frightful images of thick dark blood, of torn flesh and broken bones. Feeling off balance, he walked to the front door. As he turned the knob, the woman's words intertwined with the music. *Free your heart.*

Alex turned and found Mary as she had been moments before, sawing away and bobbing her head to the music. He pulled the door open. A breeze rolled in, disturbing the chimes. He stood on the porch, trying to decide what to do, where to go from here, then shoved his hands into his pockets and searched the sky. The urgency in Mary Whitewing's tone stayed with him as he stepped off the porch and walked past tidy rows of Victorian homes toward Joe's. If Mrs. Schell was home she'd call the police, sure as hell. *But only if she sees me.*

At the corner, Alex stopped and looked at the sidewalk, studied it with the intensity of a kindergartner learning to add two and two for the first time. Something was missing from Mary's story.

"Shit." A sharp pain bolted through his shoulder, making him wince. "Goddamn it!" Alex shot his balled fists out as if striking at an invisible adversary. He cursed with each punch and kicked at the darkness in an uncontrolled frenzy of frustration.

"You want me to save him?" he yelled, jabbing a finger into the night. "You fucking do it! I'm done with this shit!"

Alex ran. Images of rot and blood and death chased. The cool wind slammed against his body. He kept running, hoping somehow to leave his emotions behind, but erratic, fragmented pictures filled his head. He saw himself kneeling in the street, face smeared a reddish brown. Blood clung to his hair in sticky clumps. His hands were stained. It had taken days for the scarlet to disappear from his fingernails. He had run out of Joe's house with shrieking sirens rattling his teeth. Flashes of light surrounded him. "Upstairs," he'd told the faceless blue uniform before falling to his knees on the pavement. He had stayed there until the ambulance screamed off in a dizzying circle of red and blue light, fading, fading.

He's fading.

He never saw them load Joe into the vehicle, didn't remember calling for help. All he saw was a flowing river of obsidian blood and Joe being swallowed by it. All he heard was Joe's weak voice saying two words. *Help me.* Then, in dreamlike motion, he was being lifted. Someone had taken him by the arm. Pale green eyes looked into his. The word *shock* reached his ears through a non-stop stream of chatter in his head. The word hung in the air, echoed inside his head in an eternal scream. The planet turned upside down. He was unconscious before he hit the pavement.

Alex had seen death before but hadn't known what it sounded like until that moment. It was lonely, dark, afraid and empty. And quiet. So quiet. *Help me.* He knew Joe could see it coming, greeting him with cold, stiff arms. It was in his haunted blue eyes, in those two words when he had whispered them. In his calm expression. He was not asking Alex to save his life; he was begging for help in ending it. When Alex first realized this, he'd vomited all over Dr. Lyn's green pumps, and then spent his next two therapy appointments apologizing for the mess he'd made.

Breathing hard, Alex found himself standing in the Thrifty parking lot, staring at the flashing red sign. A few of the letters had gone dark and Alex watched R-I-F-T spell out his fortune for the night. Below, the word *SAVE* blinked in a frantic strobe. The steady buzz of neon lights made him dizzy, filled his veins with more apprehension.

Inside the store, Charlie Dugan stood behind the cash register, helping a pretty woman who kept brushing her amber hair back from her face and smiling. Charlie seemed oblivious, a shy giant of a boy shuffling from foot to foot, head down. Alex felt a sudden flash of envy at the normalcy of it all, at the possibility of it, and thought about going in and saying hi to the pretty woman at the counter, because that's what any normal eighteen-year-old straight boy would do. But he wasn't normal. Nothing about his life was normal. So, he stood on the other side of the tempered glass window and envied Charlie his awkwardness, envied Charlie all that possibility.

6:27pm

Joe pried his eyelids open. He blinked up at the ceiling as a claustrophobic gloom gathered outside. He had to pee so bad it hurt.

A voice lingered in his ears, but he could not remember the words it had spoken. *Just a dream,* he thought. *A bad dream.* He turned his head and glimpsed a bloodied palm lying inches from his face. Joe realized the hand belonged to him and a series of unclear recollections spilled into his mind from the vast, empty place he'd been.

Distant thunder rumbled. Joe pulled his heavy arms in toward his body and propped himself up on his elbows. Trying to orient himself in time and space, he glanced at his blood streaked torso and groaned. *Fucking can't get it right.* Wincing, he eased back to the floor. The carpet around him had stiffened with blood, several spots still sticky and wet. Joe pressed the back of his mutilated hand against his forehead and straightened his curled fingers. The partially healed flesh tore open, trickling blood into his hair. Taking deep breaths, he tried to slow the manic images skidding through his mind, but something caught his attention and held it.

A sound. Like a toilet running, which made his bladder contract painfully.

Joe raised onto his elbows again and looked at the carpet beyond his feet. Clear liquid streamed from the glass and bars of the mirror, pouring onto the rug just past his toes.

"God. Damn. It." He lay on his back again. *Am I awake?*

Joe shifted onto his side and rolled up onto his forearms and knees. Perspiration stung his eyes as he fought for control of his shaking, pain-wracked body. The room felt blistering hot and humid despite the open window and cool breeze. He rocked back onto his feet and squatted with his knuckles on the floor for balance. With a heavy grunt he straightened his legs, knees popping in protest. The room spun in dizzying circles and he groped the air for something to hold on to. Flashes of light zipped by his eyes in blinding bursts as a dark tunnel closed in. Spinning, he fell backward and landed on his side.

"Damn. Fuck." He lay on the floor for several long minutes then rolled over and began to commando crawl, inching his way to the bed. He put his forearms on the bed and leaned against the mattress, willing his aching body to stop shaking, hoping the darkness would just take him once and for all. He looked at the mirror through clumps of sweat drenched hair. Liquid surged from the glass, cascaded from the brass bars, filling the humid air with a briny smell that made his stomach lurch. And, like stubborn harbingers of doom, two brick colored stains the size of watermelons stood out on the rug, loud in their accusations. On either side of these, further apart, were two smaller soils—blood from the wounded palms he now pressed together as if praying. All four spots ran in a perfect horizontal line. *Connect the dots and see where they lead on this map to perdition. God, I'm tired.*

"Okay." Joe put his forearms on the bed and stood up. Stars burst open before his eyes again. He stood still until they subsided.

Shuffling to the bathroom, he stepped into the tub, leaning on the wall for support. He turned on the shower and stood under the downpour, letting his bladder empty out and wishing he could get the water hot enough to penetrate his bones to stop the shivering. Pale pink water ran down his legs into the pool rising around his ankles. He inspected his wounds. The cuts on his ribs needed stitches.

Fucking failure.

Joe stepped out of the tub and gingerly toweled off, leaving smears of red on the terry cloth material. He gathered all the towels, bedsheets, and blankets from the linen closet, carried them to the mirror and dropped them to the floor, knowing it wouldn't make any difference. Moving like an arthritic old man, he went back to the bathroom, opened the medicine cabinet and stared at the rows of bottles and boxes of bandages, feeling sick. His stomach suddenly twisted in a violent lurch. He flung himself over the toilet, but nothing came up. The vertigo worsened. His head felt like a balloon filled with hot water. He clamped his sweaty face in his cold hands and opened his eyes, peering at his reflection in the bathroom mirror. A stranger stared back and Joe jumped, startled by the haggard, withered appearance of his face.

He soaked his stinging hands in cold tap water and splashed his face. With a small pair of scissors, he cut several strips of surgical gauze and taped them to the worst hacks on his ribs. His right side was worse. He could see the bone where the glass had cut deep, and he stared, fascinated by the way the ropy sinew clung to his skeleton. With practiced precision, Joe wrapped his hands. *You're a real fuck-up Joe Schell. You can't even die properly.*

As he searched for clean underwear, the mirror sprung another forceful leak.

"Goddamn, fuck it all!" Joe pulled on a too-loose pair of faded jeans and a tattered long-sleeved shirt whose band name had long since worn away. Head still zinging, he stepped over the russet stains and carried a ball of dripping towels to the tub, leaving a wet trail. His bandaged hands began to prickle immediately upon contact with the brackish fluid, but he tried to concentrate on wringing the towels instead of the nauseating sick rising into his throat. For the first time in a long time, he felt like he could cry. He carried the towels back to the mirror, dropped them to the floor, and stared at the soggy heap, helpless.

I need coffee. Strong, black, with a hefty dose of rat poison. He fished in his pockets for a cigarette and wondered where

Mrs. Schell was. Not that it mattered. She worked four days a week at the church daycare and helped in the admin office almost every night and on Sundays after services, and she was not one to stray from her routine. *What fucking day is it?* He glanced again through the open window at the approaching storm, then looked at his bandaged hands, the gauze and tape completely soaked through. Peeling back the surgical tape, he peered at his palms in the dim light.

The sky rumbled, splitting as a sudden flurry of raindrops hammered the window. Several drops struck Joe's cheek, startling him with their force.

The gouges in his palms had healed, leaving shiny pink scars. Bloodied strips of wet gauze slipped from his fingers and fell to the floor. His head spun, reeled, and he heard someone whimper from very far away. Joe ran into the bathroom and vomited steaming bile into the toilet. Shaking in violent spasms, he retched a second time, insides burning, churning. Streamers of light exploded in front of his eyes.

God make me disappear too. I don't want to be here anymore.

Heavy footsteps pounded up the stairs. Alex bolted into the room, hair and shirt damp with the beginnings of rain.

"Hey, your mom's car is gone—" He stumble-spun toward the spouting mirror, eyes growing wide. "What the fu—"

Help me, Joe thought, holding out his hands. *I can't make it stop, Rex. It won't stop.*

Alex looked at Joe with a mixture of puzzlement and panic, letting Joe's unspoken plea clang around inside his skull before recognizing the hopeless desperation he heard in Joe's thoughts. There was chaos there, too, and deep sobbing cries. Alex scrambled to the middle of the room and looked around, not sure what to do. Joe's thoughts continued to ram up against his own like a semi trying to get through a brick wall—*I can't make it stop—it's dark—it's coming through—screaming—it's coming*—Alex saw the piece of glass on the floor, scarlet stains on the carpet, and his anger flared. He opened his mouth to speak, but the words stuck in his throat when he caught sight of the mirror.

An eerie, hypnotic haze permeated the glass, sweeping like a lazy storm into the dim room. Alex tried to back away, but as he watched icy smoke fingers wrapped around his ankles and squeezed, anchoring him where he stood—and Joe's thoughts suddenly let go. Alex watched as Joe stepped to his side, brushing his arm, and moved a few steps closer to the glass, wonderment on his pale face. His reflected features looked grossly distorted, undulating in waves of disjointed motion as the mirror continued to weep.

"Joe, no." Alex croaked, trying to lift his arm. His legs felt like they had cement blocks wrapped around them.

Joe turned and looked at him, a trace of enraptured fear in his glassy eyes, and took two more steps beyond Alex's reach.

"Joe, what're you doing?" His voice sounded like it had traveled through torrents of water, thick and indistinct. Alex reached to grab the back of Joe's shirt and missed, falling forward onto his hands, feet anchored where he stood. He watched in helpless horror as Joe stepped closer to the mirror.

"Joe, don't—"

A brutal wind erupted, howling in Alex's ears like a rush of devil's breath. The room came alive in surging gusts of hazy movement and the fog took on the sharpness of distinct facial features, stretched at impossible angles. Oblong craniums bent and folded, jaws disfigured and warped. Yawning maws bared needle-sharp teeth, like hungry ghosts starved for eternities. The damp air filled with a moaning freight train snarl. Twisted, grasping talons slashed at Alex's skin, pulled at his arms, tore at his hair, leaving cuts and bruises that quickly vanished. Feet anchored, he flailed at the unearthly entities, unable to get enough air into his constricting lungs. The mirror opened, revealing a gaping, undulating throat-like tunnel. Joe stood at the opening of the cavernous pit, clear liquid splashing at his bare feet, wind whipping his long hair into a frenzy. Misty finger tendrils coiled around his body, pulling him closer to the spiral gullet. Joe lifted his hands and began walking toward the glass as though entranced.

The familiarity of it all struck deep in Alex's bowels. His bladder suddenly felt full. He yelled Joe's name, still punching at the corporeal fog. It felt like a hundred crows dive-bombing him at once, stripping away bits of sanity a little at a time. He could feel clumps of hair leaving his head, skin peeling from his arms and face, all leaving no trace of the assault on his body.

It's okay, Al. I have to go now.

The powerful wind shifted direction and became a vacuum. Coke bottles flew by, pelting Alex so hard he almost fell over. Wolfgang's cage sailed past, smashing into the closed door. Posters ripped from the walls, books and cassette tapes rode the powerful one-way tempest. The folding closet doors pulled loose from their bottom track and flung open, letting loose a deluge of clothes, which hit the mirror and fell in piles to the soaked carpet. A convoy of Joe's makeshift bone arrows soared through the air—one pierced Alex's low back, another buried itself in the back of his left arm. He screamed in pain and fear.

Suddenly, Joe spun and dove, clutching in desperation at the carpet, panic filling his eyes. Off balance with the sudden shift in the air, Alex belly-flopped to the floor, reaching long. His fingers met Joe's outstretched hand briefly before Joe skidded backwards, dragged by gnarled fingers of vapor. As if in warning, another demon howl thundered in Alex's ear and he threw his arms over his head to drown out the hell-beast growl. Something still had a grip on his ankles and he kicked harder against it when he saw Joe being jerked upright, hovering like a puppet on a madman's string. Joe groped for the brass bars on the side of the frame and clung to them, face knotting. His hair whipped around his panic-stricken face as his legs swept through the liquid glass, dangling into the ominous throat. The brass bars bent and groaned with the weight of his frail body. A rapturous moan filled the room, sounding like the all-encompassing laugh of Satan himself.

Alex lunged with all his strength and scramble-crawled to his feet. He reached, fingers wrapping around Joe's wrist just as Joe lost his grip on the riot of brass bars and was pulled deeper into the moving abyss. Alex held tight, the deafening freight-train roar of rushing air drowning out all sound. Water poured over his head. His stomach lurched. A bilious taste flooded his tongue. He tried to swallow over the nauseating lump rising in his dry throat and move out from under the steady stream spitting from beyond the glass, but a relentless push-pull force flattened his face and body against the icy glass, making it impossible to breathe. His arms and hands, holding Joe's thin wrist on the other side, felt like they'd been set afire. Saltwater sprayed into Alex's nose and mouth. He felt the air leaving his lungs and panicked.

"Joe, grab my arm with your other hand!" The growling wind swallowed his voice.

Joe fumbled, trying to catch hold of the edge of the frame. His legs flailed, unable to find ground.

Alex managed to plant one knee against the glass and brace himself. He pulled hard, but the writhing, grasping fingers of mist held strong and yanked Joe farther into the circular cavern. Alex grunted in pain. His shoulder wrenched, and he let out a yell as his knee slipped and he slammed into the cold glass, face flattened against the unyielding mirror, his hold on Joe's arm slipping.

I can't hold on. Joe's words were breathless and paper-thin inside Alex's head. *You have to let me go.* Joe's grip on Alex's wrist loosened. The strained muscles in Alex's shoulder separated from the bone and he gritted his teeth. The dive-bomb attack resumed from behind.

"No way," Alex seethed. "Fight, goddamn it, like you always do!" With every bit of strength he could muster, he pulled Joe up a few inches and gasped when he saw Joe's eyes. Pure darkness beamed through the wide orbs and everything went black for a second. With a thunderous clap, Joe ripped free of Alex's grip and fell, swallowed whole by the pulsating throat.

Alex shouted as he was hoisted, slamming face first into the solid glass. In a blinding flash, he flew backwards across the room, his head striking the bathroom doorjamb with an angry crack. A wave of darkness washed him away.

part two

*If once you start down the
dark path, forever will it
dominate your destiny;
consume you it will.*

-Yoda

four

Brothers

Makate, the son of Midnight, and Wabishk, the son of Dawn raced through the valley, searching. Along the way, Makate painted the hills with rainbows and Wabishk sang a lonely song.

"What is this sad song you sing?" Makate asked. "I have not heard it before."

Wabishk leapt to a mountaintop and said, "It is the song of Darkness and I heard it in the reflection of the red river."

Makate said, "Show me so that I may know this song and sing it with you."

Laughing, Wabishk ran through the valley with Makate chasing close behind, tossing color to the wind. They came to rest at the stream's edge and Wabishk knelt, silencing the waters. Makate listened carefully but did not hear Wabishk's lonely song.

"You must close your heart and think only of a night without stars," said Wabishk. "Then you will hear the sad song of Darkness and know its meaning."

So Makate concentrated and he did hear the soft moans of the lonesome song but did not like the way it made his heart feel. When he looked closer into the reflection of the river he saw Wabishk's face next to his, but his brother's features looked like the monsters One Who Walks Across The Sky spoke of. She told them never to let the fiends see inside because they will claim your heart for their own and Darkness will laugh, causing violent storms and the broken spirits of the people.

Makate began to tremble and the sky shook with force. He stood up and took Wabishk by the shoulders and looked into his eyes and there he did see the light fade. Makate hugged his brother close and cried out, "Why did you let it see you, my brother? Why let Darkness have a say?"

Wabishk hung his head low. "I could not resist. The song is too sweet, the promise too strong."

Makate bathed Wabishk in his tears, but it was not enough. Wabishk's light soon went out, and Makate was lost.

May 26, 1984

He heard a single flute through the humming in his ears. The idea struck him funny. *Why would there be a flute in Hell?*

Jagged noises played like a skipping record. After a long period of deciphering, he realized the noises were voices. Familiar voices. Without effort he sat up and looked around. His mother curled in a chair by the window. Her head rested on a pillow. He smiled. She looked so pretty, but her cheeks were blotched pink.

Someone entered the room. A tall nurse who looked like he hadn't shaved in two days. Alex greeted the man but received no response. Alex looked behind him at the figure on the bed. It was him—at least he thought it was. His heart thumped once, so hard it jolted his body, and he scrambled out of the bed and away from the horrific thing lying under the blankets.

His face was smashed, almost unrecognizable. Bloated purple and green bruises rose on his forehead and the right side of his face. His right eye was swollen shut. A strip of white tape covered his bent nose, barely hiding indigo swells under both eyes. A thin hose ran from a hanging plastic bag to his hand and disappeared under a patch of gauze taped there.

That isn't me, he thought, knowing it had to be.

Fear took hold. Alex backed away, unable to take his eyes off the disfigured thing in the bed. He turned and reached for his mom's hand, but his fingers passed through her flesh as if it were air.

"Mom!"

Elizabeth Knapp's head snapped up from the pillow. She looked around the room, dazed.

"Mom."

Elizabeth frowned.

Alex knelt and looked at his mother's weary, tear-blotched face. *This is how she looked all those weeks with Dad in hospice*, he thought, trying in vain to take her hand. She looked right at him but saw nothing.

"Mom, I'm here."

Elizabeth stood up. She went to the bed and sat next to the broken person lying there. Her lips brushed his forehead. She combed her fingers through his dark hair.

"I know," she whispered. "It'll be okay."

The hum-buzz sound returned to Alex's ears along with the familiar voices. Muffled music came from very far away and somewhere behind him. Alex looked toward the window and saw someone outside.

Joe stood there, naked body drenched in blood. Venous liquid ran in steady streams from his long hair, bathing his pale chest and a blazing cross carved into his torso. He opened his arms wide and smiled, a thick red wave appearing behind him. Alex pressed his hands against the glass and screamed Joe's name. He slammed his fists against the window, but it wouldn't break and made no sound. A milky bloodshot wave undulated toward Joe and Alex could do nothing but watch in helpless, silent horror as it devoured his friend.

On the bed, Alex opened his eyes and blinked in the bright light. Wild-eyed, he stared at the ceiling and whispered. "He's alive."

11:11pm

"Who's the president of the United States?"

"Ron Reagan," Alex replied.

"What city and state do you live in?"

"Rogue River, Oregon."

"When's your birthday?"

"March second nineteen sixty-six."

Doc Abraham blew at a strand of gray hair hanging in front of his glasses. "Okay. You bonked your head pretty good there, buddy, and nearly got your arm pulled clean out of its socket. Concussion is nothing to sneeze at. If you don't do everything I tell you, you'll be in the shits for a long time. Got it?"

Alex tried to nod, but his neck was so stiff it felt like it was in a vice grip. He'd been asked the same questions every ten minutes by an assortment of medical staff since waking up and it was starting to wear him out. Doc Abraham continued.

"You'll be here a few more days, just to be sure there's nothing going on that I don't already know about. But even after you get home there are going to be rules, mister."

Tapping his clipboard, Doc moved toward the IV and re-positioned the bag. He went on, working his glasses back into place by contorting his face and scrunching his nose.

"Rest is the most important thing right now. You'll experience some blurred vision, headache, nausea, lack of appetite. We were able to relieve the edema in your noggin with meds, but your brain could start swelling again, so no exertion whatsoever and you gotta take the dexamethasone to keep the inflammation down. We'll start physical therapy for your shoulder, strengthening, range of motion, the whole bit, but not for a few weeks. You gotta keep it slinged and give the strained connective tissues a chance to heal some." Doc walked to the door and opened it. "Could've been a whole lot worse, kiddo. Good thing you're young. You'll be back on your feet in no time."

The door swept closed.

"Water?" Elizabeth asked, reaching for a plastic cup.

Without thinking, Alex lifted his chin to nod. Deep, throbbing pain shot down his spine. Beads of sweat sprung on his upper lip as Elizabeth guided a straw into his mouth. He swallowed a cup and a half before his throat felt less scratchy.

"How long have I been here?"

"Three days." She brushed a hand across her tired eyes.

"*Three days*? How did I—?" Alex swallowed. "Where's Joe?"

His head began a deep throb and his eyes felt like they were being sucked from their sockets.

"Mom?" He started to sit up, but she put her hand on his chest. Wincing, he lay back and watched Elizabeth. His lips had gone numb.

"He's in the intensive care unit on the fourth floor, Alex." She squeezed his hand. "He's unconscious and not doing well. His head ..." She looked at the floor then stood and walked to the window. She peered beyond the glass into the night.

"Norma found Joe sprawled on the front lawn and called nine-one-one, then found you lying in a heap in Joe's room. She said the room looked like a tornado had hit it and you two must've had one nasty fight."

Alex squeezed his sore eyes shut.

"The police are involved, Alex, and the newspapers, mostly because of Norma's big mouth. 'Violin virtuoso Alexander Knapp found unconscious at local residence.'"

She still hadn't turned to face him. He needed to see her eyes, to know that she was okay.

"Mom, I'm sorry." Alex's thoughts tried to float away like bubbles on a breeze, but something picked at his brain and the persistent buzzing in his head kept him alert.

Elizabeth gazed out the window, arms wrapped tight around her body. "There's a lot you don't know about Joe, Alex."

"No argument from me on that point." He fingered the strip of tape on his nose.

"Years ago, Mary Whitewing told me something that I'd forgotten until I saw you collapsed in Joe's room. She told me a story about a looking glass, that some are able to absorb energy while simultaneously reflecting it back. She said some are gateways to the soul, avenues to the innermost psyche, a place of absolute truth. Mary calls it 'the god place.'"

Elizabeth turned away from the window and Alex saw her bloodshot eyes, the exhaustion behind them.

"I asked her why she was telling me this fantastic tale and she said I would need to know for the child I was carrying. Two days later I learned I was pregnant with you."

Elizabeth eased into the chair by the window and rubbed her face.

"I knew the day would come when I would have to tell you what I'm about to tell you, but I'm still ill-prepared." She took a big breath and launched in. "When she was five months pregnant with Joe, Norma's two-year-old son Isaac drowned in the pond at Grove Park."

"I know. Joe told me."

"Did he tell you Isaac had Down Syndrome?"

Alex blinked. "No."

"When Norma noticed Isaac had wandered from the sandbox, she went looking for him. It was thirty minutes before she found him. She tried to wade in after him but got such severe abdominal cramps she almost drowned. A couple of men were jogging through the park and saw her in the water, screaming, hysterical. One of the men was your dad's boss and he told us what happened."

Elizabeth took a deep breath. Alex listened through the steady buzz-whine in his head.

"After Isaac's funeral, Norma seemed excited about the baby she was carrying, which in retrospect now seems like an inappropriate response to everything. I even thought she and I might become friends since we were about a month apart in our pregnancies. But she quickly became irrational, paranoid, obsessive. Marcus told me she tried to make herself miscarry by beating on her stomach. Early one morning she threw herself down the stairs, hoping she would lose the baby. Then Marcus found her in the bathroom one night. She—Norma ..." Elizabeth covered her eyes. "Norma had taken a wire coat hanger and tried to abort the baby herself. She told him she was carrying a demon inside her and that it had killed Isaac. Marcus had no choice but to get her psychiatric help. It was very hard on him. He was so scared. He admitted her to the psych ward at Rogue Valley Medical in Medford a few weeks after Isaac drowned."

Alex felt hot tears on his cheeks but made no move to wipe them away. His chest had taken on a crushing weight.

"Norma was delusional. She kept telling the doctors that she was the chosen vessel for God's holy children, but that something had gone wrong, that she'd been polluted and that her baby had turned into a demon and she wanted it out of her. The doctors were afraid she'd try to harm her unborn child again, and she did. Somehow, she'd gotten into the meds and downed half a bottle of sedatives. They had to pump her stomach and keep her confined and moderately sedated from then on. She was watched twenty-four-seven. Norma's official diagnosis was manic depressive insanity with paranoia, but they also identified several personality disorders. One of them was acute narcissism."

"Jesus," Alex breathed. "Christ."

Elizabeth reached for a tissue and blew her nose.

"On her due date, Norma was transferred here, to Providence Medical, where they induced labor, but Joe was breech and that made his delivery very difficult. You were born here, too, as you know. You and Joe share the exact same time and date of birth, as you know. But what you don't know is that I went into labor five weeks before your due date. Doc tried to stop it with medications, but nothing worked. My water broke and there you were. You were so small and had trouble breathing on your own. Doc Abraham ran tests, thinking that your dad's chain smoking in the house while I was pregnant might have had something to do with it. You were underweight and had to stay in the neonatal ICU for a couple of weeks, but you still weren't gaining weight."

"Like Luke," Alex mumbled.

"Yes. Just like Luke," Elizabeth said. "But, unlike Luke, all your tests came back fine. Doc never figured out what the issue was and determined you were just eager to be on the outside."

Alex rolled his eyes to look at his mom's exhausted face. "Sorry I keep scaring you."

Elizabeth gave him a weary smile. "It's cool. Page eleven of the Mom Handbook prepares us for things like this."

Alex tried to smile, too, but his face felt like a bloated balloon.

Elizabeth went on. "Joe cried constantly, so hard that he'd turn purple, and nothing could get him to stop. Your dad was working long hours, so he wasn't around much. I refused to leave you in the NICU by yourself, so I wasn't getting any sleep. Marcus was exhausted, a real mess after everything that had happened with Norma. He hadn't even had a chance to grieve for Isaac. So, one afternoon, out of sheer exhaustion, I laid Joe down next to you."

Alex watched his mother's face. Elizabeth leaned forward with her elbows on her knees.

"It was magic. Joe looked right at you, right into your eyes, and for the first time in twelve days, he stopped crying. You two just stared into each other's eyes and made little baby sounds. It's impossible, I know, but I swear it was like you two were communicating somehow, like you hear about twins doing. It was like you recognized each other from another time and place. Right then I should have known."

"Known what?"

"That you two would be together for life, no matter what happened. And that's exactly how it's been for eighteen years."

The sharing, Alex thought. *It's a real pain in the ass sometimes.*

Elizabeth continued. "That night the two of you slept side by side. Marcus slept too, but I watched you and Joe. I watched as you and Joe reached out in your sleep, found each other's hand, and intertwined your tiny fingers together. I honestly thought it was a dream until—"

"—Mary." Alex held back tears, knowing how much his head would hurt if he started bawling.

"Yeah. Whitewing strikes again. So, Marcus and I buddied up since your dad couldn't take time off work and was always so exhausted when he got home. Marcus had no idea about formula because Norma had breastfed Isaac, but that man was an expert diaper changer, so we took turns. And he loved that baby, just like he'd loved Isaac with every cell of his body. He told me he felt for the first time in a very long time that there was light back in the world. Hope, too. Joe was a beautiful boy, with flaxen hair and enormous blue eyes, and so happy. He had a belly laugh you could hear a block away." Elizabeth's face darkened. "Norma was released from Rogue Valley on Joe's sixth birthday—your sixth birthday. She crashed the party."

"I remember. That's when you stopped letting me go to Joe's house to play," Alex mumbled.

"That was one of the hardest decisions I've ever made as a parent," Elizabeth said, rubbing her face. "You two were joined at the hip."

Still are, Alex thought.

"They were able to stabilize Norma with a combination of medications, and she seemed to do okay for a while, but I still thought she might try to hurt you. When she came home, she was different. She smiled a lot and said nice things. She became more active in church, but …"

Her voice trailed off. Tears spilled down her freckled cheeks.

Alex squeezed her hand weakly, his mind too dulled by painkillers to fully grasp everything. Distant humming filled his ears and he heard his mother's voice in the drone.

"I didn't know what to think," she said. "All of a sudden, Mary's story came back to me."

"Wait," Alex mumbled. "Rewind. I missed something."

Elizabeth leaned forward. "Where did he get that horrible monstrosity anyway? It's the most hideous thing I've ever seen."

Alex jerked his head and groaned as instant arcing waves of pain wracked his shoulder blades. He sucked air through clenched teeth, perspiration springing on his forehead. An invisible knife twisted in his chest. After several excruciating minutes, he said, "You saw the mirror?" His voice came out thick and scratchy. He could barely hear himself over the pounding in his head.

Elizabeth nodded. "Norma called the police then called me. I didn't like standing in front of it. I felt uneasy, like someone was watching from the other side. That's when I remembered Mary's story." Elizabeth pulled out a tissue and blew her nose. "I know Joe didn't do this to you. He's not that kind of person, and why would he? You would never strike him, but you wouldn't just stand there and let him beat the hell out of you either. Whatever happened was *not* between you and Joe, and when you're better you're going to tell me exactly what happened in that room."

1:33am

Elizabeth flipped on the hall light and pulled off her sneakers. She ran cold water into the kitchen sink and filled a glass before heading down the hall to her bedroom. She passed Alex's room and peeked in at the disarray. His violin case lay open on the floor. As she knelt to flip it closed, she glimpsed the edge of a photograph among the sheets of music lying on the floor and pulled it from the pile of papers.

Luke and Alex stared back at her with big grins spread across their boyish faces—Luke standing on tiptoes to wrap his arm around his big brother's shoulder, Alex half-lifting Luke so he could reach. Elizabeth had snapped the polaroid just before the boys' first rappelling lesson. She'd been so nervous she was afraid the picture would turn out blurry.

Elizabeth held the picture for a long time, studying her sons' sweet faces, then reached to arrange Alex's sheet music into a neater pile. A second photo fell into her lap and she looked at it, solemn. She'd taken the second picture minutes after the first. Alex had wrapped his rappelling rope around Luke's neck in a playful display of brotherly torture. Luke had crossed his eyes and opened his mouth wide, tongue wagging, purple from the grape candy he'd been eating all morning.

Fighting tears, Elizabeth put the two photos together and finished straightening Alex's music. She didn't make a habit of going into her son's room, unwilling to invade his privacy, a concept her own mother could never understand. But she was glad she'd seen the pictures. Since Joe's problems had begun, she often wondered if Alex had blocked out the good memories of his father and brother along with the bad.

A hot shower beckoning, she stood and turned off the light, closing the door behind her—and stopped short in the hallway. The door to Luke's room stood open a few inches. Wary, Elizabeth pushed it open and hit the light switch. Movement caught her eye and she stepped back, startled, then watched as a small white feather descended through the air. The plume took several seconds to reach the hardwood floor and when it did Elizabeth made no move toward it. Instead she looked up, expecting to see a bird that had gotten trapped in the house.

The room was still, except for the silent motion of the carved owl's wooden wings stirring the humid air.

1:33am

In the dream, a small man with skin the color of onyx danced shadowless in a snow-white desert. He was alone and wore only a long tunic, which billowed and blew as he moved in the bright sunshine. Black hair hung in spiraled ropes to his heels. He chanted, dancing in pronounced movements. Garbled words and unintelligible sounds blended with the soundless wind.

Alex was there but not there. He felt the warm sand between his toes and the air brushing against his bare body. *This man sees,* he thought. *Touch his skin and you will see, too.* Alex knew if he could do this he would have enough strength for the battle, although he didn't know who his enemy was or what he was fighting for.

The man grew still and tilted his face to the sun. A slow smile pulled at the corners of his mouth as he thrust his hands into the air, and then laughed and hollered and whooped. After a while he resumed the strange dance.

"What does this mean?" Alex couldn't hear his own voice when he spoke, but the small man stopped and turned. Smiling, he winked at Alex, one eye as ashen as the white sand, the other as black as coal. Without a word, the man turned and danced away, leaving Alex alone in the silent gusting wind.

Alex looked around the dim hospital room. The painkillers had worn off and a dull ache pulsed in his temples. The dream was exactly as Joe had described. Looking at the window, Alex remembered Joe's blood-soaked image, thin arms outstretched as though inviting a macabre lover. It was dark beyond the open curtains and he could just see a slice of moon. He glanced at the wall clock. *Well after midnight. Good.* Given all his unplanned visits to Providence Medical over the years, he knew staff would be sparse and preoccupied with late night Letterman or Carson. They'd removed the IV and catheter, but the oxygen monitor was still taped to his index finger. He listened for any movement or voices in the hallway. All quiet. He would have to be quick.

Alex grabbed the bedrail and gritted his teeth at the pain ripping through his back and neck. The sling binding his right arm to his body greatly hindered his mobility and strength. Holding tight, he struggled to a sitting position, temples pulsing. The numbers on the monitor display spiked. He eased his legs over the edge of the bed and took deep breaths, watching stars explode in front of his eyes. It seemed like a long way to the floor. He slid his butt down the side of the mattress and planted his feet on the cold tile. A shiver squirmed up his spine and instant dizziness and nausea swept over him. His head felt water-logged. *Maybe this isn't such a great idea after all,* he thought, and then, *you really are a fucking coward. A bona fide wimp, just like Joe says.* Alex stood straighter and steadied himself, then reached under his gown, grabbed the lead wires stuck to his chest, and yanked them off. He tossed them to the bed and peeled the oxygen sensor from his finger then limped as quickly as he could toward the door, trying not to scream with each step.

The corridor was deserted. Crushing waves of pain bore down, almost bringing him to his knees as he crept along the hallway toward the elevators, his route mapped by years of practice. Twenty feet from his room, he heard a deep voice. Alex jumped, shockwaves arcing through every muscle. He turned, the room tilted, but he caught himself on the wall.

A very tall man with a perfectly shaped bald head, closely trimmed beard, and dark skin strode toward him wearing faded jeans and a gray sweater with a blue collared shirt underneath, the sleeves rolled up to his elbows. A small gold stud glinted from the man's left earlobe in the dim fluorescent light. He stopped and crossed his arms, giving Alex a reproachful look, but the intense warmth of the man's eyes reminded Alex of melted milk chocolate, comforting and sweet somehow.

"I'm pretty sure Doc Abraham told you to stay put," the man said, voice so deep it seemed to come from inside the Air Jordans on his feet.

"I was just …" Alex's voice trailed. He cleared his sandpapery throat and squinted at the tag on the man's sweater.

The man smiled. "Doctor Romulus David."

"You don't dress like a doctor," Alex said, realizing his words sounded stupid.

"Well, I wouldn't be a very good one if I let patients roam the hospital corridors all night, would I? I happened to be watching the monitors up front when you suddenly blipped off the radar. Knew something was up. Things just don't tend to be that exciting around here."

Alex looked at the floor, which seemed to move under his bare feet. His head threatened to explode. "I was looking for Joe Schell's room. He's in the ICU. Do you know where it is?"

Alex thought he saw a light go on behind the doctor's expressive eyes. The man nodded slowly, studying Alex's battered face for several uncomfortable moments.

"Are you sure you want to see him?"

"I have to."

"Okay then. Stay here." Dr. David disappeared through a door and returned a moment later with a wheelchair. He helped Alex into it and started down the corridor.

"You really do look young to be a doctor, Doctor David," Alex said, trying to fill the awkward silence. He pressed the elevator button using his good arm.

"Call me Rom. And you look too young to be the greatest violinist I've ever heard. I saw you at Oregon State a couple of years ago, and at Collier Center a few months before that, Portland Center for the Performing Arts. I happened to be at a medical conference in Berkeley a number of years ago. That was the first time I saw you perform. Caught you on Johnny Carson a couple times, Letterman, too. So damn young, so damn gifted. I was in awe. That sonata you wrote is exquisite."

"Which one?" Alex asked, trying to remember what those days felt like, when music sang in every cell of his body, rather than the fearful loud silence that now saturated his very being.

"The one that sounds like a million butterflies fluttering in faint streams of sunlight on a warm day. The kind of day where you just want to lie in the grass and listen to Big Mama Nature tell her stories. The way you worked in the flat notes and minor scales to pull out the refrains. Gave me goose bumps. I have them now just thinking about it. You make it look so easy."

Impressed, Alex smiled, but his face didn't light up. He thought it ironic that the doctor remembered one of the many pieces that he himself couldn't recall composing. Many times, he would play the standards—Bach, Beethoven, Vivaldi—and then it was as though someone else would enter his mind and body and he'd play a composition he'd never heard before. At the time he thought it was cool, the way it used to be when music would find him out of the mist without forethought or initiative. Now he wondered. Now it scared him.

They stopped in front of a closed door. ROOM 113. JOSEPH SCHELL. AUTHORIZED PERSONNEL ONLY. LAW ENFORCEMENT.

Alex looked up at the doctor, a flash of panic on his bruised face. "I gave them a statement. They can't do anything unless I press charges, right?"

Rom shook his head, solemn. "I don't think it's going to matter, Alex. I sent the police guard back. Joe's in bad shape. Just want to warn you." He pushed the door open and wheeled Alex inside.

Joe lay motionless on the middle of the bed. An oxygen tube looped over his ears and disappeared into his nostrils, an IV fed fluid into his arm, a urine catheter drained it back out. A bolt had been screwed into his left temple, patch of hair shaved down to the skull. A wire led from the bolt to a monitor displaying numbers Alex didn't understand. Heartrate leads snaked from a monitor and disappeared beneath the blankets covering Joe's thin form. Except for all the hardware and the bolt in his skull, he looked like he was asleep.

"He doesn't look that bad," Alex breathed, relieved.

Rom frowned, clearly stunned by Alex's words. "Excuse me? This boy has got hacks in his flesh the length of knitting needles, scars everywhere, he's underweight, his color is pallid—"

"He always looks like this." Alex's mouth had gone dry. He realized again, too late, how stupid he sounded.

"*He always looks like this?* The only time I've seen a body this carved up was after an autopsy. He looks like a walking museum. What's with the body art? Is he into scarification or something?"

Alex held the wheelchair arm tight, feeling nauseous again.

"Does he do this to himself?" Rom's voice was laced with anger and confusion, making it sound deeper than it naturally was.

Alex nodded, recalling the first time he saw Joe's naked body as an adult. But it had been covered in blood then. He couldn't remember anything else.

"Why is that bolt in his head?"

"It's an ICP—" Rom shook his head. "Uh, sorry. It's an intracranial pressure monitor to measure cerebrospinal fluid pressure in the brain."

"Oh." Alex's lips felt numb again. "It's bad then."

"Well, cops say he took a dive off his roof, so I'd say a lot of things in his world are bad." Rom ran his palm over the top of his head. "Man, I hate shit like this."

"Wouldn't he be more, I don't know, *broken* if he fell that far? It's a three-story house, well, counting the basement. Vaulted ceilings, too."

"It's complicated, and a lot about Joe's current condition doesn't make medical sense."

"What do you mean?"

Rom sighed and sat in the chair on the other side of Joe's bed. "I'll spare you the doctor-speak, and I shouldn't be telling you any of this since you're not family but screw it. The CT scans show what's called a mild intracerebral hematoma. That's when vessels in the brain bleed, resulting in swelling, and is usually caused by a traumatic injury like a blow to the head. In some cases, it can be life-threatening. Joe's hematoma is located in the limbic area, which controls emotional states, moods and responses. Right now, his amygdala—which is closely associated with anger and aggression, fight and flight responses—and his hippocampus—which is associated with emotional memory—are leaking blood from these broken vessels. These two systems in the brain work together to transfer and store memories." Rom scratched his beard.

Alex narrowed his eyes. "Okay. There's something you're not telling me."

"No," Rom said, leaning in. "There's something *you're* not telling *me.*"

Alex moved to stroke his nose but changed his mind when he realized the amount of pain it would cause.

Rom took a deep breath. "How I've described Joe's injury makes it sound horrible, but his condition is actually not that serious—nothing we can't monitor and treat, like we are now. There's very little buildup of cerebrospinal fluid at Joe's injury site, and the bleeding is minimal. Joe's basically got a bruise that will heal relatively quickly. His injury is simply not conducive to the massive, violent tumble they *say* he took off a roof. So, yeah, he would be more *broken,* to use your word. Bones. Teeth, definitely. He hasn't got a mark on him. He's got no external or structural injuries. Based on what we know and can see, there is no physical rhyme or reason as to why he hasn't woken up."

Alex closed his eyes. His fingers had started to tingle.

"You hear about people who never come back," Rom continued, "and you wonder if they really want to. I do, anyway. There's an emotional component to what's happening here, Alex. And I have a feeling you can help. I mean, we can tube feed him, hydrate him, keep him alive, but if he doesn't want to come back—if there's nothing for him to come back to—he'll keep slipping away until—"

"—he dies."

"You want to know something else?"

Alex looked at Rom through the dim light, eyelids growing heavy.

"They brought Joe in minutes before you arrived. He had cardiac rhythm but wasn't breathing. I was on-call in critical care. We ventilated, but it didn't work. Then the damnedest thing happened."

Alex tried to raise his eyebrows.

"The team was just about to call it when Chelsea, one of our trauma docs, came in. She happened to say your name, I guess because she knew I'd seen you perform and she wanted to tell me you were on your way in an ambulance. As soon as she said your name, Joe started breathing. On his own. Just like that. I like to think that means something." He looked at Alex and rose from his chair. "I'll be back in a few minutes to help you back to your room. Take your time with him. Talk to him."

Alex studied Joe's motionless form for a moment then pushed himself up and sat on the bed. He stared at his friend for a long time, brushed blond hair from Joe's calm, pale face. He put his hand on Joe's hollow cheek. His skin felt unnaturally cool.

"Joe."

Joe's chest rose and fell with a natural rhythm, his lips cracked and colorless. His eyelids were red-veined, making him look vampiric, haunted. Dark shadows filled the sunken crevices beneath his eyes.

"Can you hear me, bro?" Alex watched for any response. He leaned close, Joe's breath hot on his face.

"Where are you, man?"

Joe's lips moved. Leaning closer, Alex watched his friend's ghostly face.

"C'mon, bud," Alex whispered. "C'mon back. Fight like you always do."

A weak moan came from Joe's throat.

"What?"

Another sound, louder. Alex put his ear to Joe's mouth.

"Feather." The word came out in a forced rush of breath. Heart thudding, Alex turned slowly to look at Joe's gaunt face.

Joe uttered another word just as Rom opened the door and stepped into the room. "How we doing?"

Alex couldn't move.

"You're pale," Rom said, taking Alex's elbow. "We need to get you back to bed before Doc Abraham kicks both our asses."

Alex got up, holding the doctor's arm, chest tightening with every breath. Lowering himself into the wheelchair, he covered his battered face with a shaking hand and started to cry. Rom swept him out of the room and into the hallway.

"I knew this was a bad idea," Rom said, deep voice echoing down the empty corridor, although he spoke in a whisper. "It hurts when something happens to someone you love and there's not a damn thing you can do. It's the most helpless feeling in the world."

He wheeled Alex into the room and helped him onto the bed. After Rom hooked him back up to the web of wires, Alex turned onto his side and buried his face in the pillow, spine throbbing with the intensity of his sobs.

"Hey," Rom said. "I'll be back in an hour if you want to talk. I'll have William bring you more pain meds."

The door closed. Alex fought hard to get Joe's final word out of his mind. It bounced around inside his skull like a scream that wouldn't end. He groped for a tissue on the stand and blew his nose. Caked blood sprayed from his face into the wad of tissue he held in his trembling hand.

The unshaven nurse entered, gave him some pills, watched him swallow, and left without a word. Alex lay back on the propped pillows, staring at the ceiling, stomach burning. His heart ached in an all too familiar way. *I can't. I can't think about it. Not now.*

Through blurred vision, movement caught his eye. An object appeared out of nowhere against the off-white color of the ceiling. He looked away, thinking it a moth or some other insect, but as the thing floated closer he was able to see it more clearly. Struggling to sit up, Alex watched the thing glide within reach. He stretched out his hand and caught it before it hit the bedsheet.

A small white feather rested on his palm.

Alex eased back onto the propped pillows, tears streaming down his bruised face. Yearning for dreamless sleep, he pressed the feather to his chest and whispered Joe's last word aloud.

"Lucas."

June 2, 1984

Alex lifted a glass of orange juice to his lips and winced. It had taken five full minutes of painful movement to get out of bed, but he'd done it. Doc Abraham had sent him home with strict instructions to rest and not exert himself, but he was determined not to spend any more time on his back than he already had.

Elizabeth smiled at him from across the kitchen table. "Your face looks much better. How do you feel?"

"Okay," Alex said, spooning warm oatmeal into his mouth. "I'm going stir crazy."

"You need to take it easy," she said, sipping tea. "You'll be okay while I'm at work?"

"Yeah. I'm going for a walk today, maybe go see Mary. I need some fresh air."

His mom sighed, standing and taking her cup to the sink. "It's only been a week. You take it easy or I'll kick your butt."

Alex grinned. "I have no doubt that you could, Miss Karate Kid."

Elizabeth turned and threw a perfect sidekick in the middle of the kitchen with a mighty kiai. "And don't you forget it!"

Alex laughed. "Badass mom of the year."

"I'll call you later," Elizabeth said, pulling on a rain slicker. "I'm working in research today if you need to call."

"Okay," Alex said, swallowing the last of his juice. "Hey, Mom!"

"Yeah?" she called from the front door.

"You look like a librarian."

"A librarian who can kick some ass!"

Alex smiled. "Love you, Mom."

Elizabeth walked back into the kitchen and kissed his cheek. "Please don't overdo it. I don't need any more phone calls from the hospital, okay?"

"Got it." He took her hand and kissed it.

Alex waited for the sound of her car to fade before getting up and shuffling to the door. He slipped his feet into his running shoes, stooped to tuck the laces into the sides, then threw his windbreaker over the sling binding his right arm to his body and slipped his left into the sleeve. He stepped into the morning sunshine, shivered in the cool breeze, and started the eight-block trek to Mary's. Bits and pieces of what his mother had told him at the hospital picked at his brain. It was all he had thought about since learning the circumstances surrounding Joe's arrival into the world. The odds had been against him from the beginning.

Lost in thought, Alex arrived at Mary's quicker than he thought he would. He turned the doorknob and stepped inside. Dozens of people milled around Mary's shop, peering into glass cases filled with handmade jewelry, flutes and drums, decorative scarves and wraps, intricate dreamcatchers, and polished river stones, which Mary would make custom pieces with. Vacationers sat on the couch looking through photo albums of Mary's famous creations, hoping to order a one-of-a-kind Whitewing original, business that kept Mary working year-round, although tourist season had officially begun.

Through the crowd, Alex spotted Annie Sanford behind the glass counter, smiling at the patrons, long auburn hair tied back from her porcelain face, green eyes shining as she wrote down credit card information and gift-wrapped items. She, Alex, Joe, and Charlie had gone to school together, but she had been a year ahead of them. Alex liked the way she moved, the way her full hips swayed so confidently. He thought about the two of them eating lunch together every day in elementary school and how he'd happily swap his creme-filled chocolate cupcakes for the awful whole-wheat tofu sprout sandwich her flower-power mom always made her … how she would help him with his 8th grade algebra in the library after school … how she had visited after Luke died and didn't know what to say … how he had cupped those full hips at junior prom and how the two of them had slow-danced together, their bodies pressed against one another, Annie's warm hands clasped behind his neck. Alex grinned at the memories, glad his hippocampus had done its job storing them, then, suddenly, she was walking toward him, smiling, hands in the pockets of her Whitewing Original Art & Woodworks smock.

"Hi, Alex!" She reached up to hug him and he wrapped his good arm around her waist, just above those confident hips. She smelled of wintergreen and sandalwood. He breathed her scent in deeper.

"Hey, Annie, how have you been?" He fingered the tender bridge of his nose.

"Good! Classes are good. Biology major. Perfect for a science nerd like me. Hey, you're off to Juilliard soon, right? That's so exciting!"

"Um, yeah. Soon, I guess," he stammered, taken aback. School was the last thing on his mind.

She peered at him closer. "What happened to your face? Were you in an accident?"

"Yeah, kinda," he said, feeling even more awkward now. "But I'm okay."

She nodded.

He stood there.

"It's been busy here this week," Annie said.

"Yeah. That's good. For Mary."

"Hey, maybe we can get coff—"

But Alex had spotted Mary waving her arms at him above the crowd, motioning him toward the kitchen.

"Sorry, I—uh," Alex said, pointing. "Mary's waiting for me."

"Yeah," Annie said, "I have to get back to work anyway. But maybe I'll see you around over the summer."

"Yeah, that'd be good," Alex said, absently. He dodged around clusters of tourists toward the kitchen door.

"Sit," Mary said, setting a steaming mug of cardamom ginger tea in front of him. She disappeared through the swinging door, leaving him there to think of something to say. Several minutes later, she reentered the kitchen and sat at the table. Mary removed her glasses and looked at him for a long time.

Alex stroked his sore nose and studied the grain of the wood table.

"You're hurt," Mary said.

Alex nodded.

"What happened?"

Alex scoffed, irritated with the question. "Don't you know? Don't you know everything?"

The old woman squinted, folding her hands on the table, patient as always.

"Where is he?" Alex leaned forward. "This isn't one of your stories with the brilliant parable ending. I need to know so I can help him, like you said."

Mary reached into her smock pocket and pulled out a wad of tissue, tears filling her keen eyes.

"I feared this would happen," she said, husky voice cracking. "I fear it's too late. I fear Joseph has lost his battle with the darkness."

"'Fear is not the path,'" Alex said, throwing her own words at her. "I won't accept that. I know he's alive, but empty, or *emptying*. I feel it. You told my mom about all of this before I was even born. This isn't the end of the story. I'm not going to lose anyone else. I won't do it." He rubbed his puffy eyes. "Tell me what to do, Mary. Help me bring him back."

Mary nodded. She took his hand. "Your heart beats in time with his. What *he* feels, *you* feel. What pain *he* has, *you* carry, and vice versa. You know this, you've tasted the blood of your friend on your tongue. When death touches, death leaves a mark, and death makes claims, just as life does. He is very weak. He is in a place of darkness, somewhere between this world and the next, and you cannot reach him."

"The hell I can't," Alex said, defiant. "You're always telling me that if I open my mind and trust my heart I will never fail. You told Joe too, but he never listens. I listened, and I believed you, goddamn it!"

Mary nodded slowly, a crooked smile spreading across her sage face. She lifted her hands and brought them down hard on the table, rattling the tea mug. She leaned close, a grave scowl overtaking her usually calm features. "You are powerless until you free your heart of the burden it carries."

Alex shook his head, stomach sinking. "I don't know what that means. I don't understand this burden thing."

Mary stroked his hand. "Joe has locked himself up inside. You know how that is, don't you, dear? To retreat so far into yourself that the only way out is with the help of a friendly guiding light? I know you understand this. Maybe *you* have to go back to that dark place within yourself to help your friend, your spirit brother. What did you learn there? What did you see?"

A shiver ran the length of Alex's spine, but he tried not to show it. "Nothing. There's nothing."

Mary pushed away from the table with a heavy sigh. "This is the problem. Close your eyes."

"What? Why?"

"Just humor me, please. We haven't sung together in a while. I think it will help."

Alex stiffened. "No." He bumped the table as he reeled out of the chair. "I don't want to go back there, Mary. I can't do it right now." Tears tumbled from his eyes in a rush and he watched through blurred vision as Mary came to him. Familiar, safe arms hugged him tight. He smelled the woman's anise-and-smoke essence and lowered his head to her shoulder, shuddering.

"Alexander," she said, cupping his chin and wiping his eyes with her soggy tissue. "Sometimes a person's own mind can be his worst enemy. Victory can be found in the darkest corners, but you must first be willing to subject yourself to whatever is lurking there."

Alex shook his head. "He's going to die. And I can't. I just can't." He searched her clear dark eyes. "I don't want to die, Mary."

Mary peered at him closely. "Remember, for every speck of dark there is a spark of light. The universe has a way of balancing itself. Joseph has created his own hell where fear, denial, shame and guilt reign. These will batter the life out of him if he does not welcome hope back into his heart, embrace his lost innocence, and forgive. He could use a little light right now, don't you think?"

Alex could not stop shaking. His face hurt.

Mary placed both hands on his shoulders. Alex looked at the old woman, swiping at his nose with her shredded tissue, and saw something in her eyes that he'd seen only one time before, just after Luke died. A quiet yearning, a calm desperation, a hint of tacit fear. She took his hands into hers.

"*Nizaagichigan.* My beautiful treasure," she whispered, softly crying now but earnest in her tone. "*Bizindan bawaadan. Bizindaw gibawaajigan.*"

Alex swallowed hard.

"Listen to your dreams," Mary said. "Listen to your dream spirit."

10:13am

Alex walked, staring at his untied shoes, thinking dark thoughts. Joe never tied his shoes. *Why doesn't he tie his fucking shoes?* Alex shook his head. Having such an irrelevant thought annoyed him. He shuffled through the parking lot of the Thrifty, the buzzing of the red blinking neon adding a bass drone to the high-pitched ringing in his ears. The morning sun felt good on his face, although inevitable rain clouds had begun a dark cluster in the sky. He pulled the glass door open and went to the refrigerated section for a soda, grabbed a pack of gum and stood there, captured by the bizarre headlines on the rag magazines.

Sasquatch Gives Birth to Sextuplets, Alex read. *Well it's good to know the missing link is doing well. Woman Marries Two-Headed Alien from Jupiter.* Alex dug in his pocket for some cash. *Hope she's happy as hell.* Next to these, the Rogue River Courier and Medford Tribune blasted ominous headlines about a missing child, trickle-down economics, and—in the bottom right corner—a small headline with his name in it. He looked back at the two-headed alien.

"Hey, Alex. Haven't s-seen you in a while. M-missed you and Joe at graduation last year."

Alex looked up. Charlie Dugan smiled at him from behind the cash register, offering his very large hand in greeting. Alex motioned toward the sling cradling his arm.

"Oh, h-hey, that's cool," Charlie said. He grabbed Alex's left hand and shook it heartily. "H-heard you got into J-Juilliard, man. That's really s-something. I'm still s-slummin'. You know, j-junior college and shit."

Alex nodded. Charlie used to boast that he'd be the greatest quarterback on the planet some day and had backed up his claim by achieving All-State All-American every single year of high school. He aspired to play for USC and had big dreams of following Bradshaw, Marino, and Montana into the pros, grabbing up Heisman trophies and Super Bowl rings on his way to cereal box superstardom. Charlie had been handed a full athletic scholarship—dorm, meals, and work study included, as far as Alex knew. But there the big guy stood, striped button-up shirt jammed into his expanding waistband, black pants too short, blue vest adorned with a plastic tag that read *My Name is CHARLIE I'm Happy to Help*! His stuttering seemed to have gotten worse. *He didn't make it*, Alex thought, the heaviness in his chest gaining a few more ounces.

"What about football?" Alex pulled a five from his pocket and placed it on the counter.

Charlie shrugged. "You know. My, uh, m-m-mom said it wouldn't be so g-good to play ball anymore. She says I m-might get hurt and she'd m-miss me a lot."

Alex picked up his drink, a deep sadness sinking low. "That's too bad, Charlie. You're a great quarterback. Led the Chieftains to State more times than I can count."

"Yeah, well, uh, it's c-cool. I'll just d-do somethin' else. My m-m-mom's checking on m-medical school." He handed Alex a fistful of change.

Alex looked at the boy shifting his ample weight and struggling to spit out the sentences his brain formulated, and his heart dropped. For a second Alex thought he would vomit right there on the glass countertop that kept people from stealing the scratch-off lottery tickets.

"You'd be good at that too, Charlie. Thanks, man. See you later."

"Uh, y-yeah," Charlie stammered. "Hey, Alex?"

Alex stopped at the door and faced him. Charlie fought to get a grip on his words then took a big breath, rounded the counter, grabbed Alex's good arm and pulled him into a back room where he paced like a kid worried about a sick pet.

Alex cut a glance toward the front door, the sunshine beyond. "Charlie, what's goin—"

Charlie came to a halt and dipped his head. He stood a good eight inches taller than Alex's five-feet-nine and outweighed him by at least a hundred and fifty pounds.

"I heard something."

Alex frowned. He'd never seen Charlie so agitated.

Charlie shuffled from foot to foot and ran a huge hand through his mop of curly red hair. He studied the floor, eyes tracking, searching his brain files for information. "I heard my m-mom and Joe's mom t-talking." He looked at Alex. "I think something b-bad's gonna happen again."

A rush of anxiety let loose in Alex's bloodstream.

"I help out. V-volunteer, you know? I don't mind changing dirty diapers and I like playing with the k-kids. Kids are cool. They don't j-judge. There's a n-new one now. He has cerebral palsy. His name is Stevie Snider. I call him Snider Spider and he has the best laugh I've ever heard. He's four. Only four."

Alex watched as Charlie's thoughts faded out and away. The big guy slumped onto a crate of root beer bottles and hung his head.

Alex resisted the urge to run out into the sunshine. "Charlie, I don't have any idea what you're talking about, man."

Charlie spoke to the floor. "I think she's gonna do something. Just like Jessica Kappy. She could still give you a good hug, even with her s-stubby little arm that looked like a dolphin's fin. I told her she could swim in the Olympics if she wanted. She was only twenty months. Not even two."

Alex's patience got away from him. "Charlie. What the hell are you talking about?"

Charlie's gaze snapped up and Alex saw the terror in his wide blue eyes. Tears brimmed there, which made Alex's heart thump harder.

"I know w-what she did to Jessica," Charlie whispered. "Happy Kappy never woke up. I-I won't let her do that to Snider Spider. N-no way."

Alex squinted at his forgotten friend through the fluorescent light. The incessant buzz in his head made it hard to concentrate. "Charlie?"

Charlie didn't blink. "I think something b-bad's gonna happen. Like before."

10:57am

Alex made his way toward Joe's house, each step more painful than the previous. He sipped his soda and hoped with everything he had for the house to be empty. The last thing he needed was Mrs. Schell's vicious wrath if she found him on her property.

Like a clumsy commando lacking any knack for stealth, Alex approached the house and peered through the garage window. Mrs. Schell's blue Bonneville was gone. He relaxed a little and moved toward the front door, knowing the place would be locked down like Fort Knox. It was, but he pressed the doorbell to be certain no one was inside then tried to think of something to say if she happened to be home.

Silence.

Alex moved to the yard, set his half-drunk soda on the ground near the maple, removed his jacket and loosened the straps of the sling cradling his arm. Gritting his teeth, he slipped it off and crammed it into his jacket pocket. He straightened his elbow. Sharp pains coursed down his back, making his jaws clench tight. He sucked air through his teeth while carefully lifting his arm overhead. Muscles popped and cracked with every movement. He put his windbreaker back on and focused on the leafy maple branches above his head.

"I can do this," he whispered. "No problem." He leapt up and caught the lowest branch with both hands. His shoulder instantly screamed hot. Tendons wrenched, pulling against bone. He dropped to his knees, holding his arm, seething through clenched jaws.

You're such a pussy, Al.

"Fuck you." Alex got to his feet and eyed the branch again. He jumped up and caught it with his left hand, pulled himself up and swung his leg to straddle the branch, watching a dizzying rainbow of bright lights burst before his eyes. His heart thundered. His stomach clenched. The whistling in his pounding head grew higher in pitch. Gasping, Alex rolled up and sat in the connecting point of two thick branches, then reached for a higher branch and stood up. He tried to rally his energy by reprimanding the person who had caused this whole shitshow in the first place.

"Goddamn piece of shit, Joe. Son-of-a-bitch. Psycho fuck."

The mental tirade seemed to help. Before he knew it, he was level with the roof outside Joe's bedroom window. Alex stepped onto the red slate and stood there, breathing hard. Points of light burst through his blurred vision and he focused on lengthening his exhales. He placed his palm on the windowpane and then felt something wet on his upper lip. He swiped at his mouth. Blood dripped from his fingertips.

"Damn it." Alex tipped his head back, feeling blood run into his throat. He coughed up a hefty wad of mucus and spat the stringy red gob onto the roof at his feet. More blood spilled from his nostrils, running into his mouth. Gagging, Alex ran a sleeve over his bruised face and spit again. Scarlet drops spattered his shoes and jeans.

"Shit."

He couldn't breathe. Bloody mucus clogged his nasal passages and throat. *I'm hemorrhaging,* he thought. *Doc's gonna be pissed.* An image of himself sprawled on the ground under the great maple, covered in blood, shoulder wrenched from its socket, face the color of corpse-rot flashed in his mind—and he started to laugh. Then he knew it was serious, because he couldn't stop. Alex leaned over, blood spraying from his nose, strings of red drool hanging from his lips, and thought, *I am dying now. Joe, I'm really sorry I can't help you, but I'm on my way out. Hope you get out of hell real soon. Sincerely, your spirit brother who is also a world-class fuck-up.* The floating fragments of thought made him laugh harder and he started to wheeze with asthmatic breath. Vision darkening, Alex sank to his knees and fell onto his side. Still smiling and choking, he closed his eyes and tried to breathe through his mouth. Just as his consciousness was about to take a final leap into oblivion, he heard the familiar feminine voice in his ear. It roused him like a blast of freezing air.

Alex, please. The leaves of the trees rustled and shimmered in the breeze.

Filling his lungs, he pushed himself up and looked at the dark window, catching sight of his reflection. Blood bathed his face, shirt and jacket, streaked his dark hair a ruddy scarlet. He coughed more bloody snot out of his raw throat and staggered to his feet.

He waited.

Alex … please … dying … Her voice trailed. It sounded weaker than he remembered, more distant.

"Wait. Help me find you. Is Joe with you?"

Dark … consumed … darkness … Her voice drifted, faded.

"Don't go." He got up, holding the window frame for support, and hacked up another stringy mass onto the roof. Rustling leaves answered. Alex put his palm against the windowpane and pushed. It didn't move. He tried again, but it wouldn't budge.

"She locked it," he mumbled in disbelief. "She hasn't stepped foot in that room since Joe's *accident* but went in to lock the window thinking he's not coming back. Psycho fucking bitch!"

Alex peered over the rain gutter at the quiet street far below and wiped his face with the cuff of his jacket. He considered breaking the glass but feared her re-entry into the room—for whatever irrational reason—and she'd immediately know it was him who broke in and that would cause a world of hurt.

The faint cry of a train whistle reverberated off the low hills as Alex shuffled along the red slate to a section where the uppermost roof sloped closer to the roof he stood on. He peered into the backyard. The swing set Marcus had put up for him and Joe and Luke a lifetime ago stood with tall weeds growing around the poles and seats. The metal and chains had rusted to a muddy orange color and the plastic seats had faded to dirty yellow-white. When they were four, Alex had stuck a dyed Easter egg inside one end of the hollow crossbar. He wondered if it was still in there, stinking up the yard. Not that anyone would notice the sulfur smell. Norma's impressive rose garden flourished in all its glory, taking up most of the yard with sweet-smelling, carefully attended blooms. Alex shook his head, heart heavy, realizing the woman took more time nurturing plant life than she did cultivating a relationship with her own son.

Alex stared at the rusted swing set and had a flash of Joe and Luke flying high and back-flipping right onto one of Norma's huge madonnas, flattening it. Joe had landed on his belly, laughing and gasping for breath. Luke landed on his feet, which had earned him the title of Reigning Champion of the Swing Set Kingdom. He pumped his fists in the air like Rocky Balboa, chanting "Rematch! Rematch!" Then they got up and did it again, Joe chasing Luke all over the backyard, his lanky 9-year-old legs too long and always in the way. But Luke was fast. Had to be, with all the teasing he endured. To their surprise, Norma hadn't gotten angry with them for trashing her flowers.

Alex's stomach burned. A thought, inconceivable at first, began formulating in his weary mind, and he heard Luke's mantra in his ear. "Enemies close, bro. Enemies close."

The locomotive sped by, vibrating the shingles under his shoes.

4:48pm

Alex's hand hovered above the doorbell. There was no reason to think this should work, but he didn't have anything to lose, really—she'd already slandered his name all over town. He heard Luke's words again.

"Keep your enemies close," Alex whispered. Luke ought to know. Kids had picked on him a lot because of his size and weakened stature. They made fun of the nine-inch scar on his chest, calling him Frankenstein and other less kind names. But Luke always ended up winning them over. At this very moment, Alex hoped to channel a bit of his brother's charm and ingenuity. He pressed the button and listened as faint chimes filled the house. He poked his sore nose and tried to keep hopeful thoughts.

The door opened. When she saw him, she immediately tried to close the door, but Alex put his hand up and stopped her. He started talking—*fast.*

"Wait, Missus Schell, I came to apologize for all the trouble I've caused, I'm so very sorry, you were absolutely right about Joe being, well, *you know,* and I wanted to tell you that I plan on never associating with him if he ever gets well, I'm just going to go to college and study and get on with my life, I realize now I should have listened to you over the past few months, he's caused more damage to my life than I want to remember, I just wanted you to know you were right about him all along and I'm really kicking myself right now for not believing you."

Breathless, Alex stopped and looked at her. He'd wedged his foot between the door and jamb. All he could see of her face was one heavily outlined, angry eye and the corner of a painted, twitching mouth. She pushed harder and he winced.

"I'll call the police if you're not off my property within ten seconds. *I will have you arrested.*"

"I'm going," Alex said, trying not to let his disappointment show. "I just felt I had to tell you before I leave for school in a few months, that you were right. He was never my friend. He just used me for his psycho mind games. A sane person would never beat the shit out of someone who was trying to help. Sorry for my language, ma'am. There's something very wrong with him, and now I know his problems have nothing to do with you. You did your best with what you had to work with. There's something evil in him, like he's possessed. By demons. I realize that now, and you've reminded me that God doesn't give us anything we can't handle, right Missus Schell? I'm lucky to be alive. I just wish I'd listened to you before, and I wanted to tell you that."

Alex unwedged his foot and the door slammed shut. He heard the deadbolt and chain move into place.

"Thank you for saving my life, Missus Schell," he called. "Goodbye and God bless you!"

Alex let out a long breath and turned toward the silent maple. He looked up at the sky beyond the leaves. It hadn't gone the way he would have liked, but he knew it wasn't going to be easy getting on her good side. If she even had one. He thought of Charlie's story and shuddered.

The chain scraped, and Alex turned. Mrs. Schell opened the door a few inches and glared at him.

"I'm leaving," he told her, quickly.

"If he wakes up you call me immediately, you hear? The police will contact you first. I told them to contact me only when he dies so I can make funeral arrangements. I don't want anything to do with that heathen otherwise."

Alex nodded, trying hard to mask his hatred for her. "I will. I've got a few charges to file myself. Attempted murder for one."

She started to close the door.

"Missus Schell?"

The woman hesitated, leaving the door open a crack. He couldn't see her face, only a very still shadow.

"I'd really like to do something for you," he began, hoping. "I feel so bad. I know how it was just hanging out with him a few hours a day. You had to have him in your house *all the time.*"

Alex shook his head and looked at his shoes.

"If there is *anything* I can do for you, *anything at all,*" he paused, still wagging his head. "I trusted him, and this is what I got for it." He pointed at his bruised face. "If you hadn't found me and called the ambulance, I would've died. What impresses me most is that you didn't let your dislike of me get in the way of helping me. I don't think I could've done that for someone I hated. You really are a godly woman, Missus Schell. A true example of Christ's teachings."

Her muffled voice came from behind the door. "You were bleeding all over my carpet. I had no choice. I did it for selfish reasons."

"I don't believe that for a second," Alex said, quickly. "I think you did it because you knew it was the right thing to do, the Christ-like thing to do. You put your animosity aside and helped someone you don't care for. A sinner. That's a very righteous act and I think the Lord is smiling from ear to ear because of what you did, and you *will* be blessed for it. The rewards of Heaven are yours, Missus Schell. Definitely." He willed tears to his eyes and succeeded a little.

She pulled the door open an inch and scowled at him, eyes narrowing with suspicion. He continued, not wanting to disrupt his rhythm now that he'd gotten her attention.

"Missus Schell, I know we trashed Joe's room during the struggle." He looked at his shoes again. "And if you'd let me, I'd really like to help clean up. I'm sure you've been in there to straighten up by now, because you've always kept an impeccable home, but if there's anything that's too much for you to lift I'd be more than happy to help. I do remember knocking over that chest of drawers. I think it's oak. It's probably very heavy."

Putting on his best innocent face, Alex ran his finger along the bridge of his nose.

She eyed him through the crack of the door. "You're injured."

Alex looked up. "The shoulder's still a little stiff and sore, and I do still get a little dizzy from the concussion, but I'm sure I can get something done up there for you. It would be a privilege, ma'am. A small gesture of atonement."

"You'll fix everything and go," she stated, pulling the door open and glaring at him. Her black eyebrows furrowed in an intimidating scowl, thin lips caked fluorescent pink. A shiver of victory made Alex's hair prickle.

"Believe me," Alex said, sincerity dripping like sap, "I will never come here again, unless *you* need something. I've learned my lesson. He can just go to Hell as far as I'm concerned. The world'll be a better place without him in it." It pained him to talk about Joe like that. The words almost didn't make it out of his mouth, but he remembered Luke and stepped inside, closer to his enemy. "Thanks for hearing me out. I appreciate the opportunity to show my gratitude, my penitence."

Elated, Alex followed Norma Schell upstairs, watching her large butt sway back and forth with each step. He was so happy the sound of her pantyhose rubbing together almost made him laugh out loud. She pushed Joe's bedroom door open and Alex's jaw genuinely dropped in shock. The saddest sight lay at his feet. Wolfgang's lifeless body lay on the damp carpet. A gooey mass had oozed from the rat's ears. One eyeball hung by a bloody thread from the socket and Alex wondered if the suction from the mirror had literally pulled the poor creature's brains out.

Norma stood in the hallway outside the bedroom door and watched him, stony gaze taking in his every move, arms crossed and buried under mountainous breasts.

Alex glanced at her over his shoulder. "I'll, uh, take this with me so you won't have deal with it." He picked up Wolfgang by the tail, wrapped the rodent in toilet paper from the bathroom, and put him in his jacket pocket.

Just about everything—bed, dresser, desk, books, cassettes, papers, clothes—lay in a giant heap in front of the mirror. The bathroom door hung on one set of hinges. Empty soda bottles lay everywhere. Marilyn's torn face stared up at him, sleepy doe eyes sad, restless and knowing.

Protecting his shoulder, Alex managed to pull the chest of drawers across the carpet to its original place near the closet. The drawers lay on the floor under the window, contents spilled into the corner by the mirror. He reset them and folded each item of clothing, watching for anything he may need to investigate later. It was hard to concentrate with Norma's eyes shooting beams of contempt at him. Positioning the desk under the window, Alex glanced at the lock. Sure enough, Norma had latched it.

"I didn't realize he had so much junk," Alex said, loading books, papers, cassette tapes, and magazines into the desk drawers. He kicked a bunch of empty Coke bottles into a pile.

She stared at him, expressionless.

Alex stooped to grab the box spring mattress and hesitated. He still hadn't come across the bloodied wedge of glass and didn't want her to see it before he could pocket it. Straightening, he took a deep breath and looked around.

"You're bleeding," Mrs. Schell said, waving a hand in the direction of his face.

Alex touched his upper lip and went into the bathroom for some tissue.

"It happens when I overexert myself," he explained. "I just have to slow down a little. Joe really beat the crap out of me."

She narrowed her eyes, the corners of her mouth twitching, and said nothing.

"If you have a screwdriver and a hammer I can fix the bathroom door and put the curtains up before I leave. I'll load the bottles into some trash bags and—"

"That's not necessary." She tightened her arms across her body.

"Well," Alex said, panic rising. *I need to unlatch the window so I can get in later, you fucking cow!* "I'd really like to do anything I can, so you won't have to bother yourself with his stuff. I know you don't like to come in here, so it's no problem for me to do it. Then I'll be on my way."

She was silent.

"I just want to repay you in any way I can." He smiled, cranking up the Lucas Knapp charm a notch.

"Do not leave this room," Norma ordered.

"Yes, ma'am," Alex nodded, panic subsiding. Mrs. Schell turned and went downstairs.

Alex waited until he heard the connecting door to the garage close, then reached over and turned the latch on the window. He shoved the mattresses away from the mirror. No wedge. He pulled them out further and noticed a wooden case the size of a large shoebox, hinged on one side and locked with a small padlock on the other. Alex picked it up and frowned. He'd never seen the box before and wasn't sure where to put it, so he crammed it into a desk drawer just as the sound of scratching pantyhose found his ears. Moving fast, he pulled the mattress out to the middle of the room to make it look like he hadn't been slacking off.

She bent, pantyhose scratching audibly, and laid the tools on the carpet just inside the door, then somewhat frantically wiped her hands on a dish towel she'd brought up with her.

"Thanks," Alex said, trying not to focus on her odd behavior. He picked up the screwdriver and hammer and put them on the desk then pushed the box spring against the wall by the bathroom and went to retrieve the mattress. She stared at him from the hallway, still wiping. He had a sudden familiar urge to punch her in the face and knock out a few colorful teeth.

Alex rehung Joe's Speed Racer curtains, concealing the unlocked latch. Marcus had made them for Joe's fourth birthday and Joe had refused to take them down. Alex focused on long exhales, willing tears to wait until he was out of the clutches of Norma Schell. He finished replacing books and papers, hangers and clothes from the closet, and other random items on the floor by the south wall. When he was as done as she would allow him to be, Norma led him downstairs and opened the door. Dragging two lawn bags stuffed with empty Coke bottles, Alex stepped onto the porch and looked at Joe's mother thinking she was the cruelest person he'd ever known. But his strategy had worked. She'd let him in. He almost felt gleeful.

"Missus Schell," he asked. "What do you plan to do with Joe's things?"

"Burn the clothes. Donate what's left to the church charity." She reached to close the door.

A stab of fear twisted in Alex's chest. He cleared his throat. "*All* of it?"

"He's not welcome here," Norma continued. "And neither are you."

"Oh, I won't bother you again," Alex said, thinking *believe me*. It took everything he had to mask his mounting panic. "I'm very sorry for everything and I hope someday you can find it in your good graces to forgive me." He offered his hand. She glanced at it and lifted her stony gaze to his face.

"It's not me you should ask forgiveness of, boy," Norma snapped. "It's God Almighty. You should be on your knees pleading forgiveness for what you did to that child. Do you hear? Begging and beseeching every day for deliverance from the ultimate sin!"

Spit flew from her lipstick-caked lips. Her jowls shook with the force of her words. Alex concentrated hard on keeping his composure. He had no idea what she was talking about but, remembering his mom's words, had a feeling it had to do with his brother's accident. Fear and panic rose in him like a wave.

"I-I'm very sorry, Missus Schell," Alex stammered, voice shaking. "I won't bother you again."

He turned and hurried down the driveway, resisting the urge to break into a full speed run. Her voice rang in his ears like a shrill whistle.

"On your knees, boy! Repent! On your knees! There's only *one* who can forgive what you did!"

Dragging bags of empty soda bottles behind him, Alex broke into a painful run and didn't slow down until he was at Mary's front door. She was ready for him. The aroma of fresh cinnamon spice cookies filled the shop and she had tea waiting. Alex looked around the main floor. Not a soul in sight.

"I closed early today, Alexander," Mary called from the kitchen. "I had a feeling of song."

Alex didn't say anything, breathless and weak.

Mary bustled into the foyer, carrying an ornate wooden trunk that Alex had never seen before. "Well?"

He saw the mischief in her clear dark eyes and groaned. "This can't be good."

"Pah! Where's your sense of adventure?" She set the box on the floor and motioned for him to sit.

"It's packed away with all my other moments of glee." Holding his aching arm, Alex gratefully slumped onto the world's most comfortable couch and reached for a cookie, then thought better of it. His stomach churned hot.

"You sound like Joseph."

"Go figure," Alex said, rubbing his shoulder.

"What's with the bags?" She nodded toward the front door.

Alex had forgotten about the bottles. He shook his head. "Long story."

Mary opened the strange box, peered inside and clapped her hands together, grinning like a child who had just discovered a new and wondrous species of insect. "Alexander, call your mother. You will be staying here tonight."

6:36pm

Mary's throaty song filled the house. She sat cross-legged on the floor, eyes closed, lost in song and Spirit. Alex sat across from her, watching the old woman sway in the faint light, although he wasn't supposed to be peeking. On the floor between them, tendrils of smoke twisted up from a wooden bowl filled with burning cedar chips. The dimness made him sweat.

Mary stopped the song and opened her eyes, which seemed blacker than usual to Alex. Her face appeared less lined and her hair hung in thick gray ropes down her back, fanning out on the floor around her body.

"Shadows, reveal," Mary said. She inserted a flattened hunk of metal into one of the slots on the contraption housing the candle. "First there was the earth."

Alex looked at the shadow on the wall. A violent shiver wound up his spine, making his hair stiffen. He licked his dry lips and felt a hand on his knee.

"*Egawaateseg* cannot hurt you, Alex," Mary whispered. "The shadows are only here to show us. To open."

Alex pulled his gaze from the looming shape and nodded.

Mary retrieved a second caster and placed it next to the first. "Then there was a boy."

The candle flame cast another misshapen image on the wall. Alex tried not to look, sure those hulking shadows would soon come alive and leap from the walls to devour his mind and soul.

Mary patted his hand and offered a reassuring smile. "These belonged to Wilbur. This is how he knew we would marry. I haven't cast them since Lucas died."

"Why did you use them when Luke died?" The shadow boy lurched forward in the flickering firelight. Alex ran a hand across his perspiring forehead.

"To see, Alex. Only to see."

With a brief incantation for each, Mary placed caster after caster into their unique slots. Shadows filled the room. Alex counted twelve in all, plus the sun-shaped one throwing a spiked image onto the ceiling. Mary reached for Alex's hand.

"Eyes open."

Alex licked his lips again. "Right."

The old woman sang an ancient prayer in Shiloh then gave the casting wheel a spin. The flame danced. Alex held his breath as the room came alive with motion, swirling in blurred shades of black and gray. Shadows chased one another across the walls, leapt off at the corners, ran across Alex's sweating skin and Mary's newly unlined face, and jumped back to the wall again. Images flickered and danced—a boy, a wolf, an arrow, the deafening screech of a wood owl, the lonely moan of a single flute from the sun above. Alex felt dizzy. He felt the floor shift and thought *I'm falling* but couldn't stop the pitch of his body. The chasing shadows circled like predatory beasts until one of them, the wolf, sank its teeth deep into Alex's forearm and pulled him across the wood floor. Alex shut his eyes against the pain, grappling with the realization that he had no control here. Hot panic took hold in a wash of fear.

"Eyes open."

The sensation of falling, of being dragged, ceased. The pain let go. Alex opened his eyes to see a man, as old as time itself, sitting across from him on a mat woven with bold colors of red, yellow, black, and white that formed a circle in the center. The ends of his braided hair lifted with the breeze. He smiled. Alex smiled back.

"Gaawiin gotaajiwin gidaa-biminizha'anziin," the ancient man said, and Alex knew what it meant.

"Fear is not the way. I know, but—"

The man held out his cracked hands, a large flower cupped in his palms. One side of the flower bloomed in long blue petals, the other half dried in the wind, brown petals sailing up and away. Riding the wind, Alex followed them across the prairie, along the river and over the mountain where he came upon an identical flower that bloomed on the opposite side as the first. He pulled it up by the roots, digging deep, and carried it over the mountain, along the river and across the prairie, back to the ancient man who waited on the mat of bold colors. Alex placed the flower in the man's cracked hands and watched as the two blossoms merged into one full bloom with two separate stems.

"Bezhigwanoon nibowin miinawaa bimaadiziwin."

Alex nodded. *Death equals life.* The bloom changed shape, grew wings and lifted into the air. A child's laughter rose with it.

"Eyes open."

Alex watched the shadows fall away one by one. The sweet scent of oatmeal spice cookies and hot honey tea found him once more. Mary's concerned face floated out of the vast emptiness, peering at him as if he were a strange new bug she'd just discovered.

"Alexander?"

Alex ran a trembling hand over his damp face. His mouth felt like it had been stuffed with cotton. Sitting there on Mary Whitewing's wood floor, Alex watched a shadow leap from the wall. Before he could move, darkness took him.

five

Reflections

Joe saw it and blinked. A pinpoint of light in the impenetrable darkness. He wasn't sure at first, but— He blinked again. An almost imperceptible dot of light flashed in the distance. He was about to call out but stopped, afraid the nightmare had come to life, so instead he pressed against the wall and held on. It was the only thing of comfort he had, the only stability he'd found in the blackness, so he hadn't ventured far from it.

Something took hold and started to drag. He'd been distracted by the light and let his guard down long enough for one of them to get a grip on his hair. He could feel the needle-like talons trying to sink in, to open his skull and scoop out the secrets and memories buried in layers of gray matter and guilt. They'd been so persistent since he'd arrived, but he'd been able to keep his mind closed to their prying wisp fingers. He knew what they wanted, had known for a long time, so he swung his balled fists violently and yelled until his throat became dry, voice hoarse. He tried to take hold of the thing that had him but felt only freezing vapor when his hands grasped at the air. It was strong and there were many, their never-ending howls loud inside his head as tendrilled fingers grabbed, gouged, clawed at his chest and head. The gnarled shapes dragged him away from the wall, away from the only foundation he'd found, the only stable thing he had. The farther they dragged him across the stinging sand, the more intense the pain in his gut grew.

He knew suddenly, without question, that he was going to die, and he thanked God for it.

Then something yanked him forcefully out of the dark things' incorporeal grasp. At first, he thought another of the fleeting creatures had decided it wanted him all to itself and was going to fight for him, but then he felt warm hands on his skin, replacing the cold, choking chill. He knew who it was and reached, tried to hold on, but couldn't find her in the pitch darkness.

He called out. Unintelligible words. Meaningless.

Distant scraping answered and above him the darkness began to stretch, to open in a gaping maw of shifting color. Eyes wild and wide, Joe watched the horrible images play out and knew the demons had gotten in through a moment of weakness and distraction, knew they had been able to pull something out of him and pile it up like ropes of bloody entrails on red clay dirt … The man and woman doing it again. His helpless cries, her painted smile … his bare skin, her bare soul … his blood, her lash … him protecting, her madness. Joe wrapped his arms around his head and watched the memories descend on him like a murder of ravenous vultures. There was nothing he could do but let the scavengers drop and bury their hungry recollections deep within his brain. Moving pictures from a life of denial. Mutterings of the long-dead. Joe watched the man and woman—his agony, her ecstasy—and could not look away. Holding out his shaking hands to ward off the assault, Joe screamed, and for the first time in a decade hot tears splashed out of his eyes like baptism.

June 3, 1984

In the dream, Alex dug, fingers unearthing bits and pieces at a time. Roses bloomed hot, their thorns like a crown around his head. Flesh tore loose in his hands, slippery so he couldn't hold on to the parts, the important parts, the parts that mattered most. Just as he had settled one piece into place, the others would jump away, dragging bone and sinew out of reach and he'd have to chase them through the thorns. The thorns made him bleed and when he looked up all he saw were rings of thorns, like crowns hovering over his head. *Sir Alex, ye are defeated.* Warm, saltsweet liquid filled his nostrils. He breathed in the flowery scent until his veins ran thick with it, then got back to digging.

6:42am

Alex stood at the stove, staring into a pot of simmering water and listening to the radio DJ issue ominous warnings about the weather. Heavy rain pounded at the windows. He glanced at the clock. He'd gotten up shortly after the dream, unable to go back to sleep, unable to keep horrifying visions of blood and rot from infiltrating his mind. He'd walked home from Mary's in the warm predawn rainfall. He could have sworn days had passed since then. He looked at the wall clock again. Mrs. Schell, a judicious creature of habit and ritual, would be leaving for God's Grace Daycare Center in forty-five minutes. Willing himself to be patient, Alex turned back to the steaming pot, pulled two poached eggs from the water, buttered some toast, poured a glass of juice, and swallowed the steroid pill Doc Abraham had prescribed to keep his brain from exploding. Eating slowly proved more difficult than he'd anticipated. He gulped the last of his juice and looked at the clock. Seven minutes had passed.

"Shit."

He heard his mom's alarm start to beep in her bedroom at the same time an emergency broadcast system alert came through the radio in bursts of obnoxious blasts. Another flash flood warning was issued for Cutters Grove and surrounding areas. The DJ proceeded with the morning news report—a piece about library funding, the frenzy of anticipation over Prince's summer film release, a kid missing from her home in Rogue Valley, the escape of six death row inmates from a prison in Virginia, the Edmonton Oilers winning the Stanley Cup—and then played Lionel Richie's song *Hello*, which Alex liked and Joe hated. He said it was 'sophomoric shit,' overly simple in its chord arrangements and unexciting, but Alex liked the sentiment behind the lyrics. So, they argued about it.

At that very second Alex looked toward the kitchen entrance, expecting Joe to come bursting—soaking wet and excited as a little kid—into the kitchen with two Mary-built sailboats clutched in his hands so they could go sail the ships down the gushing gutters near the Thrifty, where the water always rose high and fast for three blocks. Joe wouldn't need to call first. Alex, knowing, would simply be ready when Joe arrived. Sitting there, Alex realized that he'd lived his entire life believing their way of communicating was normal. But nothing was normal. Joe lay unresponsive and probably dying in a hospital bed, alone and taken. Alex shook his head, stood and pulled the curtains away from the window just as lightning lit up the backyard. In different circumstances he would have sacked out on the couch and watched TV all day, or practiced that tricky part in Shostakovich's concerto one, or let Joe drag him to the estate at the top of Knob Road to watch the lightning and water slide on their bellies down the slick grassy hill.

The noise in Elizabeth's room ceased and he heard the shower in her bathroom turn on. Alex looked at the clock. Thirty minutes to go. His temples throbbed. The painkillers Doc had prescribed were on the dresser in his room, but he decided to take regular aspirin to stay sharp. Padding down the hall toward the bathroom, he remembered the look on

Joe's face as he lost his grip. Peace. Childlike wonder. Light pouring from him like lightsaber beams. Every time Alex pictured it, he couldn't stop bone-wracking shudders from taking control of his body.

Alex reached to open the medicine cabinet and froze when the thing caught his eye. A white feather exactly like the one he'd tucked away in the top drawer of his dresser was taped to the corner of the mirror. He leaned close and looked at the fibrous strands, brushed them with his calloused fingertips. *I'm not imagining this.* The thumping in his head worsened. He swallowed the pills and flipped off the light, his mind a jumble of thoughts, none of them helpful.

Alex stopped cold in the hallway. Luke's door stood wide open. It was closed when he passed it. *Wasn't it?* Hesitant, he stepped inside.

His violin bow lay on the floor in the middle of the room. Alex wavered before finally picking it up, hands shaking. It felt heavy against his fingers, the weight comfortable, famil- iar. Lifting it to his nose, he inhaled the faint scent of rosin and horsehair and wondered if he would ever play with the excitement and passion he had once possessed. He stood there with the stringed rod held to his face, feeling the gen- tle brush of taut horsehair against his cheek. *Music is your fearless companion. It heals and it guides,* Mary always said. Tears came quick and hot. Alex left the bow and hurried from the room, closing Luke's door with force behind him. He grabbed his jacket and ran into the pouring rain, letting the heavy drops wash the salt from his cheeks.

7:46am

Blinking rainwater from his eyes, Alex closed the window and looked around Joe's dim bedroom. It was exactly as he'd left it the day before. A boom of thunder pushed his heart into his throat, and he swallowed hard. His vision blurred, focused, blurred again. He slipped off his jacket and set it in the bathtub to let it drip, then stood in the middle of the room eyeing the mirror. Nothing out of the ordinary. Just a big hunk of tarnished brass and glass with his exhausted image reflected in its smooth surface.

The desk drawer squealed when he pulled it open. He removed the odd wooden case he'd discovered on the day of his close call with Norma, fished one of Mary's small screwdrivers from his back pocket, and got to work loosening the hinges. Alex wrenched the lid up.

There were photographs on top. The first was of Mrs. Schell and a husky blond boy who looked not quite a year old. Alex held the picture close in the dim light, noticing the boy's wide-set eyes and happy, mischievous smile. A much younger Norma Schell smiled as well, but hers was the look of a haunted woman—the forced smile of a woman who had just received a diagnosis of terminal cancer and was trying to put on a happy face. The smile of someone desperate and willing to bargain.

The second photo was of him and Joe holding handmade wooden swords, a serious *don't mess with us* look on their faces. Marcus Schell had taken the picture mere minutes before Joe had to go to the emergency room to get stitches in his chin after falling off his bike and skidding six feet on the asphalt in front of his house. They'd been having a good time until that happened.

Alex lifted a third picture and frowned.

Luke.

His brother hung upside down from the bigleaf maple in Joe's front yard, cheesy grin plastered across his freckled face, T-shirt bunched up around his neck and under his dangling arms. Alex looked closely. He could just make out the vertical scar running the center of Luke's chest.

All Alex remembered about Luke's birth was his mom crying and telling him that his baby brother was very sick and may not come home to live with them after all. Alex remembered wishing hard. He wanted to be a big brother, to have someone to protect, to play music for and teach him how to play, too. He wanted someone who was his, someone like him, who came from the same place. But Luke had always been different, stubborn and excitable. Always talking, moving, laughing. When Luke laughed, everyone laughed.

Elizabeth tacitly blamed Luke's health problems on Thomas's four-pack a day habit, and Alex knew it. His father's outright refusal to smoke outside had been the source of many arguments. Alex remembered in vivid color the last time he and his brother saw their father alive—six years ago, just after Alex's twelfth birthday. They'd left the hospital room to get a candy bar while Elizabeth stayed behind to read aloud from *Alice's Adventures in Wonderland*. It was Thomas's favorite story. Alex still hadn't figured out why, and every time he asked his father would look at him and say, "I like the roses better when they're white."

Thomas Knapp's last words.

"What a nut," Luke had said, leaving the room and the wheezing sound of tanked oxygen and labored breath behind.

"Don't say that," Alex whispered, nudging him. "He's sick."

"It's his own fault, Ally," Luke had said. "He was given a choice and he's choosing to die. He's choosing to leave us and Mom. I swear to god, if I end up like him, tied to tubes where I can't even pee by myself, just shoot me. I mean it, bro. Seriously. That's no way to go. He's a nut and a chicken with no balls."

"Hey, where'd you learn that?"

But Luke was down the hall, leaping high, trying to touch the ceiling. "I swear, Ally. If I knew I was gonna die a slow, long, painful, terrible, sucky death like Dad, I'd just do it myself. I'd wanna die like a man. Like Superman!"

"You'll never die, Lucas," Alex had called. "You and me are gonna live forever!"

Three years later Luke was gone. He'd never forgiven their father for being so weak on so many levels. Luke's body may have been frail, but his mind and spirit were stronger than anyone Alex had ever met.

"Little whirlwind," Alex echoed Mary's words. "Strong like the ancient winds."

Alex eased down to the still-damp carpet. Raindrops smacked the slate roof outside, sounding like a thousand marbles bouncing down flights of stone steps.

There was an old Bible, the corners of the wrinkled pages torn and dog-eared. The cover, once black, had turned gray with time and use. Several page markers stuck out from the top. Alex turned to the first of them. Underlined in red pen were specific lines from the 51st Psalm. Joe hadn't marked all of the verse, only certain phrases that seemed to appeal to him.

Surely, I was sinful at birth, sinful from the time my mother conceived me, Alex read. *Cleanse me with hyssop, and I will be clean. Wash me, and I will be whiter than snow. Let me hear joy and gladness, let the bones you have crushed rejoice. My sacrifice O God is a broken spirit, a broken and contrite heart, you God will not despise.*

Joe had written in the margins with the red pen. The small, tight letters were hard to decipher, and Alex's heart began that familiar descent into his gut as he read what Joe had scrawled. *Cleanse me with blood and I will be free. Bathe me with tears and I will see. My heart is dead. My body too. Why have you forsaken me?*

There was more red ink, but Alex couldn't bring himself to read further. Something gnawed at his brain, something he couldn't put his finger on. He flipped to another marker.

The soul who sins is the one who will die. The son will not share the guilt of the father, nor will the father share the guilt of the son and the wickedness of the wicked will be charged against him.

In the margin Joe had written, *Stand alone, demon push pull evil Body moan, child scream twisted First free, pleading mercy Take me, stop crying forgive me father?*

The sinking feeling anchored in Alex's chest. He set the book on the floor and looked into the case again. He pulled out folded papers, stiff with ink, and read the finely lined words: *there can be no forgiveness without the shedding of blood there can be no forgiveness without the shedding of blood there can be no forgiveness* … It went on and on.

Alex held the pages close in the gloom. There were three in all, each repeating the phrase over and over. Every inch of space was filled with Joe's tiny handwriting, but something was different about the ink on the pages. Alex drew his thumbnail across the word *blood* in the first sentence. It flaked off, dotting the once white paper with red specks. Alex let out a shuddering breath. Papers fell from his grasp and came to rest near his soaked feet. He wiped his palms on his damp jeans, focusing on his exhales and blinking the blur from his vision.

That's when he saw them—scrolls. At least thirty of them had been tucked into the bottom of the box, all but one bound by white thread. Alex lifted the only one tied with red thread and unrolled the parchment.

Music.

Alex read the title—*sundance*—and his breath hitched and caught. Joe's name was scrawled under the title and beneath that were the words *partita for solo violin in d minor.* Eyes wide, Alex scanned the notes and suddenly there was music, loud and distinct, playing inside his head. It was bright, crisp, and familiar, as if he'd heard it in another lifetime and it had found him again in this one. The melody lifted him up and out and swept him away into a world of butterflies and air and rainbow light.

"I played this," Alex gasped. "I fucking played this. How——?"

Alex yanked the threads from every scroll and read the music, each composition specifically for solo violin, each one different and perfect and *familiar.* Each one rang clear and profound inside his head. Each one bore Joe's name as the composer, and each one held something unexpected, dynamic, brilliant. Alex turned toward the mirror, a slow realization taking root. His fingers tingled, ached for the strings.

"The sharing," he breathed. *Your heart beats in time with his. Follow the rhythm.*

Alex turned the box upside down, dumping its contents, and snatched up a spiral sketchpad.

The first drawing in the pad took him by complete surprise. It was an exceptional pencil sketch of him. Alex studied the lines and contours of his own face—downcast eyes, furrowed brow, intense scowl of concentration. His jaws were clenched tight, as if biting back a feral scream. He looked angry and sad and lost. Alex turned the page.

Joe's shadowed face stared back at him. Fear haunted the one eye Alex could see clearly. Half of Joe's gaunt face was bathed in a shadow cast by something—or someone—just outside the frame of the picture. Alex held it at arm's length and closed his eyes, a trick he'd learned in high school art class. When he opened them, he noticed the silhouette of a hand in the background. As if in offering, a man's boot dangled by its laces from a twisted, elongated finger.

Next, an exquisite drawing of the young woman who had appeared in the mirror. Her somber gaze penetrated the paper so lifelike that Alex felt them bore into his soul. Those mournful eyes filled him with a deep sadness similar to the debilitating sorrow he felt when he tried to play his music. The delicate angles of her face filled the page. Alex rested a finger on her cheek, lost in her haunting gaze.

A flash of lightning illuminated the room. In that instant, Alex saw it—the outline of a boot reflected in the iris of her left eye. He blinked, thinking the light was playing tricks on his unstable vision. Holding the pad at a distance, it became obvious.

The last drawing was the only one in color. Joe's bony back was visible through a light haze. His arm stretched in front of him and disappeared into a clear liquid wall. His profiled face exuded wonder and bewilderment.

Alex put everything back into the wooden box, closed it and ran his fingers through his hair, pulling hard, trying to think—and then froze. He thought he heard a voice mingled with the sounds of rain and thunder.

Another rolling boom. He listened, the hair on the back of his neck standing up.

Free your heart. Thunder tumbled.

He watched the mirror.

As if propelled by a will of its own, a steady wisp of smoke permeated the glass. Bathed in an ethereal amber glow, the wisp curved and twisted toward him like a phantom serpent. As he watched, the serpentine trail of smoke began to change in shape and color. The end of the stream sectioned off, forming slender fingers. Knuckles rose from ghostly white flesh along with a delicate wrist. Unlike the sinister claw that had pulled Joe through the mirror without mercy, this lovely hand floated through the air, leaving a vapor trail of haze in its wake, enveloped in a supernal halo of light that reminded Alex of a maple leaf caught in direct sunlight, shimmering golds and greens.

Alex slowly got to his feet and reached out his hand.

The spectral hand retreated several inches. Alex stepped forward. The room darkened, chilling the humid air. The incorporeal limb moved toward him, graceful in its unearthly dance, and glowing amber fingers interlaced with his, feeling as warm as he'd expected.

"You're real," Alex whispered.

The soft fingers released his hand and brushed his cheek. Alex closed his eyes, catching his breath as fingers trailed over his neck and into the collar of his shirt. The hand rested on his injured shoulder, massaging the strained muscles.

"Wait," Alex croaked, then grew silent as pain left his body.

Her other hand slid under his shirt and caressed the tender muscles of his chest. The spectral hands seemed to move through him rather than over him, penetrating his flesh, touching not only his skin, but deep inside as well. Glowing fingers skimmed over his bruised face, lingering on his eyelids. It felt as though a thousand hands were on him, caressing every inch of his embattled body, but it wasn't sexual. It was healing.

Surrender.

Alex opened his eyes, expecting to see her there, but he was alone. The room inverted. He staggered and reeled backward, falling to the floor. The wispy trails of smoke were gone. The room had grown dimmer with ominous clouds hanging low in the sky. Drops of rain struck the window, startling him back into real time. He lay there, blinking in the gloom, then let out a long breath and ran his hands over his sweat-slicked face.

"Are you there?" His dry throat burned.

A strange scratching answered, like opposing pieces of Velcro tearing apart in quick succession. Alex frowned, trying to place the sound. He turned, and panic flooded his bloodstream as he watched the doorknob begin a slow rotation. Before the thought even registered, he was in motion, scrambling across the carpet like a crazed toddler. *The bathroom. No, she'll look there—shit, my jacket!* He slid the bi-fold closet door open on its track and tumbled onto a pile of filthy clothes just as the bedroom door swung open. Alex eased the closet door closed, leaving a crack to see through. Mrs. Schell stepped to the middle of the room. *How the hell did I not hear the garage door? Fuck. Why is she in Joe's room, she hates this room. Fuckfuckfuck!*

From his hiding place, he could clearly see Joe's wooden box on the floor next to the desk and the imprints of his size tens in the damp carpet and he kicked himself for not being more careful. He glanced up and saw that Speedy's curtains were in disarray and chastised himself more. *Had she been in the house the whole time?* Mrs. Schell stood there a full minute—during which Alex's heart kept up a steady beat that made his head pound—and then she walked to the window and straightened the faded curtains. She turned to Joe's desk, opened a drawer, extracted something small and shiny, and stepped back to the center of the room.

The small hairs on Alex's ears prickled, suddenly aware of a sound like a kitten mewing somewhere in the house, which created an off-chord pang of anxiety, which worsened as he watched Joe's mother approach his hiding place. *Shit, I should've just run right past her, or confronted her, or— Fucking coward.* He rolled onto his back, thankful for another rolling boom of thunder, and scooped a pile of sweat-stinking clothes on top of him. He could hear Norma's pantyhose rubbing together as she neared, then stopped just shy of pushing the closet door open. Through the crack, Alex watched the painted woman cock her head as though listening intently. Then she left his range of vision, moving fast. Alex heard her talking to someone in the hallway and let out a long breath when the bedroom door closed. *Shit, she's probably hosting another of her holy hypocrite parties. I'm gonna end up stuck in this stupid closet till she leaves in the morning. Smart move, dumbass.*

Alex sat up and pushed Joe's rank-smelling clothes off him. He ran his sweaty hands through his hair and peered into the bedroom. Outside, he heard a car engine turn over. He slid the closet door open and crawled to the window. Peeking over the sill, he spotted Mrs. Schell's blue Bonneville pulling down the driveway. Alex sat on the floor, rested his head against the wall and concentrated on getting the shake in his hands to stop. He knew she'd seen the box on the floor, and the haphazard curtains were a sure give away. He hoped she'd been too distracted to sense his presence. *Wishful thinking. As usual.*

Alex got up and stepped toward the mirror, studying his reflection in the glass. The bruises on his face seemed fainter. He rubbed his shoulder. It felt stronger, almost normal, and he found himself wishing those spectral hands could reach into his mind and heal that, too.

Alex placed his palms on the glass. He tried to see beyond the smooth surface and into the place Joe had been taken, but saw only his own face staring back. He studied the riotous mass of bars and knobs framing the glass like tangled knots and gnarled tree branches and thought about the Hardy Boys— maybe there was a secret way in. To the right and high up, he spotted the phoenix necklace Joe had taken from Mary's on that eerie afternoon when everything went weird. Alex was sure it hadn't been there when he had cleaned up the day before. He pulled the chain loose. Stony turquoise eyes met his, offering no answers. The chain also held Marcus's gold wedding band, the only relic Joe's father had left behind before deserting his family and abandoning the one person who needed him most. Joe had worn it on a chain around his neck since the day his dad had gone missing eight years ago, as though the thing were a magical talisman that could somehow reveal the path Marcus had taken and maybe lead him back home.

Alex eyed the mirror. "Can you hear me?"

Rain tapped at the window like rattling bones.

"Joe?"

Thunder answered.

"Where are you?"

Lightning, followed by another loud crack in the darkening sky.

"Joe!" he yelled, frustration mounting. Helplessness gave way to pure anger and he slammed his fists against the glass. The sky rumbled, shaking the window in its pane.

"Answer me goddamn it! I know someone can hear me! Let me in!"

His chest burned. Blood smeared his upper lip. Resting his forehead on the glass, Alex closed his eyes and listened to the rain beat at the window. He chanted to himself, afraid that if he stopped it would bring his worst fear to life.

"Please don't die, please don't die, please don't die …"

He snatched up the box. All the way home, he couldn't get that persistent mewing out of his head.

Joe found it by accident. He dropped to his knees and dug his hands into the sand, searching for the cold thing that had jabbed his big toe as he walked blindly through the darkness. The deafening noise had settled, but it would resume with renewed intensity, untying him and surging through his skull in unexpected gusts. At times, he thought he could feel blistering cold fingers caressing his skin and hair, so he walked and walked, afraid that if he stopped moving they would get a grasp and not let go. He would not be able to resist them much longer. He was weakening with every garbled syllable they uttered into his fatigued mind. The incessant whispers had become more and more intelligible even as he tried hard not to hear what they had to say. He didn't want to look into their hollow eyes and see himself staring back. He would, though. *He would.* So, he steeled his will against accepting the reason he was there all while their wicked thoughts brushed up against his own and he found it easier to let their vague mutterings form clear thoughts inside his head. At times, his thoughts and their thoughts seemed both creations and reflections of one another.

His hand skimmed it and he dislodged it from the powdery earth. Pure, hot excitement coursed through his veins as he pressed the wedge of broken TV glass to his cheek, relishing the cool smoothness and the comfort it offered. At least now he had a weapon. Even though he knew it would be useless against them, he could turn it on himself and relieve the torment. Exhaustion gripped tight as he tried to stand. He hadn't slept, afraid one of them would take the opportunity to— Suddenly he didn't care. He knew only that he could not take another step. Joe sank to his knees and curled up in the sand, the wedge of glass pressed to his chest with both hands. He slept until the nonsensical chattering began in his ear, reminding him that this was what he had wanted for a long time. This was exactly the punishment he deserved.

June 5, 1984

In the dream, Joe was in darkness, but Alex could see. He watched Joe fumble, struggle against the suffocating night, thrashing his arms and legs against fine white grains of sand. He moaned and screamed in agony, fighting. *I need my sword. I have to help him,* Alex thought, but fear anchored him. He spoke without moving his mouth.

Remember the sundance.

The scene changed. Joe lay bloodied and beaten, gutted and lifeless on the milk-white desert, an orange orb of sun low in the sky. His blood trickled through grains of sand, staining them bright as rubies. The monstrous shadow trailing from his battered feet rose long-limbed from the ground and stretched its clawed fingers toward Joe's throat. It tore into his body without mercy, grunting like a starved animal, ripped Joe's heart from his chest and devoured it like a hungry ghoul. The beast turned toward Alex, and he saw—the monster's eyes were *his* eyes. The monster's face was *his* face. Blood dripped from his chin. A grin spread across his feral face, revealing sharp, jagged teeth. Joe's newly dead flesh and sinew hung in shreds from his smiling lips ...

Alex bolted up and skidded off his bed, landing on his injured shoulder. Holding his arm, he scrambled to his feet and backed away from Joe's Bible, which had landed on the floor. A highpitched whistle sang in his head. Alex threw open the bedroom door and ran to the bathroom. Hot vomit splashed into the toilet, but wasn't enough to wash away the taste of blood still fresh on his tongue. Blood from his nose dripped into the fouled water. The copper taste of it made him heave again. He coughed strings of red mucus out of his throat and tried to catch his breath, heart straining against his ribs. Once the heaving subsided, he sat on the bathroom floor and wiped tears from his eyes. His knees knocked together, and his hands shook with force. Sweat ran down his back, soaking his shirt. The brutal images strobing through his mind made the trembling worse.

"I killed him," Alex whispered, holding his throbbing head. "I'm a monster."

He heard the front door open but didn't try to stand. Instead, he clasped his shaking hands together and placed them in his lap. She called his name from the entry.

"In here," Alex called.

Elizabeth appeared in the doorway and flipped the light switch up. She rushed to Alex's side and knelt, grabbing his damp head in her hands.

"What happened? Are you sick?"

"Where did you get the feather?" His voice was louder than he'd intended. He slumped against the tub, feeling sick again.

Elizabeth's dark eyes searched his. Without a word, she reached for a washcloth and held it under a cool stream of tap water. She sat and blotted his face.

"Mom," he whispered, hot bile rising in his throat. "Tell me."

She looked at him. "Your brother sent it to me the night you woke up in the hospital. I thought I'd put it in here so you would see it and we could talk about it."

Alex tried to focus on her face, but her features kept warping. "Why do you think it's from Luke?"

"I don't know," Elizabeth said. "A feeling, I guess. He always wanted to fly. I think he's trying to tell me everything is okay. It's crazy, I know."

"I got one too," Alex whispered. "The same night. It just floated out of nowhere, but I had dreams before it happened. We were having the same dream and didn't know it until right before he went through—" Alex stopped and lowered his head.

"What happened, Alex? In Joe's room?"

Frightened, tired, hopeless, Alex looked at her. "There's something wrong, Mom. I-I think I'm dying. Nothing makes it better." Shaking, he lowered his head into her lap.

Elizabeth held him. "I'll make tea. We need to talk."

She helped him stand and walked with him into the kitchen. Alex listened while his mom spoke with Doc Abraham on the phone for what seemed like an hour, but when she hung up he couldn't remember a word she had said. Elizabeth set two steaming mugs on the table and sat down.

"Doc said all of this is normal. The fatigue, the emotional swings, the noises that sound like voices—especially when you don't follow doctor's orders."

"No, it's not."

"What?"

"It's not normal. None of it."

"Alex—"

"Goddamn it!" He slammed his fist down on the table, spilling tea from both mugs. "There's something wrong! I see things! I hear things! It's not normal, Mom! I'm losing my mind and there's nothing anyone can do because *nothing is fucking normal!*"

Blood ran into his mouth and he cursed again, tilting his head back.

"I can't do this anymore," Alex said, reaching for a napkin. "I want my life back. I want my music back. I'm sick of being worried and sad all the time."

"Sad?" Elizabeth picked up her tea.

"Mom, I've been sad since Marcus left, since Dad died. And then Luke and Joe and now—"

"What? Your concussion?"

"No." He blew his nose. "Worse."

"Tell me," Elizabeth said. She slipped off her shoes and crossed her legs under her. "I'm ready to hear it."

Alex stared at the table. "You're right. Joe wasn't the one who hurt me. We didn't have a fight. He was already gone by the time my head got bashed in."

"He was on the roof?"

"No, Mom. No one was ever on the roof. Joe is gone. I don't know where he is. His body is here, but—Mary said it's like his soul, or consciousness, has left him and gone somewhere else, a place he may not be able to leave. He's trapped inside and *in-between*, or something."

"The mirror in his room," Elizabeth said. A sharpness came to her eyes. "What is it?"

"I don't know," Alex said. "But that's where Joe is. Something came through that thing and took him."

12:15pm

Alex sat in the bathtub, hot shower water raining over his clammy skin. He drew his knees up and let the steady stream beat on his back. He knew his mom didn't believe everything he had told her. No sane person would. He'd watched her face as he'd described some—not all—of the things in Joe's writings and drawings and she had cycled from sympathy to horror to tears. Images from Joe's drawings swam through

Alex's mind like drugged fish with no sense of direction. He stared at the water pooling in the bottom of the tub and searched for an answer among the scattered, disjointed scenes in his head.

Joe's words, written in tiny red script in the margins and note pages of his Bible and on yellow-lined paper, painted a disturbing portrait of Norma Schell as a twisted, paranoid woman whose line between reality and delusion had progressively blurred since her discharge from the Rogue Valley Medical psych ward. She often referred to Joe as 'Marcus' while she beat her son with everything from crucifixes to hairbrushes to wooden spoons to lashes. She forced him to pray for hours at a time and used ice baths to get the demons out of him. The abuse had begun shortly after she returned home and continued until Marcus's disappearance four years later. Then it was as if Joe, too, had vanished off planet Earth. From that moment, his mother seemed to look through him, rarely acknowledging his existence, and never laid a hand on him again. He'd become invisible to her, and, in a weird way Alex didn't understand, Joe had felt abandoned all over again.

"Marcus," Alex whispered, an idea forming, hazy at first, like a mirage on the horizon.

He turned off the water, tied a towel around his waist, and rushed to his room. Thunder rolled overhead. Alex flipped through Joe's Bible. He cursed himself for not noticing it from the beginning. On several pages, in tight letters, was a familiar phrase: *forgive me father.* Fleeting thoughts raced through his thumping head and he tried to hold on to one that made sense. Alex skimmed through the pages at the back of the book, where Joe had scrawled notes. The word *father* stood out more than anything else. There was nothing special or strange about the way the word was written, but it struck Alex odd that the letter *f* wasn't capitalized in any of the phrases repeated throughout the book. The realization came slowly. It was simple, so simple that he had trouble wrapping his head around it. With as much exposure as Joe had had to religion, he would know to capitalize the word when referring to God.

Alex looked out at the lightning flashes beyond his window.

"He's not asking *God* to forgive him," he whispered. "He's asking his *father* to forgive him."

Alex's frown deepened. *What the fuck does that mean?* He dressed and put Joe's Bible in the wooden case with everything else. Leaving his room, he walked past Luke's door and without a thought grabbed the knob and pulled it closed.

"Mom."

Elizabeth turned away from the counter where she was slicing carrots to add to the salad. "Feel better? I ordered pizza."

Alex grabbed a slice of cucumber. "Mom, do you remember Joe ever doing anything bad? I mean really horrible? Unforgivable kind of horrible?"

"No," she said, thinking. "Well, when you guys were around seven, he put a dead cat in his mother's car."

"Really? Why?"

"He told me he wanted her to take it to the doctor, so it could get well again. He said its soul was lost, which I thought was a weird thing for a little kid to say, but Joe's always been different. Norma threw the cat back into the street. That bothered Joe for a long time."

"Did his dad get really pissed at him for doing that?"

Elizabeth laughed. "No! He thought it was sweet. He was more upset with his wife for handling it the way she did, but he never got mad at Joe. For as long as I knew Marcus, he treated Joe like he was the only person who mattered in the world. He loved that kid with all his heart and soul. Your father could've taken lessons on gratitude and humility from that man."

"Sounds like Marcus Schell is the perfect guy." Alex grinned. "Anything ever *develop* between you two? More than friendship?"

Elizabeth's mouth dropped open. "What?! No! I do remember times when I wished your dad would be more like Joe's, but there was never anything romantic between Marcus and me. Yes, I got to know Marcus pretty well before Norma came back. We had formed a kind of partnership—a *non-romantic* partnership. We basically co-parented you and Joe and Luke. I like Marcus a lot *as a friend*. He has a good heart. His leaving was a loss for everyone."

"What exactly happened, Mom? I remember you telling me that Joe's dad had gone away, but I don't remember hearing details. Joe never talks about it. Says it's ancient history."

"I don't know all the details myself," Elizabeth said. "Marcus took his reasons with him when he left. There was talk that he'd hopped a train. He was fascinated with them. His grandfather had been a railroad engineer, so Marcus spent a lot of time around trains when he was a kid. He could tell you anything you wanted to know about them."

The doorbell rang. Alex went to retrieve the pizza. He set the box on the kitchen table and grabbed a couple of Cokes from the fridge. They sat and loaded food onto their plates. Elizabeth was quiet.

"And?" Alex coaxed.

Elizabeth shook her head. "And that's all I know. He seemed okay on the rare occasions we crossed paths after Norma came home. Maybe quieter, now that I think about it. Then he left. That's when Norma's health really took a downturn. From what I remember, she was sick with the stomach flu a lot. And she would go out of town for a couple of days every six months or so, leaving Joe here with us. She always said she had church business in Eugene or Grants Pass or somewhere, but I wasn't so sure about that."

Alex spoke around a mouthful of pizza. "Really? Why not?"

A hesitant look came over Elizabeth's face. "You have to promise not to tell Joe this, okay?"

Alex set his slice down and nodded.

"Marcus told me that Norma had a miscarriage about a year after she was released from Rogue Valley Medical. But he also told me that they had not had sex since she returned home. When he confronted her about the pregnancy, she told him that the Holy Spirit had impregnated her. She refused to answer any more of his questions. He told me that she would disappear for days at a time and he would have to go looking for her. He found her on a few different occasions at a rundown motel in Eugene, just watching TV with fast food bags and greasy containers all over the place. But there was another time, about a month before he left, that he found her way over in Astoria, and that time she was with a man."

Alex swallowed hard.

Elizabeth leaned forward. "Marcus called me, absolutely distraught. He didn't know what to do. He was upset and crying. He didn't want his family to fall apart. Despite all of the challenges with Norma, he loved her and believed they could be happy again. You know, she didn't start acting so fanatical or wearing that gawdy makeup until after Isaac died. It's as if she's trying to mask her sadness or something. So, if you think I talk about Marcus like he's a saint, yes, that man has put up with a lot. Maybe that's why he finally left. I just don't understand—" Her voice broke then. "I don't understand how he could do that to Joe. Just leave him like that."

"It sounds like his struggles run deeper than any of us will know, Mom. You never really know what's happening inside a person."

Elizabeth smiled. "Yeah. Thank you. I need that reminder. I get angry when I think about it. Being human is tough. In my next life I'm going to be a huge tree, something sturdy, rooted, and calm."

"Naw," Alex said, shaking his head. "Then all the birds and squirrels'll poop on you. Bark beetles and root rot. Nope. You'll be a mom next time around, 'cause you're good at it."

12:15pm

Norma Schell spotted the boy and his mother the moment they walked through the door of God's Grace Daycare Center, an affordable daycare for special needs children run by Our Holy Mother Ministry, although a variety of children attended the program on a regular basis. She smiled broadly, rose from her seat at the finger-painting table, and walked over to the woman, pudgy hand extended in greeting.

"Hello! My name is Miss Norma. What's yours?"

The blond boy slung over his mom's shoulder did not respond.

"Jonathon doesn't talk," the woman said.

"I see. Hi there, John–John. I'm Miss Norma."

"It's *Jonathon*," the mother said, pointedly. She lowered the boy to the floor next to an older boy with orthopedic braces on his legs. Jonathon lay staring at the ceiling, arms and legs stiffening in palsied movements every few seconds, eyes wandering.

Norma's smile never faltered. "Jonathon. Of course. Would you like an information packet about the programs we offer here at God's Grace?"

The mother looked around, breathless from carrying a sixty-pound child in from the rain. Dark circles ringed the woman's eyes and her brown hair was shot through with new grays, though she couldn't have been older than thirty.

"He'll only be here for a few hours three days a week, just so I can have a br—" she looked at her pale hands. "So, I can get a few things done. Errands. Groceries. Sometimes it's just easier. My husband disagrees with the idea of daycare, but then complains when I don't have dinner ready when he gets home, or when his shirts aren't picked up at the dry cleaners."

Norma's smile did not waver. "Of course. I have a little boy myself. I know how busy they can be, believe me."

The tired mom pulled her gaze from her hands. "Just a few hours a week."

Norma took the woman's pale hand and gave it a pat. "Come with me and we'll go through all the information you need. I think Jonathon will like it here. We have very special ways of caring for very special children. They *are* God's children, you know. Especially the flawed ones. They are our Lord's way of reminding us to be humble."

From the home living play area, Charlie Dugan watched the young mother speak with Norma Schell, a burning knot tightening in his stomach. As soon as the two women went into the office, he shot out of his chair where Libby was serving him invisible tea and plastic muffins and scooped up the blond boy lying on the floor. Charlie held the child close and brought him over for some of Libby's delicious desserts. Sitting on the floor next to a tiny purple chair, Charlie glanced at the newspaper article he'd had clutched in his hand since that morning. *Four-Year-Old Missing Since Sunday.* He hadn't seen Snider Spider in two days.

"Don't worry, Sir Jonathon," Charlie whispered into the boy's small ear. "I won't let anything happen to you here."

With a crooked grin and focused eyes, Jonathon reached out an unsteady hand and grabbed Charlie's nose.

5:22pm

Alex heard the doorbell but didn't move. He stood in his bedroom, staring at the wooden case lying open on the bed.

A second thin stream of blood topped the narrow edge of the box from the inside and slid down the outside past the padlock. It vanished into the green bedspread, leaving no trace of its existence.

"Because it doesn't exist," Alex mumbled. He leaned forward and looked into the box. A third droplet of blood inched up and topped the edge. Alex slammed the lid closed and turned away, sure he heard a squeal of pain as the lid came down hard on the small red bubble. He turned back, facing the case. Serpentine ribbons of deep red blood poured down the sides and front of the wooden box. The lid bounced up and down as spouting blood pushed against it from inside. The pressure grew stronger as Alex backed away. A putrid smell permeated the room—the carrion stink of decay and death, rotted meat and disintegrating flesh.

"It's not real," he whispered.

The lid strained then wrenched off as a gushing geyser exploded from inside, spraying the room with scarlet. Scalding drops hit Alex's skin like acid and he jerked, swiping frantically at his arms and face, smearing the gore everywhere it landed. His flesh bubbled, melting away as the searing plasma clung to his arms, hands, face and hair. It streaked his clothes, drenching him in the nauseating sweet-sour stench filling the room—the stench of burning muscle and bone.

"It's all in my head!" A steaming crimson wave rose up in front of him. He wrapped his arms over his head and backed against the dresser.

Nothing happened.

Lowering his arms, Alex watched as Joe's blood-soaked form emerged from the vile viscous wall and smiled, exposing a swollen black tongue and deep gashes around his mouth filled with caked brown blood. He had no eyes, only gaping holes. Alabaster maggots writhed from the sockets and crawled over what remained of Joe's skeletal face. Venous fluid spilled from his mouth. He reached for Alex, rotting arms spitting ruby and said, "You're the only one who can bring me back." His voice sounded thick and wet.

Decomposing hands wrapped around Alex's throat and squeezed. Joe's septic breath felt like ice on Alex's face and he fought for air, grabbing at Joe's decaying wrists. Lacy ropes of flesh and muscle came loose in Alex's hands and he gagged, tasting bile. He thrashed his legs as Joe lifted him from the floor, face puffy with the gasses of rot. Everything went black. Alex fought against the darkness until without warning there was light and … Mary. Her face hovered above his. She spoke, but he couldn't hear over the roar in his head. He was lying on the floor but didn't remember falling.

Alex sat up, dazed, head pounding. Mary's lips moved, but he did nothing but stare at her stupidly, unable to comprehend what was happening. A thought occurred to him, *she must've come in and found me struggling with Joe. But that doesn't make sense. Joe's at the hospital … or in the mirror … or dead.*

Mary grabbed his face in her wood-dusted hands, instantly bringing him to his senses.

"You were dreaming," she shouted into his face. Her breath smelled of licorice.

He looked at her, blank, unfocused.

"It was a dream, Alex," she said, and he wondered how she could know that.

He looked at the window, trying to jar the recall mechanism in his brain

"What time is it?" His throat felt dry and sore.

"He visited, didn't he?"

"Huh?" He squeezed his eyes closed. He needed a scalding hot shower. The image of Joe's decaying, maggoty face filtered through the darkness of Alex's lids and he snapped his eyes back open.

"You said he's dead," Mary said. She slipped her arm around his waist to help him up.

"I did?" He got to his feet, leaning on Mary's steady shoulder, then eased onto the bed next to Joe's case. "He was right in front of me, but—wait, how did you …?" He grimaced, stomach flipping, and looked at his hands, the texture of rotting flesh still fresh on his palms. Wiping them on his jeans, he stared at the floor, silent.

"You have to go now, Alexander." Mary held up his windbreaker and helped him into it. "The roads are flooding, but you have to go. *Now*." She clapped her hands together loudly and was gone in a cloud of wood dust.

Alex bolted straight up on his bed. He eyed the wooden case, then grabbed it and flung it full force into the wall.

5:58pm

Alex stood outside ROOM 113, running his thumb over his callused fingertips. He turned the knob and peered into the dim room. Too dark. He flipped on all the lights and gazed at the thin, motionless form on the bed. A large, knitted blanket covered the bed. Brilliant blues and magentas fanned from a center circle. Joe's ribs were visible through the thick material, his cheeks gaunt and white, long blond hair matted, his breathing shallow. He looked so small.

"My Ol' Ma made it." Rom said from the chair. "It always made me feel better when I was a kid. Still does." He had replaced the small gold earring with a diamond stud, the only bright spot in the room despite the fluorescent lighting.

Rom extended his hand. Alex shook it, sullen. "You're here late."

"Yeah," Rom nodded. "Just pulled a sixteener. Now you know why doctors are famous for their great bedside manner."

Alex shook his head, picking up on the doctor's sarcasm. "You're an exception, I think."

Rom smiled. "That's because I still love what I do. I'm not burned out yet. Give me a few years. I'll be just like some of these grouchy old geezers."

"Doubt it," Alex said. "You're different. You care."

"They all cared once. Then they got tired."

They watched Joe in silence then Alex moved to the window, pulled open the drapes and commented on the rainy weather.

"Joe and I used to sit on the lawn of this huge estate in our neighborhood when we were kids," he said. "It'd be pouring down rain and we'd sit up on the hill and watch the lightning and the trains and talk about stupid kid stuff. If it rained enough, we'd water slide on our stomachs down the grassy hill toward the wrought-iron fence. We never slammed into it, though. Always stopped just short of breaking bones." A lump rose in his throat. "Guess those days are over." Alex shoved his fists into his jeans pockets and paced.

Rom's brow creased. "Sorry, man. Hey, can I ask you—what's with his mother?"

Alex halted. "What happened?"

Rom scratched his beard. "You hadn't been released yet, so it had to be a couple of days after you two were brought in. Sandi, one of our physical therapists, was working on your friend when this strange woman came huffing in. She threw water on him and all around the bed. Made a big mess. She was mumbling the whole time. Sandi said it sounded like she was praying in some weird language. She finally pushed the call button, but the woman left before the attendants got to the room. She did refer to Joe as her son, though."

"Yeah," Alex breathed. He sat on the foot of the bed and ran his finger over his nose. "She's a fuck-nut."

Joe sat straight up.

Alex reeled backward off the bed.

Rom bolted from his seat.

Joe's wide eyes searched, unseeing. He stared in front of him, pointing. Rom spoke firmly but calmly into his face, "Joe! Can you hear me? Joe! Can you …?"

Alex shook in violent jolts, head spinning. Electricity sizzled through his veins. He couldn't breathe. Rom motioned him closer.

"Talk to him, Alex."

"I-I can't," Alex gasped. His heart jack-hammered in his chest.

"Do it now," Rom said, stern.

Alex moved toward the bed, knees knocking together. "Joe. W-what're you looking at? What do you see over there?" He glanced at Rom.

Joe's dry cracked lips moved.

Alex continued. "Joe? Can you see me? I'm right in front of you, bro. I'm right here with you. Can you hear me?"

Joe's mouth worked, eyes blank and glassy. He whispered something. Alex moved closer, watching his friend's deathly white face. Joe's words came out slurred and weak.

"Lucas soars."

Like an unattended puppet, Joe's body went slack. He slumped forward, eyes closing, and rolled backward onto the pillows.

Alex felt all the blood drain from his body. The room turned, caved in. He hit the floor with a slap but felt no pain.

6:27pm

"Who's Lucas?"

Alex stared at the carpeted floor of the small office and pressed an ice pack to the knot on the side of his head.

"Friend of Joe's?" Rom sat on the edge of his desk and waited for an answer.

"My brother," Alex said, meeting the man's eyes. "He died three years ago in a rappelling accident. We'd both taken lessons, but—" He lost his voice and looked at the floor again. "He fell. Hanged by one of the ropes. Or so they tell me. I don't really remember."

"I'm sorry." Rom placed a big hand on Alex's good shoulder and squeezed. "Joe said *Lucas soars.* Does that mean anything to you?"

Alex shook his head. "I was there when it happened. There was nothing I could do. His head was—" An electric bolt shot through his skull. He closed his eyes. "Can we talk about Joe?"

"He's never done this before, that we know of." Rom sat in his desk chair and studied Joe's chart. "Like I told you, he's quite the challenge."

"Tell me about it." Alex looked at the doctor and adjusted the ice pack, pain piercing his temples with every breath.

Rom leaned forward.

Alex shifted in his seat. "Rom, were you practicing eight years ago? I mean, were you here in the area?"

"Yeah, I interned right here at Providence. Why?"

Swallowing hard, Alex pulled the ice pack from his head and held it in his hands. "Do you remember a young woman, maybe sixteen or seventeen, who was attacked in Cutters Grove? Would have been July twentieth of seventy-six?"

Rom stared at Alex. "That was my second night in critical care."

"You remember her?"

Rom's eyes narrowed. "Hard to forget, man. She was in a coma. Deep. Bad prognosis. Her father didn't believe in western medicine, said white people don't know how to die well and honor the process, said doctors do nothing but steal grace and dignity from the people who are doing the bravest thing a human will ever do. I'll never forget his words. He took her home. I checked the obits and newspapers every day for three months. Doc Abraham finally told me to stop, said if I did that with every case it would debilitate me. He said to celebrate the victories and let go of the rest. There's no doubt in my mind that she died as a result of her injuries, no way she could live with that kind of bodily trauma and no medical intervention. Sometimes families decide not to list the death, though. Too hard for them. And there may be some cultural customs involved with her family that I don't quite understand. There were a couple of follow-up news stories, but the media quickly forgot about her. Why report on the brutal attack of an indigenous girl when there are baseball scores to talk about, right?" Rom scowled and looked down at his tightly folded hands on the desk. "So, yeah. I remember her."

Every breath Alex drew felt like water flooding his lungs. He could barely get the words out. "What was her name?"

Rom sighed. "You know I can't tell you that."

"I need to know her name," Alex said.

"I can't tell you her name, Alex. Patient confidentiality. And she was a minor." Rom's eyes widened, and he stood up. "Hey, you okay? You're pale again."

"We thought she died right there on the grass that same night. There was so much blood. The rain washed it down the hill, so it ran over our shoes. I remember watching it, but I couldn't move. Joe never took his eyes off what was happening. It was like he was entranced or something. Stuck. I don't remember everything, not even walking home. We went back the next morning and Joe found a necklace, a sterling silver phoenix with turquoise eyes." Alex looked at Rom. "Joe's dad had left a month before. We never told anyone about what we'd seen. Maybe she would have lived if we'd gotten help."

Rom held Alex's arm, deep concern etching lines into his face. "You're telling me that you and Joe witnessed this girl's attack?"

Alex nodded. "July twentieth, seventy-six. Close to midnight. We were ten."

"And you never learned what happened to her?"

Alex shook his head and glanced out at the low fog stirring the sky. "I need to know her name, Rom. Something happened that night between Joe and this girl and … and me. Her voice. I hear her voice calling out to me to save him.”

“Man, I don't know what the hell is going on.” Rom took a deep breath, forehead creasing more. “Okay, I can give you dates and locations, but that's all. Understand?”

Alex nodded. “Yes, sir.”

“I have to step out and hunt down her file in archives. Wait here.”

“Yes, sir.”

“Stop calling me *sir*,” Rom said, opening his office door.

Alex nodded. “Okay. *Rom.*”

Twenty minutes later, Rom returned, holding a manila file thick with medical documents. He sat down and opened it, flipped through several pages and stopped, then looked at Alex.

“July twentieth—”

“—eight years ago,” Alex said. “Eleven forty-eight PM.”

Rom glanced back at the file, then at the wall clock, then at his pager. Just then it started beeping. He silenced it quickly.

“Alex, I'm sorry. I have to check on someone.” He looked Alex dead in the eyes, stood up, and said pointedly, “Under no circumstances are you to look in that file while I'm gone.” He swept out of the room once more, leaving the file wide open on his desk.

Alex smiled and shook his head. He got to his feet and circled the desk. He quickly skimmed the typed notes.

Timberwolf. Jade. Grants Pass.

That was all he needed.

June 6, 1984

Microfiche images scrolled by on the screen. Alex searched the files by date—July 20, 1976. Nothing had popped up yet. Rogue Valley wasn't exactly a newsworthy metropolis. Elizabeth had suggested library archives, so he'd been waiting outside since 6:00 AM for the library to open.

Alex watched newspaper articles skid by. He and Joe had snuck out to watch the lightning that night. Joe had brought along his bow and animal-bone arrows in case they ran into any wild animals or bad guys.

"Bad guys," Alex breathed. "Jesus." He stretched back in his chair and rolled his neck. A headline skidded by. Alex stopped, leaned close. "Indian Girl Assaulted in Cutters Grove," he read, scanning the text printed in the *Portland Observer* on July 25th. "Shit. This just gives a basic summary."

The only other article he could find was dated three days later. Squinting at the computer screen, Alex read. *Buck Timberwolf of Grants Pass, father of the girl who was brutally attacked late Friday night in Cutters Grove, has removed his daughter from doctors' care in Medford. Timberwolf, adhering to the customs of his Native Indian beliefs, has insisted on taking his daughter home to be cared for. Timberwolf is a member of the Shiloh Nation. Doctors say the seventeen-year-old is in critical condition and should not be removed from their care. The girl has been in persistent coma since her attack on July 20th ...* There was a picture of a man with tired eyes and ink-black hair scowling into the camera.

Alex turned to the phonebook next to the microfiche machine and looked under residences in Josephine County. *Buck Timberwolf.* There was one residential property address listed.

Alex sat back in his chair and let out a long breath. "Guess I'm driving to Grants Pass."

six

Stones

Her house was forest green.

Alex had thought about calling before driving his filthy white VW Beetle fifty-five miles north along the Rogue River on I-5 but decided against it. He wasn't sure her parents would even speak to him, but he needed to see where she'd come from, what kind of life she'd had before she died and began haunting his own existence.

He pressed the doorbell and crammed his hands into his jacket pockets. At least it wasn't raining.

A big man with short ink-black hair and strong angular features threw open the door and Alex immediately recognized him from the newspaper article. He stared at Alex, eyes piercing, the loose skin around them puffy, deeply lined, and dark, as if he hadn't slept in decades.

Alex eyed the man's thin T-shirt and faded blue jeans and stammered, searching for words. "Uh, wrong house. Sorry." He spun around, but the man's gruff voice bellowed. Alex turned.

"Well, look here," the man said. He smiled, unveiling two rows of yellowish teeth. "What happened to your face? Get hit by a tank?" Howling with laughter, he waved his huge arm for Alex to come closer. Alex took a step backward.

"C'mon in," the man puffed, wheezing from his hearty laugh attack. "I got to tell you, son, you're the last person on Mother Earth I thought I'd find standing on my doorstep."

Alex shook his head. "Sir, you don't know me. My name is Al—"

"Alexander Knapp, violinist extraordinaire! Concert master extraordinaire! Of course, I know who you are." The man hung his head for a moment, then turned and strode into the house, leaving the door wide open. Alex hesitated a moment before stepping over the threshold.

The house smelled a little like Mary's place—cedar, cherry, sage, cinnamon—but with an underlying hint of toilet that hadn't been cleaned in months. Cat fur hung in the air. Faint meowing periodically broke the silence and every few seconds Alex caught a glimpse of a tail.

"Be right back," the man mumbled, disappearing through a double-swinging door.

Alex stood at the dusty fireplace mantle and peered at a black and white photo of his ghost. It was surrounded by numerous framed military awards, a Medal of Honor, Distinguished Service Medal, and Purple Heart among them.

"S'cuse the mess." The man reentered the room nudging several cats out of his path with his socked foot. "I've had a hard time keeping up on chores since—" He handed Alex a paper cup containing an amber liquid and peered into his own cup, head low. "Thank Spirit for friends and family is all I have to say."

The smell of the drink made Alex gag. Or maybe it was the smell of the house. He set the cup on the hearth and tried to decide where to begin. He'd come here for some clarity, some understanding, and to explain to Buck what he and Joe had seen that night—to offer some clarity and understanding in return, if that was even possible.

"Sir—"

"Name's Buck," the man said.

Alex nodded. "Buck, I came here to talk to you about your daughter."

"Oh, sure. I know that."

Alex blinked. "You do?"

"Oh, sure," Buck said. "Jade told us you'd be coming by. She loves your music, first saw you play when you were just a little thing all done up in a tuxedo and shiny shoes. She was hooked from the get-go of your career. You're a prodigy, you know it?"

For a moment, Alex got stuck on the name and hearing it out loud—*Jade*—then he shook his head, remorse deepening. The man had obviously had a hard time letting go. "Sir—Buck—I was there when your daughter was, um, the night Jade's life was … you know. That's what I came to speak to you about. I don't remember anything about that night that would be of any help to the police, and the only person who *does* remember anything is in a coma and may not survive. I came here to apologize."

Buck stared intently at Alex, and Alex wasn't sure if the man was trying to decide whether to punch him or hug him. He could see the resemblance to Jade—the high cheekbones, strong jaw and cinnamon skin, the same knowing in their eyes. Traces of Buck's former life still shone there, although muted by fatigue now. In just a few short minutes, Alex had gotten a sense of the man Buck had once been—a noble man filled with pride and honor, respected and confident. A true hero, now fallen, crippled by loss and mourning, worry and grief obvious in the way he held his body, shoulders slumped forward as if to protect his heart from breaking further.

"I'm very sorry, sir," Alex said.

Buck hung his head again, tears shimmering in the corners of his bloodshot eyes. He downed the remainder of his drink, set his cup on the mantle, and reached to shake Alex's hand.

"Thank you, son. That means everything. I wish Jade's mother was alive to hear you say that. But I tell you, what happened would've been a truer tragedy if they hadn't caught the guy. Thank Spirit for small mercies."

Alex shook the man's rough hand and blinked. "Excuse me?"

"You didn't know that, did you?" Buck took a deep breath. "'Course not. You were just a little kid."

"They caught the man who—" Alex tried to wrap his head around this new detail.

Buck nodded. "Sure did, thanks to my daughter remembering the little asshole's name and telling the paramedics before she fell unconscious. Still had handfuls of the little shit's hair clenched up in her fists when they got to her. When the cops went to his house looking for him, he was there drinking Pabst Blue Ribbon and listening to records. Just sitting there, bleeding all over his mother's sofa with clumps of hair missing, ripped shirt, face and neck and arms and back all clawed to hell, like it was any ordinary day. He denied everything, but all the evidence was good enough to send him to prison for a long time. Seventeen-years-old and already had a record. Tried and sentenced as an adult. Jeffrey Dennis Kendall, kin to the devil himself. May he rot." Buck's eyes blazed hate mixed with victory.

Alex's eyes widened. "Jeffy Kendall? I remember him. He used to bully my brother and me." It made sense when Alex thought about it. Jeffy and his twin brother Jimmy had caused trouble everywhere they went, leaving a trail of destruction in their collective wake and making more kids cry than Alex could count. Joe was the only kid who ever stood up to them. Then Alex realized something.

"Wait. You said Jade told the paramedics Jeff's name? How did she know his na—"

"Could you tell me something?" Buck interrupted.

Alex nodded, still trying to comprehend.

"Could you tell me what you *do* remember? Anything?"

Flashes of bloody hair and scared eyes, opaque fog and blood-drenched rain filled Alex's head. He shut his eyes as Joe's recollection played like a slasher movie on the insides of his eyelids.

"I remember it was raining. My friend and I had snuck out to watch the lightning, but the fog was too thick. We heard something and saw Jade on the grass. He—Jeffy—had cut her. Her blood … I remember her blood on my shoes. But Joe kept watching. It was like he was anchored there, frozen, and I think Jade saw us, saw Joe. There was a bright flash of light and … and that's all."

Alex opened his eyes to find Buck squinting at him.

"Joe?"

"Yeah. My friend. He's in the hospital with a head injury. He may not wake up."

Buck nodded. "That's some bad shit for a coupla little kids to see."

Alex swallowed hard. "I'm very sorry for your loss, sir."

"Me too," Buck said. "You know, she tried to get me to one of your shows once, but it's just not my thing. Blues. Now there's some great music."

Alex nodded, smiling a little. "Stevie Ray. *Rude Mood.* Amazing finger work."

Buck nodded appreciatively then said, "Well, Alex, time's wasting. Ready?"

"For what?"

Buck offered a coy smile and waved his big hand. Puzzled, Alex followed the puffing man down the hallway, side-stepping half a dozen cats along the way. Buck stopped in front of a closed door. "Wait here a second." He turned the knob and disappeared into the room.

Alex heard voices, Buck and a woman. He glanced at the photographs lining the walls—Jade as a baby, Jade as a toddler, Jade as an adolescent, Jade as a teenager—and the remorse he felt sank so deep it churned the bile in his stomach.

Buck opened the door and waved Alex through.

Alex stepped into a small room containing a single wicker chair and a huge potted tree and stopped short, losing his breath. Newspaper and magazine clippings papered every inch of wall space. The dates varied. One *Good Housekeeping* article showed him proudly holding his new baby brother. *Time* pronounced him a musical prodigy in their article on gifted children. His own face stared from the cover of a *People* magazine, which had promoted the "hot new talent" in conjunction with his first three-state tour at the age of nine. In the picture, the *Six Million Dollar Man* held Alex upside down by the ankle with his bionic arm while Alex played his violin, a huge smile on his face. There were photos of him with Johnny Carson, Phil Donohue, accompanying Don McLean on *American Bandstand,* sparring with Rocky Balboa at the Oscars, chatting with Casey Kasem at the studio microphone, all taken a lifetime ago.

Alex stepped closer and read the first paragraph of an article taped to the wall by the door. *Violin Prodigy Alexander Knapp will perform selections from Mozart's Great Violin Concertos and Beethoven's Sixth Symphony during what has become a winter tradition at Oregon State University. Knapp, known throughout the United States and Canada as the 'magician of musicians,' is known for his energetic, passionate, theatrical performances and astonishing pizzicato finger work. Knapp has become a staple in the Oregon Symphony's Christmas and Fourth of July Repertoires, as well as Toronto's Summer Music Festival. At age fifteen, this will be Mr. Knapp's fifth outing as concertmaster with the Oregon Symphony. He will also be performing a solo interpretation of Bach's Third Concerto to top off what is expected to be a well-rounded evening of music and fun, performed by one of the most gifted young talents of the decade."*

Alex grew sullen. A vast emptiness blew through him as he stood there, staring at remnants of a life nearly forgotten. All but one of his public performances had taken place before his brother's death. The kid on the walls was a stranger to him now, a sliver of who he used to be.

"Alex?" Buck said gently. The big man filled the frame of a second door to the left that Alex hadn't noticed in his distraction. Just then he heard it. Music. *His music.* From the first album.

Buck waved at Alex to follow and disappeared into an adjoining room.

Alex's stomach hitched up into his throat when he stepped over the threshold.

She reclined on a bed, propped up on pillows and covered by a colorful quilt made with vibrant patches of red, yellow, black, white, green, and purple material that formed a circle in the center. She wore a bright tunic that mirrored the colors of the quilt. An array of items surrounded her—stones, mostly turquoise, and baskets of what looked like plants and herbs. A good-sized rock water fountain gurgled in the corner. Cedar and sage-scented incense burned on the sill of an open window. Bright sunshine poured into the room, casting more light onto the beautiful quilt and the thin woman who lay under it. A plump older woman with bobbed salt-and-pepper hair sat by the window. She did not look up to greet Alex but hummed softly, busying her hands with something he could not see. A young woman with Asian features, sturdy arms, and asymmetrical purple hair looked up from massaging the bedridden woman's hand and smiled.

"Hey, I'm Kiki. I've been looking at your face for a long time now, so it's good to finally meet you, Alex. I enjoy listening to your music."

Alex stood frozen as ice and just as cold until a sharp pain shot through his belly, lodging in his chest and sending him stumbling into the wall by the door. All the air left his lungs. He slumped to the floor, gasping.

Buck stooped at Alex's side and grabbed his shoulders. "Whoa, boy. You okay?"

Alex nodded. The man's breath smelled fermented, rotten—a mimic of the stink the day before when Joe had grabbed him with his rotting hands. Alex felt everything leave his stomach. Before he could stop it, vomit spilled from his mouth onto the carpet. A scrawny black cat appeared.

It sniffed then licked at the semi-digested contents of Alex's stomach. He heaved again and lay back against the doorjamb, watching specks of light burst in front of his eyes. He wiped his mouth on his sleeve and watched Kiki scoop up his mess with a handful of paper towels.

"I'm okay," he told the haggard, ruddy face bobbing in front of him. "I'm okay. I-I thought …"

"I know, son. It's all right now." With massive hands, Buck lifted Alex to his feet and steadied him. "Alexander Knapp, I'd like to introduce my daughter Jade Sky-Timber-wolf. She's waited a long time to meet you."

The bedridden woman's cheek twitched. Her amber-brown eyes were open and moving, roving the room. Alex stepped forward, still trying to comprehend.

"Dreaming is important for the battle she has been called to," Buck said, sitting on the bed and stroking Jade's long sable hair.

Alex swallowed hard. He searched Buck's tired eyes and reached to touch Jade's wrist. "How …?"

"Good medicine," Buck said. "Our *nenaandawi'iwed*—sorry—our healer, Aala, is doing good work. She has been able to cast protection while Jade fights. She will be fine." Buck gazed at his once-healthy daughter. "She will win."

When Alex tried to catch her eye, Kiki turned away and continued massaging Jade's skeletal fingers. The visceral remorse anchored deep in his chest and stayed.

"Kiki, let's give Jade some time with Alex," Buck whispered. "She'd like that."

The aged woman sitting in the corner stood and walked out without a word, still clutching whatever was in her hands. Cutting a sideways glance, Kiki wiped her hands before heading out of the room. "It was nice meeting you, Alex. I hope you can visit again very soon."

Buck closed the door, leaving Alex alone with the woman who had been haunting his existence for months. He sat in

Kiki's chair and watched Jade's cheek twitch, watched her eyes roam and search. He took her hand.

"Tell me what to do," Alex whispered, holding Jade's fingers to his lips. "Tell me where to begin."

Jade's free hand spasmed up into the air. Alex felt her entire body jerk. Her long, thin arm flailed like a broken wing for several seconds before growing impossibly still, hovering, pointing. Alex turned and saw a closet door. He bolted out of the chair, grabbed the knob, and twisted.

"It's locked. I can't open it. It won't—" Alex came to a halt mid-step toward the bed. Jade's eyes had grown wide. Her mouth moved silently, her arm held its position mid-air above her frail body. "What is it? What do you see? Jade?"

Save him. The words—her voice—came from deep inside his head.

"Tell me where to start." He took her hovering hand and pressed it to his pounding chest. "I need your help."

Jade turned her face toward him, eyes searching then steadying and meeting his.

Sing the song—

"—of *songaona*," Alex whispered, eyes locked with hers.

It's the music that touches—

"—it's the music that heals," Alex said. "I know, but—"

The door opened and Kiki crept into the room, her expression urgent. Jade's gaze wandered away, hunting once more, the brief connection broken.

"Sorry to interrupt," Kiki said, easing the door closed. "I wanted to catch you before Buck comes back in."

"No problem," Alex said, fighting to keep his irritation at bay.

Kiki sat on the edge of Jade's bed, hands working the air to emphasize her words. "I'm really worried. He doesn't sleep. I've been staying later and later, sometimes all night, even though Aala is here twenty-four seven, because I'm afraid something bad will happen. I'm afraid that in his sleep deprivation he'll leave the stove on and the house will burn down. Or he'll drive to the store and fall asleep behind the wheel and die." Kiki's features darkened. "Or worse."

"Worse?"

"Yeah." She leaned forward and whispered, pointing at her head. "I think he's losing his mind."

Alex stroked Jade's long fingers and tried to ignore the rush of anxiety coursing through his arteries. "What makes you think that?"

Kiki's hands flew. "About a year ago Buck told me he saw something in here, in Jade's room. He thought it was a devil coming for his daughter. He said he felt an ominous presence and told me he believed Jade's condition was caused by supernatural forces, not by what the doctors said about blood loss and trauma."

"What do you think Buck saw?" Alex asked, feigning calmness.

"I don't know," Kiki said. "But I know people hallucinate when they don't sleep. Now, he won't leave Jade's side. Aala never leaves—that's an important part of the healing custom—but Buck sits and watches, like he's waiting and, I don't know, *guarding her*, or something. Next thing I know, it's gone. I have no idea how he got it out of the room, but it's definitely nowhere in this house."

Alex rubbed his forehead. "Wait. What's gone?"

Kiki pointed. "The thing that used to take up that whole wall. It was huge. *Enormous*. Looked like something out of a Stephen King story. Or Poe. Have you read *The Shining?* So good. I'm a lit major. Anyway—"

Jade's hand slipped from Alex's grasp. His heart jack-hammered up into his throat. "Wait. Was it a mirror?"

Kiki's hands worked the air. "Right. A mirror. That's what I said. Buck would sit there and stare into the mirror. All day, all night. Anyway—"

"Wait," Alex almost shouted. "There used to be a mirror on that wall, and it vanished? What happened to it?"

Kiki sighed. "Will you listen? That's what I'm trying to tell you. I heard from Missus Evans that Buck gave it to a woman up the street and she got thirty dollars for it at a yard sale. If you ask me, whoever bought it *way* overpaid. What kind of nutcase would buy such an ugly thing? Anyway—"

"Wait. Did it leak?" Alex tried to stay calm, focused on his exhales.

"What?"

"Did you ever see water? On the floor? Or on the glass itself? Anywhere?" Alex stared at the bare wall. There were still holes drilled where the thing had been bolted into place.

Kiki pulled at her lip, thinking, then nodded. "Actually, yeah. I remember because it was my birthday and I was upset about having to clean it up."

"Kiki, do you have a key to that closet?"

"No, but I can get it open for you." Kiki left the room and returned a moment later with Buck in tow. Aala trailed in behind him and sat down in her chair, hands still busy.

"You gotta jiggle the knob," Buck said.

"Buck, why don't you sit with Jade," Kiki said with a practiced soothing tone. "Alex and I can get it open."

Buck eased into Kiki's chair.

Alex grabbed the knob and twisted.

"No," Buck bellowed. "Up and down, up and down!"

Alex shook the knob and the latch let go. He pulled the door open, peered inside, and saw something lying on the floor. He reached in and lifted it, blowing dust bunnies and cat fur from the case.

"Ha! I remember when she bought that thing. She's good at saving money. Been working odd jobs since she was thirteen, mostly over in your neck of the woods. Babysitting sick and disabled kids, cleaning houses for older folks, volunteering at the hospice, stuff like that. She likes to take care of people. She was going out to the car one night after babysitting when—" Buck's face grew pale. He stared into nothing for several long moments, lips moving, then mumbled, "She had just got her driver's license."

"Buck, did she play?" Alex opened the case and ran his fingers over the smooth maple wood and curled neck. The violin looked brand new.

"Yep," Buck said, attention snapping back. "She's so taken with you that she made me get her lessons. Before, uh, everything happened she used to play your cassettes over and over on that very same player right there, so we keep it going. She used to play along with you, too. She's pretty good. Talented." He looked at his wasting daughter, tears shimmering in his bloodshot eyes. "She'll get back to it. She just needs to dream for a while."

"She likes my music," Alex whispered, glancing at the beautiful woman on the bed.

"She sure does," Kiki said. "We all do."

Buck bobbed his big head. "Music, dance, and prayer. Good medicine. Oh! And she has secrets, this one."

"Like what?" Alex trailed his callused fingertips along the taut strings, the same strings Jade's soft hands had rested on while playing music along with him. He drew the bow across, sending a soft, low drone into the fur-filled air, and felt his hands immediately tense up.

Buck chuckled. "She says she can hear music and songs in her head. Says the notes come *through* her, not *from* her."

Alex smiled. *The hymns of the spirits, right Jade? That's what Mary calls them. The songs of the gods. They find you from the god place, the wakwi, the dwelling place of the soul, from where they are birthed and to which they return.*

Alex tried to sound casual. "So, Buck. Is this how Jade's room has always been?"

"Yep," Buck said. A white cat leapt to the bed, curled up in the center of Jade's lap, and started a loud purr. "Well, Kiki's been putting up your clippings for years, adding to Jade's collection, and I had to get rid of that horrible thing that was on the wall over there." He pointed a shaking finger.

Alex glanced at Kiki. "Oh, yeah? What was it?"

Buck shuddered and ran a wide palm over the top of his head. "A mirror. Huge. Took up the whole wall and was downright ugly. Had all kinds of knobs and bars hanging off the sides."

Alex prodded. "It sounds like an interesting piece of work. Where did she get it?"

"Jade's Grandmother Sky gave it to her on her thirteenth birthday. Made by a shaman she knew in Arizona. He said it was a special mirror and that Jade was meant to have it, said the ancestors willed it so. Said it would help her learn and understand the realms of the backward way. So, Jade's grandmother brought it back."

"The *backward way*?" Alex rubbed his nose, anxiety mounting.

"Yep," Buck said, nodding solemnly. "Jade was a breech birth and my people believe that when a baby enters the world backward they have outsight, the ability to see outside themselves and deep into others, into their layers all the way to their core self. They can see where the shadow remains unseen and the spark of Spirit we all carry inside us. Sky said the mirror of truth is hard to look into, but that Jade would learn to command it."

"*Heyoka!*" the woman in the corner yelled. Alex jumped. He'd forgotten she was there.

"Yes," Buck said, nodding. "Not easy work. She enjoyed her time with Grandmother, learning the legends and ceremonies and mastering her gifts. She kept up on her studies until ..." He took his daughter's hand and pressed it gently between his wide palms. The room stilled, the gurgling of the water fountain the only sound.

"Then one day not long ago, they came." Buck's eyes showed the whites.

"*Maji-manidoo*," the woman in the corner said in a low ominous tone.

Buck nodded, eyes fixed on the blank wall. "Devils. I showed 'em. I chased 'em away. Mess with my kid. I don't think so." He heaved a heavy sigh. "I busted the thing down and put it out. Guess a woman a few streets over on Mystic Way snatched up the pieces and sold it at a garage sale. What's her name again?"

"Missus Bradenburg," Kiki said. "Wilma, I think? Shiloh tribal affiliation for sure and, um, Whitewing clan, I think?"

Alex's heart thumped hard against his chest. *Whitewing?* He felt queasy again and exhaled a steady stream of air. He leaned the violin case against the empty wall and told his mind not to spin out.

"That is some story, Buck. I have to get going, but I appreciate you letting me spend time with Jade."

"Sure you can't stay for supper? Kiki makes a damn good lasagna."

"We call it second lunch," Kiki said. "Like in *The Hobbit*, only not breakfast. Great book. There's plenty."

"It's getting late," Alex said, eager to get into fresh air.

"Well, c'mon back any time," Buck bellowed, getting to his feet. "You're always welcome here. And tell that friend of yours to stop by when he wakes up. Any friend of Alexander Knapp is a relation of ours. I hope he makes it through." He hung his head and slapped Alex on the back.

Alex went to Jade's bedside, leaned to kiss her ashen forehead, and heard her words again.

It's the music.

Alex brushed her cheek with his dry lips. "I know," he whispered. He stepped toward the door but was stopped by a firm hand on his arm. He turned to find Aala looking up at him. She took his hand and placed a small woven pouch in his palm.

"What—?"

Buck stood tall, giving the old woman a knowing and reverent look. "Our healer has made a medicine bundle for you."

Alex looked at the pouch and saw the same pattern of colors that were on Jade's quilt.

"Oh, um, *miigwech*. Thank you," he said, not fully understanding her gesture.

"*Weweni biminizha'an gaa-pawaadaman*," the woman said.

"She says you should pay attention to your dreams," Buck said.

"*Biizaabin.*"

Buck nodded. "She wants you to see what is inside the medicine bundle."

Alex turned the pouch upside down. Four stones spilled into his hand.

Aala picked up a deep green stone speckled with red. "*Mii ge-wiidookook da-bagakaabiyan.*"

"This one is bloodstone," Buck said, "for clear sight, intuition, and courage."

Aala picked up a pale translucent stone from Alex's palm. "*Mii ge-wiidookook da-mikwenjigeyan.*"

"This one is quartz, to unlock memory."

The old woman chose another stone, bright green. "*Gigizhaanig wa'aw, awedi bezhig dash, mii iw zhawenindiwin.*" She gestured toward Jade.

Buck smiled, tears coming to his weary eyes. He struggled with getting the words out.

"This stone is—" The big man stopped and gathered himself. "This one is jade. Jade blesses whatever it touches. Jade will help you realize your full potential, your calling. It is for protection, healing, and unconditional love." Buck wiped his tear-streaked face with the back of his hand.

Aala picked up the last stone, blood red, and Buck frowned, hesitating. He said something to her that Alex didn't understand.

"*Booch,*" Aala said with a firm nod of her head. "Yes."

Buck looked Alex directly in the eyes. "This stone is red jasper. It is for protection in both the physical and spiritual realms. It cultivates honesty with self and—" He glanced at Aala, who nodded firmly again. Buck continued, "It is for safe passage to the afterlife."

Aala brought her wrinkled hands to Alex's face and gently cupped his cheeks between her palms. She peered into his eyes, smiling so the lines in her face deepened. He smelled peppermint on her breath.

"*Gaawiin geyaabi gotaajiwin,*" the woman whispered.

"There is no more fear," Buck said.

Aala scooped the stones from Alex's palm, dropped them back into the pouch, and curled his fingers over the bundle. She looked into his eyes and nodded, then went back to her chair in the corner and sat down, busying her hands once more.

Alex stared at the pouch, a riot of emotions erupting. Mostly he was stunned and didn't know what to say, so he stood there until Buck asked if he was okay.

"Yeah," Alex breathed. "What does this mean?"

Buck put his hand on Alex's shoulder. "Aala is a seer, not an explainer." Buck paused then said, "Are you sure you don't want to stay a while?"

"No. I gotta go." Feeling numb, Alex followed Buck and Kiki down the hallway and pulled the front door open, a cool blast of air rousing his senses. He stepped onto the porch and looked at Jade's father. "Buck?"

Buck lifted his fatigued gaze.

"Do you remember the exact date you put out the looking glass?"

"Yep. Fourteen months ago Saturday. Thing was a bear to get out."

Alex thought, doing the math. *Norma bought the mirror one week later.*

"Alex," Kiki said. "Please *do* visit again. *Soon.*"

"Sure," Alex said. He looked at Buck. "Jade will make it back from wherever she is, sir."

"Oh, sure!" Buck bellowed. "She's a fighter. Came out that way."

Alex stepped off the porch and walked to his dirty Beetle. He heard Buck's gruff voice on the wind, "C'mon back anytime, son!"

Waving, Alex slid behind the steering wheel and stared up at the gray sky, thoughts and emotions racing. *The mirror was hers. The backward way. Afterlife. Whitewing. Does Mary know? Fuck me.*

He pulled away from the curb and caught a glimpse of Buck through the living room window, standing slumped and solitary. Kiki waved from the porch. Alex drove toward home, thinking only of a scathing hot shower. He was more than halfway there before noticing the fur-covered violin case on the back seat.

3:09pm

Alex climbed the huge maple, Jade's violin strapped to his back, vaguely aware of sharp pains piercing his shoulder and neck. Hoisting himself onto the red slate roof, he peered through the windowpane into Joe's darkened bedroom. The frame squealed when he shoved the window up. The room was hot and humid, the air still. He wrenched the window down, moved to the center of the room and stared into the looking glass, trying to see the world beyond, hoping Jade would appear to him as she had before, healthy and whole.

A train rumbled by. Alex groped at his chest and held the phoenix amulet and gold band in his fist. He thought of Aladdin. *Maybe if I rub it.* He retrieved the quartz and bloodstone from the medicine bundle. *To unlock memory. To see clearly.*

A freight whistle cried far away. Alex sat on the floor, pressing the stones between his palms, and closed his eyes.

He didn't pray. He listened for the silence between the notes and asked the questions—*why did I go into Joe's house that night? What did I hear? What did I see?* The stones blazed hot. The whine of the train faded and died out, leaving only the calming sound of rustling leaves and a distant drum of thunder. Alex set the stones in front of him and reached for the violin, expecting his hands to clench up as usual and was surprised when his fingers stretched wide. He brought the violin up to rest under his jaw and placed the bow on the strings. He took a deep breath, let it out slow, and began.

A low hum filled the room. The strokes came long and slow at first, then rushed and forceful. Notes sailed across the insides of his eyelids. His fingers knew just where to land on the strings. Sharp pangs twisted in his shoulder, but he barely noticed. He was lost in a familiar world of sound and color, of sadness and ecstasy. His world, where he knew exactly who he was and everything fell into place like puzzle pieces, edges blending together into one complete picture.

He played *Joe's Song*—strong, crisp, stubborn, funny, beautiful, lonely, sad. So sad.

The side of Alex's shoe tapped the carpet as a metronome. The sounds rose and moved through him, filling him, heart, bones, and soul before wending out into the ether. He became the song, lilting and weightless, taking flight, lifting up and out. Away. He could no longer feel the floor under him, could no longer feel his physical body, only the music and the spaces in between. Jade's soft voice intertwined and floated with his music, tangible and audible, ethereal and real, on the outside of his mind rather than inside his head, part of the ether.

"Save him."

Alex played the music, didn't miss a stroke.

"Free your heart, Alex."

His mind answered, *i don't know how i don't know from what*

"Why did you go in?"

i don't know
"Free your heart."
help me do it
"Free your heart."
why did i go in
"Free your ..."
i heard something a voice loud
"... heart."
it was joe he was screaming he was screaming he was scream-
ing screaming
"Why did you ..."
you promised you'd never leave me
"... go in, Alex."
i promised you promised you'd always take care of me you
shouldn't have done that shouldn't have come after me shouldn't
have left me left me holding the bag should have gone together
"Go in, Alex."
i saw you said we'd stay together be okay reaching slipping
falling on the clay
  pushing me falling down
  falling
  i believed you i was coming reaching
  slipping falling on the clay
  boot on the tracks with the blood bones
  i hate you i hate you hate you for what you did i wanted to go
should've been me not you not you
  daddy dead on the tracks
The music screeched to a halt. Alex slammed back into
his body hard and heavy. The rainbow colors faded into a
nauseating milky green. The violin and bow fell to the floor
and Alex wrapped his arms around his pulsing head. Blood
red liquid memories surged through his skull, piercing his
lucidity, probing the darkest corners, dragging him away
from the borealis of light. He clenched his fists tight and
let them take him.

He stood on the narrow walk leading to the front door. Madonnas bloomed. The heady rose perfume made him dizzy. The summer solstice heat felt sticky, stifling.

The house was dark. He turned away. The yelling began. Above. Primal, angry, accusing, sorry.

The sounds took shape, becoming deeper, more guttural, more decipherable. The sounds became words, the words became sentences, a familiar voice. Joe' s voice, but younger.

Joe's voice?

Panic. Fuck! The door's locked!

Joe!

He smashed his body into the front door until it gave way. Torrential air dragged him, slowed him as he waded through it, up the stairs, heart pounding in his ears.

His beating heart. His beating heart is bleeding out.

Not now. Not ever. Please.

Something had him by the ankles. He couldn't lift his feet. It was a … a hand. A smoky claw anchored him to the cream-colored carpet where he stood just inside the bedroom door.

Fuck! No! Joe, no.

The air, walls, floor, ceiling—everything—flowed with neon red. Shiny, like new paint. Blood sprayed down. He staggered, falling with Joe's life dripping into his eyes. Crawling, he dragged himself into the bathroom, the claw-thing reaching for his numb and useless legs. He pulled Joe from the bathtub and pressed against him, trying to stop the blood pulsing in red ribbons out of his body.

Joe's eyes rolled into his head, showing dead white. Help me, Alex. Please help me. Help me go.

Alex felt something snap inside.

You fuck! It's not this easy! Goddamn it Joe! I won't let you!

Numbers. What were they again? Nine …

Not now. Please.

Sirens. He stumbled down the stairs, slamming into the wall. He ran through vermilion waves into the street. Swirling lights, making him sick dizzy.

It's okay. We're on a ride. It's okay, it's okay, it's okay. Lifeless. Someone has taken his life.

The earthquake came. Everything shook, tilted, and Alex fell into dark, ravenous caverns, shadows reaching, clawing at his skin and senses until he thought his head would implode.

Alex blinked opened his eyes. He was sitting cross-legged on Joe's bedroom floor, hands clenched together in front of his chest. He knew what he held in them, could feel their heat and a tangible vibrating energy—the stones, phoenix charm, and Marcus's gold wedding band still on the chain.

Marcus.

Emotion welled like poison injected into his jugular, so visceral Alex could feel it thickening his veins. His head hurt. His heart burned. He ached, inside, outside. In the deepest, secret places of his being.

Chest tight, Alex opened his hands and let the offending objects fall to the carpet. He wrapped his sore fingers around the violin neck and stood up, staring at it as if it were a foreign object, a relic from a lost life. He gripped the instrument, mouth twitching. Anger swarmed his mind like fire ants, red and black and quick. He stepped toward his reflection.

"Let me in now," he seethed through clenched jaws. He held the violin like a baseball bat.

Nothing happened.

Without another word, Alex leapt at the mirror and swung. Before the instrument could connect with the smooth glass, a blast of cold air surged. He stumbled, reeled across the room, and crashed into the wall by the bathroom door. His breath left him. Muscle and tissue strained in his shoulder. He scrambled to his feet—and froze.

Beyond the glass, a boy hung from the side of a rocky incline, the top of his head visible through a film of floating dust. He thrashed his legs, helpless. Below, nothing but hungry darkness.

"Don't let me fall," the boy pleaded, terror in his voice. "Please don't let me fall."

Alex recoiled at the boy's words. He took a wavering step. Somewhere, a child began to cry.

Save him, Alex. Jade's voice. Inside his head.

"I—" Alex's face knotted. "Luke?"

The white owl on the roof outside Joe's bedroom window fluttered and Alex startled at the sudden movement. He looked back at the images in the glass and winced.

"Luke, I-I'm sorry. I'm so sorry I let you down. Forgive me, Lucas."

Forgive yourself, Jade's voice whispered. *Free your heart.*

Alex pressed his palm to the glass, breath billowing, crystallizing before melting away. The mirror gave way and his arm penetrated the smooth surface.

The owl outside shrieked, dancing on the red slate.

Alex wrapped his fingers around the kid's thin wrist.

"Don't let me fall, Al."

"I—" His hand slipped. Alex squeezed tighter, his body pressed against the freezing glass. His shoulder wrenched painfully. He sucked cold air into his lungs. Ice formed on the brass knobs and bars and the mirror began to fog with frost. Somewhere a child cried in long, hard sobs.

"Luke?"

The boy looked up into Alex's eyes, but it wasn't Luke's face Alex stared into through the dusty frost and ice. It was Joe's. The gash in his upper lip widened when he grinned, but there was no humor in his pale blue eyes when he spoke.

"You didn't save him, and you can't save me." Joe peeled Alex's fingers from his wrist and fell, grinning, into dark nothingness.

Dazed, Alex stumbled backward, legs drained of strength. He landed on his butt, unsure of anything that had happened since he'd first crawled through the window. His drenched fingers tingled in a familiar, sickening way. He rubbed his hands together, staring into the quickly warming air.

"Luke?" His voice came out hoarse, strained.

The owl extended its wings wide. Alex jerked his head toward the movement but couldn't see clearly. Dizziness swept over him, making his stomach flip. Anger and fear burned deep in the pit of his stomach. He crawled to the window. The visitor greeted him with a friendly coo and an excited flap of its wings.

He ran blindly, stumbling, breathing hard. Wings beat overhead, determined not to be knocked off course by the driving rain. Alex wanted nothing more than to lie down in the filthy gushing gutter and let it sweep him away, but he ran like he did as a child to the only person who could help him understand. Stalking shadows loomed at every turn, ready to attack and drain the last drops of life from him. He would fight but he couldn't win, and he knew it. Death would come for him with cool, comforting hands eventually.

Mary tossed a blue towel over his head and gave it a tussle, then took his elbow and guided him to the sofa. He buried his face in the cloth while she went to brew tea. The familiar scents of wood, paint, clay, and cherry tobacco were of little comfort as he sat with stinging tears rolling down his cheeks. He stared at a ceramic statue of a young man on horseback, holding a long spear high over his head, ready for battle. Alex wondered if the man was scared knowing he might not make it back, knowing he would watch his brothers die in the fight.

Mary sat and offered Alex a cup of steaming brown liquid. He looked away. The woman removed her spectacles and placed them on the stand next to her pipe. Her steady stare never left Alex's flushed face.

"Alexander?"

"Did you know she had the mirror before it wound up in Joe's room?" His back hurt when he spoke, and he wondered if he'd cracked a rib when he hit the wall in Joe's room.

Mary watched him intently. She reached for her pipe.

"I went to see her father this afternoon." Alex wiped his face with the towel and reached for his cup. Cardamom mixed with honey and ginger flooded his tongue, not too hot, just the way he liked it. He gulped it down. Mary relaxed into her chair and nodded, a distant look in her eyes.

"Joe's dying," Alex said.

"Yes," she nodded. "He does seem between worlds."

"There's nothing I can do, Mary. I-I can't."

"You can." Mary leaned close and took Alex's hands into her own. "There was a time when you could know his thoughts and feel the rhythm of his heart as it beat in time with your own. I'm sure it all feels fragmented now as Joseph has locked you out, but this does not mean you can't get back in. You are the key to unlocking his suffering. You must find the strength."

"Mary," Alex whispered, swallowing hard. "I'm dying too. He's taking me with him."

Mary shook her head. "Strength and bravery lie in the willingness to know your truth. Free yourself first. This is the way."

Alex thought of Aala's words—*honesty with self*—and watched Mary.

"Mary were you a breech birth?"

Her eyes seemed to spark in the flashes of lightning that lit up the room. She offered a small nod and Alex thought he saw a hint of a smile pull at her lips.

"Do you know what the burden is that's keeping me from connecting with Joe like I used to? Can you see it inside me?"

"I have some ideas," she said, "but only you know for sure and it's important that you come to it on your own."

He rested his head on the back of the couch and listened to the patter of raindrops at the window. The melancholy rhythm made him drowsy; he was so very tired. Thoughts skittered through his mind, unfocused, ungrounded.

"But there's definitely something."

"Something. Yes."

Alex nodded, eyelids heavy. He heard Mary's voice, but it seemed to be coming through a tunnel.

"There always comes a time when we must be willing to stand in the dark corners and light a candle to see what's there seeing us. You must open the dark side of your mind and face it, embrace it, redefine it. You must open your hands to let go and to receive. Shame, guilt, and regret are bold thieves of the human spirit."

"It's my fault," Alex mumbled, barely awake. "I never should've let him go down first, too dangerous."

He felt someone brush the hair from his forehead.

"His spirit is soaring," Mary whispered.

Alex drifted off with the woman's last words. As he slept, he dreamed of warm long-fingered hands reaching down from the heavens and saving him from drowning in a sea of his own tears.

10:10pm

"It's late," Elizabeth said, outline silhouetted in the frame of Luke's open door. "You missed your appointment with Doc Abraham today."

Alex sat on a cardboard box marked *games* in black ink, staring out the window at the star-speckled sky. A cool breeze swept in, disrupting the model planes overhead. He'd been there a while, staring into the night, numb and exhausted. Elizabeth glanced at the violin and bow lying on the floor. She stepped over them and joined Alex at the window.

"Pretty night after all that rain."

Alex was quiet.

"Luke loved nights like this," she continued, leaning on a box across from him. "He thought the world would look better from way up in the sky. Wouldn't be able to see all the pollution and violence. All the *people twubbles*, he used to say. He was a smart kid. Makes me proud to have sensitive, intelligent boys."

They were silent for a while as rainwashed wind rolled over them.

"Why can't I remember what happened that day, Mom?" His voice was barely a whisper, more like escaping air. "I think I remember holding his wrist. There was a lot of sand and rocks. He just—" Alex swallowed over the lump in his throat. "He started to slip. All I had was a piece of his T-shirt in my hand. I don't even know how the paramedics found us."

Elizabeth nodded.

Alex pointed at the darkened sky. "Mary told me that when a person dies a new star, brighter than the rest, is born. That's a yearround one. It never disappears." He looked at the calluses on his fingers. "Did you know the Shiloh people believe there are all kinds of death guides, both living and in spirit form? Some advise the souls of the dying if they get lost and afraid. Others receive the dying in the *wakwi* after their long journey. There are guides who create and play music for the dying, so they can find their way to the *wakwi*, the final destination. The goal is to not get stuck anywhere, and the music parts the veils between worlds so the dying can follow it to the receiving guides, who are waiting to help the person make choices to complete their journey. I did that for Luke. Played all night. Not sure it worked, though."

Elizabeth nodded, chin quivering. She took Alex's hand and kissed it. "That's really beautiful. Luke loved when you played for him. The first time he ever smiled was when you played *Twinkle Twinkle Little Star* for him. Remember?"

Alex grew quiet.

Elizabeth gave his hand a squeeze. "Is that what were you thinking about when I came in?"

"Yeah, I was trying to decide what to play when Joe dies. It's a tough one. He's a challenge."

"Alex," Elizabeth said. "Joe is not going to die. We won't let him."

Alex shrugged. "Maybe he won't. But I think I'll brush up on Mozart's *Requiem* anyway. I could use the practice. And it suits him."

Elizabeth shot off the box and grabbed Alex's face in her chilled hands, startling him.

"Listen to yourself," she said. "You're giving up! He needs you more now than ever and you're—"

"Marcus is dead, Mom."

Elizabeth's eyes searched his. "What?"

"He was hit by a train and killed."

Elizabeth sank back onto the box, her face white. "How …? That can't be. There would've been evidence. If a body had been found, we would have heard about it, especially in this town." She made Alex look at her. "How do you know this?"

"I remembered some details about the night I found Joe. I remembered hearing him—or not *him* exactly, but *some-one*—screaming up in his room. It was the most terrified sound I've ever heard. Like a little kid getting torn apart by a dog, or something. For eleven months, I haven't been able to figure out why I felt compelled to go into his house that night. It was because I heard someone, Mom, and I thought they were being ripped apart. Everyone thought the paramedics busted in the front door, but I did it. I had to get in."

Alex got up and paced, directionless, anger mounting. His foot hit his violin on the floor, sending it skidding into the wall with a whine.

"Wait a minute." Elizabeth shook her head. "We would have heard about this. Are you absolutely *sure* that's what Joe said—"

"Mom!" Alex stopped and looked at her. "Think about it. Norma would never want anyone to know. She'd want all the attention that a poor abandoned wife and mother would get. That makes *her* a victim and *him* a horrible man. That makes *her* the strong, resilient survivor and *him* the failed husband and father who was so weak that he left his wife all alone to fend for herself and her young son. Her churchies are still eating that shit up eight years later. They all think Marcus is the devil. And you know, just like I do, that people eventually forget your grief after someone dies. It's been six years since dad died and three since Luke. How many people are busting down our door with casseroles and condolences now, Mom? Exactly none. You said she's got some psycho paranoid disorder, right? The doctors said she's got—what is it—strong narcissistic traits, right? Oh, she's milking the poor abandoned wife performance for as long as she can."

Elizabeth was still shaking her head. She pulled at her lip. "Alex, there would have been remains. There would have been police, a coroner—"

"I don't know what happened to him after, Mom, but I run those tracks. One minute there's a dead animal and the next minute it's either picked clean or been dragged off to be picked clean. It was late spring when Marcus disappeared, right? The rain would have washed away any blood, and that red clay soaks up everything. You said Norma was a nurse? Maybe she had some friend from the morgue help her out. Probably incinerated the guy on the spot."

"Oh, Alex. That sounds too far out there, even for her."

"I don't know! Fuck!" Alex slammed his fist into the wall, leaving a jagged hole the size of a grapefruit.

Elizabeth stood up. "Alex. Stop. I mean it."

Alex glared at her, furious tears straining but he held them back. "Mom, that's not the worst of it."

Elizabeth shook her head very slowly. "What do you mean?"

Alex suddenly felt drained. "I-I think Joe saw it, saw Marcus …" He slumped to the floor and let the tears spill from his eyes. "Joe doesn't want to come back and I don't blame him. All he wants is to disappear, to be invisible. It's simpler for him that way. He's said it so many times, but I never *heard* him. He told me once about Norma's shrine. That's what he called it, *the shrine of the dead ones*, pictures of Jesus and Mary and Isaac all over her bedroom. She worships them, prays to them, makes offerings. But there's no Marcus and no Joe *anywhere.*"

Elizabeth drew a deep breath. "And Joe's been carrying the weight of this for eight years?"

"I think so."

"And there's absolutely no evidence."

"Not unless you count the memory of a dude in a coma that a bunch of magic stones helped me see."

Elizabeth stooped down and hugged him so tight that all the breath left his lungs and he winced at the pain in his upper back. "Not sure I understand that last part, and I'm still working this around in my head, but I keep coming back to this—there's a reason this is happening."

Alex shook his head and couldn't help but smirk. "Whitewing strikes again?"

Elizabeth loosened her grip on him and smiled.

"And you believe what she says, Mom?"

"She's been trying to prepare me for this for nineteen years, Alex. How can we not believe her?"

"Yeah," Alex muttered. "How can we." He picked up the violin and bow and placed them side-by-side in the center of the floor, just as they had been when he first entered the room.

"You're keeping them in here now?"

"No," Alex said, yearning for sleep. "They keep showing up in here. I knew you weren't moving them 'cause you never mess with my stuff, so …"

"You think we have a ghost?" Her voice was a whisper.

Alex grimaced at the thought of another one interfering in his life. He looked at the instrument on the floor and shrugged. "Probably," he said, needing to change the subject. "I'll fix the hole tomorrow."

"Yes, you will."

Alex pulled the door closed behind them.

Outside the window, the white owl tucked its beak into its chest and closed its crystal-clear eyes.

seven

Knots

Joe lay on the sand and thought about the wreck. The dark road had been deserted except for the other car, crunched and folded and upside down, and the little boy hadn't been much older than him at the time. The kid lying on the ground had blond hair, too, but his was matted and thick with something that looked like grease. A pool of shimmering red surrounded him as he lay there so still, eyes open and shiny like glass. Fast spitty rain in the headlights made it hard to see. The sirens hadn't arrived yet.

"Don't look, Joey," Daddy had told him. "Just put your head down and cover your eyes and stay here, okay?"

Daddy pulled off to the side and pushed the flasher button so their car bled red light onto the road like the warning lights down at the train tracks by his house. It illuminated Daddy as he knelt next to the boy.

The moon hid in the rain, a silent glowy shadow in the night sky.

God's eye, Joe remembered thinking as his small self walked on his knees across the front seat to look out the driver's window at the boy lying in the road. Daddy had scooped him up and was holding him close now, taking him to the side of the road. It reminded Joe of a time when he had held his daddy like that.

Joey put his finger on the window and tried to push it through to touch the boy's face. *Can you feel that?*

"Daddy?" Joey said when daddy got back in the car, coat smeared with that red grease from the road, eyes leaking and all knotted up.

"What, Joe?"

He liked it when Daddy called him *Joe*. It made him feel bigger than four.

"How come he doesn't get up?"

Daddy didn't answer right away.

"Daddy?"

"He can't get up, Joey."

"But how come he can't?"

"He's hurt bad, Joe. We have to drive to a pay phone and call an ambulance, and then we have to come back here and wait for it."

Joey thought about it for a second then said, "Is he dead like Baby Isaac and Casper Fish?"

Daddy let out a long shaky breath and the water in his eyes leaked into the hair on his cheeks. "Yes, he is, Joe. Just like Isaac and Casper Fish."

"But that boy is too big to put in the potty like Casper, Daddy."

"Yes, Joe. He's too big." Daddy's voice sounded like a bug got caught in his throat.

"Where will they put him if he can't fit?"

"In the ground, Joe. His family will bury him in the ground."

He watched Daddy's hands, tight on the steering wheel as they pulled back onto the road. "Daddy?"

"What?"

"Is that where Isaac is? In the ground?"

Daddy breathed out for a long time again. "Yes. Isaac is buried in the ground."

"Daddy?"

"Yes, Joe."

"That boy will never cry anymore. Even if he touches the stove. He's dead like Baby Isaac and Casper, but now he's happy in Heaven and nobody cries in Heaven."

The rearview mirror framed Daddy's leaky eyes. "You're right, Joe. Nobody cries in Heaven."

Two years later, when his mother came home, Joe remembered wishing he could lie down in the red grease next to the kid in the road and stay with him forever. It became his favorite memory because he knew if all else failed he could always just lie down in the street, or on the tracks, or in a grave, or on this cold fine sand and never get up again.

Then the images shifted, blurred, changed, accompanied by hushed howls and low growls. Somewhere in the deepest pit of his brain, a disconnected memory emerged and took shape. But it was more than that, like before, tangible and visceral. The scene opened in front of his eyes, like a mirage seen through a telescopic lens. Through a shimmering gold haze Joe saw his small self again, but he was not alone. Two other boys sat with him on the grass under a towering elm. Their young faces seemed familiar, as though they'd once visited in a dream. The town spread out in all directions below. The sun dipped low in a majestic show over the trees and a few heavy raindrops tumbled from the sky, bringing more electricity to the atmosphere. The boys spoke in excited, hushed voices, but Joe knew what they were saying without really thinking about it.

"Brothers forever," the dark-haired boy said, pricking his finger with a needle. The other two nodded, grinning, and held out their index fingers, eager to be part of the game. The smallest boy couldn't have been more than seven, but he showed no fear when the point pierced his flesh and blood bubbled from beneath the surface. He brushed long sandy-brown hair out of his eyes. He was used to needles taking his blood. Doctors had been doing it since he was born.

The blond boy watched a perfectly round ruby bead rise on the tip of his finger. Joe knew what he was thinking; the boy's thoughts bumped up against his own. *Do it again. Make me feel it.* He pulled his long bangs down over his face and stared at the red dot through stringy clumps of hair.

"Hey, Speedy," the dark-haired boy said, nudging him. "Wake up." He turned to the smallest boy. "You ready, Spritle?"

The boy smiled. "Ready, Rex Racer!"

"Brothers forever," they said in unison.

Each boy opened his mouth and let the other two touch their pierced fingers to his tongue.

"No matter what," the dark-haired boy told them, "we'll always look out for each other and keep each other's secrets. We share the same blood now. We're brothers for life. Blood brothers. Agreed?"

The other two nodded. The dark-haired boy pointed to the smallest kid. "Luke, what's your code name?"

"Spritle, sir!" The kid jumped to his feet and saluted.

The dark-haired boy pointed to the blond kid. "Joe, what's your code?"

"Speed Rac—"

The sky lit up. A deafening crack of thunder exploded overhead and they all looked up in time to see a thick, smoldering branch tear free of the trunk and start falling toward them. The blond kid jumped up and threw himself at the younger boy. The smoking elm branch fell to earth, just missing the soles of their shoes. The younger boy thrashed and yelled.

"Get off me, Joe! I can't breathe! Get off!"

The blond boy rolled onto his back and blinked up at the darkened sky, heart thudding. Drops of rain hit his face, but he didn't move or blink. The dark-haired kid crawled to them on all fours, face dead white, eyes frightened, searching.

"You guys okay? Shit Joe. You saved Luke's life."

The blond boy said nothing. He wasn't really there. They only *thought* they saw him. In reality he was invisible, wishing with all his might that the branch had fallen and crushed the life out of him. He held the gold band at his chest tight and thought about Bilbo's magic ring. Bilbo could disappear with his ring, turn into something else. The sky cried, dotting the boy's cheeks with pretend tears, because he couldn't cry anymore and never would again.

The golden rays faded and went out, leaving Joe wrapped around himself in darkness, phantom noises and a hot chill caressing his limbs, probing his chest, his abdomen, his weakening mind. Scraping, whispering sounds, closer than ever, inside and outside. A collective.

They're coming for me. Thank you, sweet baby Jesus, they're finally coming for me.

Joe closed his eyes, never noticing the tiny holes he'd dug into each fingertip with the pointed wedge of TV glass.

June 7, 1984

Alex woke knowing something was wrong. The air felt different. The dull ache at the base of his skull was strong. He pushed himself up and tucked his hands into his armpits, shivering. Clouds of crystallized breath puffed from his mouth. The digital clock read 3:13 AM, but he felt like he'd been asleep for days. He got up and stepped into the dark hallway. His mother's door stood open a few inches, as always—evidence of Elizabeth's fear of not hearing her children in the night. Alex padded down the hall and looked in at his mom's sleeping form before turning away and walking toward Luke's room. He pushed the door open and stepped back with a start. Model planes spun overhead, crashing into one another, spinning wildly out of control.

That wasn't all.

Sheet music filled with his own sloppy scrawl covered the wood floor, illuminated by moonlight pouring through the open window. A dozen pages floated to earth as he watched, rooted where he stood. As the papers settled, Alex's heart bounced hard and began a quick beat that he could feel in his temples. A figure standing by the moonlit window turned and Alex thought it was her, Jade. The image came more into focus and he felt the blood drain from his limbs. The air grew colder.

"Remember, bro," Luke said. "You did it out of love. Is there a better reason for doing anything?"

Nonsensical syllables clanged around inside Alex's head, and then sharpened into Aala's voice saying something about unconditional love.

Luke's voice seemed very far away. "When you played, it always made me feel safe. You've lost your touch, but your healing has begun. Remember the sun, Ally. And the light."

Luke lifted his hand, palm up, and blew out a steady stream of air. A cloud of frost obscured his face and when it cleared there was only a small white feather seesawing toward the paper-littered floor.

5:05am

Dim sidewalk lamps shone like beacons in the misty dark, guiding him through headstones that loomed up in the early morning fog as he wove between them, careful not to step on the many graves. Compelled, Alex had veered from his running route on the third go-around to head for the cemetery. It was dark except for pinpoints of yellow light in the mist. Heavy air cloaked him in moisture. Death hovered at every turn like life-sucking shadows, but sometimes even the tiniest pinprick could drive them away. Complete, abject darkness was a different, unbearable story. They thrived there. Monsters lurking, waiting to drain him into a soulless husk.

He stopped. Before him, shrouded in supernal gray fog, a sea of green grass stretched ahead. Beyond that lay Luke's grave.

Alex started across the expansive lawn, slipping on the wet grass, and tried to remember the last time he'd visited his brother's final resting place. Three days before Joe's suicide attempt. Too long. Rainwater sloshed into his shoes, making his feet heavy.

He arrived and gazed down at the small headstone. Chiseled into the granite were the words he and his mom had mulled over for days. When Alex had finally said them aloud, Elizabeth had broken down and sobbed into his shoulder.

Lucas Daley Knapp. June 28, 1969 - August 15, 1981. Free To Soar.

Overwhelmed, Alex sank to his knees, buried his face in the wet grass covering his brother's body, and wept until dawn.

Alex arrived home just past dawn and headed for the shower, stopping in the kitchen for a glass of grapefruit juice. Elizabeth was still asleep. He pulled her door closed so the shower wouldn't wake her and started down the hall toward the bathroom.

At Luke's bedroom door, Alex heard a click and stopped short. Backing up a few steps, he turned and watched his brother's door creak open an inch, then another two. Alex took a long exhale, squared his shoulders, and gripped the medicine bundle in the pocket of his gym pants. An elusive, peripheral memory tiptoed a little closer. He stood there, willing the vague thing in his mind to come out of the darkness.

Let it go, he heard Dr. Lyn say. *Whatever you're holding on to is holding on to you.*

"No more fear," Alex breathed, squeezing the bundle tighter in his fist. Ice cubes clacked inside the glass he held in his other hand, spilling juice over the rim.

The door opened another inch.

The blurred memory became sharper, more focused. Alex stepped forward.

"I'm not afraid," he whispered, releasing the bundle in his pocket and taking another step.

The door eased open, but before it could stop again Alex pushed his palm hard against it. It flew wide, sending sheets of handwritten music arcing into the air and planes swaying in the sudden breeze.

The unfocused, fleeting recollection came skidding full force into his consciousness.

Luke. Last night. Here. He was real.

Off-balance, Alex stepped into the room and the door clicked closed behind him. The glass slipped from his trembling hand and crashed to the hardwood floor, spraying the sheet music with pink liquid. He was alone with his music and violin and … something else. A haunting vision bubbling beneath the surface of his psyche. He wracked his brain, trying to remember the words his dead brother had spoken.

You did it out of love.

Those six horrible words came screeching out of blackness, dragging with them a vision so unspeakable and entering his mind with such force that Alex instinctively threw his hands up to protect himself. His knees buckled. He lost his balance and slammed to the floor. But even after he landed, he had an unrelenting sensation of falling through dark and light, life and death, love and hate, pain and pleasure. It went on and on and on …

Then there was nothing except a long-buried memory galloping out of the dense layers of his mind—a hideous beast, all of his nightmares and fears embodied by one grossly deformed entity. It dropped on him, suffocating him with its foul stench of death and decay, denial and guilt. It ripped at his mind with jagged talons, tearing gaping holes to let the repressed memory spill out like the guts of a fresh kill. It shredded his sanity and replaced it with an understanding so horrible, so unbearable, that the weight of it crushed him harder against his dead brother's bedroom floor, pinned him there to watch and see and hear and taste and smell and feel the hopeless horror of it all. He wished he could rewind it, press a button to pause it, to stop it. But the images landed, cold and empty, and came in the form of himself pressing a twelve-year-old boy's ruined face against a wadded-up sweatshirt and saying, "I'm sorry Lucas I'm sorry Lucas I'm sorry sorry I'm sorry …"

You did it out of love.

Six horrible words. The crushing weight of them squeezed his lungs. He couldn't breathe. Couldn't exhale.

"No," Alex moaned, writhing on the floor. "No nononono …" He covered his face with his hands, clawed the offending air, tried to ward off the assault. "I would never hurt you, Lucas. I would never hurt you. Never never never …"

Then, suddenly, he was standing at the bottom of the incline, living the nightmare again, vision so sharp he could see each particle of dust hanging in the air, smell the late summer hemlock baking in the sun, feel the loose rocks and gravel under is shoes. Except this time, he knew the outcome, knew with horror-stricken certainty how Luke's life would ultimately end. Alex finally understood why he couldn't remember the details. *The details, goddamn it.* It was too much to bear, even now after three tormented years filled with static. A channel had been changed and the images flooded in. He felt himself being swallowed in the surge.

Drowning … I can't breathe. And then the memory was there, crisp, unbidden and vicious.

He stood next to his dangling brother after frantically rappelling down the last half of the rocky cliff. But he hadn't been able to go fast enough because his goddamn rope had gotten jammed in a goddamn crack. Luke spiraled downward, out of control, into the black hole below, screaming his brother's name. The rope, the fucking rope had come untied.

Because I forgot.

At first, Luke caught himself, clutching at the crumbly earth in desperation while Alex reached for him. He'd gotten a good grip on Luke's small wrist, but then ... then Luke started to thrash and choke and panic and fall.

Halfway down the cliff, Alex wrenched free of his harness. He held the rope and skidded the rest of the way down the incline on his back, rocks and roots peeling away layers of skin, the rope flaying the flesh of his hands.

But what he found, hanging by its neck two feet above the flat ground, was not his brother. This person's head was caved in on one side, the eye bulged out of the socket. This person's brain was visible where parts of the skull had been ripped away by the sharp, jagged rocks above. This person's neck was bowed out on one side from the taut snap of the rope that had gotten wrapped around it. And yet this person was not dead. An alien rasp emanated from somewhere beyond the protruding tongue hanging like a rag from his shredded mouth.

Because I forgot.

Alex wrapped his arms around Luke's legs and lifted, freeing his broken neck from the rope. He worked his brother's limp body out of the harness and laid him gently on the ground, careful not to aggravate his left leg, which had turned around at the knee. His hips twisted at an impossible angle. Alex sat on the ground and cradled his brother's shattered body in his arms. Luke's breathing sounded like a shallow trickle of water flowing over a bed of pebbles, liquid, wet.

Alex screamed, but no one heard. No one came. So, he rocked and prayed, rocked and prayed, holding Luke close. There was no one to help. No one to tell him what he should do. No one. He looked down at his little brother's smashed face and for an instant he saw Luke as he'd been when Mom brought him home from the hospital after thirteen agonizing weeks of uncertainty and worry. *Would he live? Would he laugh? Would he run and jump and play?*

"Run and get your violin, Alex," his mom would say. "Play Twinkle Twinkle for Lucas and it will help him feel better."

He'd run as fast as his three-year-old legs could go to gather his violin and bow.

And he would play. And Luke would smile.

Alex started to scream. His voice echoed back from the jutting cavern walls, hammering at his mind until he realized Luke was moving his torn lips and looking at him through the film of mucus forming over the one eye visible through all the blood and ripped flesh. For an instant, Alex denied what he saw in his brother's soft gray iris. For an instant, he ignored the fact that he knew what Luke was trying to tell him. For an instant, he felt sheer terror.

"Can't … feel."

Alex's heart stopped. His mind stopped. Everything stopped at that moment and he felt himself lifting, floating.

Because I forgot.

"No," Alex groaned, his face contorting with anguish. "No Lucas, no Lucas, they can fix it. They can."

The gray eye stared at him, unable to blink. Blood gushed from Luke's mouth, washing over his flattened chin. He began to choke, his body convulsing in spasms.

"Don't leave me, Lucas. Just hold on—"

Hold on to what? Would he live? Would he laugh? Would he run and jump and play? Or would he be bed-bound, tied to tubes like their father after fighting so hard for a healthy life.

Because I forgot.

Alex loosened the sweatshirt still tied around Luke's waist and wadded it between his chest and what was left of his brother's face. He searched the gray iris again for a sign of hope—and it took a lifetime of moments for him to acknowledge that there was none. This person was not his brother. This person would never fly his mechanized planes high in the sky again. This person's chance at life had been ripped away in a matter of terror-filled seconds.

Because I forgot.

And no one was coming.

"Luke?"

The words came out garbled, wet, almost indecipherable. "Not like Dad," Luke whispered. "No fear."

An uncontrollable shake took over Alex's entire body. "No, Lucas. No. No."

Blood ran from Luke's mouth with a final word.

"Wings."

His lungs strained for breath. His battered body convulsed, visible eye rolling back, showing dead white.

Dead white … dead.

Because I forgot. I forgot the backup knots.

Alex broke. Inhuman sounds filled the darkening cavern. He lifted Luke's bludgeoned face toward the wadded gray hoodie, held his hand firmly against the back of Luke's head, feeling the moist softness of his brother's brain where chunks of skull had peeled away. Blood spurted from Luke's mouth again, soaking the sweatshirt and running into his long brown hair.

There was no struggle, no resistance. Only the sound of Alex's hoarse cries echoing as his brother left him. The gray iris rolled skyward. As his brother's breath grew still, Alex looked into Luke's filmy eye and tried to see beyond, deep into his mind, his playful soul. He tried to see God there, searched for all the answers to all the questions. But what he found did not assuage his anguish or his guilt. He saw quiet. He saw peace.

I forgot. You always backup square fisherman's knots when tying two ropes together. For safety. Always.

Alex's sobs came hard, spilling freely from the crack where his heart had wrenched open. Burying his face in Luke's bloodied shirt, he cried until there were no tears left, emptied himself into the earth and his brother's quickly cooling skin. He stayed hunched over Luke's twisted, broken body for a long time and when he finally lifted his head and opened his swollen eyes he saw that a deep darkness had closed in. But there was something more—monstrous shadows reached from the yawning depths of the cavern, springing from the darkest corners of the jutting rocks to draw the life from him and steal his brother's sweet spirit.

He held Luke tight. "It's okay, Lucas. I'll protect you. Don't be afraid."

But Luke couldn't hear him. Luke was dead.

Because I fucking forgot.

Beams of light, piercing the hot night, skidding across the rock walls.

Men's voices high above, mumbling, yelling.

Engines.

A flash of light in his eyes.

A man's unshaven face, mouthing words that Alex could not hear, but understood anyway. "Jesus Christ, son. Jesus H. Christ."

They took his brother away, leaving him with a light blue hoodie clenched in his blood-drenched hands, which later had to be pried open by a doctor with a shiny metal tool.

But he had never let go.

The fog outside hadn't lifted. Alex could tell when he finally opened his eyes and blinked up at the bellies of Luke's multi-colored planes. When he saw them, his eyes flooded again with hot, stinging tears that streamed over his temples and into his damp hair. He covered his face with his arms, a painful sob rending from his throat, a hoarse rasp laden with remorse and grief. A part of him had been ripped away. The best part.

A train whistled in the distance, its echo filling Alex's head with a despairing, lonely sound that reminded him where he was. Home. Safe. Alone. Utterly alone, the torturing darkness only imagined, something he'd created to protect himself from an unthinkable memory that his mind had not been ready to acknowledge until now. *Why now?*

"Should've been me," Alex breathed, sitting up, eyes nearly swollen shut. He got to his feet, looking for something, not sure what.

"Should've been me," he said louder, anger seeping into his veins. "I should've gone down first, like we planned, but he just flew over the edge. I should've checked the backup knots. My fucking backups were fucking fine!" He spun around, ripping sheet music under his shoes. His hands found the violin on the floor. Without a single note of hesitation, Alex reeled sideways and smashed it into the wall, splintering the finished oak body and loosening the neck. Smoldering anger ignited into a roar. He beat at the model flyers overhead until every last one lay broken and crippled on the paper-littered floor.

Exhaustion coursed through his muscles. Alex slumped to the floor, holding pieces of his violin in bleeding, trembling hands. He sat and wrapped his arms around what was left of the destroyed instrument.

"It should've been me. He had all the light."

Save him, Alex.

He heard her voice—inside his head—loud and on the verge of surrender.

"No," he whispered. "Get out of my head. Leave me alone."

Dying, she said, her voice urgent.

He pressed his hands over his ears.

Please, Alex …

"I don't care," he breathed. "It doesn't matter anymore."

There was a long pause and Alex almost felt grateful.

"He is with you now." Her voice filled Luke's room, audible and loud.

Alex squeezed his eyes closed.

"Play for him, Alex."

Alex opened his eyes and squinted through the gloom.

The white owl perched on the ledge just outside Luke's bedroom window. The night bird stared through the glass, crystal-clear eyes looking into Alex's anguished heart, penetrating his mind, and he had a flash — Luke running with his arms held like wings, an indisputable look of innocent expectation that at any second he would surely lift from the ground to soar high above the world and frolic with the winged creatures of the universe.

"I'm flying! Look, Ally! I'm really flying!"

In his mind's eye, he could see the back of Luke's body, sandybrown hair flying behind him, feet never touching the ground. Luke was always moving, laughing, running, challenging big brother to keep up. Most times, Alex couldn't. Luke would be a speck in the distance before Alex could take his first step. He often wondered if his brother really ly did have wings tucked away, and suddenly, sitting there watching the bird watch him, he felt certain of it.

Something popped. Alex heard it in his head but felt it in his chest and hands. It was loud, like a cork popping, and let loose a current of bubbly warmth throughout his body. His hands opened. He looked at them as if they belonged to someone else, unfamiliar sensations flooding his fingers and palms. He stood up, swollen eyes held by the owl's hypnotic gaze.

"His spirit soars. Play for him."

Alex trembled.

The owl spread its magnificent wings and lifted into the air.

"He smiles with the music ..." Her voice faded away, weary, her final words barely audible inside his head. *Your heart is now free.*

June 9, 1984

Alex crept like an amateur bandit along the dim hallway toward Norma Schell's bedroom. Charlie's early morning call had taken him by surprise, but it was the big guy's frantic, almost incoherent rambling about kidnapping and sacrifice that had made the hair on the back of Alex's head stiffen. He would have taken Charlie's nonsensical blathering as a joke if it hadn't been for the gut-knotting sobs breaking through on the other end of the phone line. He knew Charlie. This was no joke.

Alex heard it then. A soft mewling, like a trapped kitten. He reached for the gleaming doorknob and gave it a quick turn, hoping it would be locked so he wouldn't have to deal with whatever the woman had hidden beyond. He stood in the open doorway of Mrs. Schell's bedroom, absently pulling on his nose. Photos and paintings of the dead ones — Jesus, Mary, Isaac — filled the room. Joe's and Marcus's likenesses were nowhere to be found.

The overwhelming scent of lavender—even stronger in the bedroom—created intense pressure behind his eyes. Alex tugged harder on his nose, noticing a huge framed picture on the mahogany dresser. Mrs. Schell smiled into the lens of the camera, holding baby Isaac. She wore no makeup and was actually quite attractive, slender with bright blue eyes just like Joe's. Except the light in Joe's eyes had dimmed to near nonexistence. Alex quelled the disdain and hatred blooming in his chest.

Heavy draperies covered the window, blocking out the light. A refined wooden altar curved into one corner by the head of the bed and ended just short of the windowsill. Dozens of flickering candles cast an unearthly glow into the room. The light reflected off the vaulted ceiling, casting bobbing shadows on the walls and over the faces of the silent dead ones, allowing Alex to take in every disturbing detail. Tens of dozens of pictures and religious idols had been meticulously placed on row after row of wooden shelves, the night stand, the headboard of her king-sized bed, even on the top shelf of her closet, which stood open as if not to lock them in. The chest of drawers seemed reserved only for the special photo of the mother and her beloved firstborn son. Alex moved further into the room. Everything gleamed with detailed cleanliness. He was careful not to disturb anything, knowing she'd be able to sense if someone had been in her room. It was Sunday and he knew she'd be at church and God's Grace most of the day.

An ever-present feeling of menacing evil came from this room and grew stronger as Alex approached the bizarre altar. With uneasy apprehension, he stood behind a large quilted pillow, apparently used for kneeling, and looked straight up into the eyes of a crucified figure, expecting to find the sad, empty face of Christ gazing down at him, but his breath hitched into his throat. His legs wobbled, and he slumped to his knees on the cushion, eyes fixed on the withered young face of Isaac Schell. His grayish body hung from a wooden cross bolted across the corner where the walls met. He gazed downward toward the bed, his expression just as hopeless as that of Christ in all the paintings and sculptures Alex had ever seen. The boy seemed to be keeping a protective watch over his mother's sacred space.

Alex closed his gaping mouth, overcome by a need to touch the boy's feet, warmed by tiny flames leaping from the many glass cups on the altar.

"What kind of sick …?" A terrible sadness crept into his heart.

The flames suddenly flickered. Alex stood and spun toward the door. Before he could dive for cover, it opened.

She stood there in a tight orange skirt and blouse that pulled apart at the buttons, exposing a white bra. She narrowed her eyes and pointed a long fluorescent pink fingernail at him.

"I-I just came to see how you're doing, Missus Schell. To see if you need anything?" It was the only thing he could think of and he mentally kicked himself for not coming up with something more intelligent, more manipulative.

She curled back her lips, revealing brightly lipsticked teeth, and took a step toward him. "You have trespassed on a sacred house of God!"

In the dim fluttering light, Alex saw specks of spit fly from those painted lips and, for a reason he did not quite understand, became very frightened. The musky lavender aroma of the room battled with the sickening sweet smell of her rat poison perfume. An indistinct buzzing came from somewhere and he thought he heard someone call his name from very far away.

"Really," Alex said, watching her. "I just wanted to see if you're doing okay—if you—"

"You are a child of Satan. A murderer. You and that other one. Murderers! Your souls cannot be saved. The devil is your master!"

Trembling with the force of her words, Norma stepped forward and raised her hand, aiming a small gun at Alex's face. He blinked in the uneven light and took a step backward, momentarily stunned. Insane glee and deranged excitement lit Mrs. Schell's pale blue eyes. He remembered Joe writing about the look she sometimes got.

"It's God's will," she said calmly.

Disbelieving, Alex stepped forward to get a better look at her face.

"You know," he said, eyeing the crucified boy on the wall. "You're a fucking nut case. I wouldn't be surprised if you killed Isaac yourself."

Her hand shook, face visibly paling beneath layers of pancake and rouge. She glowered at him.

"My son died for mankind's sins, to save the souls of pathetic, undeserving humans like you," Mrs. Schell said, soft and steady. "My son was born of the Holy Spirit and now resides with Our Father in Heaven, a place you will *never* know. My son was chosen and the only way to redeem your despicable soul is to get down on your knees before him and plead for forgiveness."

Alex stared at her, very aware now of his name being called from somewhere in the darkness of his mind. "Y-you don't really believe …?"

But he knew she did.

Alex circled the bed slowly. The small pistol in her hand tracked his every step. He stopped several feet from her and extended his hand, searching for any sign of rational thought in her light blue eyes. But he saw only a deranged, paranoid woman and nothing more.

"Thou shalt not kill," Alex said, thinking of Luke's broken body, the pleading desperation in his eyes. "Which commandment is that, Missus Schell?"

"It's too late for you," Norma said, adjusting the handgun in her grip. "You are beyond redemption."

Alex nodded, sweat sliding down his back. "You're probably right, Norma. But it's not up to you to decide my fate." Her hands had stopped shaking and her face had relaxed, which sent a jolt of hot panic through Alex's chest.

"God has spoken to me. It is His will that you be confined to the flaming house of Hell from which you came."

He stood only a few inches from the short barrel of her gun, heart straining against his chest, head filling with a loud, steady beat. He went on anyway, pushing his luck and the voice of reason telling him to keep his mouth shut.

"Just what was it that pushed you off that edge, Norma?" He wasn't being facetious, he really wanted to know before she pumped a bullet into his body, stopping his heart once and for all. "Was your mother cruel to you? Your father?" Her face tightened. "I didn't think there was anything that could make a mother stop loving her child. I thought unconditional love was part of the agreement. What did Joe do to deserve this?"

"You don't know anything about me. You don't know what you're saying."

Alex bluffed, his gaze never leaving her meticulously painted face. "Joe told me *everything*, Norma. He told me about the day his dad died. About you. I know exactly what I'm talking about, and you know it."

"Liar!"

"I know about the boot," Alex told her, recalling Joe's haunted drawings. "I know what you did."

She grimaced, thin lips pulling down over colored teeth. *"Lies."*

"No." Alex shook his head.

"I told him to never tell. He would never disobey me. You're a liar and a murderer. You sacrificed your own flesh and blood to the Beast. It's God's will that you be punished for your sins." She held the gun tighter, knuckles turning white, long fingernails digging into the flesh of her palm.

"Who sacrificed who, Norma?" His expression became stone, his voice low and steady. "I think you're a little confused. I know everything. And *you* are going to hell for *your* sins against *your* flesh and blood. One way. Non-stop. Bon voyage."

His accusation struck somewhere deep inside her paranoid mind. He saw it on her face. Her mouth worked soundlessly for a moment and she staggered backward, arm raised to fend off his words.

"Liar!"

"You make me sick, Norma."

Norma's voice screeched through the humid air, words spewing out of her painted mouth like venom. Something moved by the open door. She didn't notice—the door was behind her—but Alex saw it and froze.

A thick stream of ashen smoke slithered snake-like along the gleaming white carpet and he heard his name again, louder this time, but still very distant. Alex stepped backward, surprised he could move. He heard Norma's voice, but her words faded into the background as he watched a rope of mist slowly climb the air behind her, appearing above her head. Her mouth worked tirelessly. Her features became more contorted in the dancing candlelight. She was oblivious to the presence behind her and continued babbling on about demons and hell in a tone filled with insane rapture. Alex watched the smoldering serpentine tendril branch off into long, knotted fingers twisting and curving toward the ceiling before folding down to hover above Norma's bottle blonde head. Pointed talons curved from the tips. Like a nightmarish crown it hovered, curling and straightening its claw-like appendages.

Mrs. Schell stopped talking and glared at him, still holding the pistol at arm's length. Alex had forgotten about the weapon pointed at his face, had forgotten the haunting realization that he'd helped his brother die. He'd even forgotten about Joe and Mary and Jade and Buck and Aala and his mom. The only thing he could focus on was the sinister hand pulsing above Norma Schell's head and the second stream of vapor now creeping along the white carpet directly toward him. The two wriggling tails of mist disappeared into the darkened hallway and he knew exactly where they led. Alex backed away from the oblivious woman, eyes fastened on the unearthly fingers working the air just inches above her halo of yellow hair.

"Wait," he breathed, raising his hand. The second stream wormed closer. Sweat ran into his eyes. His plea came too late. Just as he started to dive out of the way, the thing grabbed her, and Norma reflexively squeezed the trigger. The bullet caught Alex just below his left collar bone. The momentum of his dive pitched him sideways into the mahogany dresser where he crumpled to the pristine white carpet in a shower of framed photos, hand to his chest, bright red streaming through his fingers. A heavy weight pinned him there and he watched, choking on the humid air, as the claw-thing lifted Norma off her feet and began shaking her like a baby rattle, her head snapping from side to side in violent jerks.

Alex couldn't stop himself. "They've come for you, Sister Norma," he gasped, watching a familiar blackness close in from the periphery. "Have a nice trip. I'll see you in hell."

The last thing he saw before that familiar blackness scooped him up in cool arms and carried him away was Norma Schell tumbling, falling, cascading like a colorful waterfall from the apex of the vaulted ceiling and landing on her head with a sickening crack.

part three

What is a friend?
A single soul dwelling in two bodies.

-Aristotle

eight

Sands

The boy Makate went searching for Wabishk, who had run off like it was a game, but instead found Old Man surrounded by snow and sitting beneath a confused tree that looked like a broken spider. Makate sat with Old Man for a long time while he played a flute and let the wind whisper secrets in his ear, then asked, "Akiwenzii, why does Wabishk run so far?"

Old Man stopped his song and lowered his flute, keeping his eyes closed. "Because the fear is in him, and it pulls him along like a strong gust of wind."

"Can I hold him so he does not run?"

Old Man said, "Yes, but the wind is strong and does not lie."

The boy Makate asked, "Will it help if I sing to him?"

"Oh, yes," Akiwenzii told him. "It is the music that guides, it is the music that heals."

Makate said, "Debwewin nindakonamawaa," and stood up on the soft snow, but the ground kept moving under his feet and he could not stand straight to hold Wabishk's truth. The broken spider tree leaned far over to whisper something into his ear, but he did not hear. He watched Wabishk walk across the desert sand with his heart in his hands and became frightened. Then he heard Old Man's voice in the song of the flute.

"Hold him very tightly so you don't fall."

Makate leapt to the top branch of the spider tree and pounced on Wabishk, wrapping his body around his brother and letting the lying wind come.

Makate's song filled the vastness, and still Wabishk fought him.

~

The looking glass flickered, brightened into a solid wall of white light. Alex shaded his eyes with both arms and let the light embrace him. Someone called from the other side of the glass, but it wasn't Jade. This voice sounded childlike and much more frightened—the same voice that had beckoned him to Joe's room that bloody night almost a year ago. From somewhere within and beyond the glass, he heard the child scream and begin to cry in heart-wrenching wails. The sobs rose and fell then faded into troubling silence.

"Luke?" His own voice trailed toward him as though from a very far distance.

Alex heard his name again. A shock of fear rattled his senses. *But there's no fear here. Only light and warmth.* He dropped one arm from his face and held out the other for balance. Sliding his shoes along the carpet, he moved toward the illuminated mirror like a blind man feeling his way until he stood inches from the glass. Brilliant luminescence enveloped him, surrounding him with heat and an unmistakable sense of peace and calm. Water poured from his eyes, drenching his face with salty tears as he peered up through the streaming rays at Joe's bedroom ceiling. It seemed so far away.

Someone said his name again, the small voice scared, weak, alone. Blinded, Alex raised his hand to touch the glass, but there was nothing solid there. Only glaring light and a tired, hopeless voice whispering from its depths.

Another long primal wail followed by soft shuddering sobs.

Alex swiped at his face, held out both his hands, and walked further into the light. Something grabbed, and he yanked his hands back. Familiar fingers locked with his, urging him forward, deeper into the warmth, into the peace. A child whispered his name from below and above and suddenly the guiding hands were gone. Unable to see, Alex took a step backward, hot panic washing through his senses.

"Jade?" He heard the echo of fear in his voice.

A child answered.

Alex closed his eyes against the blinding white nimbus and nodded, knowing. "I'm coming, Luke."

Alex held his breath and sprinted headlong into the light. One final thought drifted through his mind before he realized he was falling—*the wicked shall find no way to escape, their only hope is death.*

He landed hard on his right side and convulsed as jolts of hot pain shot through his body. Twitching with each agonizing arc, Alex tried to catch the breath that had been knocked out of him on impact. He lay there, legs and arms spasming against the ground.

A drumbeat found him on a steady rush of wind. Alex realized he still had his eyes closed and that the colorful streamers of light he'd fallen through were gone. Red fire licked at him from beyond his closed eyelids. He didn't want to look, didn't want to see the hell he'd been pulled into. Nausea took hold. Groaning, he rolled onto his knees and threw up, bathing his hands in steaming vomit. He retched a second time, heaving until his ribs hurt and his throat burned. His skin prickled and tingled in electric jolts. His head felt heavy and his mind whispered from darkness. *Welcome to hell. Enjoy your stay.*

Alex stood on his knees. He put his filthy hands over his face and with every ounce of will he possessed opened his eyes. No deformed demons stood ready to attack. No blackened pits spit hellfire. No human souls roasted by their heels over glowing coals. There was only him, the raging sun low in the azure sky, and a snow-white desert stretching toward the horizon in all directions, the sand rippling gently in the soundless wind.

Alex knew where he was. He let out a long breath and pulled a handful of sand from the ground. The powder sifted between his fingers onto his faded jeans and clung there, held by the salty clear fluid that had drenched his clothes, hair and skin. He scooped up fistfuls of desert and rubbed it on his arms and hands, scraping away the quickly drying vomit. An orange orb of sun blazed hot as he got to his feet. Between the soft earth and his quivering legs, it took some time to find his balance. He stood for some time, scanning the familiar white vastness, a silent breeze brushing over him. Alex shuddered and shaded his eyes, looking up at the sky. Smooth and cloudless, it stretched down to meet the desert in the distance. A speck of white appeared against the indigo heavens then vanished, making him think he hadn't seen it at all.

Compact sand filled his shoes as he walked, but he ambled on, following the faint drumbeat, ignoring the increasing weight of his feet, searching the vastness for a lone Joshua tree and a tiny dancing man with hair down to his toes.

June 9, 1984

The bedroom door stood wide open. When Elizabeth looked in on her way to the kitchen, she had to catch herself on the jamb to keep from falling. Luke's room looked like a tornado had touched down, destroying everything that had the misfortune of being in its path. Spilled juice and broken glass sprayed hundreds of sheets of music, all written in Alex's broad scrawl. Broken biplanes, twin beeches, ancient bombers and space age jets littered the floor from wall to wall, but it was the sight of Alex's smashed violin that brought tears to her eyes. She knelt and picked up the splintered neck. Every string had been ripped from its hold, leaving ugly gouges in the wood. The only thing left unharmed and intact was Luke's carved wooden owl—the one he'd made with Mary when he was just four—whose broad wings began to move as she watched. A single sheet of music hung from its carved beak. *Luke's Flight.* Elizabeth scanned the page. Dropping the remains of her son's violin, she ran to the bookcase at the end of the hall and pulled down Grammy's old Bible. Flipping through, Elizabeth found Job 11:20 and read. "But the wicked shall find no way to escape; their only hope is death."

Hands shaking, she pulled on a rain slicker, grabbed her keys, and tried to go the speed limit all the way to the hospital. The words Mary had spoken during their visit the day before looped through her mind like a needle stuck in a record groove. The old woman had talked of living spirits and conjoined souls, of guiding music and soul-killing shadows, of layers of suffering and redemption, and then put some stones in her hand and told her to believe. Elizabeth shuddered, remembering Mary's final, cryptic refrain. *Without truth, denial reigns. Without love, fear reigns. Half a spirit cannot exist.*

10:16am

Beyond the heavy drapes and vertical blinds, sunlight fought for equal time with the rolling fog. Elizabeth pushed a wheelchair into ROOM 113 and closed the door before flipping on the light. The thin, gaunt form in the center of the bed remained motionless, the only sound that of a faint motor and periodic beeps from a monitor. For a moment, Elizabeth thought she was in the wrong room. She leaned over the bed and peered into the still figure's white face. She stifled a sob, realizing that the deathly pallid face against the pillow did belong to the little boy she used to shovel hot ginger cookies into on freezing winter afternoons. Fine red spider veins trailed over his eyelids and down the length of his nose. Sharp ridges of bone jutted from below his sunken eyes, which appeared ringed in dark charcoal smudges. His down-turned mouth was open slightly, once ruby lips now cracked and drained of color. The stench of his breath made her nostrils flare. She leaned close and planted a firm kiss on Joe's bluish forehead.

"You're not going anywhere, kid," Elizabeth whispered. She stroked his hair and choked back a cry when a handful of blond strands came loose in her fingers. Lifting his hand, she pressed Joe's palm to her cheek, then gasped at the sticky warmth oozing between his fingers. Bewildered, Elizabeth watched blood flow from a round hole in the center of Joe's palm and then, as suddenly as it had appeared, the scarlet stream vanished, leaving a smooth patch of skin. Shaking, she reached for Joe's other hand and caught sight of the last vestiges of blood as it faded into nothing.

Elizabeth held both of Joe's hands to her face. "It's going to be okay, Joe. You're going to be okay. Don't leave us."

Blinking away tears, Elizabeth lifted a four-foot ficus plant from the seat of the wheelchair and placed it as close to the head of the bed as possible. She put an enormous fern on the window bench and set Mary's stones next to it, an eerie sense of déjà vu picking at her brain.

"I've done this too many times," she mumbled, opening the drapes to a gray Sunday morning. She plugged in Alex's boombox, inserted a cassette tape, and hit the play button. A soft, lilting violin filled the room. Elizabeth smiled. Her son's music always made her smile.

Armed with a toothbrush and toothpaste, cotton swabs and nail clippers, baby wipes and a bottle of lemon sandalwood oil, Elizabeth yanked off Joe's blankets and began the task of helping him remember love.

The man was very small, no taller than an average second grader, and thin-boned but with clear angles in the muscle of his arms and legs. The top of his head barely came to Alex's ribs, his dark face a maze of fine lines and deep cracks that looked like they should hurt. He wore a simple white wrap around his narrow waist, which fluttered and blew in gusting streams of air that Alex could feel but not hear. The drum was smaller than it sounded and hung by a leather rope from the man's narrow neck. The echoing sound of it seemed not to come from the black stretched canvas at all, but from inside the man's own body. *Like a heartbeat,* Alex thought, entranced. The man's long, knotted salt-pepper hair flew around his body, set in motion by the soundless wind and his movements as he danced a strange dance, seemingly oblivious to Alex's presence a few yards away.

The enormous Joshua tree's elongated limbs reached into the clear indigo sky, looking like a crazed, multi-legged creature trying to decide which way to go. It did not cast a shadow across the desert sand, despite the orb of sun at the horizon, nor did the man cast a shadow as he stomped the earth, sending great puffs of white powder into the air from his feet. Alex's misshapen shadow stretched across the ground as far as he could see. Frowning, he opened his mouth then shut it when the man stopped his dance and lifted his hands above his head, fingers spread wide. He stood very still for a very long time. Alex stepped forward, feeling the pulse in his temples quicken. The man turned a half circle and strode the few paces to where Alex stood. He stopped, bare toes touching Alex's shoes, and tilted his head back, face expressionless yet oddly alive with motion … laughing … crying … birthing … dying … *with stories*, Alex thought.

Alex peered down into the face he'd seen in his dreams since childhood and studied every line, curve and crevice. The man had no eyebrows and Alex wondered if the hot sun had withered and blown them away. The iris of the man's left eye blazed as white as the desert sand, the other glowed as black as his ebony skin. His pointed cheekbones threatened to poke through the parched skin of his face, full lips pursed slightly in what Alex read as mild amusement. Slowly, the corners of the man's mouth turned upward, and Alex waited for him to tell him what he needed to know. But the man did not speak. He looked deeply into Alex's eyes, unwavering and unblinking, and Alex reached out to touch a deep crease at the man's right cheek. Alex raised his other hand and touched the coarse hair hanging in twisted spirals to the man's heels. He expected a shock of realization, a clear path revealed, all questions answered, but the profound sense of power and knowing he had dreamed about didn't come. After tracing every webbed line and curve of the man's familiar face, Alex found his voice.

"Am I dead?" He didn't take his hands off the dancing man's warm skin.

Without speaking or moving away, the man brought his hands close to Alex's face and smacked his palms together in a sharp clap, barely missing the tip of Alex's nose. Alex blinked with a startled jolt. The man smiled, flashing a mouthful of brilliant white teeth, the creases in his face deepening, and Alex had the strange, gut-heavy feeling that this man knew everything there was to know.

The man spun on his bare heels and danced away, kicking up clouds of sand as he went. Alex followed, knowing with deep profundity that he had just spent several extraordinary moments staring into the time-ravaged face of God.

12:01pm

Elizabeth saw a tall, dark-haired young man standing alone in a desert of snow. He did not seem afraid, but she sensed a needle of fear piercing his calm demeanor. He walked across the ground, leaving a trail of footprints in the sand, which quickly disappeared with the wind. He stopped and stood very still, listening. He turned in slow circles, scanning the distance in all directions, then broke into a full-throttle run. At that moment, she saw it. The shadow trailing across the sand from his heels transformed, becoming elongated and crooked-limbed. It grew to a hideously monstrous size, separating itself from the young man's feet as he ran. The thing loped after him, twisted fingers dragging in the sand, leaving rivers of blood in the deep ruts.

The young man looked over his shoulder, fighting to keep his footing, but couldn't get far enough out of the beast's reach to escape. The monster locked its malformed hand around the young man and yanked him to the ground before grabbing his head and opening its needle-toothed mouth wide. Before it clamped its jagged jaws onto the struggling boy's head it turned, and Elizabeth saw the creature's distorted face. Alex's wild animal eyes glared out of the thing's incorporeal skull, looking directly at her for a single moment before sinking spiked teeth into the terrified boy's face. The sound of bones caving and splintering reached her ears. A musky-sweet smell permeated the air and she realized it was the innocence being drained from her son's body …

Elizabeth slid out of the chair and landed on her butt on the hard hospital room floor. Dazed, she swiped drool from her mouth and tried to orient herself. The room was dark, but she sensed someone with her other than the still figure on the bed.

Something moved. By the door. Something big.

She scrambled to her feet and hit the buttons for the headboard light and the nurse at the same time. The light on the wall above Joe's head flickered before steadying.

No one.

Heart hammering, Elizabeth sank back into the chair and tried to clear the cobwebs from her mind. Her head throbbed.

The door flew open and a very tall, very handsome man rushed into the room. His eyes grew wide when he saw her, and he stopped short. He stood there like a deer caught in the mesmerizing glow of headlights then stepped forward and extended his hand, a smile inching across his expressive face.

Elizabeth eyed him, noticing his perfectly shaped bald head, his kind smile, and the almost imperceptible ruby stud in his left earlobe.

"You're Doctor Rom," she said.

The man raised his eyebrows.

"Elizabeth. Alex's mom."

"Good genes run in the family," the doctor said, then shook his head in an expression of instant regret. "I didn't mean that in a creepy way. I just never would've believed you have an eighteen-year-old son if I didn't already know it as fact. You could be his sister."

Elizabeth stood, took his still-extended hand, and whispered, "Now *that* would be creepy."

Rom chuckled, shaking his head again. "I'm sorry. That was very unprofessional."

Elizabeth smiled again, noticing the warmth of the man's demeanor. *No wonder Alex likes this guy. Good bedside manner.* She slipped her hand out of his and sat down, legs unsteady, and reached for a cup of water. Soft violin music filled the room and she realized the boombox was set on a loop and had been going for nearly three hours straight.

"Ah, Ludwig. Is that Alex playing?"

Elizabeth nodded, rubbing her forehead.

"I thought it was Alex when I saw the light go on at the front station. He's the only one who comes to see Joe. I was surprised to find someone else here. Obviously." Rom grinned again.

Elizabeth nodded, forehead tightening. "Has Alex come by in the last couple of days?"

"No, but I'm usually gone by the time most people start their day. I get here between nine and ten at night and try to leave before noon, depending on what's going on around here. We've probably just missed each other the past few days."

"Probably." Elizabeth pulled at her bottom lip, recalling Luke's beaten planes piled on the floor, Alex's ruined violin.

Rom sat on the foot of Joe's bed. "Is Alex okay?"

"I don't know," Elizabeth said. "I haven't seen him since night before last." She swiped at her nose and looked into Rom's intelligent brown eyes before resting her worried gaze on Joe's deathly pale face.

"How long have you been here?"

Elizabeth glanced at the wall clock. "Not long. But I'm not going anywhere, so don't try to get rid of me."

"That's the last thing I'd want to do," Rom said, sitting in the chair by the bed. "In addition to your presence and the music being good for Joe, now I've got someone to talk to besides Mister Conversation here." He patted Joe's leg. "We both win."

"Alex says Joe's going to die."

Rom's face suddenly looked very tired. He glanced at Joe then down at his folded hands. "He's weakening. He doesn't respond to stimuli. MRIs indicate that the emotional control structures of his brain are shutting down. As a man of medicine, I'm not sure he'll make it. As a human being, I wish to god he would. I'd sure like to meet this kid."

Elizabeth watched the doctor's expressive face as he spoke. She heard the tenderness and caring in his tone and thought, *this is what a man should be.*

The doctor looked at her. "My telling you all that was a blatant violation of patient privacy. Also, very unprofessional."

Elizabeth smiled and held her finger to her lips. "Our secret."

Rom's pager went off, startling her, just as the door swept open and a stout young man wearing surgical scrubs rushed

into the room. "Doctor David, they need you in emergen—"
The intern stopped short, eyeing Elizabeth. His eyes shifted from Rom's face to hers while he stammered.

Rom stood. "I'm on my way, Greg."

Greg stepped closer to Rom. "It's that kid, that violinist you like. Gunshot wound—"

Elizabeth shot out of her chair. Rom made a grab for her arm, but she was already out the door and standing in the hallway, trying to decide which way to go.

"Hold on," Rom said, following her.

Elizabeth took Greg's shoulder as the intern tried to brush by. "What happened? Where is he!"

"Elizabeth," Rom started. She looked at him and he must have seen the nineteen years' worth of worry and heartache in her eyes because he reached out, touched her arm, and gave it a reassuring squeeze. "We'll go together."

Elizabeth walked with Rom, trying to keep her breaths even. She coached herself as she often coached Alex during his panic attacks. *In through the nose, out through the mouth, in through the nose out through …* They arrived outside a double-door and Rom turned.

"You have to wait here."

"No," she said, starting past him.

The doctor took her gently by the shoulders. "Elizabeth," he said in a calm baritone. The tone of his voice had an immediate grounding effect on her, and she reminded herself not to lose her shit. She stepped back and nodded, keeping the tears at bay.

Rom disappeared into the room for an eternity.

2:37pm

"Someone, a Miss Carpenter, called nine-one-one after hearing what she thought was a gunshot while out walking her dog." Rom put a cup of hot coffee into Elizabeth's cold hands. "When the paramedics arrived, a woman—Schell—" Rom stopped and looked at her. "Guessing I know who that is. She told them there were demons in her house and that they were trying to kill her."

Elizabeth never took her eyes off Alex's sedated form on the bed. *So still,* she thought.

"She was completely irrational," Rom continued. "When they found her, she was in the hallway dragging herself toward the stairs and babbling about how demons had broken loose and were coming to take her back with them. Seems she has a history of mental illness. We don't know what happened exactly yet, but they found Alex in this woman's son's room—also guessing I know who that is—bleeding from a bullet wound in his chest. Missed his aortic artery by centimeters."

Elizabeth watched her son breathe. "She shot him."

Rom sat in a chair and cleared his throat. "Something went sideways in that house, Elizabeth. A firearm was discharged. Do you think Alex might have gone there to provoke—"

"I have to talk to her," Elizabeth interrupted, pushing the doctor's words out of her mind. *Alex would never hurt a living thing.*

Rom sighed. "I'll let you in, but it won't do any good. She's unconscious. They sedated her in the ambulance because she put up such a fight. She doesn't know who she is, let alone who you are, so don't expect to get any information out of her, especially anything that might make sense."

They boarded the elevator and rode up two floors. Outside Norma's hospital room, Rom stopped and looked around.

"The police have to be notified when she wakes up, so they can take an official statement," he said. "Remember, Elizabeth, she isn't coherent. I don't know what you expect to gain by going in there now. You should wait a couple of days and then try to talk to her."

Elizabeth pushed past him. Rom followed.

Leather straps with silver buckles bound Norma Schell's arms and legs to the railings of the bed. A padded plastic vest encased her torso; metal rods attached to the middle of the vest jutted upward, bolted to the steel halo encircling her forehead. She was completely immobilized, make-up smeared like a garish mask across her swollen face. Norma muttered in her drug-induced sleep, but Elizabeth could make no sense of the woman's words—until she heard Alex's name. She stepped closer and leaned in. Norma's eyelids fluttered as if she were trying to wake up, but the drugs in her bloodstream held her captive in fitful slumber.

She mumbled Alex's name again, but it meant nothing.

Elizabeth steeled herself against the rage knotting in her abdomen. *What kind of person would shoot a kid?*

"She has a couple of fractured vertebrae in her lower cervical and a serious concussion," Rom said. "Not sure yet what the outcome will be, but her left arm and leg seem to be affected."

"Serves you right," Elizabeth whispered.

"Took him … took him," the woman slurred, clenching her right hand into a tight ball.

Now Rom stepped closer and peered at Norma.

"Satan's claw," Norma hissed, tightening her fist. "Took him … hell."

Elizabeth straightened at Norma's words.

"It's the meds talking," Rom said.

"No," Elizabeth breathed. "It's not."

She spun around, headed for the door, threw it open, and broke into a run for the elevator. Rom's voice boomed behind her, but she paid no attention. She didn't slow down until the humid afternoon air hit her skin, and then it was only to grope in her pocket for the car keys. Elusive thoughts skidded through her numbed mind, but one seemed all too familiar. And there was something else, something she could no longer deny, a gnawing feeling she'd had since finding Alex's cryptic note hanging from the wooden owl's beak. Through the panicked haze of her mind, Elizabeth began to comprehend Mary's insistent story about Alex and Joe—that they were two halves of one spirit, each protecting the other. Able to 'see inside' the old woman always said.

A panic so pure and hot washed over Elizabeth that she started to weep and found that she could not stop. Mary had always known, had seen it the day she'd held Alex's tiny breathing body in her strong hands, and Joe's, too. Now Elizabeth understood also. Words like *inseparable, able to read one another's mind, twins born of different wombs, the sharing* drifted like wayward ghosts out of the past. For eighteen years she had denied the obvious, looking, searching, hunting for any other possible explanation.

But now she knew.

Half a spirit cannot exist.

The words screamed through her head as she drove back to Cutters Grove through layers of fog. Elizabeth joined the chanting in her head. "The wicked shall find no way to escape, their only hope is death."

The small man stopped. Alex, lost in thought, almost ran into him. He'd led Alex away from the Joshua tree and up an incline. Shading his eyes against the harsh sunlight, Alex turned in circles and scanned the rippling sea of sand stretching in all directions. He lowered his hands and looked at the man.

"Which way?" He wondered if the man was ever going to speak, let alone lead him to Joe.

"You're asking the wrong questions," the man said, his voice much deeper and booming than seemed possible for someone of such diminutive stature.

"You have a problem, son," the man continued. "Your mind harbors fear. Fear is the opposite of love. You want to find peace and salvation and forgiveness. You want to take your friend back, to rescue him, but you want this for only yourself, because you are afraid to die. Love is the way. Not easy, but simple. And the outcome may not be what is hoped for. The illusion can be strong, but everyone must one day face what they have created. There is no wrong answer. There is no right answer. But there are outcomes."

Alex squinted at the man. "I thought you'd never speak."

"I speak Truth," the man said. "It is my language. The fact that you can understand me means it is your language, too. It means you are one step closer."

"To finding Joe?"

"That is not the question."

"Okay. Who are you?"

"I have many names, but I like Te. It's short and easy to pronounce, but also sounds powerful, yes?"

"Te," Alex repeated. "What is this place?"

The man squinted, the crevices around his eyes deepening even more. "You tell me. You created it."

Alex frowned and shook his head. "I didn't—"

The man smiled, the stories in his face livening.

Alex stepped closer to the man and forced the words out in a rushed whisper. "Is this the *wakwi?* Th-the afterlife?"

"Like me, this place has many names. But what you see here, Alex, is only a reflection of the contents of your mind, your consciousness, sent back to you by the mirror of truth, the mirror of evolution. It will be important to remember that."

Alex frowned and shook his head again. "I don't understand."

"I know." Te smiled. "Think of it as one of many *betweens.* One of many layers."

"Layers of what?"

"You tell me," Te said again. The features of his face changed then, darkened into a riot of conflict and battle.

"The challenge is that this is not your between alone. It is a shared place, and that complicates things."

"Joe," Alex stated.

"Yes. Among others. More reflections, more truths, more stones."

"I have to find him and take him back."

The man looked deeply into Alex's eyes. "Why?"

Alex blinked, confused by the question. "What do you mean *why?*"

"Is the question not clear?" the man said, gaze unwavering. His voice seemed to travel from the ether. It was everywhere and nowhere.

"He's my friend," Alex stated. "I don't want him to die."

Te nodded. "I know you believe that. But your belief comes from fear, not from knowing."

Alex tried to keep his desperation at bay and Buck's voice saying *no more fear* out of his head.

"Do you know where Joe is or not?"

"He is not near, and he is not far. Remember there are layers. *Betweens.*" The man did not break eye contact.

"Between what?"

"You have all that you need right here." Te placed his small palm on Alex's chest and looked into his eyes. "I believe in you, Alex. Perhaps right now that is everything."

Te glanced up at the sapphire sky as if waiting for something to fall from it.

"People have it wrong about redemption," he said. "No one can redeem another. It must come from the inside, from a place of knowing and accepting the truth that things could not be any different than they are." Te paused. "Do you remember when Joe was with you after Luke died?"

Alex took a step back at the unexpected question. "N-nobody knows about that except us."

The man smiled. "Show him. Understand. Understand?"

"But I don't know which direction to take."

Te tilted his face to the sky and smiled. "Hmm," he said as though tasting something delicious. "It is good to have choices."

Shadowless, the man danced away in a cloud of fine powder, a steady rhythm of drumbeats riding on the soundless wind.

Joe heard his own voice through the mechanical grinding that had grown louder during the past minute—hour?—day?—week?—he didn't know how long.

"Yes," he mumbled in a languid haze. "I remember."

He sucked on the filter of a pocket-mangled cigarette and held the smoke deep. A red-tinged fog swirled through his head, whispering, filling his mind with movement, color and fear. He stared into the pinkish air as it opened, parting like a sluggish red sea through that telescopic lens. Beyond the snaking tendrils of ruby smoke, he saw a woman and a child, bathed in fluorescent light. Joe looked up from where he sat on the soft sand and saw a ceiling—the same ceiling he'd stared up at as he lay in a bath of his own blood, waiting to die. Small clothes lay in bunches by the open door. Plastic covered the yellow tile floor. The kid stood motionless, covering his penis with both hands. He shook, knees knocking together, and Joe felt goose bumps rise on the boy's thin arms and legs. Limbs and head heavy with exhaustion and powerlessness, Joe tried to crawl across the sucking sand to the little boy standing naked in the bathtub, wanting only to wrap himself around the kid's tiny body and protect him from what was coming.

The woman loomed over the tub and stared down at the boy. She held a large stainless-steel bucket above the boy's head and whispered, *the blood is the way.* Joe mouthed her poison words, crawling closer on his hands and knees, the sand pulling. *The blood of the Holy Lamb will cleanse your sinful soul.* The little boy nodded, tears appearing in his clear blue eyes, but he didn't dare cry. He jerked when the crimson liquid splashed over his back and shoulders, showering his shaking body and mixing with the shallow water around his ankles. He didn't flinch at all when she poured the thick fluid over his chest, arms and belly, but he did close his eyes and tighten his hold on his penis.

She muttered fervently while she worked, concentrating on the words of her prayers, spit flying off her painted lips. Light from overhead glinted off the lipstick on her teeth, making her mouth seem bigger than it was. Big enough to take a bite out of his soul, big enough to gnaw into his very being.

Joe writhed in the sand, hands pressed into his crotch, mind straining against his skull, mouth forming the words that the little boy could not. "Don't, don't, don't," he chanted. "I'm clean, Mama. I promise. I promise. I'm clean *you fucking BITCH!*"

She held a big red gardening bucket over the boy's head and poured ice-cold water over him, still mumbling, sweat beading on her stenciled brow. Joe jerked against the ground, groaning. The boy stood stone still and silent now, moving only with the force of the water when it hit his skin.

I forgive you. You will read now, Joe said, mirroring the woman's painted lips. *Two hours until your father comes home. I want verse later.*

Fighting the tremors wracking his small body, the boy nodded and stepped onto the plastic tarp. The woman left, closing the door behind her, and Joe caught a fragment of the little boy's thoughts—*I have a whole week till next time. A whole week!*

The red curtain of haze closed as slowly as it had split, and Joe's last glimpse of the child was of him reaching for a black leather-bound Bible and opening it. "There can be no forgiveness without the shedding of blood," the boy read.

Joe nodded, closing his eyes, hands pressed tightly between his legs.

When he opened his eyes a minute—hour?—day?—week?—later, the scene had changed and the hoarse muttering in the darkness had grown closer, colder, hotter.

Absently, Joe had dug a hole through each palm with the wedge of TV glass. He held up his hands and squinted, only able to see darkened smudges. The earthy scent of fresh blood filled his nostrils and he realized he was hungry. *So very hungry.* He licked his lips and put his tongue into the hole of his left palm, sucking at the sweetsalt fluid. Then he used the precious drops to write the words on his pale skin

strings

life

fly

forgive

die

He slipped the sharp wedge of glass into the front pocket of his jeans with his lighter and pulled his knees up to his blood-streaked chest. Joe closed his eyes and thought of a time in another life. A time when he felt joy and light running through his veins instead of boiling guilt and shame. A time when he could fly without effort. A time when he could cry.

Then the scenes in his head shifted and he had the sensation of watching again from very far away through a telescopic lens. A white curtain of haze parted. A procession of doleful, sagging faces marched robotically through his house and took their seats, some crying, some stone-faced, some abnormally vacant as if trying to remember if they had turned the stove off before leaving the house. Many rushed to the painted woman's side to offer support and sympathy—mostly other painted women, with strained botoxed smiles etched into their faces. Fresh lilies filled every vase. A gust of wind belched through the open living room window, sending several vases toppling off the table where casseroles had been set. Because people bring food in times of crisis. In times of abandonment and uncertainty. The wind belched again and lilies sailed through the air in seemingly slow motion. One of them smacked fat Mrs. Dugan on the head and she stumbled backwards as if struck by a stray arrow.

A blond boy watched it all with empty fascination. No one noticed him as he walked to the extravagant altar his mother had set up so the churchies could light vigil candles and pretend to care. Money sat piled in an offering basket, so the poor abandoned woman could provide for her poor abandoned son. Faint bits of conversation reached the boy's ears and he wondered why everyone was talking backward and nothing made sense. Fire licked at his face. He stood on tiptoes and watched in silent rapture as flames bobbed and wavered on the wicks directly in front of his eyes. He counted ten, same as his age. Beyond the fire he glimpsed a stranger watching from the glass of a mirror. A boy like him—trapped—with glassy dead eyes.

The boy touched a flame. Fire encircled his fingertip and a tangy scent filled his nostrils. His fingernail turned red, then ash gray, then black. It bubbled and warped like a plastic milk jug left too close to a hot burner. A thin stream of sour-smelling smoke twisted into the air from under his finger and he watched, captivated by its easy swaying grace. The smoke took part of him away. It lifted him and carried him to a safe place. A place of warm white sand and clear azure skies. No one noticed him. For the first time, the boy was invisible.

A whispery growl filled Joe's head. *They never wanted you. You belong here.*

Something blistering cold brushed his arm, grasping, taking hold. He knew he couldn't outrun them forever. They'd keep working on him, untying him one memory at a time, weakening him. Joe got to his feet and staggered farther into the darkness, the stinging taste of blood still caressing his tongue, the stink of burning flesh still lodged in his nose, but the thing followed, reached, caught, dragged. Joe flailed against the sand, screaming at the heat searing his mind, but it had him now and the familiarity of it made him grow still, open his eyes, and laugh.

nine

Ghosts

Mary danced the dance, bare feet tracking a circular counterclockwise path through the cedar dust on the floor and keeping time with the melancholy drone of a single drum that no one else could hear. Her Grandmother Whitewing's shroud of fine white feathers hugged her shoulders, fanning from her back. The shadows cast by these giant wings resembled a bird in flight, circling, circling.

"Father Sky, Mother Earth, Grandmother Whitewing, whose counsel I hear in the winds and the waters. I am called Mary of the *binenhshiinh* and *waawaashkesh doodeman,* and your children are suffering. I come to you as one of many children of the Bird and Deer clans. Hear my prayer ..."

She sang an invocation to her ancestors asking to open her eyes once more to the shadowlands, and the veils parted. There, she glimpsed the dark and lonely place. She heard the tormentors, merciless and unforgiving. She heard a child scream into empty blackness. She felt a glimmer of hope, a light of triumph.

"Oh, wise friend of Thunderbird, come now with wings outspread in dark and rain-drenched skies. Oh, wise friend of Deer, come now and bring us peace and gentle understanding. Oh, wise friend, come now and give new hope and guidance to the young in our nest ...

Her heart beat faster. Her rhythmic summons had stopped the rain outside, and she knew her plea had been heard. She reached out her arms and held her hands as if in offering, but it was a receiving that she had prayed for and on a breath of wind through the open window it came, and landed.

"Hello, mischief!" Mary exclaimed.

The white owl perched in her open palms danced and fluttered its wings, then hopped to her shoulder and buried its face in the long hair at her neck. She stroked its feathers, tears in her eyes.

"Thank you for coming," she whispered. "There is work to be done. *Booch igo ji-niimiyaan, giin dash da-bimiseyan.* I must dance, and you must fly. It's time."

The bird let out a soft warbly coo, spread its wings wide and lifted into the air. It flew near the ceiling in a clock-wise direction, circling, circling. Mary danced, turning in the opposite direction, the wings on her back beating in a steady rhythm. The shadow of the white owl above inter-sected with the shadow of Mary's wings below. Together, they churned the dark winds. The magnificent shadow sep-arated from Mary's heels and flew high to meet the white owl. Darkness and light danced together, soaring along the walls, finding their way, and came to rest on the chest of the young man lying on the bed.

Mary continued the dance and her prayer for some time and when she stopped, she stood with eyes closed for sev-eral minutes seeing into the shadowlands and the realms of the backward way. Then she brought her hands up and clapped them once with joy.

No one heard the beat of the drum or the sounds of an-cient song and prayer rising and falling within Joe Schell's hospital room. No one saw her leave.

It was as though Mary Whitewing had never been there.

It was with him now. A cold, blackfire presence. Inside. Out-side. A collective. Red eyes ablaze. Flames for hands at the end of long twisted limbs. Needles for teeth to pierce and tear.

And it did.

The beast squeezed his neck, stretched his spine, severed his head, flung it far. It pulled his fingers off one at a time, his toes, too. His hands. His feet. Dismembering him, disintegrating him one piece at a time. One bite at a time.

His legs.

His arms.

Wrenched, rended, far-flung, pieced out, dripping flesh and sinew. Flames charred his skin.

The beast sliced open his chest, his belly, reached in, pulled out, ate. Devoured.

Mind. Body. Soul. Sanity.

It cracked open his skull. Licked his brain with a tongue of fire. Drank his blood. Drained. Gnawed his bones, tossed them aside, began again.

A freight-train roared, and Joe screamed and screamed and screamed …

… the beast squeezed his neck, stretched his spine, severed his head, flung it far. It pulled his fingers off one at a time, his toes, too. His hands. His feet. Dismembering him, disintegrating him one piece at a time. One bite at a time.

His legs.

His arms.

Wrenched, rended, far-flung, pieced out, dripping flesh and sinew. Flames charred his skin.

The beast sliced open his chest, his belly, reached in, pulled out, ate. Devoured.

Mind. Body. Soul. Sanity.

It cracked open his skull. Licked his brain with a tongue of fire. Drank his blood. Drained. Gnawed his bones, tossed them aside, began again.

A freight-train roared, and Joe screamed and screamed and screamed …

… the beast squeezed his neck, stretched his spine, severed his head, flung it far. It pulled his fingers off one at a time, his toes, too. His hands. His feet. Dismembering him, disintegrating him one piece at a time. One bite at a time.

His legs.

His arms.

Wrenched, rended, far-flung, pieced out, dripping flesh and sinew. Flames charred his skin.

The beast sliced open his chest, his belly, reached in, pulled out, ate. Devoured.

Mind. Body. Soul. Sanity.

It cracked open his skull. Licked his brain with a tongue of fire. Drank his blood. Drained. Gnawed his bones, tossed them aside, began again.

A freight-train roared, and Joe screamed and screamed and screamed ...

... the beast squeezed his neck, stretched his spine, severed his head ...

All the while, a child wept in long tortured wails and the words wrote themselves in neon red on the darkness

scars

        fault

             blood

                     sacrifice

lamb

       limb

              stay

                   kill

The child's high-pitched screeching rose and fell like a siren, blending with the roar of a train and the voice filling his head. It was everywhere. Inside, outside. A collective.

Look into the mirror and see your sins, your true self. Rid him of pain. Quench his agony. Kill the child, your innocence, and become strong. You are the only one who can silence the screams forever. Save him. Sacrifice him. You know what must be done.

Something inside him snapped. Hot hatred surged upward from his bowels, spreading throughout his body like a seeping poison. It filmed over his eyes. He saw only red rage, tinged with yellow shame, shot through with the nauseating green of contempt. He would find the screaming child. He would tear open his weak little body, rip his innards to shreds, until only an empty silent carcass remained. He would relish it. He would at last have the blessed silence he longed for.

Reassembled once more, strength returned to warm his limbs. It spiked his blood, made his feet and hands spasm. Power rushed to every part of his body, nourishing with sweet resolve. He would feed on baby flesh, a hungry ghost like the others. His prey screamed out from the magenta darkness, desperate to be heard.

Joe began to sing.

Raised tendrils of sand snaked across the desert floor, rippling toward the skyline. The hot sun, frozen at the horizon, showed no signs of subsiding and he guessed that was good—he wouldn't have to deal with night and the terror that always came with it. He pulled the back of his sweatshirt up over his head, leaving his T-shirt to protect his bare skin, but even that offered no protection against the blazing sun. When he had finally left Te and started walking, he realized he was being pulled toward something. Whether that something was good or bad, he didn't know. Mary had said there were demons in the *wakwi*. Alex had no reason to doubt her. The sound of Te's drum filled the air. Although Alex figured he had to be miles from the dancing man by now, he thought he heard random words on the silent wind—Te's voice—but dismissed it as wishful thinking, a result of dehydration and fatigue. But then Alex heard the man's voice loud and clear in his head and whirled around, stumbling.

All things die. Even hope.

"Not Joe. Not me. Not yet," Alex croaked.

You want to save him for your own sake, not for his.

"Death means defeat."

You are no stranger to me, Te's voice boomed.

"I don't know what to do," Alex called out to the vastness.

"People wear masks. People hide. His darkness will find you. It always has. Open your hands."

Alex stopped short and looked down at his hands, clenched tight in front of him as if ready to fight. He opened them, stretched them wide, and looked again into the distance. On the horizon, a dark blot hung low to the ground. Thinking it had to be some sort of mirage, he squinted through the streaming sunlight and wiped his eyes. From somewhere within the darkened mass came a child's cry—the same cry that had prompted him to run blindly into the light in Joe's room. The same cry that had spoken to the deepest wound in his heart. The same cry he'd heard as his brother's grasp had loosened and released. *Boot on the tracks with the blood bones.*

Alex ran—slowly at first, the soft sand sucking at his shoes—then halted when he felt an overwhelming sense of evil lurking within that wall of churning darkness. Someone—something—was watching, waiting. He could feel its hunger.

The ground shifted. Once. Twice. Alex watched as the black storm grew bigger, wider taller. Closer. The tempest pulsed like a diseased heart, smoky tendrils trailing into the cobalt sky like throbbing arteries. Alex clapped his hands over his ears, trying to drown out the deafening freight train sound emanating from the rushing darkness, then turned and ran in the direction he'd come. With every step, the roaring snarl grew louder, forming words that growled in his ear, words he knew he shouldn't ignore, yet couldn't help but try. *That's right boy, run so I can have him all to myself.*

You're such a pussy, Al.

Alex skidded to a halt and spun around, sweat streaming into his wide eyes. Eyeing the storm, he set his jaw and planted his feet, watching the ominous darkness roll across the white sand, reaching for him with gnarled talons. The wave picked him up and slammed him into the ground, making his teeth clack together. A great howl and thunderous boom shook his insides. He landed on his injured shoulder and cried out, hissing air, struggling against the sweeping wind to get upright. Lifted again, he couldn't find ground. Stinging grains of sand spit into his eyes and he clamped them closed, fighting for balance in the surging gusts threw him violently in every direction, at once smashing him into the ground and again flinging him high. Then, without warning, the turbulence calmed, the wind dissipated, and he crashed to the sand on his belly, all the air leaving his lungs. He lay there, panting, clutching at the grainy earth.

Alex pried open his grit-filled eyes.

Darkness—complete and absolute—encased him, pressed in, its suffocating coolness like stinging ice on his flesh. A bone penetrating chill wracked his body. He started to shake. His breath hitched and caught in his throat. Pure panic took hold. Alex whirled around, looking for light. A speck. Anything.

Nothing.

He began to scream.

In the dark void, Joe heard the tortured wails and his hunger deepened. He grinned, pinpointing where the sound was coming from, and started towards it, trudging through the neon red and purple tinge of the air. These screams sounded out of place, a different kind of terror. He knew these screams, had heard them before—on the inside, in the sharing. He recognized the spaces in between them, the silence he longed for. He switched directions, simultaneously annoyed that someone new occupied his world of shadow and amused at the possibility of satiating his desire to add more red to the air. He would have to temporarily interrupt his search for the wailing little shit and the ghostbitch protecting him, but now he could triple his pleasure.

Joe grinned.

Alex flailed and fought, trying to keep the shifting shapes at bay. Unblinking, he watched them spring to life, reach, squeeze. Their cold dampness pressed all the air out of his lungs. He yelled, kicking and punching at the darkness, then fell hard to the ground and groaned as electric pain sizzled through his body. He writhed, trying to get to his feet, trembling legs bouncing against the ground, but he couldn't be sure which way was up. Then something was on top of him, holding his head in a vice grip, and he knew he was going to die, devoured by the shadows that had been haunting him for three years. He swung blindly at the thing, feeling his fist connect with soft flesh. The beast groaned and loosened its grip but did not let go.

"Al," the thing gasped. "Stop it. It's me."

Alex quit thrashing, a different kind of fear flooding his senses. Something in the voice made the hair on the back of his neck stand straighter than it already was.

"Joe?"

"Yeah," the low voice said. "It's okay now. I'm here, bro. You're okay."

Alex groped at the figure he couldn't see, fingers tangling in stiff clumps of long hair. He felt Joe's hot hands on his face and grabbed his friend tight, clung to Joe's bare bony shoulders, and tried not to acknowledge the strong sense of dread creeping up on him. *Just the darkness. You're freaking out. Exhale.* Everywhere, misshapen shadows loomed, waiting for their chance. His knees buckled. He slumped back to the ground, pulling Joe with him.

"What the fuck?" Alex's shaking voice filled the claustrophobic air and hung there. "Where are we? Are you dea— Are you okay?"

Joe didn't answer. Instead, he did something that took Alex by complete surprise. Joe grabbed his head again and planted a firm kiss on his sweat-drenched forehead.

"I knew you'd come get me," Joe whispered. "Everything's okay now."

His voice held an unearthly edge. His breath smelled of bile and rot. Clinging to Joe's bare torso, feeling the raised scars carved into his flesh, Alex tensed and resisted the urge to run as far as he could before the waiting shadows consumed him, mind and soul.

June 10, 1984

Elizabeth stripped off her clothes and turned on the shower water as hot as she could stand it. Escaping to a hot shower had always been cathartic for her. There's was something hopeful in washing away the day's grief in a baptism of steam. She stepped into the downpour, grateful for the heat, and watched the water pool around her ankles. She'd gotten a creeping chill while driving home from Mary's in the dense fog and no matter how hot the car heater was it couldn't chase away the chills wending through her bones. Alex had inherited the love of hot shower gene from her. It offered a refuge for him to escape the challenges any kid should never have go through. Alex had had his share. And now Joe and the horribleness with Marcus. Elizabeth realized then that she missed her son. Terribly, achingly missed him.

"They are not going to die," she said out loud.

Mary had taken the news of Alex's condition in the same way she had taken in the information about Joe—stoic and patient, as though she had already memorized the words Elizabeth had gone there to speak, as though this nightmare had already been dreamed and the outcome chiseled into stone tablets like prophecy.

Elizabeth closed her eyes and let the water pour over her head. She thought of Dr. Rom and his deep, dancing eyes. She imagined him standing there, naked and wet, strong arms holding her. He had touched something in her that she thought had been buried with Thomas long ago. She'd instantly trusted the doctor, something she was not accustomed to doing. After Thomas died, she'd focused all her energy on her sons and their goals. They were her life, her passion. She had no room for anyone else.

Elizabeth soaped up, washed her hair, and stood under the downpour for another twenty minutes. She hoped she could sleep without being startled awake by dreams of loss, of life emptying. Mary's words echoed in her head. *This story is written. Now we must trust. Now we must believe.*

The phone was ringing when she turned off the water. Terror seized her. Elizabeth sprinted across the bedroom floor, leaving a wet trail, and snatched the phone from its cradle. She held the receiver to her ear, unable to speak.

"Elizabeth?"

It was Rom.

"What's wrong?" she shouted. Her temples throbbed.

"Nothing," he said quickly, deep voice calm. "I've been calling every half hour to make sure you made it home okay in this fog. You ran out of here in a hurry. I was worried. I left messages on your machine."

Elizabeth eased onto the bed and pressed her palm to her forehead. "You scared me. I thought something—"

"I'm so sorry. I should've thought it out before calling, but I got worried. The fog's bad this morning."

"Thank you," Elizabeth said, letting herself feel grateful. "I appreciate your concern. Is Alex all right?"

"No change," Rom said. "If anything happens, I'll call. I'm glad you decided to go home for a while. Please try to rest. There's a rumor that the hospital is considering putting you on staff, since you've been here so much."

Elizabeth smiled. She liked his voice and appreciated his bedside manner. The image of him naked and wet found her again.

"Well, I'm dripping water everywhere …"

Silence, and then he cleared his throat. "Get some rest. I'll be in early, around seven or eight." He paused. "Maybe we can have dinner togeth—"

"Yes," she said, surprising herself. "I'd like that."

"I'll see you later then," Rom said. "Goodnight. Or, I guess good morning is more accurate."

Elizabeth put the receiver back in the cradle and toweled her hair. She pulled on some clean gray sweats and fresh socks and went into the bathroom for some aspirin. The small feather taped to the mirror had begun to curl and fold in on itself. She swallowed three tablets and pulled the plume from the glass. Holding it gently, Elizabeth flipped off the bathroom light and picked her way through the darkness to her bed. Pressing the feather to her chest, she drifted into dark dreams of birds flapping wildly against glass, unable to free themselves.

3:00pm

Elizabeth jolted awake, a feeling that she'd forgotten something gnawing at her weary brain. The alarm clock screeched, sounding like the frightened birds she'd dreamt of, and she vaguely remembered setting it so she wouldn't sleep the day away. She reached toward the incessant noise and swatted the machine until the beeping silenced, took a deep breath and propelled herself off the bed and into the hallway, aiming toward the kitchen for some tea.

She didn't make it that far.

Elizabeth came to an abrupt halt in front of Luke's wide-open bedroom door and instantly sank to her knees. Leaning against the doorjamb, she watched hundreds of white feathers appear out of thin air near the ceiling and sail to the wood floor, accumulating there like tiny dry snowflakes. She put out her hand and caught several soft plumes, then sat for nearly an hour, laughcrying and watching the gentle flurry of feathers cascade down to pile on Luke's floor.

4:19pm

The sign in the window read CLOSED, which struck Elizabeth odd for a Monday afternoon. She entered, thankful that she and Mary would have the place to themselves.

The woman got up from her workstation, wiped the wood dust from her hands, and greeted her with a warm embrace before making her way to the kitchen to retrieve a tea tray and a plate of hot oatmeal anise cookies. Elizabeth sat and waited for Mary to settle herself. She watched the woman's face while opening the paper grocery bags she'd brought.

"I need to know what this means." Elizabeth turned the bags upside down, hundreds of white feathers spilling onto the table and floor at Mary's feet.

Mary waited until the last bag had been emptied and the last feather had reached the floor. Her piercing gaze lifted from her feet to Elizabeth's face as she bent forward and plucked a feather from the pile on the table. She held it close and studied it over the rim of her glasses as though assessing the value of a curious jewel. Then she clapped her hands together and bounced a few inches out of her seat. She leaned forward and whispered, holding the feather in front of Elizabeth's nose. "This is good."

"What does it mean?"

Thoughtful, Mary sat back. "In many traditions, and in my own, the people believe the white feather is a message, a sign that there is something beyond the final exhale, an existence beyond death."

Elizabeth swallowed hard. "They're all over Luke's room, raining from the ceiling."

"Of course ..." Mary's voice trailed, and a sharpness came to her dark eyes. "It's a communication. Someone is trying to reach you, Elizabeth. To settle your saddened heart. To offer you peace."

Elizabeth felt her face go pale. She sipped tea from the mug Mary handed her and tried to take deep breaths. It didn't work. The more Mary spoke, the more Elizabeth felt the blood drain from her face and hands.

"There are forces at work here that we will understand one day. Today is not that day for you and me, Elizabeth. So, we must trust. And believe." Without another word, Mary sat back, lit her pipe, and smiled.

7:20pm

They sat on a thick quilt on the floor of Joe's hospital room and opened boxes of lo mein, steamed rice, and vegetable tempura.

Elizabeth shook her head, smiling. "This is great. You went to a lot of trouble, though."

Rom chuckled, the sound rolling up from someplace deep. "All I did was make a call. My very good friend Jimmy at *Chang's Chinese Cuisine* took it from there. Actually, it was probably his dad. Jimmy can't cook worth a crap, so he keeps the books. Hope it's okay. Hospital food and I have a love hate relationship. The FDA should label some of that stuff hazardous to people's health." The doctor crammed a stringy mass of noodles into his mouth. Still chewing, he tilted his head toward the boombox. "Alex?"

Elizabeth nodded. "Joe would be the last person to admit he likes Alex's music. He's into that death metal stuff. He used to sneak in during Alex's performances and make me swear not to tell. Alex knew anyway. You could see it in his demeanor and confidence the second Joe walked in. Joe's only missed one of Alex's performances since they were three years old. That was a very bad night for both of them."

Rom swallowed. "Why didn't you want to sit in Alex's room tonight?" He faltered, and Elizabeth felt a flush of heat rise to her cheeks, but it wasn't caused by the doctor's question. He continued, "I just wondered. How are you holding up?"

Elizabeth breathed out and thought for a moment, trying to come up with an answer without going into psycho-sounding detail, then decided to tell him the truth.

"This is going to sound strange." She didn't take her eyes off him, tried to read every micro-expression that flashed on his face. "I believe Joe and Alex are together somewhere *inside*. I believe Alex is trying to help Joe come back. I believe he will."

Rom looked at her, dark brows drawing together. "I get it. And I don't think it's strange at all. After talking with Alex about Joe it was obvious to me there's something between them that's unique. I sensed it. Truth be told, I've witnessed some unexplainable things in this profession. I'm a firm believer in the power of desire and will, and that things are never what they seem. Sometimes we just have to trust that the universe, or god, or great spirit, or whatever you want to call it is working in our favor, even if we don't know it. My Ol' Ma taught me that."

Elizabeth felt like laughcrying again but reeled herself in. "I knew there was a reason I liked you right away. Alex told me you were a good person."

"I have everybody fooled," Rom said, winking, and Elizabeth felt that hot flush again but now it was low in her belly.

"Did you always know Alex would be a musician?"

"Yep. His dad thought I was nuts to get him a violin when he was three, thought Alex was too young and the lessons would be a waste of money. Alex proved him wrong and I think Thomas resented it. He might look like me, but Alex inherited his dad's stubborn streak. They used to butt heads over the simplest things. Luke was the peacekeeper. He used to make Alex and Thomas kiss each other, which mortified their dad. I still don't have any idea how Luke managed that. Thomas wasn't a particularly affectionate person. He was uncomfortable hugging or kissing other men—"

Elizabeth stopped short and looked at Rom. She shook her head. "I'm babbling. Tell me about you."

Rom spoke softly. "I'd like to hear more, if that's okay. Alex mentioned he'd had a brother, but I don't know much more about your son other than he's one of the most persistent and gifted people I've ever met. I've seen him perform. I even squeezed in at a couple of fundraisers for the children's hospitals around Portland. He's a powerhouse, so much passion. Has he always been that focused and energetic?"

"Yes—" Elizabeth hesitated, glancing at Joe's still form, "—well, he's struggled since Luke died, but everything got much worse about a year ago. That's when Joe's emotional problems intensified. It took a toll on Alex. It was as if he could feel everything Joe was experiencing, and it wore him out. He started getting headaches, he slept a lot, or not at all. Lost weight. Even started hearing voices. A woman calling for help and a kid screaming inside his head. The night terrors were awful. Practicing and performing became torturous for him. He started spending all of his time with Joe. Doc Abraham said it was a delayed reaction to Luke's death triggered by Joe's suicide attempt and that Alex was experiencing post-traumatic stress. I got him into therapy right away. It helped for a while."

"Wow. I didn't know about Joe's struggles, but it makes sense."

Elizabeth looked the doctor in the eyes. "Alex was the one who found Joe. Did he tell you that?"

Rom shook his head and set his plate on the quilt, listening. "That had to be extremely difficult. For all of you."

Elizabeth nodded. "It was—*is*—difficult. Alex was on his way to a performance at the Cutters Arts Center and stopped at Joe's to pick him up. By then Alex was having a hard time staying away from him. He was scared to leave him alone. Turns out he was right." Elizabeth shook her head, frowning. "That particular performance would have been an important one for Alex. It was a small venue and we thought it would be better for his anxiety, but he was overly apprehensive about it because two weeks prior something had happened that scared both of us pretty bad."

Rom leaned closer. "Something with Joe?"

"Not directly," Elizabeth said, tugging at her lip, trying to put Alex and Joe's connection into words that didn't make her sound delusional. "Alex was on stage, right in the middle of the most complicated part of Bach's Third, when he stopped all of a sudden. He just froze. His eyes got huge and he started stumbling around like he didn't know where he was, then he dropped his violin and grabbed his head. He went straight down to his knees and started sobbing. By the time I got up there, he was mumbling almost incoherently. I couldn't understand him at first, but then he looked right at me, right in my eyes, and said, 'Mom, he's in my head. He's screaming inside my head. He's scared, and I have to help him.'"

Rom's eyes narrowed. The doctor had grown very still.

"Later, when I asked him what it meant, he couldn't remember saying it. He said all he remembered was the music stopping. He saw bright lights and he told me he thought the world was ending. Then the screams started."

Rom still hadn't moved.

"He did well in his audition application for Juilliard last year, but he could've done better, *should have* done better. He shouldn't have had that taken from him by … I don't know. Alex hasn't really been able to play since that night."

Elizabeth rubbed her face and sipped tea. "Wow. I haven't said any of that out loud in a long time."

Rom's voice seemed softer when he spoke. "I'm glad you told me. Alex mentioned his brother had an accident."

Elizabeth swallowed. "Luke died three years ago in a rappelling accident. He was twelve. I'd gotten them lessons and they loved it."

Rom nodded. "Good rockfaces up north."

"Yeah, they were good at it and great with each other. Luke was Alex's baby from the second he was born," Elizabeth continued. "He grew up listening to Alex's music, so he knew sounds, rhythm, beat. He used to tell me he could hear a man unzipping his pants in a bathroom two blocks away. He knew when Alex was trying too hard or not hard enough. Alex strove for the look of approval on his brother's face, that light in Luke's eyes. That's how Alex knew whether or not he'd done well, and he sought that light every time he played."

Rom nodded, solemn. "My younger brother died two years ago. Heart attack. He was forty."

Elizabeth reached for Rom's hand. "I'm so sorry."

"It changes you. But it's nothing like losing a child."

"Yes," Elizabeth sighed. "Nothing is ever again the way you thought it would be."

Rom looked down at their clasped hands. "It changed Alex, but he's a strong kid. He'll be okay."

"Well, he's been through more than any kid should," Elizabeth said, letting the doctor hold her hand in his. "He held Luke while he died, held on to him the whole time. Luke had bruised indentations on his back from Alex holding him so tightly. The paramedics had to pry his arms away from Luke's body. It took five of them. Alex was catatonic for almost a month. It was Joe who finally brought him out of it. He stayed with Alex around the clock, fed him, brushed his teeth and hair, read to him, bathed him, even slept in the same bed in case Alex came out of it and got scared. And he played dozens of cassettes over and over. All of Alex's favorites. Joe never left him, not for a single moment. I got the feeling he knew exactly what Alex was thinking and feeling that whole time, but I never asked. I just knew Alex wasn't alone."

Rom's eyebrows went up. "I definitely need to meet this kid."

Elizabeth nodded. "It's not surprising. They've always had a connection. You felt it. They used to be able to communicate without speaking, too. When they were little kids, they'd sit for hours and talk about a man who visited them in their dreams. I asked each of them separately to tell me about the man and, Rom, their stories were *identical.* Word for word. They both said that he made them laugh when he danced, and that our friend Mary Whitewing had sent him into their dreams to teach them. I told Mary about it and she said they were visiting with the source—universe, god, great spirit, whatever you want to call it—their own personal spark of spirit. Their own inner strength and wisdom."

Rom smiled. "I think I also need to meet this Mary Whitewing. You said Alex and Joe *used to* be able to communicate without speaking. What happened to change that?"

"About three months before Joe's suicide attempt Alex started having night terrors. That's when the voices started. He said there was so much noise inside his head that it would wake him up, but he couldn't remember exact words, it was all jumbled. He said his dreams were filled with shadow creatures chasing him in the dark. Alex developed nyctophobia after Luke died and has panic attacks if there's no light. He told me once that even though he was with Joe all the time, he felt very distant from him, like he didn't know him anymore, like Joe was a complete stranger, secretive and detached. A wall had been put up. It scared him. It had never been like that between them."

Rom nodded towards the still form on the bed and said softly, "If Joe doesn't make it, what do you think will happen with Alex?"

Before Elizabeth could answer, Rom's pager started beeping. He pulled it from his waistband and studied it, a deep scowl twisting his expression.

He looked at Elizabeth. "I'm sorry. I have to go."

She nodded. "The exciting life of a doctor, huh?"

He smiled. "Always interferes with more fun activities."

"I'll clean up here and go sit with Alex for a while."

"Remember what I told you. If they see you—"

Elizabeth grinned. "They'll put me to work."

Rom started for the door, but spun around mid-stride, took Elizabeth's hand and kissed it. "Thank you for having dinner with me tonight. I'd like to do it again, in a restaurant next time."

"Me too." She stood on her toes and kissed his cheek. Rom clutched his chest and feigned a swoon, waving goodnight.

Elizabeth closed up the food containers and re-bagged everything, then headed down the hallway to Alex's room. A woman passed her, complaining about the antiseptic hospital smell, and Elizabeth frowned. With all her unfortunate experience with hospitals over the years, she never noticed the dry medicinal odor anymore. One thing that did still bother her was the hopeless look in everyone's eyes, especially on this floor. She hoped she didn't look like all the sad people she passed. She hoped she could hold it together long enough for Alex to find his way back. Outside his room, she took a deep breath and pushed the door open.

He lay on his back, so still and quiet. Too quiet. She turned up the volume on the boombox and eased into a chair, taking her son's hand and pressing it to her cheek. He appeared peaceful and she wanted him to be. She studied his long fingers, his rough fingertips, evidence of her son's passion and commitment over the past fifteen years. She tried to imagine the strength it must have taken for Alex to hold Luke all those hours, the enormous will he possessed to simply wait, knowing there was no more breath left in his brother's body.

"You never let him go, though, did you baby. Not for a single second. And you won't let Joe go, either."

Elizabeth stroked Alex's nose with her pinky, hoping he could sense her presence. She stretched his long fingers out flat on the sterile sheet, gently pulling and rubbing them as she did before and after every performance to keep the cramps and stiffness away. She massaged his wrist and forearm, digging the balls of her fingers into the tough muscle that always ached after a show.

Pulling the bottle of sage-scented vitamin E oil from her bag, Elizabeth dribbled some into her hands and reached for Alex's arm, but stopped, peering close at a narrow vertical scratch at the base of his palm. She brushed a finger over the mark, smearing a bead of blood. Another crimson droplet bubbled up from the split skin. She reached for a tissue, thinking her fingernail had accidentally gouged him, then watched as the scratch lengthened, a serpentine trail of blood rising on the translucent skin of Alex's wrist. Elizabeth sat up straight just as an invisible blade cut fast and deep into Alex's arm, opening an eight-inch gash. Blood pumped onto the sterile white sheet. Elizabeth's lungs tightened into a horrified gasp. She threw herself over the bed, groping for the call button, and when she stood she saw it—a dark red stain spreading through the white sheet over Alex's ribs. Elizabeth pushed the button a half dozen times and then ran into the hallway shouting for Rom.

ten

Shadows

Joe flicked his red Zippo. A halo of pale light encircled them, chasing looming shadows further into the darkness. Alex stepped back. His face knotted into a shocked grimace at the sight of Joe's battered body. A reddish-brown, sticky substance streaked his long hair like car grease. It gathered in stringy clumps around his head and in front of his face, which Alex couldn't see at all and wasn't sure he wanted to. Scars—some old and faded, some scabbed and too fresh—had been carved into Joe's torso, arms, and back with determined precision. Designs, symbols, and angry slashes wove through his flesh in intricate patterns. A strikingly accurate carving of Jade peered from the sliced skin of Joe's left pec, the scar almost healed. Using his own body as a canvas, he'd somehow managed to capture the pain in the girl's exquisite eyes. Reddish streaks covered his entire body. A blazing, thick-scabbed cross splashed dull scarlet through the center of his torso.

Rom's words came screeching back into Alex's head—*a walking museum.* He hadn't known what the doctor meant until now. Joe's body was a morbid, twisted, walking work of art. A moving snapshot of self-induced torture and inner anguish. A blazing testimony to consuming pain and unspoken guilt. Alex shuddered, hair again stiffening on his scalp.

"Jesus, Rex. What happened to your face?" Joe's voice sounded odd, hoarse, guttural, too calm. Too damned removed.

Alex squinted in the flickering light, wishing he could see Joe's eyes, but afraid to reach out and touch him for fear that he might not really be there, or that he might not be able to deal with what he found beyond that filthy, matted veil of blond hair.

Joe waved a bloodied hand in front of Alex's face. "You in there, bro?"

The Zippo sputtered and went out. He heard Joe trying to reignite it, but it didn't work.

An inexplicable needle of fear twisted in Alex's gut. His legs buckled, and he put his hands down to catch himself, but didn't fall. Joe had him around the waist, easing him to the soft ground, his grimy hair brushing Alex's cheek. A brackish metallic smell hung in the air around Joe's body. A combination of sweat, blood and filth, but it was the rancid odor of Joe's dying hope that made Alex's stomach contract in sick spasms and sent a wracking shudder through every aching muscle when Joe's cold flesh connected with his own.

Alex jerked away from the scabbed arms around his waist and blinked hard, commanding his eyes to adjust to the insistent dark. He'd be useless and dependent on Joe until then. That realization scared Alex even more. Panic was already tightening its death grip again, jack-hammering his heart in his chest. He felt what little control he had slipping away into the shadows, which moved and shifted at the periphery. His stomach flipped.

"What's wrong, Al? You okay?"

"*What's wrong?* You're fucking kidding me, right?" Joe was close, still holding his arm. Alex shivered. "Where are we?"

"I don't know."

"Bullshit." Alex pulled his nose, watching vague shapes move in circles around them, scraping the dry earth with impossibly long appendages. *In my head,* Alex told himself. *Goddamn crazy.*

"I don't know, Al. But she's here. She saved my life."

Joe's rank breath blasted Alex's cheek. He wrapped his fingers around Joe's thin wrist. "You saw her?"

"No, I felt her. That was a while ago. I don't know where she is now, but we have to find her. She's in danger."

"I know," Alex said. "But I can't move yet. It's too fucking dark."

"It's gonna take a long time for your eyes to see. Just hang on to me, Al. My vision is clear now. Trust me. We have to find her. There's a monster here, stalking her. We have to do something before it finds her."

"Just let me—"

"No. We have to keep moving. It's safer. Believe me, I know. We need to stick together like we used to. Isn't that why you came after me? To bring me back? We can't leave before we find her. She has something we both need."

"How do you know that, Joe?" Alex's voice shook. Electric shocks shot through his head and down his back. He rubbed his face.

"It's a feeling, Al," Joe whispered in that eerie guttural tone. "Besides, would you *want* to leave her in this place? I don't think you could. Once you hear the screams, you'll want to find her as much as I do."

Alex grabbed Joe's head in his trembling hands. He was solid, tangible, breathing peppery hot breath into Alex's face. A mass of sticky, matted hair tangled in Alex's fingers as he moved his hands over Joe's head and face, trying to convince himself that it was still his best friend buried under that layer of grime and that what he was feeling was simply an intense reaction to the dark and the phantom shapes stirring the air as they moved, creating shadows, becoming shadows. Joe didn't brush him off like he'd expected. Alex felt the warm skin, full eyebrows and dry lips, slightly turned up nose, the patch of whiskers under his lower lip … and calmed a little. It was Joe in there. Alex had no rational reason to doubt it. But he'd be more convinced if he could see Joe's eyes.

"Okay," Alex breathed, holding onto Joe's bony shoulders. His knees banged together, feeling like detached rubber bands under his body. "Just don't let go of me. I can't see jack shit. And don't fuck with me. Tell me the truth. You okay? For real?"

He felt Joe's head nod. "Yeah, man. I'm cool. I mean, it hasn't been easy here, but I feel revived. Strong." Joe's husky voice grated in Alex's ear, sending a creeping chill down his spine. "I knew you wouldn't leave me here, Al. I knew you'd come to get me."

"Joe," Alex said. "Is this hell?"

Joe's stiff hair brushed across his arm. "I don't know, Al."

"Mary said there were demons here. She said you were trapped in a world of your own making."

Joe's shoulders lifted in a shrug. "I guess so. It seems familiar. I've learned a lot since I got here. As long as you stay with me, those things won't hurt you. We've come to an understanding."

"What things?"

"Can't you see them? Those shapes? Those shadows? You'll hear them, too, whispering and muttering when they get close."

"They're fucking real?" Alex tried to exhale but his breath was stuck somewhere between his navel and his throat.

Alex felt Joe draw nearer, the stench of him making his nostrils flare. Joe whispered into Alex's ear. "Oh, yeah. And the last thing you want to do is piss them off. Just listen, Al. They know things. I've learned a lot since I got here."

"You said that already." A shadow shifted at the periphery of his vision.

"Did I?"

Alex's chest tightened. His scalp prickled with a sick dread.

~

The feeling in the hollow pit of Joe's stomach had intensified to a fever pitch, radiating through his entire body, firing up his mind and what was left of his soul.

Hate. Blessed hate.

He could hardly contain his excitement. He did his best to conceal it, leading Alex through the cavernous darkness, guided by the soft mutterings inside, outside. A collective. But he sensed Alex's hesitation. It was in his voice, in every syllable he uttered, so Joe would have to be careful. He hadn't heard the child's irritating screams since Alex got there and figured his friend's absurdly angelic presence had calmed the little fucker down somehow. Heat boiled over in Joe's chest and he stopped walking, feeling for the wedge of glass in his pocket.

"What's wrong?" Alex held the back of the sweatshirt he'd made Joe wear and now he felt Alex's grip tighten on the damp material.

"Nothing," Joe said. "Just getting my bearings." He extracted the piece of glass and pressed it between his sticky palms. Alex stood close to him, blind, ignorant. Joe pulled his hair down over his face and looked at Alex through the stringy, red tinged mass.

"Joe?" The tone sounded pathetic, fearful. Joe sneered and brought the point of the wedge mere centimeters from Alex's throat. He tried to see how close he could get it without touching the skin.

"I'm just catching my breath, Al." With his free hand, he reached for Alex's arm and gave it a squeeze. "We'll find her and then everything will be okay."

Alex's body stiffened.

Joe held the glass and drew his thumb down the sharpest edge, amused at the beads of sweat popping up on Alex's upper lip. How easy it would be to push the point through his flesh and puncture his jugular. He'd never know what hit him. But the thrill wouldn't last, and it *had* to last.

"Everything's cool now that you're here," he whispered into Alex's ear. "You're gonna help me find her. Save her." He could smell Alex's fear, bittersweet and salty. The intoxicating scent filled his nostrils, making him downright giddy. He licked his dry lips.

Alex swallowed, his Adam's apple bobbing a quarter of an inch from the sharp point of glass. He clutched the sweatshirt like it was a life preserver, blinking against the thick darkness, and Joe had to stifle a laugh. Suddenly, Alex jerked his head, almost impaling himself on the weapon held to his throat.

"What was that?" Alex tightened his grip on the sweat-shirt.

Joe slipped the wedge back into his jeans pocket and tried to sound interested. "What was what?"

Alex stumbled forward, pulling Joe with him. "I saw a dot. A light."

"No, Al," Joe said, calmly. "You imagined it. There's no light here. Believe me."

"I saw it," Alex said, yanking Joe a few more steps. "I know I saw—there!"

"Al—"

Alex rushed forward. "It's her," Joe heard him say. "We found her."

Alex stopped short, mouth dropping open, eyes fixed on the structure in front of them. Joe breathed hard and fast next to him. He coughed, and Alex heard something wet hit the ground. He pulled Joe closer.

"What is it?"

"I don't know," Joe gasped, "but I don't want to go in there. I can't go in there."

Before them, illuminated from within and without by a supernal amber light that seemed to have no source, stood a stone door with a circular handle of wrought iron. On all sides, an impenetrable blackness. Alex put his hands on the door and pushed. He grabbed the handle and pulled. The stone slab didn't budge.

"Joe! Help me!"

Joe shook his head, stiff hair pasted to his sweaty face and neck. "No way. I don't want to go in there. If I go in there I'll—"

"You'll what?" Alex tried to see beyond Joe's hair in the light wavering like a mirage around them, tried to see into his eyes, but couldn't see anything beyond that veil of filthy red-tinged hair and had the impulse to reach out and swipe all of it away from Joe's masked face. He almost did, but a sudden eardrum-shattering scream filled the darkness. Joe doubled over, hands pressed against the sides of his head, and dropped to his knees. He rocked back and forth on his elbows and shins, moaning as though snared in a nightmare he couldn't wake from. Alex spun, frantically searching for the origin of the heart-wrenching sound—and froze.

Just beyond the arc of light filtering from and through the door, a tall twisted shape moved toward him. The silhouette of its wispy form seemed part of the darkness itself. A paralyzing tremble wrenched through Alex's body. He backed against the door, eyes wide. *Don't blink.* From where he sat on the sand, Joe began singing, quiet at first then louder and louder. He articulated every syllable, stretching each word until he lost his breath. Alex finally recognized it as *Swing Low Sweet Chariot.* Each word stuck in his brain like an arrow.

Alex tore his wide eyes from the monstrous thing moving at the edge of the penumbra and looked down at Joe. Before he could tell him to get up, the skeletal figure drew closer and Alex was able to see its features more clearly— elongated face, hyper-extended arms with long knotted fingers branching off at the ends, sharp talons dragging in the sand. Its smoky skull bulged in places and housed two holes for a nose, its lips shredded and jagged. The creature advanced and Alex had the odd sensation that if he reached out his hand it would pass easily through the thing's warped body. Its form seemed unstable, as though it was only a little denser than the atmosphere itself.

Alex pressed his back against the door, using his weight to try and push it open. Joe rocked on the ground, singing and muttering. Another scream split the eternal night. Joe clamped his thin arms tighter around his head and Alex heard him say, "Just listen."

The thing raised its vaporous arms and Alex watched its fingers lengthen, branch off, reach and snake forward like the tendrils in Joe's room, like the serpentine hands that had grabbed Norma. The creature let out a low guttural growl that seemed to come from deep within the depths of the darkness itself. Alex's breath hitched into his throat. Pulse hammering, he flattened his back against the stone door and pushed, shoes digging deep grooves into the sand as he shoved with all his strength.

The outstretched limbs came to an abrupt halt where the glow of golden light met the edge of darkness a few feet away. The towering shadowthing let loose a low snarl that echoed deep in the blackness as if this dusky world were one organism made up of many and the fiend pulsing its hungry hands in the air just one more cell making up its structure.

Alex pushed harder, grunting. The thing's gnarled limbs retreated then advanced fast, a deafening roar filling the dark void. It swung a massive, vaporous hand, missing the tip of Alex's nose by inches. The sulfurous odor of burning bones made Alex's nostrils flare and he couldn't be sure if it was the creature's natural stink or if the amber glow had scalded it when it got too close. The beast howled in volcanic rage and backed away, retracting its enormous hands. Joe snapped his head up and looked at the demented shadow, hair still hiding his face. He stopped singing.

Alex cut a glance at Joe then back at the monster loom-ing a dozen feet away and saw them—the thing's eyes, pale blue, glassy—the eyes of fear itself, of someone who'd ex-perienced an intolerable amount of pain and sadness. Alex knew those eyes. There was no light, no life, and somewhere in their dead blue-glass depths Alex saw a thousand reasons to flee, to run like hell and not look back, to forget.

Joe's eyes.

In that split second, Alex tumbled into a maze and knew there was no way he could find his way out, no possible way he could put the light back into those eyes. He swallowed the horrified scream rising behind the lump in his throat and grabbed Joe by the hair. He pushed with all his strength against the door, sand-filled shoes digging deeper ruts into the ground.

The creature grew still and parted its ragged lips. For one terrible instant, Alex thought the thing might speak. It didn't. It smiled. Layers of long needle-sharp teeth glinted in the amber light, bone-white and slick with dripping sa-liva. Like a rope unraveling into the air, the thing's gnarled finger extended, pointing, and Alex's thoughts unraveled, too. This monster was different from the lurking shadows of his phobic mind. This one had a very specific goal. This one wanted Joe.

Grunting, Alex pushed harder against the door and felt it give a little.

Another heart-rending scream pierced the darkness, drowning out Joe's words—*justlistenjustlistenjustlisten*—and Alex tracked the sound to someplace behind him, on the other side of the door. He gritted his teeth, tightened his hold on Joe's sticky hair, and leaned hard.

"You can't have him!"

Alex fell backward through the door, dragging Joe with him. The shadowthing shrieked in rage, filling the vast-ness with a freight train roar. Long tendrils of snarled smoke shot out of the gloom. Alex scrambled to his feet and shoved the heavy door closed. He fell to his knees on the stone floor, his whole body shaking with the force of his heartbeats. His eyes watered with the sudden light and through his blurred vision he saw Joe curled on his side, arms wrapped around his head, still murmuring to himself.

They had landed in a small chamber with carved stone walls. Life-sized faces of men, women, children, babies—all distorted and overrun with expressions of agony—stared from the monochromatic walls, floor, ceiling. They gaped from every inch, tortured, beaten, resolute. Many sprouted more than one face, progressively blooming into more disturbing images. Their lifeless features distended, lips and eyes twisted into grotesque caricatures of human anguish.

Alex got to his feet. "What the hell."

Joe mumbled from where he lay on the floor. Alex knelt and brushed Joe's hair off his face. Joe had his eyes squeezed closed, but when he opened them Alex didn't see what he had expected. They weren't glowing red, fire didn't shoot out in searing rays. Joe's eyes were exactly as they'd been for the past year, dull and weary.

"Joe, get up."

Joe's jaws clenched tight. "I told you I didn't want to come in here. Now I might not be able to go back."

"Why the fuck would you want to go back out there? We're safe in here. For now."

Joe sat up. He looked like he'd just seen his dog get hit by a car, in shock and on the verge of tears. He said nothing.

Alex glanced at the tormented faces.

"You built this, didn't you?" Alex gave his nose a hard tug. This wasn't a dream.

Joe stared at his bare feet and raked his hair back down over his face.

A shattering scream ripped through the silence. Joe clapped his hands over his ears. Alex did the same, squeezing his eyes closed until the deafening noise faded. When he lowered his hands and opened his eyes, Joe was gone. Alex whirled around but found only the tortured faces staring from every direction in silent wails. He turned in slow circles, scanning the small space for an escape—and saw them. Seven dark circular openings in the walls near the floor, like the mouse houses in *Tom and Jerry* cartoons, only just wide enough for a person to fit through.

He heard something and froze, listening. It came from one of the openings opposite the stone door. A faint flapping. Alex dropped to his knees and strained to see into a darkened hole. He heard a soft, low voice calling his name. Alex leaned forward on his elbows, held his breath, and crawled into the darkness.

He dragged himself along, feeling his way with his hands and using his feet to push through the deep sand. The angle of the tunnel seemed to slope downward, but gravity meant nothing here and he forced his way through the heavy sand threatening to close in and suffocate him with every breath. He fought the sensation of the sides closing in, the shadows of his phobic mind reaching, grasping, squeezing. Damp earth pressed on his skin, squeezing his lungs in a cold grip and making his flesh prickle in that now familiar nauseating way. The grains felt like ice. He focused on his exhales, plowing forward. Light suddenly appeared in the distance. Alex crawled forward and found himself staring down into another chamber—or was it the same one? As his grit-filled eyes adjusted, he saw that this one was bigger with several stone pathways leading into dusky places beyond his range of vision. In the center of the room, tall stone pillars flanked two naked figures, a man and a woman, carved from elaborate marble, their faces hidden by hair and the leaves of a chiseled tree between them.

Alex scooted to the edge, dangled his legs over, rolled onto his belly, and pushed off, dropping to the ground ten feet below.

Something swooped close, yanked a few hairs from his head, then flapped away. Alex blinked up into the radiant glow. Faces were carved into the walls here, too. A white owl circled overhead before diving toward the ground and landing near Alex's sand filled shoes. The bird laid its wings flat and cocked its head, transparent eyes meeting Alex's stunned gaze.

"Where'd you come from?"

The night owl spread its wings, dipped its head and danced before lifting from the ground and flying into the dusk along one of the pathways. Alex followed.

The marble floor spiraled upward into endless empty air, seemingly illuminated from within and surrounded by dusky darkness. Alex trudged up the winding path, shoes slipping on the smooth stone surface. He hit a flat section of the floor and stopped to catch his breath when a sudden chill snaked up his spine. He grew still, sensing eyes on him. Glancing up, he found the owl perched and staring down at him from a curved lip of the glowing walkway. But it wasn't the bird watching him that had caused the chill, he realized. No. There was something else watching from beyond the owl's white form sitting like a beacon against the dusky backdrop. The owl stood stone still, looking at him with those uncanny crystal eyes.

An abrupt tremble took over Alex's body. He clasped his hands together at his chest and then felt something hot between his palms. He opened his hands, saw a green stone speckled with red and heard Buck's deep voice—*for clear sight, intuition—*

"—and courage," Alex breathed. He held the stone tightly in his fist then put it back in his pocket. He climbed the last stretch of walkway and stepped past the owl into another dim chamber of far greater expanse than the others.

The darkness was denser here, warmer, thicker, wetter. A briny tang hung in the air. Alex could taste it when he breathed through his mouth, smell it when he sealed his lips. The stone wall to his right rose high, disappearing into the hidden apex of the strange tawny glow that seemed to come from nowhere and everywhere. Enormous carved faces yawned, creating deep shadows and ridges in the protrusions of oversized lips and noses, and sad eyes that brimmed with silent tears that cascaded down their resolute cheeks before vanishing and beginning again. Some cried streams of red, some orange, yellow, green, blue … In silent surging streams of color, grief and repentance flowed.

Alex swallowed over the dry lump in his throat and tried to rub away the hotness in his chest. Far to his left, a glass wall with no beginning and no end stretched into the depths of the room and out of sight. Alex walked the expanse of the chamber but slowed his pace as he drew closer. The glass was at once reflective and transparent, and filled with a clear liquid. He could see his own image, covered from head to foot with white sand and smeared with Joe's blood, but he could also see *through* his image, and what he found did nothing to calm the tremble in his hands and shoulders. People, trapped and floating on the other side of the glass, their frozen expressions fearful, sad, horrified, hopeless. A man with a handlebar mustache and bushy eyebrows. A woman with a 1920s-style haircut and bright red lips. Some old, some young. Some black, some Asian. All races, all ages. All of humanity's suffering.

Alex touched the cold glass, beyond it a girl who looked about twelve-years-old. He stared at the girl's angry face, felt her final thought sweep through his mind, felt her final moments of resolve as she swallowed the pills—*I'll show them no more pain for me and they can all go fuck themselves.*

"No more pain," Alex whispered. His stomach burned. He lowered his hand and moved along the wall.

A boy, about seven with red hair and freckles, mouth open, eyes closed in a grimace of fear and confusion. Alex placed his fingers on the boy's cheek *don't Daddy don't touch it don't make me.* Alex lowered his hand, tasting bile in his chest. He closed his eyes and swallowed it down.

He walked along the wall, past several twisted faces, and stopped at a young woman with long brown hair and intense blue eyes. Alex put his hand on her forehead. He waited but there was no sound and he realized the world had gone silent. He closed his eyes. A looming image of a man accompanied by a feeling of sheer terror, a crushing weight penetrating his groin, a piercing pain in his throat, blood spilling over his blouse. Alex pitched backwards, off balance, stomach churning. He leaned over, bile rising into his throat. He stared at the woman's face, at the surrounding faces, all different, all knotted into expressions of eternal torment, and wondered why. *Why them? What the fuck is this?*

His gaze fell on a man with brown hair graying at the temples, eyes shocked wide, mouth yawning on the edge of a scream. Although the man's weary gray eyes were filled with the terror of his last moments, Alex saw a kindness there, a deep caring. He peered deeper into those eyes and realized he knew this man. An eternity ago. He'd watched this man cradle Joe in his arms after a topple off his tricycle. He'd helped this man rake leaves on chilly fall days, watched him go after kites caught in trees, had swung high as this man pushed him on the swing set he'd put together for him and Joe and Luke.

Marcus.

Alex touched the glass at the man's worry-lined forehead. A freight train roar instantly filled Alex's head. A steel gridiron rushed at him. A grating shriek of metal on metal. He felt his shaking hands close around small shoulders, saw a blond boy fly through the air, heard the boy scream, felt a searing flash of pain in his limbs, a brutal splatter of blood … He jerked his hand away from the glass with such force that he spun sideways, backwards, reeling, falling hard to the marble floor, sucking at the saline air. Alex stared at Marcus Schell's time-frozen face, at the deep furrows in his forehead, the dark hollows under his eyes, and let the tears splash hot onto his cheeks.

Why?

Alex seethed through clenched teeth. *"WHY?"*

Stars exploding in his vision and head swimming, he crawled to the glass wall. Standing on his knees, he breathed out, felt the heat of the bloodstone in his pocket, and pressed both palms to the glass over Marcus's anguished face.

"Tell me," Alex whispered. "Show me."

Alex's head jerked back, a chugging freight train all he could see, metal on metal all he could hear. Then, for a moment, he suspended there formless, weightless, meaningless, detached, listening to voices very far away. They were speaking backwards, making no sense. The images in his head began moving, shifting, rewinding in head-spinning flashes … He was running, stumbling along the tracks, sodden with blood, his own pulse, his own heartbeat all he could hear. He stopped, breathing hard, crying hard, and fell to his knees. A train whistle sounded in the distance. It was dark, almost midnight. *God help me. I can't do this anymore. I can't protect him. I can't even protect myself.* He rubbed his face, clawed at his beard, deep sobs tearing out of his throat and behind him he heard footfalls on the gravel, coming fast. Turning, he saw Joey running, little legs pumping, feet kicking up clay and rocks, and put his hand out as if the motion would stop his son from coming closer, from being there at all.

"Go to Alex's, Joe. Tell his mom what happened. She'll help you. I-I can't …" *Jesus, I can't.*

Joey stared at him, eyes wide, frightened. He walked closer. "I don't want to, Dad. I want to stay with you. You're bleeding again."

She took it from me. God, she took it!

His son looked at him, eyes pleading, begging. *Don't look at me like that, Joe. You're better off without me. You shouldn't have to watch, to see the things she does. You shouldn't know the things you know. I don't want you to live with this anymore.* "I only wanted a family, Joey. I'm so sorry. I'm so sorry I let that back into our home. I-I thought" … *it would be different. I thought she'd get better if I just loved her enough, with God's mercy, God's strength. But I'm not strong. I can't protect you.*

He watched Joey step onto the tracks, walk closer. "Daddy, we could move away. Like you said before, with two dogs and a tree swing. Someplace where she can't hurt you anymore. You said. You promised."

I—I can't …

Joey stopped in front of him, eye-to-eye. He held up a scroll of paper, a red thread tied around it. "Dad, look. I wrote this yesterday. For you. It's called *sundance* with a little 's' 'cause something comes before it and I don't know what but I think it's hope. We could have Alex play it for us. He'll know what comes before it."

Tears ran in streams from Alex's eyes and into his beard. *I promised to take care of him. That's what fathers do. I said. I promised.*

I can't.

"Let's move away, Daddy. You're always saying we can't let her win. You said. You promised."

Alex watched exhaust thicken the sky above the pines, forming black tendrils. He felt his heart pound, felt it pushing hot blood through his veins. He looked down at his shaking hands, at his son, at the scroll, at his blood-saturated shirt and slacks. *How could I let this happen? How could she just take it?*

Joey wrapped his arms around his neck. Alex hugged his son tight, felt his strength, his light, his stubborn resolve. He saw the train round the bend and lowered his head. He heard his son's thin voice, lost in the pulsing of his temples and the engine rumble of the locomotive.

"I'm staying with you no matter what, Dad."

The train inched closer, hot air billowing like steam from an open oven.

He's so strong. He doesn't take shit from anyone. It's the light. He's got such brilliance. He is a beacon.

Joey kissed his cheek and hugged his neck tighter. "It's going to be okay, Dad. I promise."

Alex let go of his son and got to his feet, reached for Joe's small hand, and wiped his face with a bloody sleeve. They stepped off the tracks as hot air surged in a forceful rush, a deafening metallic rumble ringing into the night, and he watched as the scroll ripped from Joey's hand and caught on the gusting wind. Watched as Joey stepped onto the tracks, reaching, eyes wide. Watched as the monstrous black machine closed in. Felt his heart explode with terror. Felt his hands close around narrow shoulders and push. Felt a searing flash of pain. Felt his limbs shatter, scatter. Felt nothing
formless

weightless

meaningless

detached

Not Joe. He's the gift, the magic. He is the light that guides.

Alex dropped his hands from Marcus Schell's face and slumped onto his side, strength drained. His thoughts churned, turned, emptied. He rolled onto hands and knees, steaming bile leaving his throat in a boiling wave, then heaved again, his stomach clenching in spasms.

"You saved him," Alex breathed. "You saved him, but he couldn't save you."

That's when he saw it out of the corner of his water-swollen eyes. A shape emerged from the darkest shadows of the huge room. It was low to the ground and moved toward him, stopping every few feet. Without taking his eyes off the figure, Alex struggled to stand and blink his vision into clarity. The figure stopped and backed up. Alex heard a weak whimper as the small shape fled back into the shadows.

"That's not one of those things," he mumbled, wiping his eyes.

Overhead, the owl swooped off in the direction the shadowy figure had gone. Alex followed, trudging upward on a barely lit pathway for what seemed like hours but had to be only minutes. He came upon another series of doorways cut into a semi-circle in the wall. He turned and spotted the owl perched in front of one of the glowing archways. The bird cocked its head and watched him, unblinking. Alex stepped through the entry, eyes widening.

There were faces carved into the walls here, too, but these faces were alive with love and laughter. Entire scenes of carefree joy covered every inch of space. Animated, children smiled and chased under a warm sun. Lovers kissed, whispered, touched. Others cried together, reached out their arms to comfort and hold.

Alex shaded his eyes, looked up, and let out a long breath. Technicolor scenes of him, Luke, Joe and Isaac played out from the glowing space above. They swung on a swing set, carved arrows from bones, rode bikes and skateboards, sailed toy boats down gushing gutters, dove into piles of raked leaves, wrestled each other in brotherly play. Two other figures peered from the closest wall, their long sable hair blending with great feathery plumes, eyes sparkling with coy humor, and Alex knew exactly who they were.

"Wabishk and Makate," he breathed. They nodded at him, a deep knowing in their dark eyes.

Marble sculptures stood in the center of the room—two young men, pensive faces turned upward. They leaned against one another, into one another, cut from the same piece of rock. Alex touched the nearest sculpture's hand, squeezed Joe's stone fingers tight, and stepped closer, his shoe hitting something on the floor. A handle protruded from the ground between the two figures. Alex bent, grasped the hilt, and pulled free a sword. Unlike the wooden ones they'd had as kids, this one was heavy and sharp. Real. Holding the weapon, he nodded, feeling Mary's warm breath on his cheek, hearing her quiet words in his ear.

"Truth, with a capital T."

A shriek of violins sounded and Alex jumped, disoriented, heart racing, mind reeling. He grabbed at his thumping chest, thinking his rib cage was going to crack apart. He'd heard a voice—a voice he knew—but the room was deserted except for the unnatural motion of stone and color. He rubbed his forehead. Joe had to be here somewhere and, as always, seemed to be making a game out of this situation too.

"Goddamn," Alex muttered, raking at his hair. He was tempted to find Te and just go home, to leave Joe's ass here, to forget the rains and the trains, to forget that they'd reached out at twelve days old and curled their fingers around each other's, to forget the sharing. He glanced at Wabishk and Makate, who were crouched down and staring at him intently, waiting for him to make a choice. *I just want to forget,* Alex thought, and Makate stood tall and pointed.

A sound interrupted his bout of self-pity. Alex stepped around the sculpture, the back of his head throbbing. It wasn't the familiar sound of wings or a voice or even the shuffling scraping of those shadowthings. A muted, childlike whimper drew his attention in the direction Makate pointed, identical to the sound he'd heard in the other room before the small shape had fled into the shadows. Something moved. He took a step toward it. The shadow turned and disappeared amid the patter of small feet.

"Wait," Alex called. Dropping the heavy sword to the ground, he followed the sound of footsteps out of the golden chamber and into a dark tunnel. Ahead, the small figure broke free of the darkness and was momentarily silhouetted against a backdrop of amber light. In an instant, Alex saw the naked boy's back, his blond hair. Then he was gone. Alex broke into a run, sprinting headlong through the last half of the tunnel and emerging into a hazy yellow glow, barely bright enough to illuminate his surroundings. Unlike the room filled with light and hope, this room felt like a dungeon cell, small, cramped, dank. A nauseating odor of decay hung heavy in the air. Tortured faces peered from all sides, too close. He felt them looking into his soul and swallowed hard.

"Alex."

He whirled around.

Jade stood ten feet away. Long hair draped over her bony shoulders and down her back, covering her trembling body. She looked thin and pale, large eyes sunk into hollowed sockets. She wore a loose tunic—the same one she'd been wearing when he visited Buck—but it was torn and worn in places. She wrapped her arms around her midsection as though to hold herself up and took several wavering steps before collapsing to the floor in a weeping heap of hair. Alex knelt and gathered her close. Her skin felt warm, her tears boiling hot.

"I've got you," he said, feeling her tangible weight against him.

Jade buried her face in his neck. "I knew you'd come. I knew you'd find us." She trembled in his arms.

Alex brushed wet strands of hair out of her eyes. "You're so weak. What—why …?"

She shook her head. "It's okay now. You're here and you can save him."

Alex tightened his hold, trying to stop the violent shudders wracking her frail body. She drew her knees up, curling into a tight ball against him.

"Save who? Joe?"

Jade lifted her skeletal hand and pointed. "The boy."

Alex looked. Barely hidden in the shadows, a small naked figure that looked about six-years-old crouched against a wall of screaming faces. He clutched his knees to his chest, peering at Alex through a veil of blond hair, gaze steady, watchful, knowing. Alex's mouth suddenly felt very dry as the little boy got to his feet and inched closer. Alex took in every detail of the boy's face—down-turned ruby mouth, blue eyes, slightly turned up nose—and knew this child instantly.

"How …?

Alex touched the boy's cheek. He looked deep into those familiar eyes but didn't see himself staring back. Instead, he saw inside, into the child's tortured mind. He saw an innocent kid, horribly brutalized by an insane woman, so he'd escaped into the darkest corners of his mind and gotten lost. His fears had grown strong, monstrous, horrific, haunting. Alex saw angry, fierce hands come at his face and flinched, but did not let his callused fingertips fall from the boy's cheek. He heard the boy's thoughts and almost cried out with the fear and confusion filling him up like a well … *i'm not evil i'm not i'm not i'm not daddy loves me daddy said he'll never leave me daddy said i'm a good boy and that he'll be my best friend forever daddy will never leave me never leave me never leave …*

Alex's face knotted, but he couldn't take his hand away from the child's baby-soft face. Another voice raged through his head. Mrs. Schell. She spoke just a few words before Alex let out a groan, mind numbing, but still he couldn't take his hand away. *He did it on purpose because you are an evil soul, a demon-infested child, and he couldn't live with himself knowing his seed had given such a thing life!* The lash connected with his bare buttocks and back, so no one would see, bits of razored metal sewn into the ends flashing with the fluorescent lighting. The child cowered in the bathtub with his arms over his face and head *don't cry, think about alex and the violins think about the music and the rainbows just pretend you're not here pretend you're invisible and you can't feel it* The lash sailed through the air. He felt thin liquid streams run down his buttocks and knew it was over. Blood had been drawn. He came back into himself from the whispering darkness of time to hear her final words, words he'd heard at least a dozen times even though she'd been home only sixty-three days: *There can be no forgiveness without the shedding of blood.*

Alex pulled his hand away and squinted at the boy in the dim light. He wanted to scream at the kid and shake him— *Why didn't you tell me! Why didn't you tell somebody!*

"Joe?"

"He forgot me. Can you take me home?"

Alex peered at the boy. "Do you know me?"

"Uh-huh," the boy said, nodding. "I see you. I saw you in the river."

"I don't …" Alex shook his head.

"In the red river. You were helping."

"The red riv—" then Alex understood. "Was that you I heard screaming?"

The boy nodded.

Alex took a long exhale. "Is it you I hear crying sometimes?"

"Yeah. I try not to, but sometimes I cry loud because it hurts really bad."

Alex barely got the words out. "Is it you I'm supposed to save?"

The boy looked at Jade, who sat on the stone floor, thin arms wrapped around her shins, expression pensive and somehow hopeful. She offered a weak smile, tears cascading down her face.

Alex pulled the boy close and hugged him, a mixture of Mary's and Te's voices resounding in his ear. *Victory can be found in the darkest corners. Show him, make him see.*

He spotted the spade lying on the sand in the exact spot it should be. The growls and howls sharpened when he touched it. The sinew of his hands and arms and side ribs remembered. Joe thrust the small shovel into the powdery earth, digging deep. He hollowed out the smaller grave in no time.

No time.

He laughed loud into the bright darkness and it laughed back. Time held no meaning in this place.

The bigger grave took longer. He hummed a forgotten hymn while he worked. When he finished, he had a strong urge to lie down in the smaller hole, but neither grave was for him.

Joe tossed the spade to the ground. His skin felt like a swarm of fire ants had been set loose under his flesh. A scorched hatred swelled in his belly and he knew he would have to let it out. That's how this all worked, after all. *He* made the choices. No one else. To cut, to bleed, to lie, to see. To create, to destroy. To share, to withhold. To step onto the tracks and change his destiny and that of the people he once cared about all in one thoughtless, selfish moment. He held the wedge of glass between his hot palms—a holy talisman that could do his bidding, a relic of bad blood, an instrument of pain and sacrifice. The freight train snarl inside his head mirrored the cries of the darkness, heralded his demise, and all he could think was, *I'm the only one who can stop this once and for all. I am chosen.* He pressed the pointed end of the glass to his chest, pushed in and dragged down, across his ribs left to right and back again. The cross cut into his torso blazed with fury and a fall of blood spilled boiling rage from his innermost core onto the fine white sand, where it took shape, grew to monstrous proportions, sprouted twisted claws and needle teeth to devour and tear. Because that's how it all worked, this madness. His sorrow, large now, wore wrath like a shield as it strode into the dim ether to join his

guilt

    shame

        innocence

            truth

                grief

The words wrote themselves out in neon red again and again. Joe turned his attention toward the fitful whimpers in the distance, toward the whiny little fuck. Toward the people standing between him and an eternity of blessed quiet. Toward his prey.

The little boy writhed in agony on the stone floor, tears streaming from his eyes. Jade crawled toward him, weak with fatigue. Alex looked at Jade, unsure what to do.

"Joe is hurting himself again," she said, slumping onto her side. She looked more gaunt and frail with every passing moment and Alex wondered if it was because he was there now and she felt she could loosen her grasp on whatever thread had been tethering her to life for the past eight years. The boy tensed and jerked in seizure-like spasms. He let out a heart-wrenching wail. Alex grimaced, took hold of the kid and pulled him into his arms. Holding the child against him, Alex was filled with deep regret. He had run away, had retreated and avoided like a goddamn coward, leaving Jade to do the work of protecting this small part of Joe he hadn't yet been able to destroy. Her armor had taken all the hits that he had dodged. *Eight years. That's an eternity to act as a shield.*

"Don't do that," Jade said.

Alex looked at her. "What?"

"Don't beat yourself up. Your burdens have been heavy, too."

"Are you still inside my head?" Alex said, trying to keep the frustration out of his voice.

Jade smiled. "No. I saw it on your face."

Alex let out a long breath. "We have to do something."

"It's not up to us," Jade said.

The boy suddenly went slack in his arms, panting, and Jade told him not to be alarmed, which was near impossible. Alex gazed down at the child's pale face. "He's out there with those things, I know it. I'll find him and drag his ass back here and make—"

"No!" Jade's eyes grew wide. "He's been blinded! They've been torturing him with every unimaginable memory! He's not strong enough!"

Alex took her trembling hand. "Okay. Okay. It's okay. I just-I don't know what to do."

"The shadows can't just take him. *He* must surrender fully to *them*, but he can't do that until he has killed all of his hope." Her gaze rested on the boy curled in Alex's lap. "Every last bit of it. Until then, they will continue to torment him with the secrets he's carried since—"

"—since Marcus died," Alex finished.

Jade squinted at him and shook her head. "No, Alex."

He studied her haunting face and the realization dawned. "Oh, fuck. Oh, fuck. God, I'm a fucking idiot. Since Norma came home! That changed everything for Joe. And me … us."

Jade leaned heavily against the wall of faces. "The moment you clasped your tiny hands together so long ago was the moment your destinies were sealed. It was already there, *songaona*, the sharing, but it strengthened into an unbreakable bond at that very moment. He fortified you and you fortified him. And then, in your grief and your guilt, you both forgot. You are the only one who can make him see his truth. You just had to see your own first."

Alex scowled. "I saw you in your bed, in your house. I met your father. I met Aala. I met some woman named Kiki. How …?"

Jade gave him a small smile and took his hand. "I like Kiki. She talks a lot. She has a beautiful little girl named Emily. I felt you holding my hand. I felt the warmth of your skin."

"But how? How did you get *here*?"

"It happened that night, Alex, on the grass, in the lightning and the masculine rain. It happened the night I nearly died. The violent man was on top of me, inside of me, hurting me, cutting me. The rain took my blood into Mother Earth. I felt my spirit leave my body. And then the man was gone and Joe was there and he said help was coming and he spoke the violent man's name into my ear and I didn't forget. I said it out loud over and over. My spirit was floating above. I could see her, and Joe could see her, too, because he's like me. He reached up into the furious rain and took my spirit and pulled her close to him and I knew she would be safe in this little boy's heart because it had been cut deep with sadness and the scar tissue was strong. So, I told her to go with him, to protect him because a red river was coming, and he knew what it was to have your innocence stolen and trust betrayed. And then my spirit was gone, and Joe was gone and there were other men and I continued to name the monster out loud. I didn't forget."

Jade looked down at the embattled boy sitting in Alex's lap. The kid reached out his small hands and she curled her thin fingers around them, smiling. "I'm the spirit that you took in and gave safe haven to. *Gibezhigomin! Giganawenji-gemin!* Right, *Heyoka?*"

The boy jumped up and hugged her neck, laughing. "I'm your hero and you're my Wonder Woman! We are protectors!"

Hugging the child tight, Jade locked tear-filled eyes with Alex, still smiling. "He saved me and now you must save him, so he can save others."

Alex sat there stunned. He pulled at his nose.

"Wait. What do you mean Joe's like you?"

Jade set the boy on his feet and he curled himself back into Alex's lap. As Jade spoke, the child periodically reached up to touch Alex's cheek with his baby-soft hand and give it a gentle stroke.

"I am a *Heyoka,*" Jade said.

Alex squinted at her. *Why does that word sound familiar?* And then he remembered—Aala had blurted it out when he was in Jade's room.

"*Heyokas* are all over the world," she continued, "but many don't know how to harness and use their gifts. They are out of touch with the ancestors and distracted by unimportant things, so they get overwhelmed with the energies, the shadows. Then they get angry or depressed because they haven't been taught the backward way and the importance of *seeing* people and their humanity. For *Heyokas* who don't understand their gifts or been taught to create boundaries, witnessing the suffering of others can be too much to bear and they can become very destructive toward people, toward the Earth, toward animals. Many destroy themselves. They don't know that what they are feeling is a gift to be channeled toward serving others, not harming them. The mirror of truth is difficult to look into, but it's necessary."

"The mirror," Alex breathed, almost forgetting.

Jade sighed. "Yes."

Sweat ran down Alex's back. *"What is it?"*

Jade pulled her knees to her chest. Alex saw goosebumps rise on her arms.

"The mirror of truth is a tool that *Heyokas* have used for centuries. We are Empaths, in the purest and most ancient sense of the word. We use the mirror to master our skills of reflecting a person's deepest truths back to them so they can see their true nature and realize their destiny, but also so they can heal the wounds they have incurred in their lifetime. I was hoping Joe would use the mirror for that purpose—to see his path as a *Heyoka* and guide. But the mirror of truth and evolution also reflects what someone *believes* to be true about themselves, and what they see is often inaccurate, terribly distorted by the wounds of others, false truths that are handed down by broken people. And sometimes those false truths come for them. Come for us."

Shuddering, Alex had a memory flash of Luke hanging from the rocky incline and turning into Joe saying he couldn't save him.

Alex nodded, thinking. "So. When you said Joe's like you …"

"He sees. He always has. You know that. He saw you, your struggle for breath, and reached out his tiny hand to let you know everything would be okay, that you would never be alone. But now he is blinded by false truths."

The little boy in Alex's lap reached up and placed his small hands on Alex's cheeks.

Alex gazed into the child's familiar eyes and asked the question without speaking.

The boy smiled. "I'm a hero."

Jade's expression grew serious. She tightened her grip on Alex's hand. "You are as integral a part of Joe as this child is, Alex. Truly one spirit split between two bodies. That's how I was able to send a thought-thread out to you. You can reach him. I've seen into your heart. I know it's broken, but it's also big enough to hold the world, and strong enough to let go of everything you think you know."

Alex shook his head. "I did something terrible. So terrible."

Jade placed her palm over the boy's hand on his cheek. "That is a false truth. Your healing has begun. You've remembered an important part of yourself, now you'll help Joe remember who he is. After giving me such a safe, beautiful place filled with music and light, we can't lose him. People need him."

"Music?"

Jade nodded. "It's been hidden in the shadows for a while now, but yes."

Alex looked at the boy. The child blinked at him with sleepy eyes.

"He got lost and forgot me, but Wonder Woman said you can help put us back together and then I can go home."

Alex swallowed hard. "Where is your home?"

The boy patted Alex's chest then shook his head. "He won't let me back in there 'cause he's scared."

"What's he scared of?"

"Crying a lot. His heart hurts and he doesn't like it. It's like sadness, only more than what's in the whole wide world all put together." The boy yawned, curled tighter into Alex's lap, and was asleep in an instant.

Jade squeezed Alex's hand again. "He wants to live, Alex. He just doesn't know how."

Alex breathed deep, watching the sleeping child, and a troubling realization needled his brain, making his mouth dry, his heart race. A little boy once again depended on him.

Then suddenly, out of the dark quiet, loud cracks echoed like tree branches ripping free of a trunk.

"He's coming," Jade gasped, pulling the boy into her arms. "It's too soon. He can't see."

Alex sucked in a sharp breath, trying to fill his lungs. His heart felt like it had been set ablaze and he clutched at it with both hands, grimacing in pain. He could feel Joe's hot rage roiling inside his own body like poison, draining his strength. It pumped through the air around them like torrents from a shit-smelling sewer. A black terror filled him.

eleven

Scars

One Who Walks Across The Sky saw her sons chasing on the horizon and knew night would soon fall. At her feet, a blue flower took root and began to grow. One side of the flower bloomed in long petals, the other half dried in the wind, brown petals sailing up and away. One Who Walks Across The Sky followed the husks over the prairie, where she came upon her sons Wabishk, the son of Dawn, and Makate, the son of Midnight. Wabishk played with an identical flower that bloomed on the opposite side, but Makate was busy painting the hills with rainbows and did not notice her. She had brought fire, now she must bring truth. One Who Walks Across The Sky placed her dying flower into the son of Midnight's hands, where it changed shape, grew wings and flew away. A child's laughter lifted with it.

"Gichi-manidoo, daga naa gikinoowizh ojichaagwan. Great One, guide this soul," said One Who Walks Across The Sky. She leapt upon the clouds then, leaving her sons to find the blue flower on their own. From up high, she could see the rainbows Makate painted, and they looked like pain and joy. One Who Walks Across The Sky had brought truth, now she must bring darkness, which saddened her deeply.

It began to rain.

Jade sat bolt upright. Alex couldn't hear what she told the boy, but he knew it was something to calm his fears. She'd been his armor for a long time.

Clutching at his scorching chest, Alex knelt beside them. "Don't leave this room. No matter what you hear or see, stay here where the light is. I can intercept him."

"They've made him strong. He—*I* feel different."

"I do, too," Alex told her.

He studied her haunted face and stroked her hair. For a single painful moment, he realized he might never see her again.

"What if I can't convince him?"

"There's nothing Joe can do to me that hasn't already been done, Alex. But ..." Her gaze drifted from his and came to rest on the boy wrapped up in her arms.

Alex frowned. "What will happen to you? If I fail?"

"You won't," Jade said.

"Your body—" Alex had to stop himself from saying more.

"Just make him see."

"I don't know what that means," Alex said. He could hear the frustration and confusion in his voice, all bound up and steeped in a visceral fear.

The boy looked up at Alex. "He's real scared now. When he's scared he hurts me."

Alex nodded. "He needs to remember."

The boy got up from Jade's lap and wrapped his arms around Alex's neck. He whispered into Alex's ear then stepped back and put his small hands on Alex's cheeks. He caressed them gently while looking deep into Alex's eyes. Alex felt the sweltering heat in his chest ease and vanish. He peered at the child in the dim golden light and said, "Okay. I'll tell him."

With a final glance at Jade, Alex turned and left the cramped room. Slow and watchful, he retraced his steps down the long walkway and back to the technicolor room. The sword was right where he'd dropped it before following the kid. Alex stooped, wrapped his fingers around the ivory hilt, and saw Makate stand tall, Wabishk crouch low. Alex squeezed the handle with both hands and stood up, nodding to the Shiloh braves who watched from above, whose destinies he knew so well. The white owl appeared, swooped low then climbed high, dove again then soared out of the room toward the chamber that held the mirrored wall of misery.

Alex followed.

As he stepped into the room, he caught sight of someone with blond, stringy hair and streaks of fresh blood splashed across his scarred torso and came to a dead stop. The figure held something long, narrow, sharp in his hand and stood unbearably still, stone-like. His tall, reed-thin body looked like an obscene piece of living art. Scars and flesh carvings moved and undulated with every deliberate breath, animated suffering come to life.

Alex held his sword low and stepped toward the person standing in the center of the stone floor. His stomach burned. Sweat rolled down his face and back. He tried to focus on his exhales.

"The wages of sin is death, Alexander," Joe said, voice hollow, empty. "And pain."

"Come back with me, Joe," Alex said, keeping his tone even, authoritative. "Come with me to the desert and everything'll be okay. I promise."

"Making promises already?" Joe drew the sharp blade back and forth against his thigh. He stood twenty feet away. "Scared, Al?"

Whispers and soft moans filled the chamber, echoing Joe's words.

scared   *Al*   *scared*

Al   *scared*   *Al*

Alex gripped the hilt of his weapon. The sweat from his palms made it hard to hold on to. He glanced up at a stone face that was oozing a puke-yellow stream from its mouth. The flow vanished and then began again. Alex swallowed hard.

"Yes. Scared for you. Scared for both of us. I don't want to hurt you, Joe. I came here to help you."

Joe clawed bloody hair down over his eyes. The movement brought the images hacked into his flesh to more vivid life. Like the anguished, weeping faces in the walls all around them, Joe's wounds bled color, creating a rainbow aura around his body.

"Very original, Alexander. For someone with such a creative mind, you can't think of something better than 'I came to help?' C'mon. I know you."

"I know you, too, bro."

Joe snorted. Clusters of bloodshot hair stuck to his face. "Yeah? Enlighten me."

"I know why you hurt him."

Joe didn't respond. The walls whispered.

The dull amber glow of the room lit Joe's red mouth and white teeth—and Alex had a sudden urge to walk over and slam his fist into that fucking mouth and knock out every last one of those goddamn teeth. He took a step forward.

"I can't let him live, Al," Joe said as if stating a universal truth. "He makes too much noise. Always in my head. It's simple. As long as the little bastard lives, I can't die."

Alex loosened his grip. His hands ached. "Joe, I don't know what the mirror has been showing you, but it's all lies."

Joe stepped forward and Alex instinctively squeezed the hilt again, ignoring the throbbing in his muscles, the hollow ache in his temples, the fire that was trying to reignite in his chest.

"What you're doing is easier than fighting. You used to fight, Joe. You and me and Luke, battling it out, watching each other's back. Mary told you about Jade, about the kid, about your path. But you chose to believe that fucking piece of glass instead. You stopped fighting."

Joe scoffed. "And now here we are."

He began to circle. Alex tracked him, watching the drapes of color and the animated scars ripple with each deliberate step.

Joe raised his sword, twirled it casually. "The more the old hag talked about the little fuck and all the other bullshit, I knew I needed to lock you out. Couldn't be sharing that info with you, now could I? I hadn't counted on you coming this far, though. Thought you'd tuck in your balls and run away like you do with everything else in your sad life. I was annoyed at first, but it's actually been beneficial having you here. I knew you—Sir Alexander with your gallant guilty heart—wouldn't leave without them. You know exactly where they are. Don't you, Alex?"

"Yeah," Alex told him. "I do. I'll take you to them, but …

"Ultimatums, too, Al? Shit."

"I get it, okay? I get that this is my penance for doing what I did to Luke and that I get a second chance. I can't let you kill that kid. He's innocent, he's you, the best part of you, and I won't let you do it." He swallowed hard and took a deep breath.

Joe raised the sword higher and closed the distance between them by a few feet. He snorted again.

"What'd you do, Al honey?" Joe's tone sent a sarcastic echo bouncing around the room. The tortured walls answered. Joe went on.

"Something serious, huh? Like jacking off in the shower? Or missing a few chords now and then? Or how about telling a few fibs? That it, Al? I know. I saw inside your head. I was the one who told your mom something was wrong that day and she sent the cops to find you. You had no choice. Lucas was dead before you got to the bottom of the ravine. And he wanted it too much."

"Like you?"

"Fucking-A."

"I know what happened at the tracks." He watched Joe's hair-covered face, tried to see through all the filth and color to the person his friend used to be.

Joe scowled. "You don't know shit."

Alex glanced at the mirrored wall—at the floating bodies, at the spot he'd discovered Marcus Schell's face pressed hard against the glass, mouth stretched wide in a silent scream—and lowered his weapon. His arms and legs felt weak, drained, and his chest tightened so much that he couldn't inhale fully.

"Your dad told me," Alex said. "I saw it through his eyes, I heard his thoughts. She beat him regularly. She castrated him and ... and made you watch. She thought he would try to put more demon babies inside her. Of course, she knew how, knew which drugs to give him, which cuts to make, how to suture. She'd been an O.R. nurse, an excellent student, top of her class. You followed Marcus to the tracks after—" Alex swiped at his eyes, feeling very tired, very old. "He was going to end his life that night. You saw into him, saw that he didn't want to die, but didn't know what else to do. You did everything you could to change your dad's mind, and it worked, Joe. It worked."

Joe had grown very still. Alex forced himself to keep talking, choking back tears.

"Your dad's final thought was of you. Only you. But you know that already, because you saw inside, and his shame and guilt and confusion overwhelmed you so it was all you could see. But he believed in you so much, believed you are a gift. And you are. I found your notebooks, your music. I never knew where it came from, only that it would choose me. It was you, Joe. You were composing fugues and sonatas in your head before I ever picked up a violin, man. We're one half of the other. When you quit hearing music a year ago it stopped for me, too."

The burning knot in Alex's chest eased a little. He stepped forward, holding the sword at his side. Joe was looking at him. He could feel it.

"I helped one brother die," Alex said, hot tears sliding onto his cheeks. "I can't go through that again. I won't."

Joe remained deathly silent.

"That kid has carried your guilt long enough. Stop pun-ishing him. You didn't kill your dad. It was an accident."

He saw Joe's head shift, heard him mumble.

"What?" Alex stepped closer.

"I said *there's more to it, you fuck!*"

Joe lunged, his blood-caked mouth twisting into a sinister snarl. His breath reeked of carrion rot. He seized Alex by the shirt and yanked him close, almost off his feet.

"But you know everything, don't you, *fuckbag!* So, you tell me!"

Joe dropped his weapon and grabbed Alex's head in a vice grip. Through clumps of red-tinged hair, Alex looked deep into Joe's eyes and the white light flaring there. The twin beams blinded him, bored deep, sucked him in.

"You tell me," he heard Joe say again, before the light overcame him and it was all Alex could see.

Alex smelled roses. Madonnas. His mother's favorite. He had a cramp in his side from running so hard and his head hurt where he'd smacked it on the hard clay. His mother held out her gardening spade and a box of lawn and leaf bags. Extra thick to hold the weight. When he refused to take them, she whacked his shoulder hard with the spade.

"Clean up your mess," Norma spat, swinging again.

He blocked her blow, sharp edge of the spade slicing into his forearm. He tried not to cry.

She dropped the small shovel at his feet then held his skinny arms tight and forced him to kneel and pick it up. She shoved the box of bags into his shaking hands and told him to make sure no one saw. He glanced at the limb lying on the grass, twisted like a broken tree branch, the bone white against meaty red. The bootlaces were still tied in a double knot.

His mother said they'd lock him up forever if anyone saw.

Alex ran back to the tracks, legs pumping fast, dragging

the wagon he hadn't played with in four years because his mother said he was too big to play with a baby toy like that. The moon watched from vast and empty blackness. That's how he felt. Vast and empty. Dark. The sky cried a little, sprinkling him with tears while he put parts into the bags his mother had given him. Daddy's skin still felt warm.

Be a good boy. It's our job to take care of her. Just do what she asks, and everything will be okay. Alex talked while he searched, "It's going to be okay, Dad. She'll call Brother Adam. He's always talking about how we can be reborn. He'll know what to do."

There were more parts than he thought possible.

He pulled the heavy wagon three blocks and up the long driveway, proud that he never stopped to catch his breath. His mother opened the back gate and told him to go to the garden and dump everything out. Alex carefully placed each bag on the grass, except for the biggest one, which had to be tilted out, then took the spade from his mother's clenched fist. She'd already removed a bunch of rose bushes to make room. No one was allowed to touch her flowers except her.

Alex dug, the sky wetting his skin, and watched startled earthworms squirm for cover through his muddy fingers.

"Deeper," she said.

She read from her Bible, spit dribbling off her chin. The moon lit up her lipsticked teeth like flashing neon. She read about how in olden days people used to eat their children, about evil deeds and God's eternal punishment of sinners, about fathers forsaking their sons. She read about sin and made sure he understood that he had sinned in the worst possible way and would have to be punished. But that was okay. He knew he'd done something unforgiveable.

Alex dug a deep hole and took great care removing parts from the plastic bags and arranging them in order, doing his best to make them fit together. When he got to Daddy's left hand, he pulled the gold band off and slipped it into his pocket. His mother didn't notice. She was too busy reading and spitting. Rainwater washed the red clay from Daddy's smashed face. Alex bent and kissed the flattened forehead, then looked up at the rings of thorns over his head. They'd been scratching his arms and making him bleed since he started, but he didn't mind. He didn't mind anything anymore. His mind had gone away.

There was a part missing. The right boot.

"Find it," she said, pointing a long blood-red fingernail at the gate.

He trudged through the rain and looked and looked but couldn't find it anywhere. It made him sad that his dad wasn't complete. It made him sad that a part was missing and that he couldn't find it no matter how hard he looked. Part of Dad had disappeared. Vanished.

His mother wasn't happy about that.

Alex wanted to disappear, too. He got down on his knees and filled in the hole. Wet dirt covered Daddy's face. All of his teeth had gotten broken. Alex lay down on the mud keeping his dad warm and let the rain pound on his back, thinking about dirt and Genesis 3:19—*you will return to the ground from which you came, for you were made from the ground, and to the ground you will return.*

His mother kept reading.

Alex prayed with all his might, *for the Lord himself will come down from heaven with a mighty shout and with the soul-stirring cry of the archangel and the great trumpet call of God. And the believers who are dead will be the first to rise to meet the Lord. Then we who are still alive and remain on the earth will be caught up with them in the clouds to meet the Lord in the air and remain with him forever.*

He waited for his dad to rise. But the shout never came, the trumpet never sounded. Alex never made it to the clouds. Holding back tears, he wondered if Daddy would be able to eat all that good food they had in Heaven with broken teeth.

~

The blazing light released him.

Gulping air, Alex slipped from Joe's grasp and crumpled over on his knees. The knot in his throat threatened to choke him.

Joe's voice came in whisper. "It should have been me, not him."

A deep sob tore loose in Alex's throat. He couldn't fill his lungs. "Why didn't you tell me? Why didn't you *tell someone, goddamn it!*" He could feel his mind ripping, tearing.

"I've seen my truth," Joe said, tone flat. "This is my destiny."

From somewhere up high, the child screamed, his anguish filling the chamber with a tangible terror. Joe lifted his sword from the floor. Alex scrambled to get upright.

"Here's your fucking truth, Al," Joe said, resolute, calm. "You're going to die now. I hope it was worth it."

Stunned, Alex scrambled backward as Joe advanced, swinging his weapon out and aiming it at Alex's abdomen.

"You, of all people, should know *there are no accidents!*" Joe screamed. "Someone's *always* to blame!"

"No … wait …" Alex reeled away from the point of Joe's sword. Stinging tears filled his eyes. He couldn't see clearly.

"You used to like sword fights, Al," Joe seethed through clenched jaws. "Let's see if you enjoy this one." He lunged. Alex side-stepped, the blade ripping through his shirt. He brought his sword up in time to block a second blow.

"You still don't get it," Joe said. "Luke is dead because of you, my dad is dead because of me. I get that. You don't. You brought me back once. It's not happening again."

Alex tripped backward and fell against the mirrored wall of floating bodies. The image of an ugly fat man drifted through his mind, screaming *how does that feel honey?* A stinging slap followed. Joe advanced. Before Alex could lift the heavy sword to block, something sharp pierced his right side just under the ribs. Joe's sticky hair was in his face, smelling old, rotten. His breath, hot, blew the stench of raw meat and blood.

"You have a choice, Sir Alexander," Joe whispered. "You can run on home and play your fiddle like a happy little camper, or you can die a painful dark death and have your stinking spirit rot here with that bitch's. What do you say?"

Joe twisted the blade. Alex sucked air through clenched teeth, vision tunneling.

"You're scared," Alex grunted, feeling hot blood run down his side. "I can feel it. Your mom's got you brainwashed into believing it was your fault and you think if you stay here and kill your hope you'll be safe from pain. There's pain in Hell, Joe. Lots of it. Listen to these voices and you'll know." The fat man's corpse-voice screamed through his head again as Alex pressed his shaking body against the glass. *How does that feel honey?*

"You think I don't know pain? You think I don't feel other people's pain *every single fucking second of every single fucking day?* You idiot."

Joe leaned on his weapon, pushing the point in deeper. Alex's face twisted. His sword fell from his grasp. He slumped forward, cold metal inching further into his flesh, and watched a familiar tunnel start to close around him. A sudden shriek ripped through the salty air and he managed to look up in time to see Jade running across the stone floor, hair flying behind her like a cape. Joe flung his free arm out. His fist connected with the side of Jade's head and she hit the stone floor with a loud slap. Alex balled up his fist and slammed it into Joe's face as hard as he could, sending him reeling. Joe let go of his weapon and Alex groaned as the length of the sword dipped toward the floor and the point shifted, tearing into the muscle behind his rib cage.

How does that feel honey?

Alex's shoes slipped out and he slid to the floor, watching blood soak his filthy shirt and run through his fingers. He knew he shouldn't have, but he pulled out the sword, letting loose a fall of blood. He pressed his palm against the puncture wound and struggled to stand.

Joe stood doubled over with his hands to his face, a blackish-red liquid dripping through his fingers.

"Can you feel that, Joe?" Alex yelled, stepping away from the fat man's taunting voice. *"Can you, asshole?"*

Alex limped a few more steps, leaving a ruby trail. He hunched over, the muscles in his side searing hot. From the corner of his eye, he saw a small naked figure move out of the shadows.

"No," Alex moaned, doubling over. Blood filled his mouth.

The child walked across the stone floor and stopped next to Alex. He faced Joe, his pale face slick with tears, a deep agony in his blue eyes.

"You have to stop now," he told Joe. "Blood has been drawn and now you have to stop. That's the rule."

Joe shook his head. "It doesn't work like that here."

Through blurry eyes and a bone-wracking surge of dread, Alex watched Joe ease down and wrap his dripping fingers around the sword hilt, smearing the ivory with crimson.

"I just want to come home," the little boy said, his tone choked with sadness. Tears tumbled from his chin, mixing with the blood pooling under Alex's running shoes. Alex inched closer to the boy. He felt like all of life's dreams were being emptied right in front of his eyes.

"Please?" The boy stepped forward. Alex, too. Joe lifted the sword high over the child's head.

"Joe," Alex said, weak. His lungs felt like they were filling with water. "You didn't do anything wrong. Let me help you."

"You're dying," Joe said smugly, his hidden eyes locked on the child. "Your worst fear. How ironic that I get to be the bringer of death. And the wicked must suffer."

Joe swung the sword, aiming at the kid's throat.

Alex lunged, shoving the kid hard and knocking him to the floor. Something cold ripped through the flesh of Alex's left wrist, cutting deep. The sound of snapping tendons found his ears. A geyser of blood lifted into the air. He didn't realize what had happened until all of his fingers went numb and he saw tiny dancing musical notes spin away into darkness. A death march sounded in his head. Somehow, his right hand found his wrist and gripped it hard against his chest. His fingers hung dead white, limp.

Someone shouted.

Alex looked up and saw Jade stumbling toward Joe, her thin arms outstretched.

"No …" Her weary voice trailed off and she crumpled into a shaking heap at Joe's feet. She pulled the weeping child to her side and tried to cover his small body with her own. A wide gash on the boy's chest bled bright scarlet into her long hair.

"Stop," she sobbed, reaching out to Joe. "Stop. You are better than this. You're a guide, a light. People need you." She lowered her head, tears falling into the child's blond hair.

Joe bent over, grabbed the kid's arm, and dragged him out of the room, his screams echoing like the wails of a terrified animal.

Alex looked up from the steady stream of blood leaving his arm and saw the white owl coming fast towards him. It veered left and flew by, smacking Alex's face with its wing. Luke's voice sounded loudly in his ear. *Show him!* The owl circled high and flew at Alex again, almost knocking him off his feet with a forceful rush of wind.

Pressing his wounded arm to his chest, Alex stumbled toward the blurred opening in the wall then stopped and turned back. Jade stood, legs firm under her, tears gone, a fearful but determined expression on her face.

Alex extended his good hand. "Let's go."

The owl took off in the direction Joe had fled. Jade and Alex followed. He could hear Joe thrashing his way through the stone structure. The child's screams sent even more color into the atmosphere, making it harder to see clearly. Alex caught brief glimpses of a streaking white flash ahead, leading the way. Gasping, he and Jade rushed into the room with the tall pillars in time to see Joe's bare feet disappear into a tunnel ten feet above the ground.

"Fuck," Alex rasped, spitting into the sand. His vision doubled, tripled. He tried to suck air into his lungs, but every breath felt like ice in his chest and he wondered if the sword had punctured a lung—or worse. He looked at his ruined fingers, tried to make them move. They didn't.

Jade ran across the room and looked up at the opening in the wall. She took hold of a knobby protrusion—the top of a stone ear—and pulled herself up, slipped, and fell to the ground. She got up, brushed herself off, and began again. Alex limped over and squinted up at the tunnel opening, vision doubling and tripling until everything looked like it was under water. He could hear Joe through the child's unbearable screams. He was singing again.

Alex pointed, tried to blink his eyes clear. "Try that one."

Jade grabbed a distended lip and started up. Alex grabbed a stone face by the teeth with his good hand. The muscles in his shoulder lit up like fire as he hoisted himself. He ignored the searing pain and set his blood-soaked left elbow on a protruding forehead. In agonizing micro steps, he inched up the wall using the faces for balance and leverage.

"Come on!" Jade reached down from the opening, wrapped her fingers around Alex's good wrist, and pulled as hard as she could, sending a cascade of sand into his face. Alex turned his head away, gasping. Jade pulled harder and he was able to launch off his left leg and lie belly-down just inside the lip of the tunnel. He pushed off again and crawled on his elbows after the wild-eyed woman through the deep sand.

The pain seemed to have a deadening effect on him. His body went into auto-pilot, his exhausted mind, too. Joe's fear and the kid's intermittent wailing created a red-violet cloud in the air, so thick Alex had to wave it away. He could feel Joe's fury coursing through his own body like a toxin, could hear Joe's thoughts of guilt and blame, familiar as his own skin. It all felt heavy and dark and so hopeless. Alex blinked water from his eyes and plowed the length of the tunnel, leaving a trail of tears and scarlet sand in his wake. The dull amber glow ahead sent a creeping shudder through his exhausted bones and Alex stopped, spitting bloody grains from his mouth.

"Wait," he called.

Jade plowed through the fine powder and he heard her inside his head—*No. We can't let his false truths devour the boy.*

Alex picked up his pace, catching her panic on the violet-tinged air, and caught up with her as they approached the end of the tunnel. Amid the singing and the cries that had grown increasingly weary, he heard a heavy wood door heave closed and knew where Joe had gone.

"He's out there. They'll come for him," Jade breathed, crawling out of the tunnel.

"I know," Alex said. "He wants them to. I can feel it. But there's also—" He cut off, unable to pinpoint what he—what Joe—was feeling. Creeping shudders turned into violent tremors and he wondered if he was going into shock or if it was something happening inside Joe. It was all as blurred as his vision. Breathing hard and shallow, Alex pushed himself the last few feet and emerged into the room he and Joe had tumbled into after encountering the monstrosity that had wanted Joe.

Alex faced the door, keeping his injured arm pressed to his chest, and spit more bloody mucus into the sand. Dots of light swam in front of his eyes and he waited for them to subside before stepping forward. Jade was quicker, pushing and pulling on the door with all her might. Alex joined her efforts. He locked his jaws together and winced at the boiling pain in his shoulder. A fresh stream of blood burst from the wound under his ribs. With a groan, he wrenched open the door. The boy's sobs and screams intensified in volume and fear, echoing from all directions, filling the blackness with terror and *something else.*

Alex stood in the frame, an amber glow showering his body, and blinked into utter darkness. Shuddering, he took Jade's hand and walked out of the light. Gloom and despair, complete and whole, fell like a heavy wet blanket, sucking at his skin, yet the atmosphere seemed alive with pulsing shadows. Intangible wisps brushed across Alex's face, chilling his bones. He breathed out. A faint haze wavered in the distance, illuminated by that strange tawny glow, and he started toward it, holding Jade's hand tight.

The child's screams abruptly cut short and fell silent. Jade let go of Alex's hand and took off at a dead run.

"Jade, no!" Alex watched in horror as darkness consumed her.

Alex staggered forward, holding his arms out in front of him, but skidded to a stop when he saw Joe surrounded by a halo of red light and a small figure lying on the sand at Joe's feet, spotlighted by the rippling surreal glow. Joe circled the figure on the ground, his skin streaked with fresh blood, hair covering his face and saturated in crimson. Joe seemed almost transparent, hazy. He held something in his hand and Alex stepped closer to the edge of the sanguineous aura. It looked like a wedge of some sort, glinting glass-like in the undulating color. Suddenly, Joe raised the object and thrust it into his side, howling in a victory whoop and dragging the thing across his torso in a fall of blood. The boy on the ground writhed in agony but had fallen silent with exhaustion, panting for breath. Joe's image flickered and wavered, his outline blurring then coming together again. Beyond the halo, Alex saw shadowy shapes close in. Joe raised the weapon in his hand, this time stabbing it into his neck and dragging it down to his hip with a sardonic laugh that filled the darkness. The child spasmed against the ground. The shifting shapes moved closer, one emerging from the dusk larger than the others, and Alex saw the words

guilt

    blame

        shame

            sins

                punish

write themselves out in neon red in the air. The edges of Joe's body blurred, wavered again. He grew more transparent, less solid, less tangible. Alex thought it was his eyes, but then realized the truth. Joe was becoming

invisible

Alex couldn't pick up his feet. They stayed fixed to the sand. And then his body remembered, his mind remembered, his half-spirit remembered … *A halo of light framed the open door and Alex saw blood, saw Joe, saw life dripping away. He looked down at his shoes, anchored to the creamcolored carpet, polished and new, the Band-Aids on his heels making them feel tight. Perspiration poured from his armpits, soaking through his designer shirt and jacket, making the itchy fabric cling to his skin. His fingers vibrated. He stared at his feet and wondered why they weren't moving, wondered what the Florsheim people would say if he got blood all over his rented shoes …*

Joe! Noooo!

The sound of his voice snapped him back and he lurched forward, hollow cries filling the void. Something grabbed his hair and dragged. Stinging grains of sand bit into his flesh. Flailing, he kicked at the thing and tried to get a grip with his good hand on whatever evil had its grip on him. He landed at Joe's feet and lay there stunned, blinking up into the faint purple light. Joe's silhouetted form towered over him. He gazed down, hair covering his face. The cross carved into his torso blazed magenta in the rusty light.

Blood covered his entire body. At the periphery of the aura, shadows circled.

"You're a fool," Joe said, turning the sharp piece of glass in his fingers.

"Joe, don't do this," Alex gasped. "Your dad didn't want you to give up. Don't let her win." He coughed into the sand and tried to stand. Invisible hands picked him up and flung him back to the ground. His head bounced hard, clacking his teeth, jarring his brain. Points of light burst in front of his eyes.

"You should've gone when you had the chance," Joe said. "You can't win here."

"I know," Alex said, trying to focus. "I'm not strong enough to save you. Never have been." The child groaned beside him.

Joe snickered. "Finally, some sense."

"But you're strong enough to save me," Alex said. "Always have been."

Joe laughed. "And why would I do that, Alexander?"

"Because we are each one half of the same soul and you are an Empath. Your ability to see into me means you won't let me die. You know that's my worst fear. My suffering would be too much for you. Always has been. That's why you locked me out. You didn't want me feeling your pain. You knew I couldn't take it. Not after Luke. You did it to protect me."

Joe didn't laugh. He'd grown very still.

"Wrong."

A dark shape descended, the blackness churning, roaring like a freight train. Red light glinted off the thing's needle-like teeth. It was all Alex could see. The thing picked him up and slammed him face first into the ground. All the air left his lungs. The hole in his side let loose a fresh stream of blood. His nose gushed, filling his throat with thick coppery fluid. Spitting blood and sand, Alex struggled to his hands and knees. He yelled over the screeching locomotive noise.

"Your dad loved you more than anything. I wonder what he would think of all this—you surrendering, forfeiting the fight!"

Cold, vaporous claws ripped at his skin. Alex rolled away, trying to get his bearings, hawking more blood into the fine white earth.

"He believed in you, Joe. We all did."

Amorphous hands picked him up again, slammed him down hard. He landed on his wounded shoulder and groaned at the electric shocks arcing through his body.

"You ... think you ... killed him, Joe?" Alex choked, bracing himself. "Nope. It was your mom. She killed his spirit, just like she's trying to kill yours."

The impact on his abdomen made him gasp. He sailed sideways, curling into a ball, skidding, rolling across the ground, out of control. The sound of his own pulse, combined with the pulse of something much larger, thrummed like thunder in his ears. Everything blurred. Blood poured into his mouth, the metallic taste coating his tongue. He couldn't get enough air into his lungs. Flopping onto his stomach, Alex pushed up to his knees, holding his side with his bad arm, breath rapid and shallow.

"She destroyed your dad and she's been trying to destroy you your whole life. But you wouldn't let her. Don't start now."

He thought he heard Joe's voice, but the beast had him again, this time by the throat. It lifted him high, higher still. The burgundy air spotlighted Joe's form, far below, hands clenching and unclenching with the rumbling heartbeat of the darkness. Alex dangled five, ten, twenty, a hundred feet above the ground.

"He knew you had a gift ... your music ... our music," Alex rasped, the incorporeal claws tightening. He looked down into the creature's blue eyes, vision tunneling, fading. "You're stronger than this, Joe. Always have been. *Save me.*"

Alex tumbled from the thing's grasp and landed on his back, bouncing once. Something inside popped and he lay still, numbness creeping through his limbs and mind. He suddenly felt unsure of anything. Unsure of this world and his place in it. Unsure of Joe's existence, of his own.

Am I breathing?

Through a curtain of ruby dust, Alex thought he saw Joe move in from the shadows, thought he heard Joe's voice, thought he heard Joe yell.

No, Alex's mind moaned. *It's just a dream. A bad, bad dream. We're five-years-old. We get to start over. We need to start over.*

Scraping noises drew near, moving slow. Everything moved slow. Even the air swirled sluggishly around him, filling his eyes with dazzling cotton candy color. Voices came, distorted as though slowed on a tape recorder with dying batteries.

Am I breathing?

He thought he heard Joe again, but it sounded like a child's shrill holler, not at all like the man Joe had become. Turning his head, Alex spotted a hand lying inches from his face, drained and white. Blood filled his throat and he started to gag, but he couldn't move. The hand wouldn't move.

Another shrill yell. *So far away. That's not Joe. Joe's at home playing checkers with his dad, not here in this endless night.*

Alex watched the hand, lifeless on the soft sand, and heard faint music carried on the shimmering borealis of color. He watched the aurora, pillowy earth beginning a slow spin beneath him, and listened as a lilting violin played. The aura parted and he saw children there, dancing with angels on powder puff clouds, amber light making their wings glow golden. *Like sunshine. I miss the sunshine.* Three boys chased under a warm yellow orb, pirouetting with cherubs, laughing from their guts. True laughter. Innocent laughter, dancing with the sun, golden rays warming their round faces, butterflies alighting in their hair. *A sundance*, Alex thought, watching from very far away. The hand lay limp. The violin played. Clearer now. Louder. Closer. *I've lost my hand*, he mused. *But the sun is so warm and the music so beautiful. I'm dancing in the sun.*

"Like when we were kids," Alex mumbled, watching the rainbow swirl into a spiral overhead. "A million butterflies fluttering in faint streams of sunlight."

The boy with sandy-brown hair and clever gray eyes ran toward him, smiling. He held out his hands, a violin bow balanced on his palms. "Take it back," he said. "For all of us."

Am I breathing?

Another scream. Loud. Close to his ear, inside his head. Rising from the depths of his throat, his own voice, carried on a rush of indigo wind. Oxygen entered his lungs with such force that he began to choke and gag and shout. He sucked at the air as if taking his first breaths of life.

"Take … it … back," he rasped.

Another shrill shout echoed.

Grunting, Alex rolled onto his side and spat thick blood. Waves of color crashed over him and he fell back. He heard a groan and thought it might have come from his own dry throat but couldn't be sure. He pried open his grit-filled eyes and sharp spikes of fear instantly twisted deep in his chest. Boiling panic surged through his veins, making his limbs vibrate.

Bathed in white light, Joe's blood-soaked body floated ten feet above the ground. A darkly transparent creature stood over him—the same vaporous monster that had wanted Joe outside the stone wall. The child, slack and unmoving, hovered next to Joe's levitated form. The shadow creature hunched over Joe's bare chest, probing his ribs with elongated, gnarled fingers.

"No!" Alex pushed up and crawled forward, his labored breath splitting the billowing curtains of colorful air. He dragged himself, clutching at the dry earth, shoes digging deep ruts into the ground. He swam through thick magenta waves, heavy sand sucking at his hands and feet. The locomotive roar rumbled closer, louder with every inch he moved. Then, in horror, Alex watched as Jade appeared out of the darkness, leapt up and grabbed the boy's dangling arm. Holding tight, she ran toward Alex, pulling the child like a kite through the rainbow air as gnarled claws stretched from the darkness after her. As they wrapped around her legs, she threw the boy with all her strength and Alex watched the kid sail toward him on a gust of green wind. Jade belly-flopped to the ground and was dragged, clutching at the grainy earth, back into the dense night. Alex pushed up, reached up, and yanked the boy out of the emerald wave. The shadows shrieked in a miasma of putrid-smelling motion. The enormous, wanting beast turned and roared, needle teeth flashing, a freight train screech filling the shimmering borealis air. Like a macabre marionette, Joe's body hit the ground. Alex held the unconscious child tight as the shadowthing's long talons shot toward him. Knotty limbs encased and lifted high, higher still … and then let go.

They landed hard. Alex screamed out, electric jolts wracking his spine. He sat up, clutching the child to him, and tried to breathe, waiting for the assault to begin again. In the distance, he spotted a dot of light and blinked through the haze of his vision. *No. It's just my eyes, my head.* Something moved nearby. He tightened his hold on the kid.

"Joe?"

The boy's eyelids fluttered, showing nothing but white. He panted, hair falling away from his alabaster face. The slash on his chest blazed a greenish light. Alex struggled to his knees. The shape moved again. He squinted into the darkness—and felt his heart thump hard against his ribs.

Jade appeared out of the blackness, expression earnest, and then was gone—yanked back with a terrible force and vanished into the ether once more. Alex opened his clenched fist. A jade stone lay in his bloodstained palm and he heard her weary voice inside his head—*for protection, healing, and unconditional love.* He squeezed it tight and held the embattled child close, peering through the colorful haze at the dot of light in the distance. It grew bigger as he watched and then took shape. A rush of wind found his ringing ears and he felt the owl's wingtip brush his face again. The night bird circled up and away, then swooped low. Dark shapes advanced.

"You can't have him," Alex rasped, thick blood coating his tongue. "You can't have him without taking me. And I'm not going."

The shadows closed in, protracting twisted limbs from the throbbing ether, and Alex did the only thing he could think of to do—he stood up and walked, followed the small bird as it flew in front of him, illuminated, splitting the darkness with its determined wings and casting the shadows into the edges of night. For minutes—hours?—days?—weeks?—he didn't know how long, he followed the beating wings, so like the heartbeat of Te's drum, shoes filling with sand and blood running in a steady stream from the wound in his side. He walked until the white owl became a blinding ray. He walked until he came to the Joshua tree and the man without a shadow dancing beneath it. Alex laid the child's motionless body on the white sand and squinted at the godman of his dreams, tears flooding his eyes.

"I brought him here … to you. Can you do something for him?"

Te looked down, his leathery face filling with stories of impossible sadness, all the world's tragedy laid out in a sea of unshed tears.

Alex curled over the boy and pressed his face to his soft baby skin, a stream of uncontrollable sobs flooding out of him. "No!" He pressed the boy to him, fingers curling into fists to hold on. *Hold on, Luke. Just hold on.*

"No! No! No! No!" Alex rocked and screamed over and over, hoarse cries filling the vastness, and then he looked up at Te through swollen eyes, beseeching.

"Not again. Please. I can't do this again."

Te remained silent, watching.

"Why?! I did *everything* you asked!"

The drumbeat silenced. "Did you?"

Alex seethed. "Fuck you. I lost my hand, my music."

The man nodded. "Hmm. Is that all?"

"What do you mean *is that all?*" Alex shook with rage.

"Did you show him?"

Tears spilled from Alex's eyes. "I tried. I-I failed. They got to him."

"Hmm," the man said again. He glanced at the child. "Did they?"

Alex's heart flipped in his chest. He squinted at the man through the bright sunlight and shook his head.

"I-I don't …"

"Remember, Alex," Te said as he danced away. "Remember the backward way. The *betweens.*"

Alex frowned. He peered down at the child's peaceful, pale face, his ruby mouth and upturned nose, and saw this child riding down his driveway on a ratty skateboard, blond hair flying in the wind. He saw this child chasing the ice-cream truck, waving dollar bills over his head, saw him sharing that ice-cream with his best friend, his blood brother and accomplice in mischief. Saw him in his inside out shirt and untied shoes sailing handmade boats down the gutter … commanding lightning, racing trains, aiming arrows. He saw this child writing secret music in his bedroom, heard that music inside his own head, felt it leave his fingertips and find the world. Saw this child fighting, protecting everyone he cared about.

Alex scanned the blinding horizon, terror tightening his throat.

"I left him."

Alex felt like he was folding in on himself, skidding downward. He fought for a hold, a grasp, something, anything. Images floated through his mind like untethered kites caught in a gentle breeze. He saw Luke, arms spread wide, soaring high above and Rom at the hospital offering a bloodied hand and saying, "We got you a new one, buddy." He saw his mom, crying, and Mary holding out her upturned palms to him, welcoming him home and whispering a message. He saw Jade, hunting with her eyes and saving a boy, saw that boy save her. Saw Thomas, raking leaves into piles so Luke could dive into them and Marcus squirting them with the garden hose, the sun bright overhead.

"Wait." It was his own voice drifting away on the soundless breeze.

No one had ever told him that monsters did exist and that they could be powerful enough to destroy the strongest of spirits, the best of heroes.

"Wait. It's not about me."

Te stopped. "What did you say?"

The sky turned neon shades of green and pink. Alex looked up through a swirling aura of color and heard a woman's soothing voice—not Jade but someone he knew— reading from a favorite story. *And now, Fox ol' friend, the time has come to say good-bye ...* He curled over at Te's feet and pressed his face into the sun-kissed sand.

"I left him. He's scared, and I left him." Alex knelt, searching the distance for darkness and listening to the soundless wind. The air moved around him in neon shades of white that flapped like curtains in a breeze.

"I have to go back."

The man put his hand on Alex's head and bright red blazed. He had the sensation of collapsing, weakening, falling, and dying.

"Wait."

part four

*Greater love hath no man than this,
that he lay down his life for his friends.*

–John 15:13

twelve

In calm surrender I
release myself to you
Your caresses soothe
my wounds
In darkness
you show me light
Sweet Mother
Death
I am lost
I am found
I am yours
I am free

-J Schell journal entry June 21, 1983

June 15, 1984

7:33pm

Wearing a white bra and cotton underwear, Norma Schell lit all the candles and eased down to kneel on the big prayer pillow, holding the altar for support. One arm hung slack at her hip and the left side of her face drooped. The padded steel support collar encasing her neck made her skin itch. Shadows flickered, chasing the dimness into haunted corners. Muttering, Norma sat back on her bare heels, raised her good hand toward the vaulted ceiling, and let loose a rush of unintelligible sounds, stirring the hot air above her blonde head with a chubby fist. Thank God Brother Adam had exorcised the house.

"Cast out the despair and the wickedness and be not afraid to smite the Devil," she chanted. "The child of Satan has no place by your side, so be gone with the evil seed. Glory!"

Like a smitten teenager, she gazed up at the small crucified figure hanging on the wall. Her Lamb, her sacrifice. The martyr stared down with unseeing eyes, sad, lost, drained. Norma held a small cross to her orange-tinged lips and closed her painted eyes. She thought it was the medication making her sweat.

"Praise you, Lord," she whispered, wiping her forehead with a tissue. "And bless me for my efforts. Although imperfect here on Earth, the children are so very worthy of your divine benevolence. The mothers and fathers simply do not see the truth about who their children are and what must be done for them … for you. I will continue my works as best I can, with your divine strength inside me, even in the assault of Satan. I serve you and you alone, my prince."

Norma held the alter edge and leaned forward, resting her damp head on the dark cherry wood, and prayed the same lamentation she'd prayed for over nineteen years. "I did what you asked of me. He bore the sacred sign, the first one, so I sent him away to be with you, his father, but the other one is stubborn. He held on inside me, wouldn't let go of my womb. I tried to tear him free once I knew the truth about where he'd come from. It should have been your seed, my husband, and I failed. I failed."

Tears streamed down Norma's fleshy cheeks and tumbled from her chin. The woman picked up the lash at her side and flung it over her shoulder with a sharp snap, the razor blades sewn into the ends leaving pink trails of raised flesh. With a quick turn of the wrist, she flipped the whip over her other shoulder and gritted her teeth against the bite of contrition.

"If this is but a fraction of what you endured, my Lord, then I deserve more for my sins." The sharp tongue of the scourge left blood trickling down her spine, pooling in the rolls of fat at her waist and hips. "I am unworthy. I am unworthy. Forgive me."

Thunder tumbled into the low hills of the Siskiyou Forest and a sudden battering of rain hammered the sealed windows. Norma mumbled her prayers, lost in a wilderness of penance and supplication. The lash took a fierce bite, but she hardly noticed. She looked up into her messiah's withered face, a sliver of drool bubbling from the corner of her numbed mouth. Candlelight threw shadows around the dim room, animating the mounted figure's gaunt features. Lightning bolts flashed one on top of the next, followed by a resonating boom of thunder.

"I have sinned. I am unworthy. I have failed." The leather strap whipped through the air with a whir, removing a strip of pale skin. Another thunderclap, another whir of the lash. Above, the savior's mouth yawned wide with sinister shadow and Norma heard his voice. *You did as I asked. You were chosen to send the special ones home to their Father. I have chosen you as vessel for the holy ones, and you alone.*

Tears streamed from the repentant woman's mascara-blackened eyes. "Why, then?" she pleaded. "Why have you not filled me by now with another of your progeny? Have you forgotten my sacrifices? Have you forsaken me, my love?"

Thunder reached down from on high, giving the house a raucous shake. Lightning strobed through the room. The crucified figure danced a maniacal jig with the sporadic illumination. Norma unhooked her bra, let it drop, and pressed her hand to one breast, trailing a long red fingernail over the nipple until it stiffened. A ripple of excitement shot through her abdomen.

"Please, my love," she whispered. "I am yours."

Norma slid her hand into the waistband of her cotton underwear. She spread her knees and slipped a finger into the warmth of her sex, readying herself.

"Please ..."

Thunder whispered and her heart quickened when the messiah's head turned.

"Yes," the enraptured woman breathed. "Please. Now."

The savior smiled down at her, his face full of love and flickering light. The peg screwed through the sculpted figure's small feet began unscrewing. It fell free and hit a candle cup, breaking the glass and snuffing the flame.

Norma moaned, fingers working her into an aroused trance, eyes rolling with pleasure. She rocked back and forth, swaying to the rhythmic heartbeat of the storm, black tears streaking her rouged cheeks. *Yes,* she thought, *come for me now. Fuck me now.*

The bolt screwed through the martyr's left hand began a slow rotation, dropping to the altar with a sound of breaking glass. Plumes from the feathered crown encircling his head sailed toward the wooden altar, snuffing a candle flame and dimming the room even more. Dangling by one hand like a macabre puppet, the figure stretched and curled his small fingers. Thunder tapered to a dull groan.

Norma's breath came hard and fast, fingers circling quicker with each beat of her heart, arteries pumping harder with every breath. The blue vein running the center of her forehead bulged. A layer of sweat dampened her neck and face. Heat radiated off her pasty skin and she let out a string of nonsensical mutterings, arching her back. *Now! Come for me now!*

The crucified boy swung away from the wall, freed his other hand, and dropped to the altar, sending several candle cups to the pristine white carpet. He perched over the entranced woman like a curious child, stretching and curling stiff fingers, then reached out and buried his cold withered hand in her hair.

Norma's body went rigid and an expression of pure virginal rapture overtook her makeup stained face. She let out a primal shout, shuddering with climax, and opened her eyes to look upon her divine lover. Through unshed tears, she held her savior's gaze, a slow realization settling in. The boy's eyes blazed with compassion and pity. He seized the half-naked woman's hair and pulled her toward him, raspy breath filled with ice, and she could not look away. Norma's slack jaw worked the hot air in silence as a terrible and vast loneliness filled every cell of her body, so deep it made her spine ache, her heart stutter, and the blue vein in her head bulge more.

Gasping, Norma fell backward. A hacking shriek found its way out of her throat before strangling to a halt mid-breath. She crawled to the bed and tried to heave herself up, but her body wouldn't cooperate. She clutched the bedspread to her breasts and turned at the sound outside the bedroom door. Someone whispered. Sweating, Norma watched as the polished doorknob began a slow rotation.

"Dear God." The sound of gushing water reached her ears and she pressed a shaking hand to the pain in the side of her head.

Bathed in sputtering flashes of light, her messiah crept across the carpet, bloodied palms turned upward, pleading eyes bleeding scarlet teardrops.

The door opened an inch.

Norma's Lamb opened his withered mouth, corpse lips pulling apart like rotted silly putty, swollen tongue darting like an engorged worm, eyes blazing eternity. Her savior reached out a wounded hand, small fingers searching, grasping.

"Mama."

The door blew open with a rush of devil's breath.

7:33pm

White light pulled at his eyeballs. He tried to move toward it but was pushed back by invisible hands. Loud, incessant beeping blared somewhere to his left and he turned toward it, trying to see what it was through the blaze. A tired face suddenly appeared, a frown creasing her features.

"Mom?" His throat felt like sandpaper and he started to cough, the taste of dry sand and salt heavy in his mouth.

"Alex," she breathed, throwing herself on top of him. He winced at the pain that seemed to have taken over every inch of his soul. She hit the call button and kissed his face.

"Mom?" he said again. "What—"

The door flew open and Rom rushed into the room.

"Well I'll be damned," the doctor boomed, shaking his head. "Welcome back, buddy. You scared the hell out of us."

"Am I at the hospital?" He had a hard time moving his mouth. His aching jaws felt like they'd been wired shut for a century and his face was numb. A familiar canvas sling held his right arm, his left was bandaged from fingertips to above the elbow. His ribs burned.

"You're disoriented, Alex," Rom said. "You lost a lot of blood."

He must've looked frightened because Rom walked over and placed a gentle hand on his injured shoulder. "You'll be okay, Alex," the doctor said. "I'll explain the extent of your injuries later."

"Tell me now," Alex said, trying to sit up.

Rom let out a long breath and glanced at Elizabeth. "We don't know how this happened to you, Alex, but you've suffered severe trauma to your left arm."

"Will I play again?" He searched Rom's troubled face and tried to wiggle his fingers.

"Alex—"

"Just tell me the truth. Please."

Rom sat on the bed. "I called in Doctor Sandra Sullivan from the Mayo Clinic in Rochester, Minnesota. She's a leading expert on peripheral neurosurgery. She worked on your arm for more than eleven hours."

"And?" Alex said.

"And now we wait," Rom answered. "Everything that can be done has been done at this point. Doctor Sullivan removed nerves from your thigh and—" Rom's voice broke. He squeezed the bridge of his nose.

Alex sank into the pillows. He was so very tired.

"Joe's dead," he stated.

Rom and Elizabeth looked at one another.

"He's still in a coma, Alex," Elizabeth started and then looked at Rom.

"Something has changed," Rom said. "His EEG shows decreased electrical signals in his limbic area—that area we talked about that is associated with emotional states—and his fMRI indicates reduced oxygen flow to the same region, but ..."

Alex narrowed his eyes and Rom leaned closer.

"It looks like his amygdala and cingulate gyrus are—" Rom shook his head, obviously bewildered. "It looks like they're *shrinking*. But his hippocampus, which plays a role in remembering emotionally charged and traumatic experiences is, well, it's almost *five times* the size it should be. And there is no physical explanation whatsoever for any of it."

Alex nodded, throat burning. *Joe's choking on the bad memories and forgetting all the rest.*

Rom's pager went off.

"Shit," he said, glancing at the screen, annoyed. "I'll be back." He leaned to hug Elizabeth and Alex saw the quiver in the doctor's chin as he walked out.

"I like him too, Mom," Alex said after a long silence.

"Is it that obvious?"

Alex gave her a worn-out smile.

She tried to smile back.

"No Juilliard, huh?"

Elizabeth reached for a tissue and blotted her eyes.

"So, you're stuck with me. For a while anyway."

"Yeah. Terrible." Elizabeth tried to smile again. She sat on the bed. "Alex, the police will want to talk to you."

Alex frowned. "Why?"

Elizabeth leaned forward. "Do you remember what happened in Joe's house?"

He thought about telling the truth, about spilling all his suspicions about Mrs. Schell, but changed his mind. "I went there to see if she was okay, if she needed anything."

Elizabeth narrowed her eyes. "Huh. She shot you. Do you remember that?"

Alex looked away. "Vaguely."

"She told the police she thought you were an intruder. She said she warned you never to step foot on her property again."

"Yeah, but …"

"I went to Joe's after the paramedics found you there in Joe's room. What were you doing in his room?"

Alex blinked, confused, remembering diving into Norma's chest of drawers and the shadows coming. "I-I don't know. I don't remember being in Joe's room at all."

"The floor was soaked with water. It was leaking from the frame of that god-awful mirror on the wall."

"Water?" A lump rose in his sandblasted throat.

She nodded. "You were covered with some sort of liquid that made the paramedics sick when it got on their skin. They're still trying to figure out what it was."

A little boy's tears. Alex closed his eyes and tried not to burst into sobs.

The door opened and Charlie Dugan's round face appeared. "Uh, o-okay if I come in?"

Elizabeth stood and hugged the giant boy then turned back to Alex. "Charlie's been coming by a couple of times a day to check on you. I'll go call Mary. She's been doing a lot of praying. And I'll ask Rom when you can come home."

Alex nodded, barely hearing her. "Mom, what time is it?"

"Almost eight."

"Morning or night?"

"Night. You need rest." She kissed his forehead and left the room.

Charlie stood there, shuffling from foot to foot, looking lost.

"It's not your fault, man," Alex told him.

The big guy looked at the floor and nodded.

"There's a key in Joe's desk drawer."

Charlie's steady gaze met Alex's.

"I saw her get it when I was hiding in Joe's closet. It's to a room in the basement. Same room she—" He let the words drop, the torturous images still fresh, the realization of what needed to be done still new. "The latch on Joe's bedroom window is broken. You can get in that way, just make sure Norma's not home. Check the garage for her car. You have to take my mom with you. You'll need a witness. She won't go home tonight, so as soon as she falls asleep, I'm going to leave here. Tell her not to worry. Tell her to trust me. And please tell her I love her."

Charlie's pale green eyes never blinked. The towering boy nodded.

11:47pm

Alex waited until his mother's breathing became regular and rhythmic before attempting to get out of bed. He worked the sling loose with the help of the metal bed railing and his teeth, shrugging his injured shoulder out of the harness, ignoring the shocks sparking in his chest. Pain ebbed and flowed, coursing through every cell, every limb. He put his feet on the cold floor, the wound in his side pulling at the meat of his ribs, and slowly stood.

Elizabeth shifted in the recliner near the window. Alex held his breath until his mom settled again, then shuffled past the potted ficus his mother had put near the window— strong healing properties, Mary always said. He didn't bother with clothes or shoes. He grabbed his jacket and pocketed Elizabeth's car keys then slipped out of the room and headed for the elevator. Once there, he got in and hit P1, rode down to the garage and found her yellow Mazda where she always parked it. He drove slow and steady through the fog, grateful his mom's car was an automatic.

Alex turned the key and stepped into the foyer. Thick mist chased him through the door. It seemed years had passed since he'd been home and he was tempted to stay, to sleep in his own bed, in his own room. But he couldn't. Not yet. He wrote the note and left it near Elizabeth's *World's Greatest Mom* mug so she'd be sure to see it, then went to retrieve Jade's violin. On his way out, he paused long enough to press his bandaged, limp fingers against Luke's closed bedroom door, then turned and walked out of his house.

Alex drove the car up the long driveway and parked in front of the garage door. It didn't matter if she saw him. Even if she called the police, he'd still have plenty of time to say two words to her. That was all he wanted. Just two words: *You win.* Norma finally got what she had always wanted.

He didn't knock. The knob turned. He pushed open the door and stuck his head in. Her blue Bonneville was parked in the garage, but the house was quiet. The overwhelming scent of lavender made his nostrils flare as he stepped inside and closed the door. The muscles around the wound in his chest spasmed with the movement. Rom had told him the bullet never exited so they were able to take it out with minimal tissue damage. *Thank God for small favors*, Alex thought, wincing. *Sure hurts like hell.*

"Norma?"

An electrical sizzling sound came from upstairs, followed by a muffled cry. Alex listened. Several loud pops, like a gun going off, made him jump. He shuffled up the steps and stopped outside Joe's closed bedroom door. Another loud bang shook the walls. Alex grabbed the knob and twisted. The door yanked open, dragging him with it. He reeled into the room—pain spiking in every joint—and sprawled face down, gasping, vision doubling. And then he saw it—the tail end of a thin wisp of smoky vapor vanishing into the glass of the mirror. Alex got to his feet and took a step toward his disheveled reflection. The hospital gown blew around his legs, animated by an indiscernible breeze.

With an ear-shattering bang, the glass webbed as if hit with an invisible hammer directly in the center. Another explosion and Alex stumbled back, splintered glass spraying his body. The room filled with a pungent rot smell that reminded him of death and hospitals and sour yellow skin hanging on cancer-ravaged bones. Shards of broken glass flew and boomeranged off the walls, coming at him from every direction. He shielded his face with his arms, backed into the bathroom, and swung the door partially closed, leaving enough space to watch as airborne glass spun out of control, gouging paint off the walls, careening into the ceiling, knocking over anything that wasn't tied down. Each sharp fragment flashed unnaturally, creating a maniacal strobe in the dimness. Then, one by one, the shards dropped to the floor in a pile.

Alex waited a moment before stepping out of the bathroom. Wary, he approached the mound of broken glass, expecting to look down and see his own fractured reflection in the pieces. He did—in one of them. The others held images of people he'd never seen before—a small girl with short blonde hair, a young boy with a patch over one eye, a bearded man who looked as old as Alex felt. Faces, many different faces, peered out from the fragments, their sorrowful wails trapped and silent.

And there on top of them all was Joe—bloodied, battered, beaten.

Standing.

Smirking.

Alex let out a long slow breath and noticed the air had changed. The rotten stench of death and decay was gone, replaced with something he had no trouble identifying.

Roses.

Alex looked at the webbed pattern of glass still clinging to the center of the frame and saw his own fragmented image. He heard a voice, very far away, and couldn't move. Then, with a startling pop, something flew from the center of the web. He flinched, putting up his hands. The thing bounced off his bandaged arm and landed at his bare feet. Alex stooped and plucked it off the damp carpet.

A tooth caked with bright orange lipstick.

"Oh, no. Fuck me." Alex took deep breaths of the perfumed air and backed toward the door.

He staggered from the room, down the stairs, and out the door to his mom's car. Slamming it into reverse, he floored it, narrowly missing Ms. Carpenter and her dog. The wheel spun in his hand. He rammed the shift into drive and took off full speed.

Alex drove through increasing fog before spotting Mary's porch light burning as bright as a lighthouse beacon in a tempest. Clutching Jade's violin to his chest, he stumbled up the walkway. When Mary opened the door, Alex fell forward and slumped to the floor. He could already hear the drumbeat calling his name in the thunder, already feel the soundless wind on his skin.

"I have to go back, Mary. Send me back."

thirteen

Innocents

Once, in the days of mist and rain, two brothers born of separate wombs wandered the land in search of strength.

"Sing the song of songaona for all to hear," sang One Who Walks Across The Sky. The boy Makate and the boy Wabishk danced a circle around their mother. Laughing, they tossed autumn leaves into her hair and she shook her mighty head and set the leaves free on the wind. Then she darkened the heavens and sent a bolt of electricity into the ground.

"A choice will be made," One Who Walks Across The Sky told them, spitting raindrops onto their heads. "Who will choose?"

"I will!" said the son of Dawn.

"I will!" said the son of Midnight.

And both fell upon the ground, laughing with delight.

Angered, One Who Walks Across The Sky sent a second bolt of lightning into the ground. Makate and Wabishk sat up and looked into their mother's scornful face, dark and filled with clouds.

Where the lightning had struck, a box lay, brimming with light at the edges.

"I want to play with the ball of daylight," said Makate.

"No," said Wabishk. "I want to play with the ball of daylight. It's mine and I will not share it!" The son of Dawn took up the box and ran away with it.

Makate gave chase and a great fight ensued. The son of Dawn and the son of Midnight battled fiercely, falling together into the Lake of Sorrows, where Wabishk pulled Makate to the bottom and clawed him savagely. Wabishk tried to drown Makate at the bottom of the lake, but Makate fought for the light. They dragged each other, pulling and tugging and ripping and biting until the Lake of Sorrows spilled over with rage. Makate and Wabishk tumbled over and over again as a massive wave caught them and swept them away. Makate grabbed bushes and rocks and trees, trying to pull himself out of the mighty surge, but it was no use. He was too weary to fight anymore, until he saw that Wabishk lay still at the bottom of the lake, clutching the glowing box in his hands.

"Daylight," said the boy Makate, and he dove into the water and swam to the bottom. He took the box from Wabishk's stiff hands and swam to the surface, but daylight had fled.

"There is only one way to find it again," said One Who Walks Across The Sky.

"How is that, Mother?" asked Makate.

"You must give it away."

Makate looked at Wabishk lying at the bottom of the lake and began to weep for his lost brother. "I will give the ball of daylight to Wabishk," said Makate, "so that he may wake up and sing again."

One Who Walks Across The Sky sprinkled gentle raindrops on Makate's head.

The boy Makate dove into the lake and retrieved his brother, laying him on the bank of the Lake of Sorrows and singing to him the song of sharing. The ball of daylight returned in the sky and grew bright, chasing away the shadows. But still Wabishk did not stir.

"The battle was too much," One Who Walks Across The Sky told Makate. "The light was his to hold, but he did not fight hard enough to keep it in his grasp. Half a spirit cannot exist, Makate. You must give it away for Truth to find you."

Makate wept hard tears, bathing Wabishk with loss and regret and shame. It was all he could feel and knew it would never end because the song of the people ceased at that very moment.

"Ninga-zoongide'eshkawaa," said Makate to his mother. "I will make his heart strong. I will give him my light, so that we both may sing again." So, the boy Makate took a handful of light from his own heart and fed it to into the mouth of the boy Wabishk to make

him strong. Makate wrapped his hands around Wabishk's fingers and blew life back into them with a mighty breath. The cold wind brother joined the warm wind brother in a joyous dance, lifting the hair of One Who Walks Across The Sky out over the earth. New, Wabikate rode on his mother's locks, singing.

This they call songaona, the sharing.

And this is how Wabikate's music guided the lost and fearful souls of the wakwi.

June 16, 1984

5:17am

Rain-soaked, Elizabeth and Charlie stood on the damp cream-colored carpet and stared at the mound of broken glass heaped in the middle of Joe's bedroom floor. The enormous mirror frame hung empty and crooked, the riot of brass bars bent, broken. Bundled in the dead center of the wooden mirror backing, an elaborate chain of knots twisted away, leading to a point with a hole in it. Elizabeth stepped closer and plugged her finger into the opening, feeling the suction grip tight. She yanked her hand away and glanced at the walls. They looked like they'd been sliced up by a madman wielding a box cutter. She stooped and picked something off the floor.

A tooth?

Charlie stood stone still, eyes moving from side to side as the cogs of his brain cranked and shifted.

"Listen," he whispered.

Elizabeth turned her head, concentrating. She nodded. A faint mewing, like a trapped kitten, came from somewhere beyond Joe's closed bedroom door. They'd spotted Norma's car in the garage but decided to risk it.

"Maybe it's the TV," Elizabeth whispered.

Charlie shook his head. "Th-that's the s-scary story sound. That's what m-me and the kids at God's Grace call it. Kids make that noise after they hear a B-b-bible story and get scared. Some kids have nightmares." Tears came to Charlie's eyes and he brushed them away with a big hand. "W-why would people tell kids such horrible s-stories?"

"We should call the police, Charlie," Elizabeth said. "They'll know what to do."

Charlie's eyes grew wide and he shook his head from side to side. "Uh-uh. They've been here before and it d-d-didn't do any good. I know what she did. I won't let her do it again. And b-besides, Alex said to t-trust him, right?" Charlie opened Joe's desk drawer and retrieved a silver key, then cocked his head, listening.

Elizabeth eased the door open and looked back at Charlie. "Are you sure about this?"

Charlie bobbed his head. "Yes. Alex t-told me about the k-key."

"I can't believe I'm doing this," Elizabeth breathed.

They left Joe's room and crept along the dim hallway. The soft mewling grew louder and without another word Charlie launched himself the length of the hall, disappearing down the stairs in a thunderous scramble that shook the walls.

"Charlie!" Elizabeth kept her voice at a loud whisper, even though she was sure Norma would have heard them by now if she were home.

Elizabeth stood there for several minutes, listening to Charlie trudge through the house, unsure what to do. When she'd awakened and seen the young man sitting solemnly on Alex's empty hospital bed, dread had filled her, but it was Charlie's emotional rambling about kidnapping and sacrifice that had made her pay attention and listen. Below, she heard Charlie's footfalls hit the basement steps in rapid succession. A loud crash, like wood splintering, sounded and

Elizabeth willed her feet to get moving, but they wouldn't. Her heart galloped in her chest and she found it hard to breathe.

She waited.

Silence.

Elizabeth took a deep breath and headed down the stairs. The door leading from the kitchen to the descending basement steps stood wide open. The basement door at the bottom of the steps leaned on its hinges, the wood splintered from the jamb with the force of Charlie's body. Holding the rail, she moved down the steps, heart thudding in her temples, wondering if the police had confiscated Norma's gun. At the bottom of the stairs Elizabeth glimpsed Charlie's wide back framed by a doorjamb on the east wall, beyond it only darkness. The trapped kitten sounds had stopped.

"Charlie?"

He crouched down and mumbled something she couldn't understand.

Elizabeth groped for the switch on the wall and flipped it up, flooding the basement with fluorescent light. Just over Charlie's broad shoulder, a small hand reached up. Charlie took it and pressed the tiny palm to his cheek.

Elizabeth stepped closer. Tears flooded her eyes when the realization struck, then a red rage filled every fiber of her body when that realization sank in. She stepped closer and peered around Charlie into a bathroom, identical to Joe's, right down to the yellow tile, but much bigger and with a few differences. This room had a drain in the middle of the floor. A stainless-steel table with wheels lay tilted on its side. A kid-sized bed was pushed against one wall, a blue down sleeping bag on it. IV stands with bags and tubes attached stood like sentinels. A soiled towel lay wadded on the tile. Buckets of reddish-brown liquid had spilled across the floor. The reek of feces and urine soaked the air along with the undernourished child sitting on the floor like a tiny doll. Cabinets with locked glass doors held vials of liquid, hypodermic syringes, and surgical instruments. Elizabeth looked into a cabinet closest to the door. A sickening knot pulled tight in her stomach, anchoring the realization deep in her gut.

Morphine … Propofol … Lorazepam … Diazepam … Midazolam … all heavy sedatives and paralytics, all drugs someone who worked in a hospital operating room would be familiar with. She glanced into the next cabinet and felt the very core of her being shift and shatter. A dozen glass jars lined the shelf, each containing a fetus at various stages of development, but none past about four months of gestation. Elizabeth's breath caught high up in her throat. She turned and leaned against the doorjamb, swallowing a scream that was quickly gathering. Tears splashed from her eyes.

Charlie gathered the filthy little boy into his strong arms and held him close, kissing the top of his dark, matted curls. Face streaming with tears, he turned to Elizabeth and smiled.

"Missus Knapp, this is Stevie Snider. Snider Spider for short. He's a superhero."

Elizabeth drew in a sharp breath, recognizing the boy's name from recent headlines.

"I want mommy and daddy," the boy said, his words labored, slurred. He wrapped palsied arms around his rescuer's neck. "Will you take me home now, Red Dog?"

"Yes," Charlie said, holding the child close. "I sure will."

Taking the steps two at a time, Elizabeth bolted upstairs and dialed 9-1-1.

4:17am

"First there was the earth." Mary's raven eyes seemed to darken.

Alex looked at the shadow on the wall.

"Then there was a boy."

Alex shut his eyes, licked his dry lips.

"Eyes open." Mary's black eyes shone in the candlelight, making her seem alien, unreal. The woman's long hair hung in ropes down her back and she swayed with the chant that Alex had come to recognize, and to dread.

Mary Whitewing inserted another flattened hunk of metal into a slot. A tree. A Joshua tree.

Alex wiped his face, hot.

Mary uttered a final incantation and gave the casting wheel a spin. Alex watched the shadows move in a slow circle. Distorted shapes and figures sailed across the west wall, leapt off at the corner, ran across Alex's sweating skin and Mary's face, jumped back to the wall, and circled again. But the images had changed from before. A boy chased a dog, the dog chased a fleeting silhouette bearing long hair, the longhaired figure ran and ran. Thunder rumbled, shaking the house.

The screech of a night owl filled the room. A wolf howled. The sun moaned. *Too hot*, Alex thought. *It's going to burn.* He felt the floor shift, the heat rise in his belly, and looked at Mary, his anchor. The woman's hair was black as ink now, her eyes blazed obsidian. An amber glow radiated off her body, filling the room with a warm light and Alex wanted it to envelope him also, but the heat in his belly rose to a fever and he curled up and pressed his hands to his abdomen, feeling sticky hotness pour through his fingers in a flood.

Shadows chased, casting the old story. The boy walked; a white wolf followed. A different boy ran away, growing smaller with each rotation of the wheel. A child screamed. The sun moaned, and the wheel spun faster. *I'm falling*, Alex thought, and felt the pitch of his body. Only Mary's blazing black eyes held him vertical, pinned him there so the ghosts could find him. The wolf leapt off the wall, teeth bared. A wicked snarl. Saliva soaked Alex's skin. The heat became unbearable and he groaned, wanting it to stop. The wolf sank its teeth deep into Alex's ruined wrist and dragged him away from Mary's sweet golden light, away from the familiar scents of anise and cedar. Away from the heat and deeper into the redness. Alex shut his eyes against the pain, fighting the realization that he had no control here. He tried to remember, but the searing pain wouldn't let him. He tried to open his hands, but the sighing sky made his fingers tighten around it and he felt stars slip through like teardrops.

The white wolf dragged Alex through a blinding redness and agonizing heat so intense he felt his flesh being flayed with every inch. Just as the heat became unbearable, the animal dropped his wrecked arm and trotted off in the direction of the drumbeat, but when Alex opened his eyes, he knew something had gone terribly wrong.

It was snowing, cold. There was no horizon, only a continuous sea and sky of white, above and below. His breath crystallized and hung in front of his face for a moment before falling away like shattered glass. Intricate spherical snowflakes as large as fists cascaded from a sky he could not see, touching his skin and burning like ice before disappearing into a desert floor covered with white feathers. Alex dipped his hands in. His body bore no scars or wounds; the stiffness in his shoulder and pain in his side were gone, his fingers alive. He let the quills tumble from his palms. The wolf stopped and looked back, waiting.

"Is this a different between?" Alex asked the animal. His voice sounded close, contained, as if he were inside a glass bubble.

The wolf, panting crystal blue breath, turned and trotted away.

Shivering, he followed the animal through a cold, vast whiteness, certain he had landed in the wrong place. Everything moved slowly, even the white wolf jogged in slow motion, stopping only to look back and wait for Alex to catch up.

Alex spotted a tree through the falling snow, but it was different from the Joshua tree of before. This one stood immense and tall, with vivid pink blossoms and snow running the length of each branch. Under it sat a little boy with blond hair and ruby lips. The wolf sat next to the boy and yawned. The boy lifted his chin, once blue eyes now colorless, unseeing. The gash in his chest seeped red. Alex frowned. The burning sensation in his gut intensified.

"Where's Te?" His voice came with an echo that vibrated inside his head and he wasn't sure he'd even spoken the words out loud.

The boy said nothing.

Alex's stomach pulled tight. "The small man. Where did he go?"

The boy stared, blind.

Alex turned and watched Joe roll out a metal morgue table. Jade lay naked and translucent, eyes open, unfocused. Joe held a wedge of broken glass and cut her vertically from throat to pubic bone. He reached in, pulled out a small fetus and threw it on the feather-covered ground, smearing the stark white a bright scarlet. Where the fetus landed, a red rose bush bloomed.

"That's me," the blind boy said.

The wolf yawned and lay down.

Alex spun around. "What is this place?"

A second Jade pushed a baby buggy across the desert, stopping at the tree. She reached into the buggy and pulled out a violin and bow, wrapped in a colorful blanket, and put them in Alex's arms. "Look what we made together," she said before breaking apart into a thousand tiny owls and flying away.

"*What is this place?!*" His words sounded faint, confined to his mouth. He looked at his empty hands, the violin and bow gone. The boy stared, unseeing. The wolf put its head down and closed its eyes. Alex stepped closer to the morgue slab. Jade opened her blood-red eyes and reached out a cold hand, wrapping skeletal fingers around his wrist.

"Show him." Blood poured from her mouth. "Make him see."

On the other side of the table, the second Jade twisted in surreal dance, long sable hair fanning around her body. Marcus stepped in and spun her faster, laughing. Beyond them, Luke built a castle out of white feathers as Elizabeth wept, pacing.

Jade tightened her hold on Alex's arm, eyes crying scarlet rose petals and growing wide. "Do you see?"

Images flashed in muted color and Alex couldn't be sure if they were inside his head or outside. A familiar scene, one Joe had shown him many times, yet different now, as though viewed through someone else's sight, experienced through someone else's senses.

Jade's hand slipped away.

Te appeared and looked up at Alex. "Do you?"

"Yes."

"Then you know what must be done."

Alex nodded.

"Leave him, then."

Alex looked at the blind boy. "How?"

"By reflecting truth. Of course." Te put the blanket-wrapped violin and bow in Alex's arms, clapped once, and danced away, kicking up feathers. Chords from *sundance* sounded faintly inside the odd snow globe container and Alex realized he was playing the violin. He finished the arrangement and held the instrument in his hands, unsure what to do next. Nothing had changed. The sightless boy sat, the white wolf slept, the small man danced, complicated snowflakes continued to fall.

Then Alex spotted a dark-haired boy racing across the desert toward the blind boy sitting under the pink-blossomed tree. As he neared, a flurry of color followed—shimmering greens, golds, and russets—and Alex saw a million butterflies trailing after the boy, illuminated in faint streams of sunlight. The little boy skidded to a stop at the tree and sat down next to the blond boy, butterflies alighting on their bodies and hair, wings beating in slow-motion.

Alex stepped close and knelt down.

"Hi," the dark-haired boy said. "What's your name?"

"My name is Alex."

The boy's eyes grew wide. "That's *my* name, *too*! But Mary calls me *Alexander*. I don't like it."

"That's a king's name," Alex said, blinking away sudden tears. "Alexander the Great. He was a warrior."

"Mary says *that, too!*"

"Did Mary send you here?"

The boy nodded. "She said to listen and when I heard the music to run as fast as I could. That's how Joe and me find each other sometimes."

Alex swiped at his eyes.

The boy touched Alex's cheek. "Are you crying because he can't see?"

"I think so. Maybe that's it."

"It'll be all right. He doesn't know I'm here, but I'll take care of him so he doesn't hurt himself. Mary said I'm *armor!*"

"Like a knight?"

"Yeah. But I want to be a Jedi instead, like my little brother."

"Jedis are knights, so you can be both," Alex whispered, letting the tears fall. He set the violin and bow on the downy earth. "Can you take care of these, too?"

"It's pretty."

"Yeah, it is," Alex said, stroking the wood with calloused fingertips. "I think you're supposed to give it to your friend."

The boy nodded. "I know. But not yet. I have to wait until he wakes up."

Alex touched the boy's dark hair, brushing away a handful of butterflies. The insects enveloped the boy, settling on every inch of his naked body like a living, breathing cloak of color.

Alex stood and scanned the whiteness, suffocating in its closeness. Joe rolled the empty morgue table away, but stopped and turned, eyes bleeding blackness.

"He's here."

The blazing sensation in Alex's belly grew with violent intensity. He heard a freight train rumble and looked down. Two black-clawed limbs punched through the feathered desert floor and wrapped tight around his ankles. He jerked backward, twisting away from the grasping talons, then stopped fighting, stopped the fear. The claws wrenched him down through freezing dampness and into the hot underbelly of darkness. But he wasn't falling, held up instead by invisible wires like a puppet on strings. He hung vertically several feet above a sand-less marble floor, arms extended above his head and secured by unseen tethers. Everywhere he looked, the wall of faces was alive with movement, sound, and weeping color. Haunted screams and the cries of the anguished filled the dark cavern. Faces yawned toward him in macabre dance, features distorted at monstrous proportions. Little boys and baby girls cried out for relief, old men wept, women sobbed. Alex watched it all, heard it all, felt it all, thinking his mind would blow apart. Their shrieks of torment filled his head, bounced off the liquid-filled glass encasement before him and came back with a vengeance. He couldn't shut his eyes against the onslaught; something wouldn't let him look away.

Then, like a ghastly caricature, his own face gaped out, stretching the confines of the glass enclosure, simultaneously reflective and transparent. Just a few inches away, the perverse reflection mimicked sorrowful tears. Alex watched as the flesh of his mirror self tightened around his facial bones, ripping the skin in long gashes and tearing away in strips. The pale mouth opened wide.

"Do you see?" the thing jeered in his own voice.

Alex tried to turn his head but couldn't. An invisible vice grip held him.

Then, emerging from the ocean of bloated faces and floating bodies, he glimpsed a figure with long, straggly blond hair, face emaciated and pallid, eyes the color of old oil, cheekbones protruding in sharp points. Dead-white lips curled in an obscene mockery of a smile as the hovering figure drew close. Hanging, helpless, Alex tried to arch away, but the freezing breath on the back of his neck sent a wracking chill down his spine, immobilizing him where he suspended. The drifting figure parted ashen lips.

"Welcome back, brother." Joe's voice sounded like air hissing out of a tire. "So glad you could join us for the final refrain."

Encased within the transparent mirror, Alex watched as Jade floated out of the mass of others, mouth open and screaming words he could not hear. She pounded the glass with balled fists, trapped. She looked swollen, magnified, as though the salty liquid had infused every cell, muscle, and bone.

Joe spoke. "Aw. That's sweet. I think she likes you."

Alex strained against invisible chains. They held tight.

Joe circled, levitating like a demented cartoon. His sunken eyes shined black as ink in the dim amber glow. His hair hung in thin strings over a misshapen head, skin translucent and blue-veined. The cross carved into his cadaverous torso blazed with a blood-orange light. The suicide scars on his arms spit red fire, while the intricate flesh carvings moved across his ravaged body like grisly photographs come to life. A sick yellow glow came off his wasted body in a rush of heat, the sweet-sour reek of rot and death strong, his breath icy, teeth sharper.

"Prepare ye to die, O slayer of monsters," Joe intoned, voice unnaturally hoarse, unreal, but touched with a menacing humor.

Another cold ache wended through Alex's bones. He tried not to breathe in the carrion stench of Joe's ruined flesh and mind, but the smell made him gag and a profound knowing settled deep and ugly—he'd lost his friend for good this time, and now he was about to lose himself. Hot bile rose in his throat and he choked it down, trying to look away so Joe wouldn't see the desperation in his eyes.

"Do you see what I see?" Joe sang, sarcasm rolling off his gray tongue in a trill. Beyond Joe, Alex saw the glass flicker.

"We're going to play a game, Sir Alexander," Joe hissed, repulsive visage floating just inches away. "It's a question game and for every answer you get wrong, you lose a bit of skin. If you resist, I'll strip you down to the bones. Sound fun?"

Alex hung there, unable to respond.

"Question number one. Where is the little bastard?"

Alex strained to look beyond Joe at the sparking mirror, but Joe held his gaze with those depthless black eyes. The stench of his dying spirit made Alex's stomach turn.

Stop this now, Joe. It's not too late.

Joe sighed a putrid torrent of breath, reached out a long, blackened fingernail and touched Alex's cheek. Scorching heat bit hard. Alex grimaced in pain as Joe peeled a strip of skin from cheekbone to jaw. Joe dangled the bloody slice of flesh in front of Alex's eyes before flinging it to the marble floor. He licked his fingers.

"Question number two. Where is the little bastard?"

Alex caught movement just over Joe's bony shoulder and he craned to see. Jade was gone, but Luke stood there, whole and healthy. Alex's heart jumped. Luke stepped to where Alex could clearly see him and crouched low. His gaze locked with Alex's and he lifted a single finger to his lips.

Alex pushed his thoughts out, did everything he could to close his mind so Joe wouldn't see.

"Oh, my dear Alexander," Joe said. "You know I can get inside if I want to. But this is so much fun. I think I'll savor it a while longer."

Joe placed a blackened fingernail on Alex's cheek, rending a wide strip of flesh that cut to the bone. Alex grunted, gritting his teeth. Joe ran the bloody strip over his tongue and flung it to the floor.

"You always were stubborn, Alexander," Joe seethed. The light emanating from the cuts in his flesh intensified. "Always choosing the wrong fight. Jesus did the same thing and died for it. Guess you'll be in good company. Fucking martyrs." Joe dragged a sharp fingernail down and then across Alex's bare chest, opening a vertical and horizontal gash. With a wave of his hand, he set the cuts afire, bringing the cross to life. Alex seethed in agony.

"Oh, stop being so dramatic," Joe said. "You like it. You've been looking for punishment since the day Luke died. You kick your own ass constantly. You like the pain more than I do. You seek it, want it, crave it. Hell, you're better at it than I am. But at least I don't pretend. You ignorant fuck."

Alex pushed his thoughts. *This isn't you.*

Joe descended to Alex's eye level, sockets glimmering dark, but Alex could see into them, could see his own soul staring back.

"*I am God,*" Joe spat. "I am Judge. Jury. Executioner."

Joe's breath stung Alex's face.

"Do you remember what you did, Alex, sweetie? Do you remember squeezing the life out of Lucas until he stopped breathing right there in your arms? Do you remember killing your baby brother?"

Alex swallowed. Joe's reflective black eyes held him and in their liquid depths he saw his brother's bent and broken body, felt Luke's wet flesh on his hands, heard his own sobs echoing through the canyon. *Because I forgot.*

Below them, Luke stood tall and planted his feet.

Joe floated close and whispered, leaving frost on Alex's ear. "I have no tolerance for people who harm innocent children."

Norma Schell tumbled out of the darkness, landing in a heap on the floor. She lay there in her bra and underwear, frightened groans escaping her throat in labored gasps.

Alex sucked at the air, unable to fill his lungs. He searched Joe's eyes, looking for intent, but saw only himself looking back from the abyss. Joe descended toward the floor. Alex pushed his thoughts.

What about you?

Joe stopped mid-turn and rose to look into Alex's frantic eyes.

"What about me, Sir Alex?"

You're going to kill that little boy.

Joe's mouth curled into a nauseating grin. "Yes, but he's not innocent."

He is innocent. You just can't see it. He—you're blind.

Joe's expression coiled into a fury. Blackness raged from his sockets. His face shrunk tighter against the bones. The fire carved into Alex's abdomen surged, internal heat flared.

"That little fuck did a horrible thing," Joe seethed. "And he will die for his sins."

You don't get to decide that.

"Don't I?" Sneering, Joe thrust his long black fingernails into the blazing slashes in Alex's belly. The heat scorched him from the inside out and he clenched his teeth, breathing hard, but he didn't release his lock on Joe's oily eyes. Beyond Joe's knobby shoulder, Alex saw Luke open his arms wide and lift into the air.

"I'll get back to you, Alex," Joe whispered, extracting his claws. "Mother requires attention." He began a slow descent, sucking blood from his pale fingers.

"No."

Joe came to an abrupt halt. He waved his hand. "You don't speak here."

"Fuck you."

Joe moved fast, flying up and gripping Alex's head in sallow hands, raven eyes blazing.

"*You do not speak here!*"

Stinging frost settled in the cuts on Alex's face, making them burn.

"Yeah? *Fuck. You.*"

The excruciating heat in Alex's belly boiled over. With an ear-shattering screech, Luke flew at Joe, pushing him so hard he collided with Alex and the thought came in a flash—*this is my world, too, asshole.* Alex wrenched free of the unseen shackles, grabbed Joe's head with both hands, and unleashed the heat blazing up from his gut. White light beamed out of his eyes and bore into Joe's blackened sockets. Their world tilted, turned, spiraled, rewound, reversed.

Pay attention, Joe. Now I've got something to show you.

Mary Whitewing set a tray full of stones on the worktable next to a bundle of sage and a pot of burning cedar chips. She watched the man who was once a boy lying on the couch in sacred dream, watched his eyes move beneath the lids like ocean waves in a storm, watched fresh wounds track through the flesh of his face and chest and then vanish without a trace.

It is begun.

She reached into the cedar chest, withdrew a colorful quilt, and fanned it over the man's body, tucking in the edges. Bright patches of red, yellow, black, white, green, and purple material formed a circle in the center.

Faith. Determination. Victory. Sharing. Healing. Magic.

Her cousin over in Grants Pass had made it special for this day. But that was over eighteen years ago. She was only now permitted to unpack it.

Mary settled into her rocker, lit her pipe, and began a story, one she had never told before, but one that both boys needed to hear now. An epic story about the importance of Truth and forgiveness, sacrifice and love. Connection and reconciliation. A story as old as Day and Night. She sat back and began the prayer, the prelude and the coda, waving her hand to bring the smoke close and breathe it in.

"Father Sky, Mother Earth, Grandmother Whitewing, whose counsel I hear in the winds and the waters. I am called Mary of the *binenhshiinh* and *waawaashkesh doodeman.* I come to you as one of many children of the Bird and Deer clans. Hear my prayer. Your children are uneasy. Now the son of Day and the son of Night must wander the between. May the sacred directions reveal their wisdom and compassion and clear the dense fog of darkness and misknowledge. May they find Truth in birth, in death, in rebirth. May your children know their path and their peace."

fourteen

Heroes

Joe walked, sheathed in a luminous white light that embraced every inch of his being. He fought it, tried to break
the holds, but the light told him to settle the fuck down
or he'd get his teeth kicked in. He looked at his hands, his
arms, his chest, all free of scars, free of blood. An endless
passageway stretched before him. He made his way through
the brightness in search of a way out, but the passage went
on and on no matter how close the end appeared. Doors
lined the corridor, the edges framed with a supernal glow.
Writing appeared on each as Joe passed. The inscriptions
whispered their meanings, but the language was foreign
to him. With each ingress he walked by, a sincere longing
filled his chest and he struggled to push it away, to ignore
the promise it held. Then whispers of tranquil reflections
began filling his mind with emotions he could not translate
and didn't know how to define. The soft sighs made his skin
prickle, the hairs on his arms stand straight, and his angry
thoughts roll out like a kite tether, setting them free on a
soundless wind. He knew the calm murmurs were dangerous and would keep him caged there in the luminescence if
he didn't break away. He shut his eyes against the brilliance,
clenching and unclenching his fists. He knew it was Alex
holding him up, keeping him there, and that pissed him off.
Stupid kid. Always doing the right thing.

Joe stopped at a door and tried to read the word carving
itself out right before his eyes but couldn't decipher it. The

longing sensation spread upward into his throat and he put his hand on the knob. The door opened, bathing him in brilliant white light. He stepped over the threshold, bare foot coming down on the asphalt in front of Alex's house. Joe plopped down on the curb, chewing a piece of two-day-old bubblegum. His goal was to chew it until it completely disintegrated, which, according to the new *1976 Guinness Book of World Records* his dad had given him, had never been done before.

Luke hit the button on the controller. The B-52 lifted a foot off the ground, flew a couple of feet, sputtered and crashed to the pavement. With a groan, he walked over and picked up the model plane, turning it over to inspect the problem.

"It's gotta be the axle," Joe said, getting up from the curb. "It looks crooked."

"Really?" Luke peered closer, squinting in the early May sunlight. "It said forty-five degrees."

"I don't think we measured it right." Joe took the plane and wiggled the front wheel. It snapped off. "Shit."

Luke's eyes got big. "You said shit."

"So did you." Joe blew a bubble and sucked it back into his mouth with a dramatic inhale.

"Alex hates it when I cuss. He says six-year-olds shouldn't say bad words."

"Yeah? What do *you* think six-year-olds should say?"

"Fuck," Luke said, grinning.

"Right on." Joe high-fived him. "We can fix it. Just need to get the angles figured out so it flies straight."

Luke didn't say anything. Joe followed the boy's gaze, watching two older boys, high-schoolers, stride toward them from across the street. Joe could feel Luke's fear come off him in a wave and it made his stomach hurt.

Jeffy and Jimmy Kendall stopped and crossed their arms, mirthless grins plastered across identical faces. They wore baggy black jeans to match their greasy black hair and identical Alice Cooper headbanger T-shirts, except Jimmy's was torn at the sleeve. They each held a cigarette. The twins had a reputation for enacting merciless torture on smaller kids, stealing their bikes, beating them up, even holding pets for ransom—cigarettes, money, alcohol. Jimmy spent time in juvie last year for vandalizing cars in the school parking lot, and Jeffy was notorious for stealing anything his grimy hands touched. If Cutters Grove had a gang, the Kendall brothers were it.

"Whatcha got, Lukey Pukey?" Jeffy said, eyeing the plane in Joe's hands.

Joe handed the plane to Luke, clenched and unclenched his fists. "What does it look like?" Joe asked.

"Looks like another faggy little baby toy to me. Guess the homo gene runs in the family." Jeffy sniggered. Jimmy nodded ignorant agreement.

"Yeah," Joe said, shrugging. "Just a faggy baby toy. Maybe you'd like to take it home with you. You could play with it while your mommy gives you a bath."

The sneer left Jeffy's pimple-pocked face. "What?"

Luke tried to hold back a giggle, but it didn't work.

Jeffy took a step forward. "You laughin' at me, you retarded little shit?"

Luke shook his head, covering his mouth.

Jeffy snatched the plane out of Luke's hand.

Luke squared off, glaring at the older boy. "Give it back."

Jeffy held the model bomber over his head. "Chill out, Puke. Just want to look at it." He wound the plane up and down in the air, making engine noises in his throat, then started sputtering, stringy spit flying off his lips in the sunlight. "Oh, no. Houston, we have a problem. I think we're gonna crash. Aaaaaahh!"

Jeffy brought his arm down quick, throwing the plane to the asphalt as hard as he could. He brought his shoe down, crushing the wood under his heel with a triumphant cry, then bent down, scooped up the remains and let the broken pieces fall over Luke's open hands.

A boiling heat filled Joe's chest and he clenched his jaws, smashing the gum between his molars.

"You keep it," Jeffy said, brushing his hands together. "I don't play with baby homo toys."

"Yeah," Jimmy echoed. "You keep it." He bent over and picked up the remote control, turning knobs and pushing buttons like a moron just handed a shiny new plaything.

Luke's eyes brimmed at the sight of the prized flyer lying obliterated on the pavement. At the sight of Luke's tears, the heat in Joe's chest spilled over and he balled up his fists. It had taken him and Luke three months and over fifteen dollars of their own money to build the B-52, and Jeffy Kendall only thirty seconds to destroy it.

Crying, Luke knelt and began picking up the pieces like they were nuggets of gold, placing them in his shirt one at a time. Joe could see the thoughts running through the kid's head, feel the grief weighing his heart. Thomas was going to be pissed. He'd tell Luke it was his fault, that he needed to be more responsible and take better care of his things. He'd tell him to be a man. Alex would try to persuade Mr. Knapp not to be so hard on Luke, but Joe knew it wouldn't work. Thomas hated Alex and the "misdirected" energy he spent playing music instead of football. *I'll go with him*, Joe decided. *I'll make him see that it wasn't Luke's fault.* Through Luke's broken sobs and his own blinding sense of justice, Joe could hear Jeffy whooping and carrying on like he'd just won a fucking sweepstakes. Blistering heat spread into Joe's arms, making his fingers tingle. He glared at Jeffy Kendall, willing a meteor to sail out of the sky and fall on the asshole's greasy empty head.

"That's right, you stunted little retard," Jeffy hollered. "Nobody fucks with Jeff-k." He took a deep drag on the butt burning between his fingers and exhaled a steady stream of smoke into Joe's face.

Joe crouched down to help pick up the bits of wood. He caught Luke's eye and grinned. "On three," he whispered.

Luke cut a glance at Jeffy, who was now poking the remote in Jimmy's hands, wiped his nose and nodded.

Joe mouthed the countdown and they both lunged, each grabbing a cuff of Jeffy's baggy jeans. They yanked hard, sending Jeffy crashing onto his back, one arm flailing, the other hand trying to hold on to his pants. Luke and Joe pulled with all their strength, dragging Jeffy Kendall's saggy jeans right off his ass. Jimmy stood there holding the useless remote, a confused look on his face. Joe balled up the jeans and tossed them to Luke, grabbed the controller out of Jimmy's hands and took off running, towing Luke with him, who let loose a victorious hoot.

"That's right, Ken-*doll!*" Luke yelled. "Nobody messes with Lucas Knapp and Joe Schell!" He added "fuckers!" for emphasis and because it felt good.

Yeah, Joe thought, running in the sunshine. *Really good.*

What are you trying to do, Alexander?

Alex didn't let go. He kept Joe inside, tight as a womb, and dove deeper into those black pools where Joe's soul had been drowned in waves of denial.

I want you to see.

It won't work.

You will see.

No. I won't.

Alex hunted, searched, found another pinpoint of light and submerged himself in it, taking Joe with him. He would gather the fragments, each and every one, until there was enough light to penetrate Joe's blind eyes. He would hunt, as Joe had hunted, and he would be just as ruthless in the pursuit.

He pushed his thoughts. *I'm here. Don't be afraid.*

~

Joe faced a second door and squinted at the word writing itself out in narrow red script, but the letters held no meaning. So he touched it, thinking maybe the importance of the command might infuse into his brain, but clarity eluded him. The longing sharpened.

He turned the knob, white light cascading in a baptism of blinding warmth, and stepped over the threshold. His bare foot came down on a cold linoleum floor and he squinted in the sparse fluorescence, spotting a hospital bed. A figure lay in the center, immobile, eyes open.

Joe stepped close. "I'm here, bro. No matter how far you run or how deep you go, I won't let the darkness take you."

It hurts.

Joe whispered into Alex's ear. "I know."

It's dark.

"Yeah, it is."

I can't.

"This is not your fault."

I can't stay in this place. It hurts too much. I have to go.

"I'll come with you."

Joe watched tears slide from the corners of Alex's blank eyes and soak into the pillow. He lay down, stretching out alongside Alex's rigid body. He intertwined his hand with Alex's calloused fingers.

I'm here, Al. Don't be afraid.

Alex wandered, lost. Joe wandered with him, making sure his friend didn't go so far that he couldn't get back. He reached out every now and then to guide Alex's direction, to let him know he was not alone in the wilderness.

Alex's keening filled the void, a terrible sound of enduring remorse and desperate regret. Joe felt every bit of Alex's grief. It washed over and into him, flooding his mind with a constant ache. It ran his veins hot then cold then boiling. It reached a fevered intensity and Alex let out another sorrowful howl, beating at the darkness with balled fists. When he fell, spinning and screaming into the chasm where it all happened, Joe fell with him, wrapping around Alex like armor to fortify him for what awaited. He knew Alex had to feel it—all of it—or his light would extinguish.

Alex led him deep inside the dusty cavern where his heart had been shredded to bloody pieces. Luke lay in the dirt, his head bulging on one side, spine and leg twisted at impossible angles. The boy rasped, breathing liquid and shallow as his lungs tried to fill with air. Above, bright lights circled, waiting to take Luke away, but Alex kept them at bay with his tears and clenched fists, with his unwillingness to let go. He held his little brother, whispering promises that could never be kept.

"You have to let go," Joe told him.

"Shut up!" Alex spat, clutching Luke tighter. "You don't know what I did!"

Joe sat in the dirt and gazed at Luke's ruined face, saw the want there, the peace. He touched the boy's hair and knew it could be no other way, knew Luke's relief in the finality of it.

"I can't leave him," Alex sobbed.

"It would be selfish not to."

Tears streamed from Alex's eyes. Joe wiped them away with the palm of his hand.

"You can't stay here. You don't belong, you know that."

Alex looked up at the darting lights. "I'll never get him back if they take him."

Luke's body lifted a few inches from Alex's arms and he tightened his grip.

"You're not being fair," Joe said. "He can't fly with you holding on like that, Al."

"I know. But I-I can't." Alex stared at him, squinting. "Why do you shine like that?"

Joe shook his head. "That's not my light, man. That's yours. See?" He pointed at Alex's chest.

"I don't see it."

"You never do, Al." Joe scooted closer. "Remember when Makate and Wabishk found the feather? The one with the seeing eye? What did it show them?"

Alex lowered his head. "It showed them the *wakwi.*"

"Right. The god place, the otherworld where the death guides are. They direct and accompany the souls who are confused so they don't get stuck in the layers."

Alex's hands tightened on Luke's shirt.

"It also showed them that only those who sacrifice a part of themselves can stay in the *wakwi* and that some people give up the wrong part of themselves—their hope, their truth—and are lost forever, drifting in the cold and warm seas between here and there."

Alex raised his chin, a flood of fresh tears tracking through the grime on his face. "I can't stay with him."

Joe stroked Luke's blood-soaked hair. "No. You have to come back with me and let Luke find his way."

Alex looked at him, plaintive and scared. "I don't want to let go."

Joe looked deep into Alex's mind and saw the shadows there, waiting to reach in and snatch his friend away for good. "I know, man. But you have to."

Alex lowered his brother's limp, bent body to the dirt and left him there for the hovering spirits to take.

"Do you see it now?" Joe asked.

Alex looked down at his chest, at the dark hole where his heart had turned to ash. A tiny ember shined there. He looked away. "No, I don't want to."

"It's okay," Joe said. "You'll see it again one day."

Joe anchored him, keeping his palms together with Alex's hand pressed between.

On the hospital bed, Alex turned his head for the first time in a month. He locked eyes with Joe.

I couldn't save him.

No, you couldn't.
I should have …
Should have what? Been a superhero?
I should have made sure.
We can never be sure, Al. That's part of the fun. And the pain.
You never left me.
Nope.
Don't leave me now.
Shit no.
I'm not strong enough.
Fuck me, Al. You're the strongest person I know.
It's dark.
I'm here. Don't be afraid.

The word scrawled out on the door. Joe thought he saw a *b* and an *o* but didn't want to see more so he shut his eyes and watched the word etch itself into the redness of his eyelids

brimstone

He turned the knob and stepped over the threshold, bare foot coming down on yellow tile. The smell of bleach made his nostrils flare. His stomach pulled into a familiar ball.

His father was crying. Marcus sat against the wall, holding empty hands out and looking at them as though at any moment they might receive the most precious gift, the best answer. Blood ran the length of his left arm, dripping from the elbow. A red serpentine trail wound toward the drain in the floor and disappeared down the Devil's throat. Joe knew that somewhere below them was a place of fire and stones and people who misbehaved and that that's where the Devil lived. He drank blood, especially the blood of children, and if you didn't behave the Devil got thirsty and the only way to make him leave you alone was to give him a drink. That's why mama did the things she did, to keep him and Daddy safe from the Devil.

Joe walked around the drain, taking a wide berth, his white undershorts too tight and slicing into the backs of his legs. He sat next to his dad on the floor and watched blood drip, tried to see where it came from. He spotted a deep gash on Daddy's palm. He'd probably tried to block it, to keep her away, but sometimes it was better to stay still and get it over with.

"Go back to bed, Joey," Daddy said, making a weird choking sound in the back of his throat.

Joe opened the plastic grocery bag and pulled out a bottle of iodine and a Band-Aid that was too small but might help anyway. He also brought a needle and thread, just in case. He got up and held a washcloth under the cold tap at the utility sink then lifted Daddy's hand so he could see the cut better and wash the wound. Day before yesterday, he got to go with all the other second graders to the firehouse and learn about first aid and escape plans. Alex had to sit down the whole time because it made his stomach hurt, but Joe liked knowing what to do. *Stop, drop, and roll,* he thought, rinsing the washcloth. *That puts out the flames.* He soaked some cotton balls with mercurochrome and set them deep in the gash on Daddy's hand, then threaded the needle.

Daddy couldn't stop crying and Joe wondered if the Devil liked to drink tears as much as he liked to drink blood because there sure were a lot of them. He sat on his heels and lay his dad's wounded hand out flat on his thigh. Concentrating, Joe poked the needle through one side of the cut, crossed the gap, and pulled it through the other side, cinching tight, but not tight enough to hurt more.

"I can't feel it," Daddy said. The choking sound rattled his throat.

Joe bit his bottom lip, leaning close and sticking the needle through.

"It was a glass," Daddy said. "She threw a glass."

"Why?"

"I forgot to rinse the dishes last night."

"Oh." Joe inserted the needle, pulled the thread through, crossed back and did it again.

"She didn't have a clean coffee cup this morning."

"Oh."

Daddy's tears landed in Joe's hair and that strange choked sound came up from the back of his throat again. "You're a champion, Joe."

He liked when Daddy called him *Joe*. It made him feel big.

"What's a *champion*?" Joe put the needle through one last time, bit off the thread and tied his best double bowknot.

"A champion is someone who doesn't give up, always does the right thing, and takes care of people, no matter what."

"Like you!"

Daddy's face fell down like it was melting. "No, not like me. Not at all like me."

"Like Superman?"

Daddy wiped his eyes with his good hand. "Superman is a pretend champion. You're a real-life champion. Always remember that for me, okay?"

"I will." Joe unwrapped the Band-Aid, but the cut was still bleeding so the sticky parts wouldn't stick.

They both turned at the sound of the front door opening and closing upstairs. Joe ran on his toes to the utility room door and closed it, but the deadbolt could only be locked from the outside. He flipped the light switch off and tiptoed back to where Daddy sat on the floor. Joe pressed the key into his dad's good hand and bunched up into a ball next to him.

"Maybe she'll think she forgot to lock it all the way," Joe whispered.

"No, Joe. Go out and relock the door and put the key back. If she finds you in here with me—" Whatever was choking Daddy's throat didn't let him finish talking.

"I'm staying with you."

A new trickle of tears ran down the Devil's throat. Joe leaned up and kissed his dad's whiskered cheek.

"Joe—"

The knob turned. Marcus stood up fast, putting Joe behind him.

A long, orange fingernail reached through the crack of the door and flipped the light switch up. The door banged open and she stood there wearing a pumpkin-colored dress, pink teeth glinting. A leather lash dangled from her hand. The bits of metal sewn into the ends glittered in the fluorescents.

Marcus stepped forward. Joe went with him.

"Norma, just let us out. You don't need to do this."

She smiled. "I'm sorry, but you know the rules as well as he does, Marcus." The apologetic tone in her voice and manner made Joe's tummy turn liquid. He needed to pee.

"I won't be disrespected in my own house," she continued, stepping onto the yellow tile in her peach-colored high heels. "I work very hard to maintain a sin-free home, but you two make it difficult."

"Norma—"

She went on. "Since you are obviously too weak to discipline him, the task is left to me. You put me in this position, Marcus. If you weren't so ignorant to The Word, if you weren't such a feeble man, I wouldn't have to do this. You understand that, don't you, sweetheart?"

Joe felt his dad's arm tremble.

"I'll punish him," Marcus said. The choking rattle made his voice sound like it belonged to someone else. "Give me the lash. I'll do it."

She smiled again and shook her head a little. "Trust, Marcus. A good marriage is built on a foundation of trust and you've betrayed mine many times over. You are incapable of keeping your word. That's why the task is always left to me." She stepped toward them.

Marcus held out his good hand. "Just me, then. I told Joey to get the key and let me out. He was just following my orders, minding his father like any good kid would."

Norma shook her head again, still smiling that tricky Cheshire Cat grin. "Marcus, you know that's not true. That boy is as wicked as they come. I knew it the moment he was conceived. But since you wouldn't let me take care of it then, I must deal with this affliction the best I can now. He's a liar and so are you. He's *your* child, no doubt about that." She took another step.

Joe's bladder burned, and he wished he hadn't drunk all that chocolate milk before bed. He stepped out from behind his dad.

"Daddy's sorry, Mama. Don't hurt him again."

She pointed a long fingernail at him. "You will learn to obey the rules of this house, so help me God. Take off your underwear."

Marcus staggered forward. "You will not lay a hand on him. I won't let you."

Norma scoffed. "You are the most pathetic man I've ever known. I make the rules in this house, rules founded on the word of God. The Lord is my only authority and if it didn't so blatantly defy His laws, I'd have divorced you a long time ago. You are nothing but an unrepentant, incompetent fool."

"No he's not," Joe said, taking a step toward his mother. He wasn't sure what *unrepentant,* or *incompetent* meant, but he knew his dad wasn't a fool. A fool was someone like the guy who talked to his shoe on *Get Smart* and Daddy didn't act like him at all.

Joe stuck out his chin. "Daddy's a champion. He always does the right thing."

His mother's nostrils flared. She glared at Marcus, crossing plump arms under her big boobs. "You see? Defiance is the influence of the Devil. Are you happy now?"

Joe looked up and saw a hint of pride in his dad's tired eyes.

"You're not touching him," Marcus said.

Joe watched his mother's face do a strange thing then. It softened, the hard lines of rouge and lipstick paled, and she looked down at her hands, at the lash clutched in her fist. Tears came to her eyes, smearing the heavy mascara so zealously applied that morning. She looked at the two of them, her face a mask of deep disappointment.

"You don't give one whit about what I've been through, how hard it's been for me. I put food on our table, a roof over our heads. I'm only trying to make a happy home, to be a good mother and wife, but my efforts go unappreciated. I want a family, a good God-fearing family. But I'm losing you both. Just like I lost Isaac. I'm failing at the one task God gave woman, the one responsibility she is required to accept." She looked at them through black splotches of makeup. "You don't love me. You detest me, and that makes me feel so alone."

Joe had never seen his mother cry before. His dad cried a lot, but not his mom. Not ever. So, he went to her, walking across the bleached yellow tile, and put his arms around her waist.

"I love you, mama," he said, looking up at her. "Don't be sad. I'll listen better. Me and Daddy will both listen better."

"I know you will, but it's no use," she whispered, stroking his head. "The Devil's in you and nothing more."

Before Joe could move, Norma's hands came down and pinned his arms to his sides. The lash swung against his bare legs, the chips of steel scratching like claws. She hoisted him up and shook him.

"I never wanted you! You did not come from me!"

Joe's head snapped back and forth, and he could think of only one thing to do—*stop, drop, and roll.* He went limp and let loose a stream of golden urine down the front of his mother's pumpkin dress. She stopped yelling and for a second her smudgy face looked like one of those scary masks Daddy had shown him at the museum, the one with the big mouth, sharp teeth, and melting black eyes. Daddy said the people who wear them eat snakes and Joe thought his mom would probably like to eat snakes because she liked to eat fish and really they were the same thing. Her face puckered up like a deflating balloon and she let him go. He landed on his feet and fell back on his butt.

Norma looked down at herself, an expression of shock and disbelief overrunning the smeary mess of her face. She gasped and dropped the lash. Flailing fat arms, she reeled into the wall, swiping at her dress with pudgy hands. Her breath wheezed out in hoarse puffs.

Joe thought his mom looked just like a clown at the carnival, twirling and dancing around like that. All she needed was a barrel and some silver hoops to juggle. He started to laugh and that made him pee more, so he stood up, pulled down his undershorts and fire hosed the floor like he and Alex had done in the boy's bathroom last year and had to go to the principal's office. Norma fled the utility room, screeching and wheezing.

"If you hurt Daddy again, I'll pee on your head while you're asleep!" Joe yelled, a final arc of urine spilling onto the yellow tile. Grinning, he turned to his dad. Marcus crouched on the floor with his good hand on his forehead and Joe saw a hint of a smile, but also a touch of cold fear. He sat down and rested his head on Marcus's quaking shoulder.

"Don't be afraid, Dad. We can read *Robin Hood* tonight if you want."

It took Norma over six months to recover. During that time, she didn't lay hand or lash on either of them.

Joe walked, reading the word on each door as he passed.

compassion

fear

believe

hate

joy

suffer

love

sacrifice

forgive

So many doors. This whole thing was beginning to wear him down and he knew that's what Alex wanted. Joe could feel him, his essence carrying him along like a leaf caught on a steady current, and he couldn't break his hold. Joe stopped at a door and watched the word appear. The yearning sensation strengthened, deepened.

Truth

No. Joe stepped back, but the pull in his chest tugged him forward. *I don't want to.*

Is the knowing so bad?

Joe frowned. It took a moment to recognize the voice, to decipher, to comprehend, to believe.

Is it?

He touched the word engraved on the door.

She's waiting for her champion.

Joe closed his exhausted eyes, knowing he had to turn the doorknob.

It was you.

"No," Joe breathed, digging his fingers into the roughness of the door. He shook his head, the sequence of events flooding his mind in a surge.

Do you see?

He sucked at the air, trying hard to fill his lungs with denial, trying hard to resist. The shadows raged and reached, but Alex held fast, keeping him in the light.

"Why are you doing this to me?" Joe moaned, covering his face with his hands to ward off Truth.

Is the knowing so bad, Joey?

Joe watched the scenes flash in his mind. He sank his fingers deep, dragging *Truth* off the door and dropping it to the white marble floor, where it splintered into a million fragments and disappeared. He clutched his head, trying to make the certainty stop.

It was you.

Joe grabbed the knob. The door eased open and he stood there for several long moments, hearing the sounds and smelling the smells. The longing deepened. Impressions burned against his eyelids like continual afterimages from a flashbulb. He stepped over the threshold, bare foot coming down in a river of blood.

The wrought iron bars felt cold and slippery in his hands. He smelled mowed grass, wet and lush, tasted warm rain and sweetsalt blood in his mouth, felt the blade sink deep, heard muffled cries of terror and bewilderment mixed with thunder. A deluge emptied from the darkness above. He glanced down at his black Converse One-Stars, at the torrent of red water pouring over them, and knew his mom wouldn't buy him new ones. It had taken three months of continuous begging for her to give in and buy these. Size six, two up from the pair his dad had bought last year, even though Joe didn't feel like he had grown at all since then. And Dad was gone now anyway, so Joe couldn't ask him for new shoes, couldn't ask him anything, including what to do about all the blood gushing over the grass and down the hill toward him and Alex.

He squinted against the storm. The yellowish property lamp above their heads made it hard to see beyond the dim halo of light. He looked at Alex standing there with his head down, mesmerized by the red river running over his shoes.

"Where's it coming from?" Joe called over the gale.

Alex stood there, unmoving. He didn't even blink the rain from his eyes.

Joe could hear the noise, could see a shape moving in the low fog blanketing the estate grounds, could smell someone's insides on the gusts of wind slamming into his body. It was a scent he knew well and had come to rely on for comfort in the month since his dad left.

"Think it's a fox?" Joe yelled. Their whole lives they'd scouted for the remains of animals down by the tracks, hauled the carcasses to Mary's and dried out the bones, fashioned medieval weapons for battle against evildoers. Usually, though, they just stole trash cans from Old Lady Walker or made spooky voices on Alex's tape recorder and played them when Mrs. Schell got home from her shift at the hospital.

Alex held the black bars tight, white knuckles like beacons in the tempest. He watched the red river, silent.

Joe grabbed the iron bars and climbed over the sharp points at the top, dropping to the lush lawn on the other side. He pulled a homemade bone arrow from his *Batman* backpack, loaded it into the bow and made his way toward the dark shape thrashing around near the top of the knoll thirty feet away. Halfway there, he stopped and turned. Alex stood on the other side of the wrought iron gate, yellow slicker glowing like neon under the light of the lamp. Joe turned back, nocked his bow and trudged up the hill. As he drew close, a monster loomed out of the billowing fog, snarling and moving in jerks and twitches, a jumbled tangle of limbs and growls, grunts and muffled screams. Joe raised the bow but stopped short of letting the arrow fly when he realized it wasn't a monster at all. It was a lady with a man on top of her, hips wedged between her bare thighs and slamming against them over and over. The lady thrashed, knuckles of one hand connecting with the man's cheekbone. The man let out a wail of pain, lifted a fist and smashed it down on the lady's nose. She sank her teeth into his shoulder, clawed at his face, bucked under him like a trapped animal.

Monster man's gruff voice carried on the rolling wind. "You take it, cunt. You know you like it." He grabbed the lady's wrists, flipped her over and lay on her back. She wrenched her arms free and elbowed him in the face. A scarlet geyser sprayed from monster man's nose and he sat up, choking on the rainwater and blood running into his throat. The lady scrambled, slipped on the wet grass, got on her feet, slipped again. A once-white tank top hung in shreds from her thin shoulders. Her half-naked body oozed crimson, heavy rain washing away the blood as soon as it appeared in the deep cuts on her arms and thighs. Joe blinked water from his eyes and watched blood seep and disappear, seep and disappear, like a weird illusion.

"Fucking bitch," the man seethed. He stood up, black T-shirt dripping, baggy pants around his ankles, a metal blade flashing in the shifting sheets of rain. The lady darted across the grass on all fours. Her hands slipped and she skidded to the ground again, coughing up water. Monster man pounced, grabbed her flailing arms and pinned them behind her, plunging the blade deep into her side.

Joe let the arrow fly. It struck monster man in the bare butt and he let out a high-pitched shriek. Joe loaded his bow and let loose a second arrow. It bit into the man's forehead, knocking his head back. With a loud war-cry, Joe ran forward, grabbed a handful of monster man's greasy hair and ripped it from his head. The man roared in pain. Glaring, he wiped rainwater and blood from his face. The lady lay limp on the grass, eyes open, seeing. Joe knew he needed to get help, knew it like he knew his dad was never ever coming back.

Monster man pointed at Joe, wet hair pasted to his pimply face, and Joe could see who it was.

"You little fuck!" Jeffy Kendall screamed.

His distorted voice sounded far away in the downpour. Joe backed up.

"I'm gonna rip your fucking head off!"

Joe took another step backward, reaching back for an arrow. He loaded the bow and took aim at Jeffy Kendall's exposed groin, pulled back the wire and let go. The arrow struck him in the belly just left of his bobbing penis. Joe backed deeper into the fog, Jeffy's howl of pain riding the storm.

"You fuckin' little fuck shithead! I'm gonna kill you!" Jeffy screamed, trying to drag his saturated pants up to his waist and give chase. He stumbled and fell with a splash, still screaming threats.

"The police are coming to get you, Ken-*doll!*" Joe spun and ran, headed for the lighted windows winking in the billows of rain across the expansive estate yard. He ran up the steps and banged on the door until someone answered— Mrs. Ma'kadalia, a round woman with tufts of gray hair who leaned over to look him in the eyes, a curious frown on her wrinkled up old face. He told her to call an ambulance because someone got hurt by the gate, then he jumped off the porch and ran back into the fog, back to the lady. Jeffy Kendall was gone and so were the arrows. Joe sat next to the lady, orange jacket soaked through to the skin. He wiped her hair away, then lay down on his tummy next to her and looked into her eyes.

"Can you see me?" he asked.

She did, and Joe glimpsed a strange light in her warm brown eyes, the same kind of light he only ever saw when he looked at Alex.

"Yes, I see you," she said, weak. A slow smile curved the corners of her lips. "I see him now."

"Are you gonna die?" Joe asked her. He put his hand on her shoulder to let her know she was not alone.

The lights in the lady's eyes brightened as she stared at him, then the twin points lifted from her irises like two stars and Joe rolled onto his back and watched them float above like fairies in the mist.

"It's okay," Joe whispered to the lights, reaching up. "You can come in."

The twin sparks exploded. A brilliant sunbeam pierced his forehead, held him there. Rainbows danced in front of his eyes. Music sounded in his ears. The rays evaporated into fog. Sirens sounded in the distance.

Inside his jacket pocket, Joe clutched the strands of monster man's slimy hair. He took it out and stuffed it under the lady's cold hand, curled her fingers around it in the wet grass. He leaned close and said Jeffrey Kendall's name into her ear and told her not to forget. It was all he had, all he could give, all he could do. He got to his feet, raking hair down over his face, and walked across the grass to where Alex stood on the other side of the wrought iron fence. A swirl of blue and red lights hurried up the street. Thunderous rainfall nearly drowned out the sirens, but not quite. In the vast darkness of all the noise, Joe heard a child begin to cry.

You gave up after that.

Fucking-A I did. It was too much. With you … and her.

But it was you, Joey.

Joe grabbed his head, watching *Truth* write out in the white light. *I didn't know what else to do!*

You did it all.

"I know, goddamn it! Shut up!" He slammed his fist against the door. "I didn't know what else to do. I-I didn't know." Joe slumped to the white marble, tears flowing out of eyes strained from trying hard not to see. The water spilled into his cupped palms and he let it whisper promises and betrayal. He felt drained, sucked dry, empty, lost in the knowing that he could be trapped in this upsetting place of light and truth for good rather than in a place of oblivion and eternal night like he'd intended. The realization made him mourn harder and the shadows railed. A fresh fall of saltwater streamed. He licked it from his lips, tasting loss and grief.

Why do you cry? It was the woman, the one he didn't save that night, the one whose light he still carried inside so he would never forget his failure.

"Shut up," Joe choked, burying his face in his arms.

Is the Truth so hard to see, Heyoka? Have you run so far from yourself that you can no longer see the good?

Joe's shoulders shook with shame and wracking sobs. *There is no good. I couldn't save him, and I couldn't save you. It's finished now.*

He felt a gentle hand on his head. Her voice was close, in his ear. "But he saved you so you *could* save me."

Joe shook his head, rocking from side to side. The sorrow expanded, coursing through his veins with such profound despair that he thought his chest would crack open with the pressure. "I couldn't. I wanted to, I tried, but … it's finished." Tears flowed over his cupped hands.

"No, this story is not over."

Joe lifted his chin and opened his swollen eyes, seeing her there. She was near, but too far away to touch.

"You did save me. But it's all for nothing if you stay between and allow your false truths to consume you." She blinked out, vanished into the white ether.

It was you, Joey. You are a champion.

Joe curled against the door, shaking his head. "I didn't—"

"Yeah, you did," Alex said, crouching next to him. "I saw her with my own eyes, man. Her name is Jade. She's not doing well. She's trapped here. And her dad misses her."

Joe felt like he was choking on heartache. It lodged in his throat like a hard ball of fire. He swallowed. "Her dad?"

"Yeah. Buck Timberwolf. He invited us over for lasagna. He said he hopes you make it."

Joe looked at his wet hands. "I can't help her now. It's too late."

Alex stood. "You can. All you have to do is let her go."

Joe shook his head. "What?"

"She's here to protect the kid. She's *mii manidoon gen-awenimigojin*, Joe, the spirit who takes care of him. When he doesn't need protecting anymore, she can go home."

"You're trying to trick me," Joe said, wiping his face. "You're trying to make me feel."

"No," Alex said. "No tricks. No lies. No more secrets or false truths."

"I don't want to go back." Joe's voice quavered. He pressed his hands together to get them to stop shaking.

"That little boy told me otherwise. He's ready for the fight, Joe. Like you once were."

Joe lurched to his feet. Fresh tears fell from his jaws in steady streams, emptying his soul. "I don't know how. I don't know him anymore."

Alex nodded. "Okay. We'll let the bully win this one then. She's already had a few victories since you gave up. Why break her streak now?"

Joe squinted through the colorless haze creeping into the periphery of his vision. His lungs strained for breath. A hole in Alex's chest bled red, a stark stain in the whiteness.

"What is that?"

"Your mother, Joe. She did this to me. You're letting her win."

"I—how …?" The air wrung out from his lungs. He sank to the gleaming white marble, watching his hands shake like frightened birds. A white blur clouded his eyes, closing in, and Alex's voice echoed.

"If you don't go back, Jade's life will be lost. Mine, too. Your dad will have died for nothing. You'll have given up on the people who have refused to give up on you, the people who believe in you most, who have seen who and what you are in the world and know you belong in it. We know you've forgotten and that the false truths your mother put in you are strong. But you let Jade inside that horrible night and gave her a safe place. You saved me after Luke died. You brought me back. You showed us that heroes do exist, even if they're in the form of a ten-year-old boy shooting handmade arrows like he's fucking Robin Hood. You've got a second chance to save her. And me."

Joe looked up at Alex through the thickening mist and tried to grasp the thoughts sailing through his head, fought to comprehend. One feeling pervaded his entire being above all others, taking on a bitter flavor that he could taste in the back of his throat and he didn't like it. He watched the word

believe

scratch out in front of his eyes and hang there in neon green. Then everything turned blinding white.

"I can't."

"Don't be afraid."

"I can't see."

He felt Alex lift him again, heard Alex's encouraging voice in his head, then saw a dark vaporous claw reach out of the whiteness and wrap tight around Alex's body. With a freight train howl, it yanked him back and Joe dropped.

fifteen

Waves

Norma Schell sat against a smooth stone wall, trying to see into the billowing veils of empyrean mist that enveloped her like a comfortable blanket. Within the illuminated white cloud, she watched shapes dart across her field of vision to merge with others or vanish altogether, lifted high on gossamer wings. Smiling, she kept her hands clasped at her breast and continued with the Lord's Prayer, unsurprised that she felt no numbness, no pain. God had healed her, His chosen, His queen. Soon He would send His angels to bring her home, where she belonged.

"Lead us not into temptation but deliver us from evil …"

A sheen of perspiration lit her face. She felt warm inside, bathed in His light. A low laugh resonated, riding the mist and rolling over her in a cool rush. She kept her eyes open, hoping to finally see her savior, her Lamb, the living light of the world. All those years of penance, of right-living and doing God's will, and here she was, elevated to heights no ordinary mortal could ever conceive of. Her time had arrived, at long last.

"Praise you," she whispered, lifting a palm high, the other pressed to her chest. "I knew you would reward my sacrifices, sweet prince. For you. Only you." She let loose a rush of unintelligible words and mutterings. *Holy words*, she thought. *The language of the divinely elected.*

The ethereal mist stirred, and she was sure she glimpsed a winged figure within the white cloud surrounding her.

"Give us this day our daily bread …"

Something brushed her hand, a solid and tactile sensation. She squinted into the ether, watching transparent shapes fuse and evaporate.

"… and forgive us our trespasses, as we forgive those who trespass against us."

A child's giggle rode on a gust of wind and Norma felt a second firm sweep against her palm. Something pulled at her fingers as though trying to get her to stand. A burst of laughter found her ears and she smiled.

The children! Of course!

Norma closed her eyes, quelling tears of gratitude and reverence at His benevolent gesture. Dozens of little fingers caressed hers with gentle strokes. She let them touch her hands in exploration, tugging and tickling playfully, childlike laughter riding the cool air in joyous song.

She'd always wondered what it would be like, how He would acknowledge her unwavering service. Sending the children, *His* children, to bring her home not only made sense now, it made her fully realize why He had chosen her in the first place. Of all His servants, only she had been up to the task He demanded. Only she had the strength to carry through. And now she knew that all the indignities she'd suffered at the hands of her mortal husband and that evil child had happened for a reason, that it had all been a part of His grand plan for her. God had tested her and now she knew she had not failed. Satan had tried to break her, yes, tried to instill doubt and fear into her mind, of course, but she'd stayed on the path to His kingdom, to His eternal glory, to the reward she now faced. A mere nod would not suffice a Queen; simple deliverance could never repay. But sending the children to bring her home? She let the tears fall, His divine validation too great, too good. *It was all worth it, my prince. For you.*

An amused titter sang very close. A child's smiling face loomed out of the mist and then was gone, replaced by another and another and another.

She recognized them all. Little Adam with his autistic head banging. Clever Shantal with her deaf ears and mute mouth. Inquisitive Ricky with his palsied legs and arms. Grinning Schuyler with her encephalitic brain. Talkative Jessica with her tiny, useless arm. And the other special ones. One after another their angelic faces appeared out of the nimbus, a glint of carefree mischief in their eyes, a touch of playful wickedness in their smiles. Norma started to smile back, started to take their hands and let them lead her home, but the sweat beading on her upper lip and the sudden ache in her temples kept her there, immobile. As the children crept closer across the alabaster floor, the throb in her head grew strong and she gasped, eyes widening in bewilderment.

While their faces were cherubic, their bodies twisted and bent in all the wrong places. They moved in stiff, labored jerks, legs wasted to bone, tummies distended, little hands grasping at the fine mist. Norma's chest felt heavy. Her heart pounded in uneven beats. But there was something more than simple fear overriding her senses like a charging freight train. Her nipples stiffened. Her breasts tingled, swelled. She pressed a hand there and felt warm liquid, sticky and wet. Their small voices rose like a chorus, mouths working the chilled air. "Feed us, mama. We're so hungry."

Norma looked up from the milky blood oozing through her fingers, the lighted mist growing dark as she watched. Fluttering curtains of haze separated and a figure shuffled toward her, taking arthritic steps as though contact with the stone floor made its heels burn. Its arms crooked at the elbows, swinging rigid at its sides. Palms dripped ruby beads onto the pristine ground, leaving a trail that made Norma think of redemption. As it neared, a fall of vermilion teardrops streamed from the figure's radiant eyes. It reached out a punctured hand, small fingers searching. The hideous thing stopped, just tall enough to meet Norma at eye level, and opened its withered mouth, corpse lips pulling apart like rotted silly putty, swollen tongue darting like an engorged worm, eyes blazing eternity. Norma pushed herself against the wall, turning away as the creature buried a cold hand in her hair. He drew close, breath hot and reeking of accusation. A gush of dirty water spilled from his mouth and she heard her baby's voice like a low whistle inside her head. The words he spoke were too old for him, as though he'd somehow been infused with all the knowledge of the universe.

Your milk runs red as sin and you filled me with it.

Norma searched the thing's shrunken face for any indication of the divine being that should have been standing there and saw a truth so visceral she could feel it surging through her veins in excruciating pulses and she saw a word etch itself into the wispy pallor in neon yellow

sinner

Panting, Norma twisted away, but the thing held fast.

"Why did you hurt me, mama?" Misery and confusion constricted every syllable. Red teardrops streamed down the boy's cheeks, the rotted putty lips quivered. A stench of moldy water and algae saturated the cool air.

With a strained wheeze, Norma flung out her arm, knocking the creature aside. Its flesh felt frigid, clammy, undeniably lifeless. The small figure righted itself, moving in unnatural jerks and jolts, once-blond hair plastered to its head, ghoulish features twisting into an expression of abject hurt.

"You make me sad, mama." It choked out the words in hard sobs, a foul fish odor filling the air. "But I still love you."

The voice, too wise, came again. *Remember the satisfaction? The contentment only a selfish woman can feel?*

A wail wrenched from Norma's throat and she held out her hands as though warding off an attack. "No, Isaac, don't."

"Was I bad? Is that why you put me in the water?" The horrid creature reached for her again, wanting, and she swatted its hand away, recoiling against the wall at her back. Frosty mist reached deep into her lungs, squeezed. She sucked at the air, a sharp pain spiking in her temple and wending down her arm.

"I—I ..." She looked into the fog beyond the aberration. Twisted children crawled fully into view like grotesques emerging from the waters of a hellish womb, and Norma heard a voice spilling truth into her mind in a wave of soiled water.

You know what you did was wrong.

"I do God's bidding," Norma rasped, clutching at her throat. "You were a special child of God. You belonged to Him, your true father."

The wasted little boy reached again, runny mud and sodden leaves spilling from his mouth. "You made Daddy go away. You make my brother sad."

Shantal's belly-laughter rode the chilled air.

The boy caressed Norma's face with an icy hand, deep blue eyes burning with accusation and puzzlement.

You say they are special, but you do what you do because you want your god to favor you, not because you believe they are bound to him.

"Favor you." The words came with a mischievous giggle that struck like an arrow in Norma's temple. She clutched her head, anchored by the inferno in the phantom child's eyes.

"No," she rasped. "This is all wrong!"

You serve only yourself. You rationalize your actions to raise yourself to a place you will never be, to quench your thirst for the pity and attention of others. Selfish woman.

"Pity," Ricky laughed. "Selfish," Adam echoed.

Norma jerked her head to search for the source of the knowing voice but could not look away from the boy's blistering gaze. In the peripheral space around him she saw the children slink closer across the smooth white floor. Her nipples leaked in steady streams, staining her bra a muted red. The pain in her head worsened, gnawed at her skull, blurred her vision.

Filthy water gushed from the boy's black mouth, spilling over Norma's heaving chest, stinking of pond scum and mixing with the bloodmilk spreading across the floor.

"I only did God's bidding. He chose me. He chose me to send you home, Isaac. And the others. He put his children in my womb. The special children. This is a mistake."

The despondency in his voice rattled her nerves, quickened the pain peaking in her head. "No, mama, you were wrong."

In a rising refrain, children's cries filled the void, growing in intensity and volume until it was all she could hear. Their mournful wails and shuddering sobs pierced her skull like blades, filling her throat with a fear so tangible she thought it would strangle her. Jessica's round baby face loomed, smiling, then the little girl sank her teeth into Norma's arm. She tried to shake the girl off, but a nip at her cheek made her gasp. She reeled away just as Ricky took a bite out of her calf and Shantal gnawed the flesh of her upper arm. Norma writhed, kicking. She heard her baby's voice high on the malignant wind, buoyed by the stench of polluted pond water.

"Mama, you should pray now."

She screamed as the children swarmed.

Alex fell through streamers of searing reds and cool violets. The thing pulled him down and he thrashed against it, tried to regain some control and just a sliver of sanity. He hit hard, splashing into the pool of saltwater and sinking deep, the might of the thing's grasp tightening, holding him within the confines of the watery prison, obviously reserved for those who had failed or quit the fight. He kept his eyes open, watching hundreds—thousands—of bodies drift in the current, their bloated faces looming close and brushing his skin. His lungs constricted, craving air. He kicked, arms pinned to his sides, but couldn't rise. Something held him there, anchored at the nadir of sorrow and grief. A profound despair began to seep in. He could feel its cold tendrils probing, searching for a way in. It felt like tiny pins pricking every inch of his body, his mind and soul. His stomach turned. Bile rose and he quelled the need to vomit. He thrashed harder against the liquid fingers probing his pores, hunting for the cracks in his soul. He began to gag, to choke on the rising nausea and the intense feelings of misery and hopelessness filling every living cell. Alex pushed the panic from his mind, refusing to breathe in defeat.

Joe stepped over the threshold, bare foot coming down on a stone floor. Amber light settled like a heavy blanket, making his skin prickle and tighten. Near the crumbling stone walls, things shuffled and scraped, waited for him to let his guard down, waited for him to fuck up. He could feel their presence in his mind, like old friends welcoming him back after a short exile. Sinister whispers prodded the barrier between his sanity and their will to make him doubt, to make him stumble, to make him fall.

Again.

Why do you do it, Joe? Why do you make yourself bleed?

Because if I don't, he will.

Who?

From the depths, a shadow stretched out a vaporous arm. Like a rope unraveling into the air, the thing's gnarled finger extended, beckoning. The beast smiled, needle-sharp teeth glinting in the golden light.

Joe swallowed, pointed. "Me."

The wail of a train whistle rang out in the near distance. He eyed the caged souls floating beyond the mirrored glass and knelt to curl his fingers around the hilt of Alex's sword. Blood had pooled on the floor. His blood, Alex's blood. The child's.

The child. Joe squeezed the sword handle. A surge of hatred flooded his veins, hot, familiar, soothing.

You are a failure, Joe Schell. An unworthy little boy.

Joe's hands clenched. He shut his eyes against the rising fear, railed against the insidious phantoms that knew him so well.

You are powerless, and you know it.

Joe's heart thumped against his ribs. He drew a deep breath and looked down at the weapon, at his pale hand wrapped around the ivory handle. He tried to lift it, but the weight was too much. His heart took up a quick rhythm, thudding like a bass drum. Sweat slid down his back. He let the weapon go, tears threatening, and wiped his face.

You are nothing.

Joe listened closely to the steady thrum of his heart. He listened to the stillness between the beats. Alex always said that was where the magic happens, in the silence between the notes.

Riding a rush of devil's breath, a screeching freight train growl shook Joe's insides. The wind pushed hard, tried to send him skidding, but he dug in.

To win, you need him, fool.

"Where is Alex?" Joe yelled over the rushing wind.

A smoky limb sent him spinning into the glass wall. The impact knocked the breath out of him. He pushed himself up. Wind-whipped hair stung his eyes. A deafening howl blasted from beyond the golden light filtering from nowhere. One stone wall split apart. Yawning faces peeled away and fell to the marble floor, shattering with a crash.

You cannot be saved without him. You are a fragment.

"I know," Joe murmured, letting the tears come. "I-I can't fight you." He stepped away from the mirror wall, searching for a threshold, a way out. His legs felt like lead. His arms hung slack at his sides, drained of energy. *No power*, he thought. *I have no strength.*

A vile howl echoed inside his head, vibrating to the core. He tried to bring up his hands to drown it out but couldn't manage the weight of his arms.

Embrace your true self.

An ominous chuckle rode the wind and Joe recognized his own mirthless voice. He looked at himself in the mirror and saw a young man who'd dove into the heart of darkness and made it his own. His face grew skeletal and blue-veined, the flesh tightened, eyes darkened. He raked at his stringy hair, staring at the horrid truth of who he was.

murderer

He's dead because of you.

Joe watched as Alex drifted out from the clusters of slack bodies on the other side of the glass, emerging from the depths like a sick joke. He looked at Joe, but the light in his eyes had dimmed to a bare spark. He didn't fight, didn't struggle. Joe caught a fragment of Alex's thoughts *hopeless … no use … too dark here* as they mingled with the despondent reflections of all the other souls, creating one singular voice inside Joe's head—the unified voice of those who gave up too early in the fight. The voice of desperation, of lives lost to overwhelming heartache, hearts and spirits broken, minds battered to bloody oblivion.

"No," Joe gasped, doubling over on his knees.

Now you can find the child and finish this once and for all.

Seething through gritted teeth, he raised a heavy arm and touched the glass where Alex's cheek was pressed. The thought entered Joe's mind with such force it pitched his palm away with a jolt of stinging electricity. *You were right, Joe. It's finished.*

Joe reeled back. He clutched his head, trying to shake the sinister voice out of his mind. His heart felt like deadweight inside his chest, heavy as stone. A visceral sorrow filled him, bones to flesh, top to bottom, inside out. Tears flooded his eyes. The stone walls tilted. He sank to his knees, fighting to stay upright. A crushing weight held him there while the wind bayed inside his head, whispering truths only he could hear. *I did this. I killed him.*

Sobs wracked his body. Distant music sang his name. Rainbows faded before his eyes, his vision going gray. Tears hit the floor, mixing with his and Alex's blood.

Now you can do what you came here to do, get what you've always wanted.

Joe looked up, saw Alex floating among the lost, and heard his friend's words.

He's ready for the fight, Joe, like you once were.

Joe's hands clenched. The pressure in his chest increased, wringing the air out of him like a dirty dishrag. He slumped forward, watched Alex grow old, watched Alex's skin wrinkle and bloat like all the others. He watched the light in Alex's eyes dim.

He's mine now, you worthless little heathen piece of shit. You're nothing.

Joe wrapped his arms around his head and sobbed. The mad moans of an angry wind swept through his psyche, wending through the spaces that had once been the very core of his being—the spaces between *then* and *now*. He couldn't turn them off. The cavernous sighs clawed at his sanity, rending strips of it away like so much burnt flesh, and he knew he couldn't win this one. All feeling emptied from him in one big exhale. The room turned sideways, and he with it.

The little fuck is yours for the taking!

A champion always does the right thing, Joey.

You are no champion.

He only pretended to love you.

Who's the pussy now, bro?

Joe thrashed, kicked, pulled clumps of hair from his head. He gouged at his skin with ragged fingernails, bit his hands in a pathetic attempt to feel. But he felt none of it. Scratches did not appear; no blood bubbled from his pores. He felt inconsequential, unstable in his body, out of control, as though he weren't there at all, but a mere figment, a shallow excuse. Through the confused fog of his mind Joe found Alex, still there, always there, and caught a whisper. *It's finished now.*

And then he saw it. A vision flashed from nowhere like a wayward note that finds its way into a new composition and fits just right. It wasn't something Alex needed to show him. The memory came clear and liquid into his mind, and it was all his own. Joe drew a sharp breath. Heat bloomed in his belly, and he winced at the precious pain. He staggered to his feet and lunged at the glass as Alex drifted up and back into the saltwater depths, vanishing.

"Al!" Joe slammed his fists against the mirror. A freight train rumble shook the walls and Joe froze, palms against the glass. He felt the smoothness of it, the cool solidity, and a recollection flashed—Alex damming up the leak with his finger just before Jade appeared in the mirror—and then was gone.

A dark shape swarmed out of the ocher depths, straight at him. Joe closed his eyes and smelled the anise on Mary's breath, the cedar-scented air, too, and heard the old woman's soft whisper in his ear, *victory can be found in the darkest corners.* Joe turned and faced the blackness coming for him, planted his bare feet firmly on the cool stone floor. He looked down at his hands, curled into tight fists, and raised them high. A wry smirk pulled up the corners of his mouth. He couldn't help it. It was all too perfect.

"Okay," Joe whispered, eyeing the tempest. "We'll do this my way. Make me bleed."

The shadow scooped him up, enveloped him in absolute blackness. Joe opened his arms wide and flew, smashing face-first into the glass.

You're little. You're nothing.

Vaporous talons yanked him up and away. Suspended by thin wisps of black cloud, Joe wiped his nose with the back of his hand and looked at it, relishing the familiar metallic taste on his tongue.

"I may be nothing. I may be small, and you just might kill the best part of me …" He licked blood from his lip and smirked, gazing deep into the abyss and letting it fill him. "But, like Alex says, I'm one stubborn son-of-a-true-bitch."

With a thunderous snarl, amorphous hands hoisted him up and pitched him into the mirror. The ribs in his back cracked. Joe groaned in agony, more precious pain. When the shadowthing pulled him back he saw water spraying from a wide crack in the glass and smiled.

Disembodied fingers tightened, night coursed through Joe's veins like thick black ink, fueling his resolve. Needle-teeth flashed. *Kill the child. Embrace your true self.*

Joe looked deep into the blue, blue eyes of darkness, saw himself staring back, and laughed.

"Bite me, motherfucker."

A cavernous black maw opened and Joe dove in. Pointed teeth pierced his skull and he felt his father's arms close tight around him. This time he held on. The heartbeats returned, and Joe paid attention to the silence between them.

The glass shattered with the impact of his body. Water arced in a cresting wave. Joe sank deep, breathing in all of the world's sorrow, all of the joy. He filled his lungs with the sacred waters and let them wash him clean.

Joe slammed into Alex with such force it sent him spiraling into a knot of decomposed men floating yards away. Then Joe was gone, sucked into the vortex of bodies writhing like bizarre dancers trapped in a madman's ballet. Alex reached, probed the waters for something to hold on to—an arm, filthy hair, anything—but the waves pushed him deeper.

Lifeless human forms collided. The dead reached, pulled him farther down into the bottomless pool. His lungs spasmed, craving air. He couldn't see. Water churned. He didn't know which way was up, which way was *out*. Big hands closed around his throat—a man with a crew cut and a scar on his cheek—and began to squeeze. The man's rotted mouth worked, as though trying to form words Alex would never be able to hear in the muted saltwater sea, even if the guy's vocal cords were still in working order. The man's stiff fingers let go when a dead woman crashed into him and sent him spinning away.

Alex hovered there, trying to get his bearings, and realized the current was moving in a specific direction. He went slack, riding the wave. The idea that the grisly aquarium stretched on forever made his stomach hurt. He rode the current, pushing the dread from his mind.

A pregnant woman sailed by, clutching her belly. A man with dark skin and large, intelligent eyes drifted near, arms and legs gone, ragged stumps still oozing blood. A teenage girl with a gaping head wound floated past, eyes empty, skin loose. Alex touched her cheek, cold and long dead, and felt a familiar remorse stalking the weak spots of his mind, hunting for a way in. He picked up speed. Water shot up his nose and the reflex to cough it out took hold. Panicked, he drew a shallow breath, inhaling the nauseating liquid. His stomach lurched.

No. No. Fuck no.

A sucking force pulled him fast. He pinched his nose closed and slammed hard into a cluster of bodies bottlenecked in one place. Elbows, feet, heads, knees and asses smashed into him, punting him around like a trampled ragdoll. He took a hard kick to the gut and bit back the urge to draw another breath. The spiral suction pulled him harder against the throng of corpses, the strong flux dragging him into a mass of stiff limbs. Cold fingers brushed his skin like slithering tentacles. Bloated faces loomed close, offering deathly kisses.

Everywhere, the dead and should-be-dead reached for him, seeking salvation, begging rescue.

Alex kicked hard. He swam deeper into the gruesome morass, grabbing bodies and using them for leverage to get closer to the exit they were clogging up. He knew he was close when he picked up speed again and the corpses ahead shot forward, towing him along in their wake. He took the stiff hand of a young woman who'd lost her battle long ago and followed her out, riding a breathless waterfall for what seemed an eternity. He spilled out of the watery cell, the furious tide threatening to sweep him up again and carry him into nightmares only the dead could dream. Jets of water roared in his ears. It was all he could hear—his head was full of it.

He spilled from the chamber and slammed hard to the ground. Water pulsed against his back like a thousand fire hoses, holding him there for several interminable seconds. His lungs cramped, ached. He inhaled as though taking his first breath of life, then gasped as a second section of the mirror shattered. A crushing swell washed over him, pinning him to the stone floor. A young boy rode the wave and landed right on top of him, his swollen baby face coming to rest on Alex's chest. Alex cradled him there for a moment, held the kid's tiny body tight and tried to comprehend the promise he once held—the promise they all once held.

Alex rolled with the next surge, setting the boy free in the saltwater graveyard, and paddled to the nearest wall. He could stand with his head above the surface, but the cresting waves and constant thrust of the waterfall made it hard to keep his balance. He needed a better vantage to search for Joe. Alex grabbed a carved face and heaved himself up a few inches. The water lapped like a thirsty beast, trying to keep him down. He set his jaw and lunged with every bit of strength he had. His legs felt like thousand-pound weights and his heart jack-hammered in his chest, but he managed to climb high enough to see out over the roiling surface.

"There's so many of them," Alex rasped, eyeing the lost souls set afloat by Joe's cocky brave arrogance. *Stupid kid. Always doing the right thing.* Alex coughed on the brackish burn in his throat and scanned the carnage for anyone with long blond hair. *Shit, so many.*

A third crack blew apart. A geyser arced high into the air. The water level rose immediately, inching up Alex's legs as the mirror emptied more of its ghastly treasure into the amber-lit room. Bodies spilled from unseen depths. Some sailed through the opening that led to the narrow pathway and the labyrinth of nonsensical rooms far below. Alex watched it all in helpless horror.

"My god." He climbed higher, holding a huge distended stone tooth with both hands. Another ear-shattering crash. Water poured from somewhere beyond his field of vision and within the newest tangle of ruined flesh cascading out of the tomb Alex saw an arm, full of life, flailing. He shook his head, blinked, held his breath.

There it was again … and then gone.

A low hum found his ears through the cacophonous noise. Water rose to his waist. Turning, Alex grabbed a stone ear and lifted up a few inches. He scanned the choppy surface.

Backed against a jutting edge where part of the wall had peeled away, he spotted someone, and blinked again.

"Jade?" He shook his head, the hum growing louder. Another thunderous crash. The water rose another full foot.

The person waved, frantic, wild brown hair like a fan in the sea, one arm flapping overhead, the other wrapped around a limp body that bobbed at her side.

Alex didn't think, he dove, stretching long, and emerged twenty feet away. He plunged again and stroked toward her, pushing bodies out of his path and fighting the current that dragged at him with liquid hands. He sputtered to the surface and wiped his bleary eyes, the taste of salt making his tongue tingle.

"I can't hold him up," Jade panted. She seemed thinner than ever, frailer, drained of her essence and whatever spark had kept her going for so long. Alex took Joe's shoulders and turned his face out of the water. Puncture wounds encircled his head. Pinpoints of blood pulsed in slow beats.

"Is he okay?"

The expression on Jade's face was all the answer he needed.

"We have to get to the doorway," Alex called over the rush of water. A dead woman twirled into him and he pushed her away. "It's the only way out!"

Jade fought the tide, fought to stay above the waterline. "No! It's not!" She reached for the wall and pointed with her other hand. "We can go up!"

Another crash boomed and the sea tilted as if pouring from a giant bowl, pulling them sideways. They held the sharp juts of the broken wall. Alex looked up, struggling to keep Joe's head above water. Amber light rained down, but Alex couldn't see what lay beyond. He shook his head. He needed to get Joe out of there. He needed to get Joe to Te. *It's not too late. It can't be too late.*

"How?"

Jade dipped under, eyes wide, and came up again. Alex could see her strength waning and wondered how long she'd been holding Joe. *Dumbass,* he chastised himself, looking into her eyes. *She's never let go.*

"We climb," Jade gasped, pushing a half-decomposed girl away. "There's a …" She dipped under again and Alex grabbed her arm, still stunned at how real she felt. "There's an exit up there. A passageway."

"Where does it lead?"

"Out, I think," she called over another bone-jarring explosion.

"Into the darkness?"

"I don't know. I just feel it's there."

A claustrophobic panic squeezed, and Alex let out a quick breath as another carcass slammed into him. He yelled over the steady roar of the water. "I can't carry Joe up a fucking wall, Jade! I don't have the strength. He's too heavy."

Jade pointed at all the bodies bottlenecking in one place. "Do you really want to try to dislodge them and swim through? That's a battle you don't need right now!"

Alex looked. Bodies crashed and spun, all sailing in the direction of the one exit in the chamber. He wiped his face, shook his head. *So much death, so much misery.*

"I have to try," he said, voice feeble.

Then he saw Jade's face, saw the determined set of her jaw and the reconciled might that had become vital in surviving this funhouse of shadows and light. She'd worked too hard, sacrificed too much to stop now.

He lowered his gaze and looked at Joe, at the ashen cheeks, ruby mouth that the girls at school had gone stupid over. Joe always pretended not to notice or did something unexpected to stun them into a hasty retreat. He always went for the shock and awe, the big gesture, to show people a part of themselves that they didn't want to see or had forgotten. Alex had spent his entire life wishing he had Joe's balls-out bravery, his backward way of doing things, his astounding capacity for compassion. He'd retreated instead, watching from a distance as Joe took on the world, pissing it off and stirring it up every chance he got.

"Why did he do this, Jade? Why make a game out of it, out of everything?"

Jade laughed, and Alex couldn't be sure if it was the ocean in her eyes or tears. "You got him to see, Alex."

The tightness in Alex's throat wouldn't let him speak. *He did this to save me.*

The waterline rose, lifting them eye-to-eye with a protruding stone face imbued with tangible anguish. Alex tucked his shoulder into Joe's abdomen, found a decent foothold, hooked his fingers into the jawbone of the carved face and heaved himself up. His whole body shook with the exertion and added weight of Joe's slight frame. Water rushed around Alex's thighs then ebbed away, pulling at his aching muscles. Periodic crescendos of shattering glass boomed throughout the structure. Stone faces loosened high above. Entire heads plummeted into the water like boulders, and Alex was sure he could hear their screams echo throughout the chamber as they fell. Jade and Alex stuck close to the wall, doing their best to avoid the flight path of the falling wreckage.

With hungry waves lapping at their hips, they tag-teamed Joe up the rocky cliffside. Alex lifted, using every muscle in his tired body to hoist Joe up. Jade pulled Joe onto the next ledge, tracking a path to the narrow rims where she could stand or sit for leverage. Together, they climbed higher into the amber light. Alex half-expected to see cherubs circling, but everywhere he looked Hell materialized. It was in the profoundly sad expressions of the carved faces and in the fetid, shit-smelling waters chasing him up the side of a hallowed stone wall, a monument erected to protect the hope Joe still harbored somewhere within that embattled mind of his.

Alex glanced over his shoulder and stifled a groan. Death twirled in the vortex below. Bodies spun like discarded mannequins. Misery permeated the humid air, so vast he could taste its greed with every breath of salted air. For the first time in his life he considered Hell as an actual place and the reality of it struck him numb. It had been there the whole time, he realized, running them down like a rabid dog. An afterlife of torment lay in Joe's placid face, in Jade's battle-weary posture, in his own guilt-blackened heart. But he fought it with every inch of water rising from that hellish womb. He fought it because that's what Joe would do, what Joe did.

With each labored pull upward, Alex's body shook, his mind numbed, his thoughts rolled out and away.

Swordfights and Cokes ... picking through the dried bones of unfortunate animals ... Luke sending plane after plane up and away, face glowing with pride and accomplishment ... boats sailing down gushing gutters ... greasy black hair stuffed into a fist.

Another section of the mirror burst, and he thought he heard a calm voice in his ear. A woman's voice. Alex's head snapped up to look at Jade as she contemplated her next handhold.

"What?" Alex yelled over the monotonous bellow of the sea.

Jade looked down at him and shook her head, wet hair plastered to the sides of her gaunt face. "What?"

"What did you say?" The tide rose to nip at his ankles.

Jade shook her head, brow furrowed in confusion and concentration.

"Sing ..."

Alex startled. It was louder now, not just inside his head but vibrating his teeth with that odd low hum.

Jade stared at him. "What is it?"

Alex cocked his head. "I thought I heard something."

Water lapped at his calves. Jade found a grip and pulled herself up onto a narrow ledge. She hooked her elbows under Joe's armpits and looked at Alex as though he'd just been mortally wounded. "Something bad?"

"I-I don't know," Alex said, trying to catch his breath. He heaved Joe partially onto the ledge and rested his head against the rough rock. His heart hammered. A teeth-rattling boom shook the wall and the stone he was standing on broke free. Alex scrambled for a hold, found one, but a second blast pitched him sideways. He clawed at the rock. Wet grit filled his eyes. Through the haze, he saw Jade haul Joe up with all the strength she had, dragging his limp body onto the lip. Alex started to follow, but the upsurge of tide sucked at his exhausted legs and for an instant, only an instant, he thought of loosening his grip and letting the sea take him. He dug in, lifting one leg then the other out of the suckling water. Panting, he pulled himself onto the slim edge next to Jade.

"How much farther?" he gasped. His eyes felt raw, sticky.

Jade peered up into the ocher brightness, studied it like it was some strange new equation in need of solving. "I can't see it. But I know it's there."

Alex closed his sore eyes for half a second. "How do you know we can get out that way?"

She gazed into the infinite glow and smiled. "Because that's how I got here."

The waterline rose, flooding over them with a fateful crescendo.

"Fuck," Alex seethed. He stood on a protruding nose, tucked his shoulder into Joe's abdomen and nodded to Jade, who took hold of an overhang and began to climb.

The glow brightened as they ascended. Alex felt its warmth on his face and inside, too, filling him with a familiar heat that anchored low in his gut.

"Sing …"

He stopped mid-reach and cocked his head.

Jade looked down at him from a narrow ledge, hands outstretched. "You heard it again?"

Alex nodded. "How'd you know?"

Jade gave him an expression as if the answer were obvious. She rocked back on her heels, took a thin breath, and Alex knew she didn't have much left. She was wasting away right in front of him, getting smaller and weaker with each second that passed.

Jade peered into the light sifting down from above. "Do you feel that?"

Alex looked up. "What?"

She leveled her gaze at him. "Hope."

A wave spilled into the grim pool below. Jade's knees buckled when she stood. She clutched a jagged rock, holding tight.

"Can you do this?' Alex called. The waterline rose fast, the dead with it.

Jade nodded, pulling herself up. "I have to!"

Another crash and the pool filled, spurring them upward. Alex hoisted Joe's limp body, rested him on a wider rim, then pulled himself up, grabbed Joe and slung him over his back. Saltwater lapped at Alex's heels. A stiff hand reached for his foot. The tide rose. The heat in his belly suddenly flared. He almost lost his balance but leaned forward against a chiseled tooth and tried to fill his lungs with air. The hotness spiked in his chest and he gasped, leaned into the wall and slid to his knees. Water rose around his legs. He heard Jade's weak voice from above.

"Alex! Hold on! Don't let go!"

Heat spread like fire through his torso. He peered up into the amber flush but couldn't see her. The glow bathed his face, and it felt good. "I won't," he said, lightheaded. *I just need to rest for a minute.*

Water rose around his calves. A dead man reached with rigid fingers and Alex wrapped his hand around them for a brief moment.

"Sing ..."

Dizzy, Alex peered into the glow. *The song.* Heat sizzled in his belly, pulsing into his weak arms like electric shocks. He bent over, set Joe on the ledge, and looked at his friend. He brushed the wet hair off Joe's face. "I remember that," Alex said. "You said it would float and you were right. You're always right."

The water rose another three inches.

"Alex! Don't let go!"

Alex looked up, but the light filled his eyes so it was all he could see. "I won't."

A crunching crash and the water closed around his waist. "I know," he said, watching the pinpricks of blood on Joe's head ebb and flow. "It's the fire." The heat bloomed hot in his gut and he doubled over, breathless. He smelled anise and cedar. Cherry.

"Sing …"

"… the song, yeah. But I forgot the words." The water rose to their chests and Alex looked up again. "Jade?"

He gazed out over the roiling surface, at the hundreds, thousands, of hopeless dead set adrift on the sea of tears, and it was like a cruel thump against his head. He reeled back, stared at the water rising above his chest and grimaced in horror. He tightened his grip on Joe's arm and looked up again.

"Jade! Keep going! I'll find you at the top!"

No answer.

He craned, trying to catch a glimpse of her somewhere above. "Jade!"

Nothing.

Alex pulled Joe up and let his slack body fall over his shoulder. He grabbed a jagged edge of stone, found a foothold and pulled with all his strength, but the water reached with liquid claws and he lost his grip, splashing back onto the slippery ledge. Teeth gritted, he tried again. His arms and legs shook with the effort, and the ravenous sea held him in a death grip, eager for more gruesome treasure.

"Fuck." The water had risen too high for him to get any leverage. He couldn't get a grip without the tide pulling him back into its clutches. He looked up again into that fantastic glow, fighting off frustration.

"Jade!"

An explosion rang out. Debris splintered and fell away from the walls. Sections of stone as big as lodgepole pines peeled free and landed in the water like bomber missiles. Waves crashed over Alex with the impact. He held the wall, pressed himself as close as he could as the tide tugged. Another bone-jarring boom and the water rose a foot. He dipped his shoulder and set Joe upright, holding him close

around the waist as water surged to their chins. Alex tread-
ed, fighting to keep Joe's face out of the water. He held the
wall so they wouldn't drift into the hordes of colliding dead.
He squinted into the bright nimbus overhead and heard the
voice again.

"Sing ..."

Another explosion and the water level rose. Alex let go
to adjust his grip on the wall just as another boom echoed
and the stone facade tilted, moved, crumbled at his touch. A
boulder plummeted into the water ten feet away. A crushing
wave arced, drove them down while the undertow pulled.
Water shot up Alex's nose and he gasped, breathing in the
brine. He clawed the air, paddling with one arm, and felt Joe
slip from his grasp. Alex groped, managed to get a handful
of dirty blond hair, then the whirlpool yanked hard, towing
Joe out into the choppy waters and under the surface.

Alex spun, searched, grasped at the churning liquid and
saw only the sorrowful sea's deadly claim floating all around,
circling like those soul-sucking shadows in the dark, like
those shapes waiting patiently to steal Luke's spirit away.
Alex's thoughts rolled out again. Running in the sprinklers,
pizza parties, but he didn't let them get far this time.

Alex dove, sweeping his arms out and away in broad
stokes, probing the salt waters with his fingers. He kept his
eyes open and watched the cast of the Reaper's sick show
sail past on the current. He came up for air and dove again,
going deep. Just beyond a woman with a baby clutched to
her chest, Joe floated, tangled in the billowing Victorian
dress of a different woman whose eyes were gone. Alex
swam down and wrapped his arms around Joe's slack body.
He kicked hard for the surface, chest on fire.

But the surface wasn't where he'd left it. The sea shook
with a muted crash. A huge boulder plunged eight feet away.
Alex reeled with the force of it, narrowly missing a head-
on with a massive stone eye. His lungs burned. The searing

heat in his gut erupted. His legs felt like deadweight. He kicked, but the surface had risen and he could barely see the amber glow now, so distant. He held Joe tight.

The glow faded. The heat in his belly raged for release. He looked at Joe's calm face, mind fogging. Through the haze, he thought he saw Joe open his eyes and smile that trademark mischief grin of his.

You're the champion.

Alex couldn't tell if the thought was his own or had come from the random misfirings of his oxygen-starved brain. The hotness surged, coursing through his veins and making his limbs smolder. He smelled anise and cedar and wanted so much to breathe the smoke in. *Just one sip, one taste.*

"Hold fast to your fire, Alexander."

The glow dimmed high above. *Will it help if I sing to him and play the song?*

"Don't let go."

I won't. Alex tightened his grip.

"Hold him tightly so you don't fall down."

We've already fallen. And I'm so tired.

"But you can rise."

The glow seemed so far away now, unreachable, unattainable. His eyelids felt like they had anchors on them. He drifted, weightless, and saw Luke soar into the air, unfettered against an indigo sky. As he flew, he blossomed into a brilliant blue flower.

"I believe in you."

Alex blinked through the blur. The heat in his belly blazed. He looked at Joe's serene face and saw the radiance there, the promise.

Don't die, man.

There are worse things than death, Al. Like giving up your soul for the wrong reason.

Alex held Joe close and put his face against his cheek. The light high above winked out and he felt the life leaving Joe's body, an ounce here, a couple of grams there.

No! Alex shook him, tried to jostle life back in, the heat an unbearable inferno in his belly. *Where's it coming from?* He looked down and saw a speck of yellow light flare just below his chest, saw the memory.

"Why do you shine like that?"

"That's not my light, man. That's yours. See?"

"I don't see it."

"You never do, Al."

Alex squinted through the murk at the puncture wounds encircling Joe's head, then down at his own chest again, at the small ember pulsing like a beacon in the storm.

What's happening?

The ocean surged from below. Alex held Joe and rolled with the force of the salt sea. He peered at Joe's face and saw himself in the guttering brightness of his friend's soul. Alex suddenly felt lighter, like micrograms were leaving his body one at a time. Tiny stars burst in the cloudy depths, showering them with sparks. Water rushed upward, lifting them toward the hidden surface. Alex clenched his jaws and held on, the hotness in his belly like a skewer through his heart. His mind lightened, numbed. He felt giddy, detached, and saw flashes of movement. Marcus weeping, joyful, Elizabeth holding Mary's hands as white feathers rained down, Luke and Jade spiraling into powder puff clouds, Isaac as a man walking away across a white desert.

The ocean circled, closed in, spun them around and around as they ascended toward the barely visible amber light far overhead. A voice whispered in his ear, inside his head, and Alex's face knotted. The heat became intolerable. *Wait! This is a mistake! He's the one with the light!*

The voice sighed again, Te's voice, echoing from that vast expanse of white calm. *"You want to take your friend back, to rescue him, but you want this for only yourself, because you are afraid to die. Love is the way. Not easy, but simple. Either way you have a choice to make."*

Alex felt mass leaving his body, felt like he was separating into meaningless flecks of dust and ash. Slivers of his essence began to fragment and float away like leaves on the current.

Alex studied Joe's face as the two of them sailed skyward, boosted from below by the thrusting tide, and saw a little boy, innocent and alive, creating secret music in his bedroom and sending it out along the sensory strand that had connected them since birth. He saw a stubborn, rebellious kid fighting, always fighting, for the ones who couldn't fight for themselves. *You are the best part of me, Joe. You are the music and the light, and you have saved me again and again. You can't go. Stay with me.*

Warm, long-fingered hands reached deep into the gulf, closed tight, and lifted him out of the roiling sea of tears. The glow brightened, and they entered it. Heat bit into his ribs. Light engulfed them, embraced them in warmth and a sublime, hushed stillness, and Alex knew then the weightless release Luke had felt as his essence lifted, flew, soared.

"Half a spirit cannot exist ... you must give it away for it to find you."

I won't leave you, Joe.

Alex watched the amber glow split into two separate rays and knew what it meant.

Separation.

The flavor of sweet anise flooded his tongue. He looked down at the ember glowing in his chest.

"It is the key to saving Joe, this heat you possess."

"You have all that you need right here."

"Choice," Alex exhaled.

He wrapped himself around Joe and set the blaze free. Blinding light flared from his calloused fingertips, penetrating Joe's cold flesh. Radiance beamed from the small jade ember in Alex's heart, opening his chest wide, and the heat poured out of him into Joe.

Breathe.

Sheathed in pure light, Alex saw himself onstage, playing music that made people weep with joy. Saw two teenagers race trains, and win. He swung a wooden sword and chased Luke, but never caught up. He heard Joe's kid-laughter, contagious and real. Saw a pair of baby boys splashing in a bathtub, amazed at the bubbles. He felt Mary Whitewing's strong hands holding his tiny body and lifting him toward the night sky and knew the prayer she spoke. *This day is kind and true, a day of birth. Great One, sprinkle blessings on this new soul and help him see his path clearly. Take him, hands of Spirit, and hold him safely. Zhawenimishinaam, zhawenimishinaam. Blessings, blessings.*

The glow bathed them in a supernal incandescence as they soared higher and deeper into it. The stone walls fell away far below, collapsing until only the blessed light remained.

Breathe, Alex.

He felt soft sand beneath his feet and the warm wind brush silent against his skin. He heard the drumbeat calling him to the god place, saw a dark-haired boy reach out and take the hand of the blind boy sitting next to him beneath a vivid pink-blossomed tree, smelled rosin and horsehair, anise and cedar.

"Fear is not the path," Alex said, and breathed it all in.

Norma Schell lay breathless on the stone floor. She'd managed to climb out of the first chamber and find a small cell to wedge herself into before the children's cries began again. No matter where she hid, they managed to find her, biting, clawing, laughing. Always laughing.

The cups of her bra filled with bloodmilk, which puddled around her fat body. She pushed herself up and tried to gather her wits, to pull herself together. She had to be ready when He decided enough was enough and she'd passed the trial. The children's giggles and hungry cries had receded, but they would return, she knew. They kept coming and coming, wanting more of her. More than she could give. More than any god had a right to demand.

Norma wiped her face with a trembling hand. The raw flesh of her jowls stung. Her hands throbbed from all the grasping and fighting. The space where her front tooth had been knocked out began to bleed again and she fought back a pathetic sob. *I don't have anything left. Lord have mercy.* She pushed herself against the wall, eyes wide in the darkness, but no hands reached, no teeth ripped at her flesh, no baby mouths tried to suckle.

Through the narrow entryway she had managed to squeeze through, Norma glimpsed a pinprick of light, brightening as it moved closer. She held her breath, wiped her swollen eyes, but she had no more energy to pray, even though that seemed the right thing to do. She tried to keep still as the light grew into a glowing orb, sending rays of bright white to chase away the darkness. It moved straight toward her, growing bigger, and her heart leapt.

Him! It's Him! She rocked forward to look closer, shielding her eyes with one arm, then fell back onto her ample butt, mouth open. A young man stood there looking down at her. Norma wiped her face and pressed her hair down, staring at the man and his overpowering light. She could barely see his face and wasn't sure she should wish it. The warmth radiating off him in waves made her heart soar. She began to weep at the benevolence, at the pure love washing over her from deep within that white brilliance.

The man knelt at her side and reached out, placing his fingertip on the scar on her face. He traced her wound gently.

"Please," she sobbed. "Heal me." She wept harder as he cupped her swollen cheek.

"You will heal yourself," he said, and the voice was familiar.

"Who-who are you?" she croaked, reaching out a tentative hand.

The young man raked long blond hair out of his face, his eyes so blue, so benevolent.

"Consider me your own personal angel of mercy," he said, taking her hand. He helped her up and together they walked out of the darkness.

coda

June 21, 1985

They stood outside ROOM 1512 at Providence Hospice and Palliative Care Center.

"Do you have everything?" Jade asked.

He turned to her, looked deep into her amber-brown eyes, and nodded. "Everything I need."

"Do you want me to come in with you?"

"He'd like that."

Joe pushed the door open and stepped to the side of the bed. Lying on his side was Johnny Lucero, age 90, decorated WWI veteran, award-winning photojournalist for *Life* magazine, husband of 68 years to Joan before her death two months ago at the age of 84, father of four, grandfather of nine, great-grandfather of two. He wore sneakers to work every day, was a die-hard Green Bay Packers fan, loved Chopin, crossword puzzles, reading the *New York Times* front to back, and straight-up vanilla ice cream without any crap in it. Two scoops on a regular cone. None of that cherry and whipped cream business.

Joe crouched down so the man could see him and looked into his watery eyes. The man smiled, placed his hand on Joe's cheek, gave it a weak pat, and Joe knew Johnny would be leaving soon.

"Thank you for coming," Johnny whispered, his voice weak.

"Wouldn't miss it," Joe said. "And that pretty girl is here with me, too."

Smiling, Jade crouched down next to Joe and placed her hand on Johnny's shoulder. "I wish for you a beautiful death, Mister Lucero."

Johnny rolled his eyes toward Jade and smiled. "Ahhhhhh, I almost don't want to leave now. Almost."

Johnny's eyes closed. Joe put his hand over Johnny's on his cheek. He could see inside, could see Johnny's regrets and sorrows, his greatest triumphs and joys, and wanted to make sure his path was clear, his journey untroubled. Joe leaned close to whisper in the dying man's ear.

"I will help you navigate the betweens, Major Lucero, so you don't get lost or stuck. There will be some scary shit along the way, no joke, so it's important for you to remember who you are. Between me and the man waiting for you on the other side, we will ensure your safe delivery. It is my honor to guide you today. Good journey, sir."

Joe stood, removed the violin from the case, and stroked the mahogany wood. He studied the instrument as though it were a limb, a part of his body that he could command and maneuver at will, then tucked the chin rest under his jaw and cradled the neck in his hand. He placed the bow on the strings. The first earthy notes of Chopin's *Berceuse* filled the air. He would play until the man's chest stilled, his final breath expired, and Joe was certain.

After a while, Johnny breathed out and did not breathe in again. This was the first layer; there were many more to journey through. It would take all night and forty-four more. Joe would play music each of those days—for Johnny, for Amy, for Heather, for Kelly, for Kasa, for Andrew, for all the others—guiding them through the betweens so they wouldn't get stuck.

He continued to play and in the silent spaces between the notes he heard Alex's voice. *Keep your wrist strong but fluid. Don't work it too hard, let the music guide you rather than you trying to control each note.* Joe's fingertips tingled, electrified, and he sent a thought out on the thread that connected his soul to its other half.

Bite me.

Grinning, he did what he was told and a caprice by Beethoven poured from the instrument. When he came back from the mist, Jade was curled up asleep in the chair and Johnny's body was gone. The staff at the Center knew Joe would stay and play while they washed and prepped the body before it was sent off to the morgue. The families knew him, knew he would stay as long as it took, and they were always grateful. He had kept every thank you card he received over the past year and remembered he needed to get a bigger box.

Jade opened her eyes and yawned. "All good, my *Heyoka* brother?"

Joe nodded, running a thumb over his calloused fingertips. "Oh, yeah."

"Awesome." She stood and stretched. "Coffee?"

"Yes, please," Joe said. "I have to call Dammasch State first and see how she's doing."

Jade nodded. "I'll meet you in the hall." She hugged him tight on her way out of the room.

As the door swept closed, Joe set his jaw, remembering his last words to his mother. *You will confess all of your sins to the police and accept whatever punishment they deem appropriate. You will be lucid, and every moment of every day for the rest of your life you will atone for the pain and heartache you have caused others. Do you understand, Norma?* She had nodded numbly, clinging to him the way a terrified refugee might cling to a lifeboat.

At the exact moment that he and Jade had opened their eyes one year and one week ago, officers from Cutters Grove Police Department arrived at the white house with red slate roof and red trim. There they found a 45-year-old blonde woman sitting at her kitchen table, face meticulously painted, fuchsia dress clean and pressed, long fingernails polished to a high red shine. Calm and composed, she told them about the bodies. She told them about her miscarriages, her heartache at failing. She told them she simply wanted to be the chosen vessel, the Holy Mother. She simply wanted to bring a savior into the world. She simply wanted to show the father that she was worthy.

Joe attended the exhumation, watched as every last madonna rose bush was shredded to muddy mulch. He stood between Shantal's mom and Ricky's dad while the forensics team meticulously dug up the backyard. When the investigators upended the swing set Marcus had installed when Joe and Alex were two, something fell out of the hollow crossbar. A pale blue Easter egg. Amused, Joe later pocketed the rotten thing, figuring he'd leave it on Mary's mantle next to Alex's urn just to annoy him—and her, of course. Joe had closed his eyes only when the larger bones were liberated from their earthy tomb. He had expected the guilt and fear to come rushing back, but instead he felt his dad's soul encircle him and then lift, finally, up and away.

Charlie Dugan was there, too, standing on the back patio like a bold giant with tears streaming down his round face. After a while, Charlie approached, took Joe's hand and pressed a silver key into his palm.

"Melt this thing down so no one can ever use it again," Charlie had said. "And come see me play in California. We're gonna kick Denver's ass and you're in desperate need of a road trip, man." He'd smiled, wiped his eyes with meaty fingers, and walked away.

Joe dialed the phone in Johnny's room. The social worker at Dammasch State Hospital for the Criminally Insane answered and told him there had been no change in Norma's condition and that she was safe and well cared for. Joe thanked her, told her he would call again in a month, and hung up. He repacked the violin, pausing to breathe in the rosin scent of the bow. The instrument had shown up in Alex's room one week after Joe was released from the hospital last year—the one-year anniversary of his suicide attempt. When he asked Elizabeth about it, she had simply smiled, said something about both her boys being world-class mischiefs, and poured him some mint tea. That night Joe had the first of many dreams that would guide him through the year to come. In it he stood in a field of white feathers, a brilliant orange orb hanging low in the desert sky and casting rays of light in every direction. Alex was there.

"You're not coming?" Joe asked.

Alex said, "I have to stay. But I won't be far."

Two little boys, one with dark hair, the other as blond as sunshine, chased each other around an enormous pink-flowered tree. Butterflies landed on their skin and hair, cloaking them in living shades of green, blue, orange, red, violet—every color imaginable. Millions of wings reflected the light, casting rainbow prisms around like dancing bubbles. The boys laughed from their guts as they played, and it made Joe's heart feel good to watch them.

Excited, the dark-haired boy ran up to Alex and he bent over so the boy could whisper into his ear, but Joe could hear as clearly as though the kid were shouting at him.

"He's not leaving again, is he?" He stroked his freckled nose and glanced at the blond boy, a worried expression on his face.

Joe crouched down and looked into the boy's familiar brown eyes. "He's not leaving again. He's going to stay here with you. The way it's always been."

The dark-haired boy grinned, then laughed and looked up at Alex, hopping up and down. "I kept it safe just like you told me to. Can I give it to him now?"

Alex nodded. "That's a great idea."

The little boy held out his small hands, a violin and bow wrapped in a colorful blanket balanced on his palms. The blond boy watched from behind the pink tree, laughing and leaping up to catch streaming bubbles in his cupped hands.

"It's yours now," the dark-haired boy said, offering the instrument to Joe. "You can take it back with you."

Joe did.

He picked up the violin case and stepped into the hallway. Jade crooked her arm into his elbow.

"Will you be at Mary's for dinner later? Papa and I are making lasagna. Well, Papa is. I watch. And taste-test. Kiki's coming, too."

Joe smiled. "Yeah, I'll be there. Rom wants me to help him clean out the garage today. Elizabeth never throws anything away and it drives him batshit. With the baby coming in a couple of months, we need to make room. Heading to the hospital in Medford around noon. Missus Ma'kadalia is leaving today."

"Oh!" Jade breathed. "I would very much like to be there for her, if that's okay."

Joe nodded, giving her a knowing glance.

They walked toward the front doors.

"Mary says your studies are going well," Jade said. "She says you're learning control and meditation techniques to help with the overwhelm. Aala has new stories for you and—"

"—new stones, I'm sure," Joe finished, sighing. The stones had been the hardest part of his studies so far. He just couldn't feel their energies like he could with people. But Aala was determined, and the more determined she got the more determined he was to give her a hard time. It was, as the old woman repeated often and with immense patience, the backward way.

"I think I'll switch her stones for those speckled jellybeans and see if she notices."

Jade smiled up at him, shook her head. "Good luck with that."

They stepped into a sunny sprinkle of rain. Watching the streaming rays illuminate each drop as it fell from the sky, Joe could feel the spaces between here and there. Often, when he played, he could hear the dying person's final thoughts as they brushed by, like sighs on a breeze. But mostly it was a touch, a grateful caress against his cheek as they took their leave. He wanted to guide them all and Mary had to constantly remind him that there were others doing the same important work and that it wasn't all on him, that death guides are often chosen, the way Marcus had chosen him, and Lucas had chosen Alex. She reminded him that Alex was waiting in the *wakwi* to help the dying complete their journeys, and that Joe would know when a good death had been achieved, or when someone needed extra guidance, because Alex would tell him. Just then Alex's voice found him on the inside saying that Sully, a recent arrival, was a funny guy who loved everyone and didn't want his friends to be sad that he was gone. Joe knew then that the man had successfully navigated the layers—the horrors and the joys, the darkness and the light—and had made the good hard choices along the way. Joe watched the word write itself out in the liquid-bright sky

love

A train moaned in the distance. Joe tilted his head back and stuck out his tongue, tasting sweet anise and home. Smiling, he closed his eyes and let the sun-kissed rain bathe his face.

author note & acknowledgments

In 1984, I wrote a short story for Penny Jackman's creative writing class at Pikes Peak Community College. I titled it *Edge*—as in the *edge* of a cliff, the *edge* of a blade, the *edge* of conflict, the ragged *edges* of sanity and love. (I would come to learn that a title should, in fact, communicate something about the actual story). After my class critique, Penny asked to speak to me. She told me I had a good story on my hands and to think about expanding it to novel length. I smiled and nodded and quickly forgot all about it. But the seed had been planted and, as you no doubt have heard from many writers, these characters would not leave me alone. These guys showed up in my dreams (always arguing, of course) and I found myself having conversations with them while driving, doing dishes, in the shower, nursing my daughter, nursing my son, and while blocking literal and figurative blows. These boys kicked and hollered, demanding that their story be told. They wouldn't shut up. The thing is, I am a fair-weather writer. I write when all is well and ordered in my world, after I've had time to process and digest, which says something about why it took me 35 years to finish this book. In those times of difficulty, I knew Joe and Alex were waiting in the shadows for me like old friends. I knew they were willing to battle not only for their own souls, but mine as well. These guys have been around longer than my own kids and have saved me again and again. The seeds Penny planted so many years ago have grown and bloomed into the story you now hold in your hands. I am eternally grateful to her.

~

A few things I need to mention:

While I have drawn on the Ojibwe language for this book, the Shiloh Tribe and the customs and legends associated with it in this story are purely fabricated by me. I intend no harm and no disrespect in the amalgamated forms I have created to tell this story, and I understand that my intentions mean diddly.

While all the characters that appear in this work are fictional, Mary Whitewing was an actual person, my grandmother a couple of greats back. I have tried to honor her ancestral wisdom and resilience in this modern story. I hope I did okay.

Heyokas are real. They are the empaths and the seers, and they are everywhere in this world. It is my belief that we should listen to them and honor those who understand and embody the backward way.

Writing is a solitary endeavor. Launching a story into the world is not. I have many people to thank …

Chelsea and Will, for inspiring me every day to be a better human and reminding me of the important things.

Mom, for presenting many opportunities to heal and understand who I want to be in this world.

Pop, for kneeling down to my level, pointing to the stars and instilling a sense of wonder and connectedness in my little-kid mind, for encouraging me to ask the big questions, find compassion at every opportunity, and be humble. He was my champion and I miss him.

Lynn, for extending her hand in eighth grade and being a friend ever since. (Moo).

Laura, for refusing to leave me in the darkness.

Jeanne, for offering me safe shelter when I needed it most.

Kathryn, for the most *interesting* conversations and for being my friend.

Allen, for always having my back.

Sandi, who read the earliest drafts of this story decades ago and has stuck with it (and me) for the long haul. This story is as much hers as it is mine. (Super shout-out to Tom, who has supported this story through time and space from afar).

Kiku Flores, Kristen Uveges, and Jason Grundhauser, for keeping me healthy and for listening to me yammer on for years about this story. My spine and I love you.

My Cambio Yoga and Yoga Studio Satya sanghas, for making me a better teacher and human.

R. Michael Burns, for the title and so much more.

Henry Snider and Hollie Snider, for believing in this story from the get-go.

Jené Jackson, for thinking big and for being one of the bravest women I know.

Debbie Meldrum, for being a great first reader and long-standing supporter of this story.

My Sparkling Hammers critique group—Chris Mandeville, Todd Fahnestock, Aaron Brown, and Giles Carwyn. Your insights, support, great conversations, mad storytelling skills, and wicked humor mean so much to me. Thanks for keeping it real.

CSFWG, my first writers group. There were many talented people in this group whose early critiques kept me going. You know who you are.

Pikes Peak Writers Conference, for opening opportunities for new writers to learn and grow.

Michael Sullivan, for helping me honor the beauty of the Ojibwe language in an authentic way. *Miigwech!*

Rashed Al Akroka, for his stunning cover art and unwavering patience with me.

DeAnna Knippling, for her excellent interior design work and for catching all the little things that could have easily turned into big things.

Billy Sobolik, for the haunting illustrations that simply elevated this book to the next level.

Liza Holbrook, for adding extra special touches to Billy's illustrations and for being a rad human.

Denise Little, who read the first 90 pages of a rough draft back in 1993 and wrote in her rejection letter that I would be a New York Times bestselling author one day. That feedback buoyed my confidence and fanned my creative embers for years. This novel would not exist without her early encouragement.

I wrote goodly chunks of this book in various spaces over the years. I am grateful for Poor Richard's Restaurant, Pikes Peak Library, and Giuseppe's Old Depot.

Melissa Etheridge, whose music set the soundscape for this story and has guided me out of my own darkness too many times to count.

River and Keanu, whose abiding friendship set the foundation on which Joe and Alex's relationship is built.

And you, dear reader. Without you, all of this would be for naught.

about the author

A voracious reader as a youngster, Morgen Leigh spent a lot of time with her nose stuck in a book and scaring the hell out of friends and family with her unsettling, dark tales. Her fiction and creative non-fiction have appeared in Twilight Times, Apollo's Lyre, The S'Peaker, The Lorelei Signal, and Mystic Signals. She is a university professor published in academic research and a yoga teacher specializing in adaptive yoga for people with disabilities. She is currently finishing a second novel and working on a memoir. Morgen writes and breathes in Colorado.

Email: morgen.leigh.author@gmail.com
Website: www.morgenleigh.com
Facebook: @morgenleighauthor
Instagram: @morgenleighauthor

If you or someone you know is struggling with suicide, self-harm, or domestic violence, please know you are not alone. I see you and others will, too. Please reach out.

National Suicide Prevention Lifeline: 800-273-8255
Self-Harm Prevention Hotline: 800-366-8288
National Domestic Violence Hotline: 800-799-7233
The Trevor Project: 866-488-7386

A portion of the proceeds from the sale of this book will be forwarded to organizations that support First Nations People and their livelihoods as well as to The Rebels Project, an organization that supports survivors of mass violence and trauma.